THE NURSE'S CHRISTMAS GIFT

BY
TINA BECKETT

THE MIDWIFE'S PREGNANCY MIRACLE

BY
KATE HARDY

D0530782

Christmas Miracles in Maternity

*Hope, magic and precious new beginnings
at Teddy's!*

Welcome to Teddy's Centre for Babies and Birth,
where the brightest stars of neonatal and obstetric
medicine work tirelessly to save tiny lives and
deliver bundles of joy all year round—but there's
never a time quite as magical as Christmas!

Although the temperature might be
dropping outside, unexpected surprises
are heating up for these dedicated pros! And as
Christmas Day draws near secrets are revealed,
hope is ignited and love takes over.

Cuddle up this Christmas
with the heart-warming stories of the doctors,
nurses, midwives and surgeons at Teddy's in the
Christmas Miracles in Maternity mini-series:

Available November 2016:

The Nurse's Christmas Gift
by Tina Beckett

The Midwife's Pregnancy Miracle
by Kate Hardy

Available December 2016:

White Christmas for the Single Mum
by Susanne Hampton

A Royal Baby for Christmas
by Scarlet Wilson

THE NURSE'S
CHRISTMAS GIFT

BY
TINA BECKETT

Published in Great Britain 2016
By Mills & Boon, an imprint of HarperCollins*Publishers*
1 London Bridge Street, London, SE1 9GF

© 2016 Harlequin Books S.A.

*Special thanks and acknowledgement are given to Tina Beckett
for her contribution to the* Christmas Miracles in Maternity *series.*

ISBN: 978-0-263-91521-1

Dear Reader,

Have you ever wanted something so badly that it consumes your every waking thought? And yet that very same desire ends up causing unimaginable pain?

Annabelle Brookes finds herself facing a tragic cycle of hope and grief as she tries time and time again to carry a child to term. Those failed attempts finally affect her health and her relationship with her husband. When he finally puts his foot down and says, 'No more', she is devastated. So devastated that she pushes him away.

Years later Annabelle comes face to face with the man she once loved. All the emotions she thought long-dead are resurrected, and she has to decide once and for all what the important things in life are. Only this is Christmas, the season of miracles, when nothing is carved in stone.

Thank you for joining Max and Annabelle as they struggle to let go of the pain of the past. And maybe— just maybe—they'll discover something more tucked among the tinsel and the holiday lights. I hope you enjoy reading their story as much as I loved writing it!

Love,

Tina Beckett

To my kids,
who are always willing to give me space—and time—
when I'm under deadline. I love you!

Three-times Golden Heart® finalist **Tina Beckett**
learned to pack her suitcases almost before she learned
to read. Born to a military family, she has lived in the
United States, Puerto Rico, Portugal and Brazil. In
addition to travelling, Tina loves to cuddle with her
pug, Alex, spend time with her family, and hit the trails
on her horse. Learn more about Tina from her website,
or 'friend' her on Facebook.

Books by Tina Beckett

Mills & Boon Medical Romance

The Hollywood Hills Clinic
Winning Back His Doctor Bride

Midwives On-Call at Christmas
Playboy Doc's Mistletoe Kiss

To Play with Fire
His Girl From Nowhere
How to Find a Man in Five Dates
The Soldier She Could Never Forget
Her Playboy's Secret
Hot Doc from Her Past
A Daddy for Her Daughter

Visit the Author Profile page
at millsandboon.co.uk for more titles.

CHAPTER ONE

MAX AINSLEY WAS happy to be back on familiar soil.

Opening the door to his new cottage in a brand-new city, he hefted his duffel bag and tossed it over his shoulder, enjoying the warmth he found inside. Six months was too long; the days and nights spent helping displaced children in war-ravaged North Africa had eaten into his soul—one painful bite at a time. Trying to meet each desperate need had drained his emotional bank account until there was nothing left. He'd needed to come back to recharge and decide what he wanted to do next.

What better season than winter? The icy weather and the festive lights of the approaching holiday should help him push aside the thoughts of what he hadn't been able to accomplish on this trip. At least he hoped so.

Three years of running from his past had changed nothing. Maybe it was time to start living in the present. To sign the papers he'd left behind and to finally let go of the past once and for all.

Shedding his parka and throwing his belongings onto a nearby leather sofa with a sigh, he surveyed the place. With its white-painted walls and comfortable furniture, it wasn't huge or fancy, but it was big enough for a landing place, at least until he could figure out where he wanted to park his butt for the long haul. Sienna McDonald had sent pictures of several possibilities that were just a short distance from the hospital, and he'd settled on this one, the cottage's quaint one-bedroom floor plan made more attractive by the small private garden off the back. This was the place.

He could finally sell his flat back in London.

And maybe it was time to call his solicitor and have him complete the process—to cut any remaining ties with a certain dark period in his life.

He spied a piece of paper on the table in the dining room and stiffened, before he realised it couldn't be from her. She had no idea where he was right now. And she hadn't tried to find him over the last couple of years. At least not that he knew of.

Wandering over to the note, he placed a finger on the pink stationery and cocked his head as he made out the cheerful words.

'Welcome to Cheltenham and to Teddy's! I've put some milk, cheese and cold meat in the fridge, and there is bread and sweets in the cupboard along with some other staples to help get you started. The boiler is lit, instructions are on the unit. I hope you're ready to work, because I am more than ready for a rest!'

She'd signed her name with a flourish at the end.

Sweets, eh? That made him smile. But he was glad for the boiler, as snow was expected to hit any day and the temperatures had been steadily dropping. His body was still trying to adjust to the chill after all those months dealing with the hot temperatures of Sudan.

He was due at Teddy's in the morning to start his contract, replacing Sienna McDonald when she went on maternity leave. She'd sent him a letter as he was packing for the flight telling him to get ready for a wild ride. There was a winter virus running through the halls of the hospital, affecting patients and staff alike. They were short-staffed and overworked.

He was ready. Anything to keep his mind off his previous life.

And the timing couldn't have been more perfect. Sienna would be there to show him the ropes, and Max would have time to adjust to being back in a modern hospital, where day-to-day life was not always a life and death struggle.

Well, that was not entirely true. In the world of paediatric cardiothoracic medicine, things were often about life and death, but they were caused by the battle raging within the person's body, not the cruel deeds done by one human against another. And with Doctors Without Borders, he had seen his share of war and the horrific results of it.

His mind headed to a darker place, and Max forced it back to the mundane tasks he had to accomplish before his first shift tomorrow morning: shave the scruff of several weeks off his face, unpack, hunt down a vehicle to use.

With that in mind, he headed to the refrigerator to find something to eat. And then he would face the day, and hopefully get ready to face his future…and his first step towards banishing the past, once and for all.

Annabelle Brookes couldn't believe how crowded the ward was. All the beds were full, and patients were seemingly crammed into every nook and cranny. The winter virus was not only sending people flooding into

the hospital, but it was sending staff flooding out—
multiple nurses and doctors had all become ill over
the past several days. So far she had steered clear of its
path, but who knew how long that would hold? She was
frankly exhausted and, with six hours left to her shift,
she was sure she would be dead on her feet by the time
she headed home.

Despite it all, she was glad Ella O'Brien had pestered
her until she'd agreed to come to Cheltenham a year ago.
Maybe because her friend had recognised the signs of
depression and the deadly spiral her life had taken after
her husband had left for parts unknown. Whatever it
had been, Annabelle felt she was finally getting her life
back under control. She had Ella to thank for that. And
for helping her land this plum position.

Head neonatal nurse was a dream come true for her.
She might not be able to have children of her own, but
she was happy to be able to rock, hold and treat other
people's babies all day long. Working at the same hospital as her midwife friend also meant there was plenty
of time for girlie outings and things to take her mind
off her own problems.

She let her fingers run across a draping of tinsel
against a doorway as she went by, the cool slide of glit-
tery metal helping relax her frazzled nerves.

Tucking a strand of hair back into the plait that ran
halfway down her back, she dodged people and patients
alike as she made her way towards the nursery and her
next patient: Baby Doe, aka Baby Hope.

The baby had been abandoned by her mother—who
was little more than a baby herself—and Annabelle
felt a special affinity with this tiny creature. After all,
hadn't Annabelle been dumped by the person who

should have loved her the most but left her languishing with a broken heart? No. Actually, Annabelle had done the dumping, but her heart had still splintered into pieces.

Baby Hope's heart was literally broken, whereas Annabelle's was merely…

She stiffened her jaw. No. Her heart was just fine, thank you very much.

Was that why that paperwork was still sitting on a shelf gathering dust? And it was too. Annabelle had cleaned around the beige envelope over the past couple of years, but hadn't been able to bring herself to touch it, much less open it and read the contents. Because she already knew what they said. She had been the one to do the filing.

But Max had never responded. Or sent his signed copy back to her solicitor.

And if he had? What then?

She had no idea.

As she rounded the nurses' station to check the schedule and see what other cases she'd been assigned for the day, the phone rang. A nurse sitting behind the desk picked up the phone, waving at her as she answered the call.

'Baby Doe? Oh, yes, Annabelle just arrived. I'll send her in.' She set the phone down.

Maybe the first order of business after her divorce should be to officially get rid of her married name. It still hurt to have it attached to her, even though she no longer went by Annabelle Ainsley.

'Miss McDonald and her replacement are doing rounds and are ready to examine the baby. Do you mind filling them in on what's happened over the last few hours?'

'On my way.' Annabelle had already been headed towards the glass window that made up the viewing area of the special care baby unit, so it was perfect timing. Arriving on the floor, she spotted a heavily pregnant Sienna McDonald ducking into the room. The neonatal cardiothoracic surgeon had been overseeing Baby Doe's care as they waited for an available heart for the sick infant. Another man, wearing a lab coat and sporting dark washed jeans, went in behind Sienna. She could only catch a glimpse of a strong back and thick black hair, but something inside her took a funny little turn at the familiar way the man moved.

Shaking her head to clear it, she reached the door a few seconds later and slid inside.

She headed towards the baby's cot, finding Sienna and the other doctor—their backs to her—hovering over it.

About to step around to the other side, the stranger raised the top of the unit. 'Her colour doesn't look good.'

Annabelle stifled a gasp, stopping in her tracks for several horrified seconds. She lifted her eyes and stared at the man's back.

That voice.

Those gruff masculine tones were definitely not the feminine Scottish lilt belonging to Sienna, that was for sure. This had to be Sienna's replacement. Had she actually seen the name of the new doctor written somewhere? She didn't think so, but she was beginning to think she should have paid more attention.

She swallowed down the ball of bile before the pressure built to dangerous levels.

The new doctor spoke again. 'What's her diagnosis?'

The ball in Annabelle's throat popped back into place with a vengeance.

It couldn't be.

Sienna glanced over at him. 'Hypoplastic left heart syndrome. She's waiting on a donor heart.'

The other doctor's dark head bent as he examined the baby. 'How far down is she on the list?'

'Far enough that we're all worried. Especially Annabelle Brookes—you'll meet her soon. She's the nurse who's been with our little patient from the time she was born.'

Annabelle, who had begun sliding back towards the door, stopped when the new doctor slowly lifted his head, turning it in her direction. Familiar brown eyes she would recognise anywhere met hers and narrowed, staring for what seemed like an eternity but had to have been less than a second. There wasn't the slightest flinch in his expression. She could have been a complete stranger.

But she wasn't.

He knew very well who she was. And she knew him. *No. It couldn't be.*

For a soul-searing moment she wondered if she'd been mistaken, that he wasn't Sienna's replacement at all, but was here to say he'd finally signed the papers. Maybe he'd heard about Baby Hope's case and had just popped in to take a look while they hunted for Annabelle.

Or...maybe he'd met someone else.

Her whole system threatened to shut down as she stood there staring.

'Annabelle? Are you all right?' Sienna's voice startled her enough to force her to blink.

'Oh, yes, I…um…' What was she supposed to say?

Max evidently didn't have that problem. He came away from Hope's incubator, extending his hand. 'I didn't realise you'd moved from London.'

'Yes. I did.' She ignored his hand, tipping her chin just a fraction, instead. So he hadn't come here to find her.

Sienna glanced from one to the other. 'You two already know each other?'

One side of Max's mouth turned up in a semblance of a smile as he allowed his hand to drop back by his side. 'Quite well, actually.'

Yes, they knew each other. But 'quite well'? She'd thought so at one time. But in the end… Well, he hadn't stuck around.

Of course, she'd been the one to tell him to go. And he had. Without a single attempt to change her mind— or to fight for what they'd once had.

Sienna's brows went up, obviously waiting for some kind of explanation. But what could she say, really?

She opened her mouth to try to save the situation, but a shrill noise suddenly filled the room.

An alarm! And this one wasn't in her head.

All eyes swivelled back to Baby Hope, who lay still in her incubator.

It was the pulse oximeter. Hope wasn't breathing!

'Let's get some help in here!' Max was suddenly belting out orders in a tone that demanded immediate response.

Glancing again at the baby's form, she noted that the tiny girl's colour had gone from bad to worse, a dangerous mottling spreading over her nappy-clad form. Annabelle's heart plummeted, her fingers beginning a familiar tingle that happened every time she went into crisis mode.

Come on, little love. Don't do this. Not when we're just getting to know each other.

Social services had asked Annabelle to keep a special eye on the infant, since she had no next of kin who were willing to take on her care. Poor little thing.

Annabelle knew what it was like to feel alone.

In Max's defence, it had been her choice. But he had issued an ultimatum. One she hadn't been prepared to accept.

Right now, though, all she needed to think about was this little one's battle for life. Max shot Sienna a look. The other doctor nodded at him. Whatever the exchange was, Max took the lead.

'We need to tube her.'

Annabelle went to the wall and grabbed a pair of gloves from the dispenser, shoving her hands into them and forcing herself to take things one step at a time. To get ahead of yourself was to make a mistake.

She hurried to get the trach tube items, tearing into sterile packages with a vengeance. Two more nurses rushed into the room, hearing the cries for help. Each went to work, knowing instinctively what needed to be done. They'd all been through this scenario many times before.

But not with Baby Hope.

Annabelle moved in next to Max and handed him each item as he asked for it, her mind fixed on helping the tiny infant come back from the precipice.

Trying not to count the seconds, she watched Max in

motion, marvelling at the steadiness of his large hands as he intubated the baby, his face a mask of concentration. A look that was achingly familiar. She swallowed hard. She needed to think of him as a doctor. Not as someone she'd once loved.

And lost.

He connected the tubing to the ventilator as one of the other nurses set the machine up and switched it on.

Almost immediately, Baby Hope's chest rose and fell in rhythmic strokes as the ventilator did the breathing for her. As if by magic, the pulse ox alarm switched off and the heart-rate monitor above the incubator began sounding a steadier *blip-blip-blip* as the heart reacted to the life-giving oxygen.

The organ was weak, but at least it was beating.

But for how much longer?

Thank God they hadn't needed to use the paddles to shock it back into rhythm. Baby Hope was already receiving prostaglandin to prevent the ductus in her heart from closing and cutting off blood flow. And they had her on a nitrogen/oxygen mix in an attempt to help the oxygen move to the far reaches of her body. But even so, her hands and extremities were tinged blue, a sure sign of cyanosis. It would only get worse the longer she went without a transplant.

'She's back in rhythm.'

At least a semblance of rhythm, and she wasn't out of the woods, not by a long shot. Her damaged heart—caused by her mum's drug addiction—was failing quickly. Without a transplant, she would die. Whether that last crisis arrived in a week or two or three, the outcome would be the same.

Annabelle sent up a silent prayer that a donor heart would become available.

Even as she prayed it, though, she hated the fact that another family would have to lose their child so that Baby Hope might live.

They watched a few more minutes as things settled down. 'We'll leave her on the ventilator until we figure out exactly what happened. We can try adjusting the nitrogen rate or play with some of her other meds to see if we can buy her a little more time.'

Sienna nodded. 'I was thinking the exact thing.' She glanced at Annabelle. 'Are you okay?'

It was the second time she'd asked her that question. And the second time she had trouble coming up with a response.

'I will be.'

'I know this one's special to you.'

Of course. Sienna was talking about the baby. Not about Max and his sudden appearance back in her life.

'I just want her to have a chance.'

'As stubborn as you are, she has it.' Sienna gave her a smile.

'Annabelle is nothing, if not tenacious.' Max's voice came through, only there wasn't a hint of amusement in the words. And she knew why. Because he wasn't referring to Hope. He was referring to how she'd clung to what she'd thought was *their* dream only to find out it wasn't.

'You said you know each other?'

When Annabelle came to work this morning, never in her wildest imaginings had she pictured this scene. Because she already knew how it was going to play out. She braced herself for impact.

'We do.'

There was a pause as the other doctor waited to be enlightened.

Annabelle tried to head it off, even though she knew it was hopeless. 'We've known each other for years.'

'Yes,' Max murmured. 'You could say that. Your Annabelle Brookes is actually Annabelle Ainsley. My wife.'

'Your...' Sienna suddenly looked as if she'd rather be anywhere else but here. 'It didn't even dawn on me. Your names...'

'Are not the same. I know.' Max's mouth turned down at the corners, a hard line that she recognised forming along the sides of his jaw. 'I see you've gone back to your maiden name.' He pinned her with a glance.

'We're separated. Getting a divorce.' She explained as quickly as she could without adding that going back to her maiden name had been a way to survive the devastation that his leaving had caused.

Even though you're the one who asked him to go.

They hadn't spoken since the day he'd found her temperature journal and realised that, although she'd stopped doing the in-vitro procedures as he'd demanded, she hadn't completely given up hope. Until that very minute.

When she'd seen the look on his face as he'd thumbed through the pages, she'd known it was over. She'd grabbed the book from his hands and told him to leave.

And just like that, he'd walked out of their front door and out of her life.

Just like Baby Hope's mother.

And like that lost soul, Max had never come back.

Until now.

She frowned. 'Did you know I was at Teddy's when you accepted that contract to take Sienna's position?'

Even as she asked it, she knew it made no sense for him to have come here. Not without a good reason.

Like those papers on her shelf?

'No.'

That one curt word told her everything she needed to know. If he'd known she was working at the Royal Cheltenham, this was the last place he'd have chosen to come.

Sienna touched a gloved hand to the baby's head. 'If you two can finish getting her stabilised, I need to get off my feet for a few minutes.' She eyed Max. 'Why don't you give me a call when you're done here and I'll finish showing you around the hospital?'

'Sounds good. Thanks.'

Annabelle was halfway surprised that he hadn't just said he was ready now. He had to be as eager to get away from her as she was to get away from him. But they had their patient to consider.

Their?

Oh, God. If he was Sienna's replacement, that meant they would share this particular case. And others like it.

As soon as Sienna had left the room along with the other nurses, Max took a few moments to finish going over the baby's chart, making notes in it while Annabelle squirmed. She couldn't believe he was here. After all this time.

And for the tiniest second, when those intelligent eyes of his had swept over her, she'd entertained the thought that maybe he really had come here looking for her. But it was obvious from his behaviour that he hadn't.

He hadn't seemed all that pleased that she'd dumped his name. How could he expect otherwise, though? She'd wanted no reminders of their time together, not that a simple name change could ever erase all the pain and sadness over the way their marriage had ended.

'Why don't you fill me in on the details of her care? Miss McDonald seemed to indicate you know the baby better than anyone else on staff.' The cool way he asked the question made heat rush to her face.

Here she was agonising over the past, while he was able, as always, to wall off his feelings and emotions. It had driven her crazy when they were together that he could behave as if their world weren't imploding as she'd had miscarriage after miscarriage.

'Social services needed someone who could report back to them on what was happening with her care. And since I'm head nurse, it kind of fell to me to do it.'

'Somehow I didn't think you would remain a neonatal nurse. Not after everything that happened.'

She shrugged. 'I love my job. Just because I can't… have children doesn't mean I want to go into another line of nursing. I'm not one to throw in the towel.'

'I think that depended on the situation.' His words had a hard edge to them.

She decided to take a page from his book and at least try to feign indifference. 'What do you want me to tell you about her?'

'Do you know anything about her history? Her mother?'

Annabelle filled him in on everything she could, from the fact that Baby Hope's mother had been hooked on heroin to the fact that she'd fled the hospital soon after giving birth, staff only discovering her absence when they went in to take her vitals. They'd found her bed empty, her hospital gown wadded up under the covers. They'd called the authorities, but in the two weeks since the baby's birth no one had come forward with any information.

The drug use had caused the baby to go through withdrawals in addition to the in-utero damage her heart had sustained. It was getting weaker by the day. In fact, every ounce she gained put more strain on it. Normally in these children, Annabelle considered weight gain something to be celebrated. Not in Hope's case. It just meant she had that much less time to live.

'Does any of that help?' she asked.

'It does. I'm going to up her dose of furosemide and see if we can get a little of that fluid off her belly. I think that's why she stopped breathing. If it's not any better in an hour or two, I'm going to try to draw some of it off manually.'

'We did that a few days ago. It seemed to help.'

'Good.'

They looked at each other for a long moment, then Max said, 'You've let your hair grow.'

The unexpectedness of the observation made her blink. 'It makes it easier to get out of the way.'

Annabelle used to tame her waves rather than pulling them back. Between blowing them out and using a straightening iron, she'd spent a lot of time on her appearance. Once Max had left, though, there'd seemed little reason to go through those contortions any more. It was only when she stopped that she realised she'd been simply going through the motions for the last half of their marriage. Having a baby had become such a priority that her every waking moment had been consumed with it. It was no wonder he'd jumped at the chance to get out. She hadn't liked who she'd become either.

She opened her mouth to say something more, before deciding the less personal they made their interactions, the better for both of them. They'd travelled down that road once before and it hadn't ended well. And she definitely didn't want to give him the impression that she'd been pining for him over the past three years. She hadn't been. She'd got well and truly over him.

'Since you're working here now, maybe we should set down some ground rules to avoid any sticky situations.' She paused. 'Unless you'd like to change your mind about staying.'

His eyes narrowed. 'I signed a contract. I intend to abide by the terms of it.'

Was that why he hadn't moved to complete the process of terminating their union? Because he viewed their marriage as a contract rather than an emotional commitment? She'd been the one to actually file, not him.

Her throat clogged at the thought, but she pushed ahead, needing to finish their conversation so she could leave. Before the crazy avalanche of emotions buried her any deeper.

'Most people at Teddy's don't know that I was married. They just assume I'm single. All except for Ella.'

Since she no longer wore her ring, it made it that much easier to assume she had no one in her life.

His brows went up. 'Ella O'Brien?'

'Yes.' He would know who Ella was. They'd been best friends for years. She was very surprised her friend hadn't got wind of Max's arrival. Then again, maybe Annabelle would have known had she paid more attention during staff meetings. She'd known Sienna was going on maternity leave soon but had had no idea that Max was the one who'd be taking her place. Maybe because Baby Hope had taken up most of her thoughts in the last couple of weeks.

'How is she?'

'Ella? She's fine.' She looked away from him, reaching down to touch Hope's tiny hand over the side of the still-open incubator. 'Anyway, Ella knows about us, but, as you could see from Sienna's reaction, that information hasn't made its way around the hospital. I would appreciate if you didn't go around blurting out that you're my husband. Because you're not. You haven't been for the last three years.'

One side of his mouth went up in that mouth-watering way that used to make her tremble. But right now, she was desperate to put this runaway train back on its tracks.

'I have a paper that says otherwise.'

'And I have one that says I'm ready to be done with that part of my life.'

'The divorce papers. I'm surprised you haven't followed up on them with your solicitor.'

She should have had that solicitor hound Max until he signed, but she hadn't, and she wasn't quite sure why. 'I've been busy.'

His eyes went to Hope. 'I can see that.'

'So you'll keep our little…situation between us?'

'How do you know Miss McDonald isn't going to say something to someone?'

'She won't.' Sienna was secretive enough about her own past that Annabelle was pretty sure privacy was a big deal to the other doctor.

'And Ella? You don't think she'll say anything?'

'Not if she knows what's good for her.' She said it with a wryness in her voice, because her friend was obstinate to the point of stubbornness about some things. But she was a good and faithful friend. She'd mothered Annabelle when she'd come to her crying her eyes out when Max had walked out of the door. No, Ella wouldn't tell anyone.

Annabelle pulled her hand from the incubator and took a deep breath. Then she turned back to face Max again.

'Please. Can't we try to just work together like the professionals we are? At least for the time you're here.' She wanted to ask exactly how long that would be, but for now she had to assume it was until Sienna was finished with her maternity leave. If she thought of it as a finite period of time she could survive his presence. At least she hoped she could.

But she already knew she'd be seeing a lot more of him. Especially if he was going to be the doctor who either opened Hope's chest and placed a donor heart in it or who signed her death certificate.

She closed her eyes for a second as the remembered sound of that alarm sliced through her being. How long before that sound signalled the end of a life that had barely begun?

'I don't know, Anna.' His low voice caused her lids to wrench apart. 'Can we?'

Her name on his lips sent a shiver through her, as did his words. It was the first time she'd heard the shortened version of Annabelle in three years. In fact, during their very last confrontation he'd reverted to her full name. And then he was gone.

So it made her senses go wonky to hear the drawled endearment murmured in something other than anger.

She'd wanted a simple answer…a promise that Max would do his best to keep their time together peaceful. He hadn't given her that. Or maybe he was simply acknowledging something that she was afraid to admit: that it was impossible for them to work together as if they'd never crossed paths before. Because they had.

And if those old hurts and resentments somehow came out with swords drawn?

Then, as much as she wanted to keep their past relationship in the past, it would probably spill over into the present in a very real way.

CHAPTER TWO

'AND THIS IS where all of that wonderful hospital food is prepared.'

Sienna's easy smile wasn't able to quite penetrate the shock to his system caused by seeing Anna standing over that incubator. Why hadn't he kept track of where she was?

Because he hadn't wanted to know. Knowing meant he had to do something about those papers her solicitor had sent him. And he hadn't been ready to. Maybe fate was forcing his hand. Making him finally put an end to that part of his life in order to move forward to the next phase.

Wasn't that part of the reason he'd come home? To start living again?

Yes, but he hadn't meant to do it quite like this.

He decided the best way to take his mind off Anna was to put it on something...or someone else.

'The ubiquitous hospital food.' He allowed his mouth to quirk to the side. 'But it's probably better than what I've been eating for the past six months.'

She laughed. 'I'm sure Doctors Without Borders feeds you pretty decently.' She paused to look at him as they made their way down the corridor. 'What was it like over there?'

'Hard. Lots of pressing needs, and not knowing where to start. Not being able to meet all of those needs was a tough pill to swallow.' Memories of desperate faces played through his head like a slide show. Those he saved…and those he couldn't.

'I can imagine it was. And living in another country for months at a time? It couldn't have been easy being away from the comforts of home.'

'I heard you had a little experience with that as well. What was the kingdom of Montanari like?' Someone had mentioned that the other cardiothoracic surgeon had visited the tiny country on an extended stay, but that she had returned quite suddenly.

Sienna stared straight ahead. 'It was different.'

Different. In other words, move on to another subject. He was happy to oblige, since he knew of one particular subject he was just as eager to avoid. 'How about your cases here? Anything interesting?'

The other doctor's shoulders relaxed, and she threw him a smile that seemed almost grateful. 'Well, we actually have a mum who is expecting quadruplets. We're keeping an extra-close eye on her but so far she's doing well and the babies are all fine.'

'That's good.' He didn't ask any more questions. Someone carrying that many foetuses made him think of fertility treatments—another subject he wasn't eager to explore.

'Apparently they might bring in a world-renowned neonatal specialist if any complications develop.'

How many times would he have loved to fly in a specialist when he was in Africa? But, of course, there were only those, like him, who had volunteered their time and expertise. Doctors Without Borders sometimes took pot luck as far as who was willing to go. As a result there were often holes in treatment plans, or a patient who needed help from a specialist that wasn't on site. That was when the most heartbreaking scenarios occurred.

Yet despite that he was already missing those brief, and often frantic, interactions with the team in Sudan, which surprised him given how exhausted he'd been by the end. Or maybe it was the shock of having to work with Annabelle that had him wishing he could just fly back to Africa and a life where long-term connections with other people were neither expected nor desired. It was more in line with the way he'd grown up. And far removed from what he'd once had with Anna. He'd decided that keeping his distance from others was the safer route.

'Who is the specialist?'

'Hmm…someone told me, but I can't remember her name. I do remember it's a woman. I'd have to look.' She stopped in front of a set of double doors. 'And this is where we work our magic.'

The surgical unit. The epicentre of Max's—and Sienna's—world. Even with all the prep work that went on before the actual surgery, this was still where everything would be won or lost. Annabelle had once said she didn't know how he did it. He wasn't completely sure either. He just did it. The same way she did her job, standing beside the incubators of very sick babies and taking the best care she could of them.

Why was he even thinking about Annabelle right now? 'Can we go inside?'

'Of course.' She hit a button on the wall and the

doors swung wide to allow them through. Glancing at the schedule on the whiteboard at the nurses' station, she said, 'Do you want to scrub up and observe a surgery? There's a gallbladder being taken out in surgical unit two.'

'No, I'm good. But I would like to observe your next cardiac surgery.'

Sienna gave a sigh and put a hand to her belly. 'Sure, but I'm really hoping to scale back by about seventy-five per cent over the next week so I can leave without worrying that you haven't carried an actual caseload.'

Maybe he should have been offended by that, but he wasn't. Sienna didn't know him from Adam. He was pretty sure that she could still carry her share of the patient load, but her comment had been more about wanting to see him in action. To reassure herself that she was leaving her little charges in the best possible hands. He was determined not to disappoint her.

'That sounds fair enough.' He paused. 'And the baby who was in crisis? Baby…Hope?'

'She doesn't have an official name. Hope is Annabelle's pet name for her. I think it's a fingers-crossed kind of thing. Whatever it is, it's stuck, and we all find ourselves calling her that now.'

That sounded just like Annabelle. Refusing to give up hope, even when it was obvious that the procedures were not going to work.

'Annabelle mentioned social services. And that the mum took off?'

'Yes. The mum came in while she was in labour. She was an addict and abandoned the baby soon afterwards. We have no idea where she is.'

Max's chest tightened. His parents had never actually abandoned him physically, except for those long cruises and trips they'd taken, leaving him in the care of an aunt. But emotionally?

'Anyway,' Sienna went on, 'I'm assigning the case to you. Make sure you become familiar with it. Your best bet for doing that is to get with Annabelle and go over her patient file. She has followed that baby from the beginning. She knows more about her than anyone, maybe even me, and I'm Baby Hope's doctor.'

Max's heart twinged out a warning. The last thing he wanted to do was spend even more time with Annabelle, because it was...

Dangerous.

But what else could he do? Say no? Tell Sienna that he couldn't be a professional when it came to dealing with his almost-ex? Not hardly.

Maybe Sienna saw something in his face. 'Is that going to be a problem considering the circumstances? I'm sorry, I had no idea you two even knew each other.'

If there was one thing Max was good at, it was disengaging his brain from his heart.

'It won't be a problem.'

'Good.'

He'd work with Anna. Until it was over. Because one way or the other it would be. The baby would either have a new heart, or she wouldn't. The twinge he'd felt seconds earlier grew to an ache—just like the one he'd dealt with on an almost daily basis while working in the Sudan. He rubbed a palm over the spot for a second to ease the pressure.

'How often do hearts come available?'

'Do you mean here in Cheltenham? Some years there are more. Some years, less.'

'How many transplants have you done?'

'One. In my whole career. We deal with lots of holes in the heart and diverting blood flow, but hypoplastic cases are rare at Teddy's.'

So why was she handing the case over to him? This was a chance that she'd just admitted didn't come across her desk very often. 'Are you sure you don't want it?'

'Very.' Something flashed through her brown eyes. A trickle of fear? His gaze shifted lower. Was she worried about the health of her own baby?

He remembered well the worry over whether a foetus would make it to term. In fact he remembered several times when he'd prayed over Annabelle as she'd slept. Those prayers had gone unanswered.

'When are you due?'

'Too soon. But right now it feels like for ever.' Her glance caught his. 'Everything is fine with the baby, if that's what you're wondering. My handing that case over has nothing to do with superstition. I just don't think I have the endurance right now for what could be a long, complicated surgery.' She pressed a hand to the small of her back. 'And if for some reason I go earlier than I expect, I don't want to pass Baby Hope over to someone else at the last second. I want it to be now, when it's a deliberate decision on both of our parts.'

That he could understand. The need to be prepared for what might happen. Unlike in his relationship with Annabelle when he'd impulsively issued an ultimatum, hoping to save her from the grief of repeating a tragic cycle—not to mention the dangerous physical symptoms she'd been experiencing.

It had worked. But not quite in the way he'd expected. This was not where he wanted his thoughts to head.

He'd do better to stick with what he could control and leave the rest of it to the side at the moment.

'Your patients will be in good hands. I'll make sure of it.'

'Thank you. That means a lot to me.' She sent him a smile that was genuine. 'Do you have any other questions before we officially end our tour and go on to discuss actual cases?'

'Just one.'

'All right.' The wariness he'd sensed during his mention of Montanari filtered back into her eyes. She had no need to be worried. He was done with discussing personal issues.

'Is the food as bad here as it was at my last gig?'

Sienna actually laughed. 'I'll let you be the judge of that. I don't mind it. But then again, I eat almost anything, as long as it isn't alive or shaped like a snake.'

'Well, on those two points we can agree. So I take it Teddy's doesn't serve exotic fare.'

'Nope. Just watery potatoes and tasteless jelly.'

He glanced at his watch and smiled back at her. 'Well, then, in the name of science, I think I should go and check out the competition. Can we save the case discussion until later?'

'Yes, I'm ready for a break as well. And you can tell me what you think once you've sampled what the canteen has to offer. Just watch out for the nurses.'

'Sorry?'

'Some of them have heard you were coming. While you're checking out the food, don't be surprised if they're checking you out.'

Would they be? He'd made it a point not to get involved with women at all since his separation. And he wasn't planning on changing that.

And what of Annabelle? She was a nurse. Had she been checking him out as well?

Of course not. But on that note, he'd better go and get something into his stomach. Before he did something stupid and went back down to the first floor to check on a very ill baby, and the protective nurse who hovered over her.

Annabelle wasn't good for his equilibrium. And she very definitely wasn't good for his objectivity. And no matter what, he had to keep that. Because if he allowed his heart to become too entangled with her as he cared for his patients, he would have trouble doing his job.

What Baby Hope and the rest of his patients needed was a doctor who could keep his emotions out of the surgical ward. No matter how hard that might prove to be.

Annabelle grabbed a tray and headed for the line of choices. She wasn't hungry. Or so she told herself. Her stomach had knotted again and again until there was almost no room in it for anything other than the big bowl of worry she'd dished up for herself that morning. Baby Hope was getting weaker. The crisis she'd had this morning proved it. If Max hadn't been there, Hope might have…

No, don't think about that. And Max had not been the only one in that room who could have saved her. Sienna would have called for the exact same treatment protocol. She'd seen the other woman in action.

Once upon a time, Annabelle had expected Max to play the role of saviour. It hadn't been fair to him. Or to her. He'd finally cracked under the pressure of it all. And so had she. At least her body had.

A few days after she'd lost her last babies, her abdomen and legs had swelled up with fluid from all of the hormones she'd been on and she'd been in pain; Max had rushed her to A&E. They'd given her an ultrasound again, thinking maybe some foetal tissue had been left behind. But what they'd found was that her ovaries had swelled to many times their normal size from harvesting the eggs.

There'd been no magic-wand treatment to make it all go away. Her body had had to do the hard work. She'd worn support hose to keep the fluid from accumulating in her legs, and had had to sleep sitting up in a chair to make it easier to breathe as her hormone levels had gradually gone back to normal. And the look on Max's face when the doctors had told him the cause...

It had come right on the heels of him telling her that he was done trying to have babies. It had made everything that much worse. But she'd still desperately wanted children, so she'd started keeping secret recordings of her temperature. Only the more secretive she'd got over the coming weeks, the more distant he'd become. In the end, the death knell had sounded before he'd ever found that journal.

Back to food, Annabelle.

She set her tray on the metal supports running parallel to the food selections and gazed into the glass case. Baked chicken? No. Salad? No. Fruit? Yes. She picked up a clear plastic container of fruit salad and set it on her tray, pushing it a few feet further down the line. Sandwiches? Her stomach clenched in revulsion. Not at the food, but at the thought of trying to push that bread down her oesophagus.

Broccoli? Healthy, and she normally loved it, but no. She kept moving past the selection of veggies until she hit the dessert section.

Bad Annabelle. What would your mum say?

She peered back down the row, wondering if she should reverse her steps and make better choices. Except when she glanced the way she'd come, her gaze didn't fall on food. It fell on the very person she was trying to forget. Max.

And he was with Sienna. Both were holding food trays, which meant...

Oh, no! They were eating lunch too.

It's what people do. They eat. They sleep. Her throat tightened. *They move away to far-off places.*

Sienna waved to her. 'Hey, Annabelle. Hold on. Would you like to join us? We can talk about Baby Hope, and you can help catch Max up on the case.'

It was on the tip of her tongue to say she was going to eat back in her office, but she'd just been worrying about the baby. Any light they could shed on her prognosis should outweigh any awkwardness of eating with her ex. Right?

Right.

'Sure. I'll save you a spot.' She tossed a container of yoghurt onto her plate and then a large slice of chocolate cake for good measure. Handing her personnel card to the cashier and praying she scanned it before the pair caught up with her, she threw a smile at the woman and then headed out towards the crowd of people already parked at tables.

Setting her tray on one of the only available tables

in the far corner, she hesitated. Should she really be doing this?

Yes. Anything for Baby Hope.

She shut her eyes. Was she becoming as obsessed with this infant as she had been with her quest to become pregnant all those years ago?

No. Looking back now, those attempts seemed so futile. Desperate attempts by a desperate woman. Max's childhood had been pretty awful, and she'd wanted to show him how it should be. How wonderful hers had been. And since he had no blood relatives left alive, she'd wanted to give him that physical connection—for the roots she'd had with her own extended family to take hold and spread. Only none of it had worked.

If her sister hadn't had a devastating experience when trying to adopt a baby, Annabelle might have gone that route after her first miscarriage. But if the grief she'd felt after losing a baby she'd never met was horrific, how much worse had it been for her sister, who'd held a baby in her arms for months only to have to hand him back over to the courts weeks before the adoption was finalised? The whole family had been shattered. And so Annabelle had continued on her quest to have a biological child, only to fail time and time again.

She popped open the lid to her fruit, realising it was the only truly healthy thing on her plate. She'd just wanted to get out of that canteen line at any cost.

Her mouth twisted sideways. It looked as if the final cost would be paid by her waistline and hips. She shoved a huge blueberry into her mouth and bit down hard just as Max and Sienna joined her. Juice spurted over her teeth and drummed at the backs of her lips, seeking the nearest available exit.

Perfect. She covered her mouth with her napkin as she continued to fight with the food, finally swallowing it down with a couple of coughs afterwards.

Max frowned as he sat. 'Okay?'

'Yes.' Another cough, louder this time, a few people at neighbouring tables glancing her way. Probably wondering who they were going to have to do the Heimlich on this time. She swallowed again, clearing her throat. 'Just went down the wrong pipe.'

Sienna, who arrived with only some kind of green bottled concoction that made Annabelle horrified at what her own plate contained, twisted the lid to her liquid lunch and sat down. She nodded at the selection. 'I'm finding smaller portions are easier to handle when I'm working. I'll eat a proper meal when I go off duty.'

Forcing herself to cut a chunk of melon into more manageable pieces, she wished she could be just as disciplined as the surgeon. Well, today was not a good day to stand in judgement of herself. Was it any wonder she was seeking out comfort food? Her husband had just landed back in her life.

She couldn't even pretend to have a boyfriend, because if there'd been anyone serious she obviously would have wanted to pressure Max into signing the divorce papers. But she hadn't.

Ugh! She chewed quickly and then swallowed, thankful that at least this time she wasn't choking.

A phone chirped and all three of them looked down at their devices, making her smile. Her screen was blank, so it wasn't Ella, who she hadn't heard from all day, which was unusual. Maybe she hadn't heard that Max was back.

Or maybe she had.

Sienna frowned, setting her drink down on the table so quickly the contents sloshed, almost coming over the rim of the bottle. She stared at her phone for several seconds, not touching the screen. Either it was very good news...or very...

The other doctor stood up, her tongue flicking out to moisten her lips. 'I'm sorry, I have to go.' She glanced at Max. 'Can you carry on without me?'

'Of course. Is everything all right?'

'It will be.' Her hand went to her midsection. And rather than responding to whoever had sent a message, she dropped her phone into the pocket of her scrubs and picked up her drink, screwing the cap back on. 'Page me if you have any questions or need help.'

'I think I'm good.' Max sent Annabelle a wry glance. 'I'm sure Anna can answer any questions about Hope or the hospital I might have.'

Or about why he hadn't severed those final ties that bound them together?

Somehow, though, she doubted he was any more eager to revisit their past than she was. But still, the last thing she wanted today was to play hospital adviser to a man who still made her knees quake. She had no idea why that was so. She was over him. Had been for the last couple of years. In fact, she hadn't thought of him in...

Well, the last fifteen seconds, but that didn't count, since he was sitting right across from her. Before today, she'd gone weeks at a time without him crossing her mind.

But since Sienna was glancing her way as if needing reassurance that it was indeed okay to leave them alone without a referee, Annabelle nodded. 'Go. It'll be fine.'

Looking a little doubtful, but evidently not enough

to want to stick around, the cardiothoracic surgeon gave a quick wave and headed towards the entrance of the canteen. Annabelle noticed she slid her phone out of her pocket and stared at the screen again as she rounded the corner.

She wondered what that was all about. But it was really none of her business.

But Baby Hope was, and since that was why Sienna had wanted to sit with her…

'Is there some news about the baby?' Maybe that was what the message was about. Could it be that…? 'Could a heart have become available?'

Hope sparked in her chest, flaring to life with a jolt that had her leaning forward and sent her plastic fork dropping back onto her tray.

Max must have seen something in her face because he shook his head. 'No. Not yet. I think she would have told us if that message had anything to do with a donor heart.'

She sagged back into her chair. 'I was hoping…'

'I know. Why don't we work on things we can control until one is available? Tell me anything else you can think of about her. The events surrounding her birth, et cetera.'

'Are you looking for something in particular?' She'd told him pretty much everything she knew back in the special care baby unit.

Max pulled a small notebook out of one of the pockets of his jacket. 'I can look at her chart and get the mechanics. But tell me about *her*. Anything out of the ordinary that you've noticed that you think might help.'

She picked up her fork and pushed around a few more blueberries, not trying to really stab any of them but using the empty gesture as a way to sort through her thoughts about Hope.

'She's a fighter. She came into this world crying as hard as her tiny lungs would let her.' She sucked down a quick breath. 'Her mother didn't even touch her. Hope was very sick and might not have survived the night, but she never asked to hold her or tried to keep us from taking her away. Maybe she already knew she was going to leave her behind and was afraid to let herself get attached.'

'You were there when she was born.'

'Yes. When the mum came in—already in labour—the doctor examined her. He didn't like the way the baby's heartbeat sounded so they did an ultrasound. They immediately saw there was a problem, so they called Sienna down.' Annabelle gripped her fork tighter. 'She knew as soon as she looked at the monitor that it was serious. So when she delivered there was a roomful of staff, just in case Hope coded on the table. They did a Caesarean section, trying to save the baby any undue stress during delivery.'

'It worked. She's still alive.'

'Yes. But she's all alone. Her mum has never even called to check on her. Not once.'

'And say what?' Max's jaw tightened. 'Maybe she didn't want to have to deal with the fallout of what might happen if it all went wrong.'

'It was her child. How could she not want to be there for her?'

'She could have felt the baby was better off without her.'

Something about the tight way he said those words

made her wonder if Max was still talking about Baby Hope and her mum, or something a little closer to home.

Had he felt she was better off without him?

Rubbish. It hadn't been his idea to leave. It had been hers. If he'd truly loved her, he would have fought for her.

But Max had always had a hard time forming attachments, thanks to parents who did their utmost to avoid any show of affection. And those long trips they'd taken without him—leaving Max to wonder if they were ever coming back. If they missed him at all. Annabelle had cried when he'd told her in halting words the way things had been in his home. Her own family's open affection and need to be with each other had seemed to fascinate him.

Maybe he really could understand how a mum could abandon her own child. In many ways, Max had felt abandoned. Maybe even by her, when she'd told him to leave.

She should have just given up when he'd given her that last ultimatum. But she hadn't—she'd wanted Max to have what his parents had denied him. And when he'd found her journal… God, he'd been so furious that night. To forestall any more arguments, she'd told him to get out. The memories created a sour taste in her mouth.

'I guess I'll never know what her true motivation was for leaving. If I had, maybe I could have changed her mind, or at least talked her into coming back to check on Hope.'

'She probably wouldn't have. Come back, that is. Maybe she felt that once she walked out, there was no going back.'

This time when his eyes came up to meet hers there was no denying that he was talking about something other than their patient.

Unable to come up with anything that wouldn't inflame the situation further, she settled for a shrug. 'Maybe not. I guess people just have to learn to live with the consequences of their choices.'

As Annabelle had had to do.

And with that statement, she made the choice to stab her fork into the slab of chocolate cake on her plate and did her best to steer the conversation back to neutral territory. Where there was no chance of loaded statements or examining past regrets too closely.

But even as they spoke of the hospital and its patients and advances in treatment, she was very aware that nothing could ever be completely neutral as far as Max went.

So she would try to do as she'd stated and make the very best choices she could while he was here. And then learn to live with the consequences.

CHAPTER THREE

'ELLA, LET'S NOT have this discussion right now.'

'What discussion is that?' Her best friend batted her eyes, while Annabelle's rolled around in their sockets. 'The prodigal returns to the scene of his crime?'

'That doesn't even make any sense.'

'It doesn't have to. So spill. I haven't seen you since I heard the big news. Not from you, I might add. What's up with that?'

She tried to delay the inevitable. 'What news are you talking about?'

Ella made a scoffing sound as she leaned against the exam table. 'That a certain ex has crashed back onto the scene.'

Crashed was a very good word for what he'd done. 'There's nothing to tell. He showed up yesterday at the hospital.'

'Out of the blue? With no advance notice?' Her friend lifted the bottle of water she held, taking a quick drink. She then grimaced.

'Are you okay?'

'Fine. Just a little tummy trouble. I hope I'm not coming down with whatever everyone else has. Wouldn't that be a wonderful Christmas present?' She twisted her lips and then shrugged. 'Anyway, you had no idea he was coming?'

'Of course not. I would have told you, if I'd known.' And probably caught the next available flight out of town. Annabelle sighed, already tired of this line of questioning. When had life become so complicated? 'I'm sure someone knew he was coming. I just never thought to ask because I never dreamed...'

'That Max Ainsley would show up on your doorstep and beg for your forgiveness?'

'Ella!' Annabelle hurried over to the door to the exam room and shut it before anyone overheard their conversation. She turned back to face her friend. 'First of all, he did not show up on my doorstep. He just happened to come to work at the hospital. I'm sure he had no idea I was working here any more than I knew that he was the one taking Sienna's place. And second, there's no need for him to apologise.'

'Like hell there's not. He practically abandoned you without a word.'

Oh, Lord, she'd had very little sleep last night and now this. As soon as she'd finished lunch with Max yesterday, she had got out of that canteen as fast as she possibly could. Even so, he'd come down to the special care baby unit a couple of hours later to get even more information on Baby Hope. Clinical information this time about blood types and the matching tests they'd done in the hope that a heart would become available.

She'd been forced to stand there as he shuffled through papers and tried to absorb any tiny piece of information that could help with the newborn's treatment. With his head bent over the computer screen, each little shift in his expression had triggered memories of happier times. Which was why she'd lain in bed and tossed and turned for hours last night. Because she couldn't help but dissect the whole day time and time again.

Sheer exhaustion had finally pulled her under just as the sun had begun to rise. And then she'd had to get up and come into work, knowing she was going to run into him again today. And tomorrow. And three months from now.

How was she going to survive until his contract ended?

'He didn't abandon me. It simply didn't work out between us. We both had a part in ending it, even though I asked him to leave.'

It was true. She couldn't see it back then, and Ella had had to listen to her long-distance calls as she'd cycled through the stages of grief, giving sympathy where it was needed and a proverbial kick in the backside when she was still wearing her heart on her sleeve six months after the separation.

'Enough!' she'd finally declared. 'You have to decide whether you want to start your life over again or if you're going to spend it crying over a man who isn't coming back.'

Those words had done what nothing else had been able to. They'd convinced her that she needed to climb out of the pity pit she'd dug for herself and start giving back to society. What better way to forget about your own heartache than to ease the suffering of someone else?

Ella had talked her into moving from London to the Cotswolds soon afterwards. It had been one of the best decisions of her life.

Well. Until now. But that hadn't been Ella's fault. It had been no one's. Not even Max's.

Annabelle's pager suddenly beeped at the same time as Ella's, and they both jumped at the noise. Peering down to look at what had caused the alert, Annabelle read.

A multi-vehicle accident on the M5 has occurred. A hired bus for a nursery school outing was involved. Several of those patients are en route— eta five minutes. All available personnel please report to A&E.

'Oh, God,' she said, reaching for her friend's hand.

'I know. Let's head over.' Her friend stopped and gripped the edge of the table for a second.

'Ella?'

'I'm okay.' She ran a hand through her hair, her face pale. 'Let's go.'

'Maybe you should go home instead.' Almost a third of the hospital staff was out due to a virus that had spread through their ranks. Hopefully Ella wasn't the latest person to fall victim to the bug.

Her friend blew out a breath. 'I hope to God I'm not...' She stopped again. 'I'll be all right. If I start feeling worse, I'll go home, okay?'

'Are you sure?'

'Yes. Now, let's get our butts in gear and go and help whoever is coming.'

Max spotted her the second she came out of the lift. She and a familiar redhead hurried past a small Christmas tree towards the assembled staff who were waiting for the first of the ambulances to arrive. The other woman sent him a chilling glare. Perfect. It was Ella. She'd always had it in for him.

It didn't matter.

His ex moved over to him. 'Any word yet?'

'I don't know any more than you do.'

Just then, he caught the sound of a siren in the distance. And then another. Once they hit, they would have to do triage—the kind he'd done during his stints with Doctors Without Borders. This hospital might be more modern than the ones he'd worked in over the last six months, but that didn't mean that the process of sorting patients from most critical to least would be any easier. Especially not when it came to those involving high-speed crashes. He had to be ready for anything, including cardiac involvement from chest trauma.

He'd never got used to the cries of suffering while he was in Africa. And it would be no easier here than it had been there.

A nursery school outing! Of all things.

Right now, they didn't even know exactly how many patients were coming in, much less the seriousness of the injuries.

Then the first emergency vehicle spun into the space in front of the hospital, another stopping right behind it. And, yes, the screams of a child as those back doors were opened cut through him like a knife.

He moved in to look as the stretcher rolled backwards and onto the ground. A child who couldn't be more than three came into view, blood covering the sheet of the stretcher. And her right arm… Her shirt sleeve had been cut and parted to reveal the raw flesh of an open fracture, the pearly edge of a bone peeking through.

One of the orthopaedists moved in. 'Take her to exam room one. Take vitals, check her for other injuries. I'll be there in a minute.' He knew that doctors hated assigning priorities to treatment, but it was the only way to save as many lives as possible. If they treated these patients according to the order they came in, they might condemn a more seriously injured patient to death. It couldn't work that way. Max knew that from experience.

A nurse directed the paramedic back towards the interior of the hospital where other staff were preparing to receive whoever came through those doors.

The assembled doctors met each stretcher as it arrived, specialists matched up with the appropriate accident victims. When Annabelle tried to follow one of the other doctors, Max stopped her. If a critical case came his way, he would need a nurse to assist. And who better than a nurse who dealt with crises on a daily basis? He'd seen her in action when Baby Hope's pulse ox levels had plummeted. She'd been calm and confident, exactly what he needed.

It wasn't an unreasonable request.

And it had nothing to do with their past, or the fact that working with someone he knew would be easier than a complete stranger. He already knew that he and Annabelle made a great team on a professional level. They'd worked together many times before, since they'd been employed by the same hospital in London during their marriage.

The next ambulance pulled into the bay. The driver

leaped out just as the doors at the back of the vehicle swung open.

'How many more are coming?' Max called. So far they'd had thirteen patients ranging in age from two to four years in addition to three nursery school workers who'd also sustained injuries. The rescue in the frigid November temperatures had taken its toll as well. Despite being wrapped in blankets, many of the patients were shivering from shock and exposure.

'This is the last one. She was trapped between seats. She sustained blunt force trauma to the chest. She threw PVCs the whole way over.'

When the wheels of the stretcher hit the ground and made the turn towards them, Max caught sight of a pale face and blue-tinged lips, despite the oxygen mask over her face. A little girl. Probably two years old. Disposable electrode pads had been adhered to a chest that heaved as she gasped for breath.

'How bad?'

The paramedic shook his head. 'Difficulty breathing, pulse ox low as is her BP. And her EKG readings are all over the chart. PVCs, a couple of quick ventricular arrhythmias, but nothing sustained.'

'Possible cardiac contusion. Let's get her inside.'

As soon as they ran through the doors, Max glanced at her. 'We're going straight to ICU. You'll have to tell me where to go.'

With Annabelle calling out instructions they arrived on the third-floor unit within minutes. The paramedic had stayed with them the whole time, assisting with moving the stretcher.

They burst through the entrance to the unit, and Max grabbed every staff member who wasn't already treating someone and motioned them to the nearest empty room. Together they worked to get the girl hooked up to a heart monitor and take her vitals. The child was conscious, her wide eyes were open, and, although there were tears trickling from the corners of her eyes, her struggle to breathe took precedence over crying.

Somehow that just made it worse.

'We need to intubate, and then I want to get some X-rays and a CAT scan.'

He was hearing some crepitus as she breathed, the popping and crackling sounds as her chest expanded indicative of a possible sternal fracture. It could also explain some of her cardiac symptoms. The faster he figured it out, the better the prognosis.

He leaned down to the child, wishing he at least knew her name. 'We're going to take good care of you.'

Within minutes they'd slid a trach tube into place to regulate her breathing. Her cardiac function was still showing some instability, but it hadn't worsened. At least not yet.

Max was a master of remaining objective during very difficult surgeries. But there was something about children who were victims of accidents that threatened to shred his composure. These weren't neat put-the-child-to-sleep-in-a-controlled-setting cases. These were painful, awful situations that wrung him out emotionally.

Needing to come home from the Sudan to maintain his certification couldn't have come at a better time. He'd desperately needed a rest; the abject poverty and suffering he'd seen had taken their toll on him.

And yet here he was, his second day on the job, feeling as if he'd been thrown right back onto the front lines.

Mentally and emotionally.

Annabelle helped him get the girl ready to move to the radiology section, glancing at him as she did. She touched the youngster every chance she got, probably as a way to reassure her. He'd noticed her doing the same thing with Baby Hope.

Those tiny gestures of compassion struck at something deep inside him.

Strands of hair stuck to a face moist with perspiration, and yet Annabelle was totally oblivious to everything except her patient.

Just then, as if she sensed him looking at her, her head came up. Their gazes tangled for several long seconds. Then they were right back at it. Annabelle was evidently willing to set any animosity aside for the benefit of their young patient.

The CT scan confirmed his suspicion. The force of the little girl striking the seat in front of her had fractured her sternum, putting pressure on her heart and lungs. A half-hour turned into an hour, which turned into five as they continued to work the case.

It had to be way past time for Annabelle's shift to end, but she didn't flinch as they struggled to stabilise the girl.

Sarah. He'd finally learned her name. And unlike Baby Hope's mum, or even his own parents—who'd been more angry than concerned when he'd been injured in a bike crash—Sarah's mum and dad were frantic, desperate for any shred of news.

Annabelle came in from her fifth trip to see them. 'I told them they could come see her in a few minutes.'

'Good.' Sarah was already more comfortable. They'd given her some pain medication, and although she was still on a ventilator they'd be able to wean her off in the next day or two, depending on how much more swelling she had. 'Why don't you take a break? Get off your feet for a few minutes.'

'Sarah needs me. I'll rest when she does.'

'Have you eaten today?'

This time she smiled, although the edges of her mouth were lined with exhaustion as she repeated the same thought. 'I'll eat when you do.'

If she thought he was calling her weak, she was wrong. She was anything but. Of course, he already knew that. He'd watched Annabelle go to hell and back in her effort to have a child. She was as stubborn as they came. It was one of the things he'd loved most about her, and yet it was ultimately that very thing that had driven them apart.

'Is that a dinner invitation?' He cocked a brow at her.

Her smile faded. 'Of course not. I just meant—'

'I know what you meant.' His jaw stiffened. 'I was joking.'

'Of course.' Annabelle began collecting some of the discarded treatment items, not looking at him. It was then he realised how harsh his voice had been. It reminded him of the time he'd finally had enough of the procedures and the heartache. He'd been harsh then too. Very harsh, if he looked back on it now.

Max moved in closer, lifting a hand to touch her arm, then deciding better of it.

'I'm sorry for snapping at you. I would say chalk it up to exhaustion, but that's no excuse.' He could envision this scene repeating itself ad nauseam unless he put a stop to it. 'Maybe we really should grab a bite when we're done here. We can figure out how we're going to work together for the next several months without constantly being at each other's throats.'

She glanced up at him. 'I think we can manage to bump into each other now and then without having a meltdown.'

This time the sharpness was on her side.

'I know we can.' He took a deep breath and dragged a hand through his hair. 'Look, I'm trying to figure out how to make this easier on both of us, since I assume neither one of us is going to resign.'

It wasn't just because of his contract. He'd known for a long time that this day was coming. When he'd have to face his past and decide how to move forward. Maybe that time was now. He could go on putting it off, as he had over the past three years, but this wasn't Africa where he could just immerse himself in work and not have to see her day after day. They were looking at months of working together. At least.

'I love my post.' The sharpness in her voice had given way to a slight tremor. Did she think he was going to cause trouble for her or ask her to leave?

'I know you do. And I don't want to make you miserable by being here.' This time, he touched her gloved hand. Just for a second. 'Will it really be so very hard, Anna?'

'No. It's just that I never expected to…'

'You never expected to see me again.'

'No. Honestly I didn't.'

'But we both knew we would eventually have to finalise things. We can't live in limbo for ever.' This wasn't the direction he'd wanted to go with this discussion. But now that he was here, he had to see it through.

'You're right.' She glanced down at the items in her

hand and then went over to throw them in the rubbish bin. Then she moved over to the exam table and pushed the little girl's hair out of her face. The tenderness in her eyes made his stomach contract. She would have made such a wonderful mum. It was a shame that biology—and fate—kept her from being one. No power known to medical science had seemed able to work out what the problem was. Or how to fix it.

What he hadn't expected was for her to shove him out of her life the second she realised he was serious about not trying again. That bitter pill had taken ages to go down. But it finally had. And when it did, he realised his parents had taught him a valuable lesson. Keeping his heart to himself really was the better way.

When she looked up at him again, all hints of tenderness were gone, replaced by a resolute determination. 'You're right. We can't live in limbo. So this time the invitation is real. If you don't have plans, I think we should have dinner. And decide where to go from here.'

Suddenly that discussion didn't look quite as attractive as it had moments earlier. But since he'd been the one to suggest sitting down and talking things over, he couldn't very well refuse. 'Okay, once Sarah's parents have had their visit, we'll head out.'

A half-hour later, Max had scrawled the last of his instructions in Sarah's chart and set it in the holder outside her door. The girl's parents were still sitting by her bedside. He'd sent Annabelle on ahead to get her things.

As he stretched his back a couple of vertebrae popped, relieving the tension that had been building along his spine. He was dog tired. Maybe having dinner with Annabelle wasn't such a good idea. The discussion should probably wait until they were both rested.

Except there'd never seemed to *be* a right time to approach their unfinished business. So they had to make time.

He went to the men's changing room and washed his hands and then bent down to splash his face. Blotting it dry with a paper towel from the dispenser, he caught a glance at his reflection.

Dark hair, still cut short from his time overseas, was just starting to grey at the temples. Where had the years gone?

One minute he'd been a happily married man, and the next he'd been on the brink of divorce and living like a nomad, going from place to place but never really settling down. Maybe he should have joined the military. Except he hadn't wanted to give up the possibility of coming back to work in his field, and he would have either had to retrain for his speciality or settled for a position as a general surgeon. He loved paediatric cardiology in a way he couldn't explain to anyone but himself. So he'd gone with Doctors Without Borders.

Only his travels had simply delayed the inevitable. He still had to face the ghosts of his past.

He didn't want to hurt Annabelle. And he wasn't quite sure why he'd never signed the papers the second he'd realised what the packet of documents contained. Maybe he'd used them as a cautionary tale of what could happen when you opened your heart up to someone. Or maybe marriage had been an easy excuse for not getting involved with anyone else—not that he ever planned on it. Some day, though, Annabelle would meet Mr. Right and would want to be free to be with him. Their old life would stand in the way of that.

So, were they going to discuss their past tonight? Or discuss how to work together in the future?

He wasn't sure. They were both tired. And probably overly emotional.

Maybe he should just let Annabelle take the lead as far as topics went. And if she decided she wanted those divorce papers signed post haste, he might just have to tackle a tough conversation after all.

CHAPTER FOUR

THE PUB WAS PACKED. And with the clanging of plates and raucous laughter, it was hard to think, much less carry on a civilised conversation. Not the kind of place to go after dealing with a twelve-hour day of work.

But the place was also dark, with just some dim wall sconces lighting the way towards the tables. A few co-loured bulbs along the bar were the only concession to the upcoming Christmas season.

O'Malley's wasn't a normal hospital hangout, but that was okay. She wanted privacy. Which was one of the reasons Annabelle had suggested it. If they were going to have The Talk, opening up the subject of their past, she didn't want anyone to overhear the conversation.

And the low lighting would keep Max from seeing her expression. In the past, he'd always been able to read her like a book. It had been no different in that treatment room an hour earlier, when he'd known instantly that he'd hurt her with his words and apologised. She hated that he could still decipher her expressions. And when he'd touched her...

No doubt he'd seen the heat that washed into her face. Well, this time she was going to make it a little harder on him, if she could.

They followed the waitress to a small table for two in the very back of the place. Max waited for her to sit down before pulling his own chair out.

The server plonked a menu down in front of each of them, having to speak loudly to be heard above the din. 'What would you like to drink?'

Annabelle tried to decide if she wanted to risk imbibing or if she should play it safe. Oh, what the hell? Maybe she should dull her senses just a little. 'I'll have white wine.'

Writing her request down in a little book, the woman then turned her attention to Max. And 'turned her attention' was evidently synonymous with turning on her charm. Because suddenly the waitress was all smiles, fiddling with her hair. 'And you, sir?'

'I'll have a whisky sour, thank you.' He sent her a quick smile, but to his credit there was nothing behind it that hinted of any interest in whatever the waitress was offering. And she was offering. As a woman, Annabelle recognised the signs, even though she had never gone the flirting route.

At least not until she met Max.

Evidently realising she was out of luck, the woman shifted her gaze to Max's left hand, then she snapped her little book shut and flounced off.

Max didn't wear his ring any more. But then again, neither did she.

'Thank you for that.'

Max tilted his head. 'For what?'

'Not responding to her in front of me.'

Up went one brow. 'Not my type.'

That made her laugh, and her muscles all loosened. 'Really? Because she seemed to think you were hers.'

'I hadn't noticed.'

'Oh, come on.' She sat back in her chair and studied him. Max had always been handsome. But in the three years since she'd seen him, he'd grown even more attractive, although there was a deep groove between his brows that she didn't remember seeing when they were together.

'Seriously. She was probably just being friendly.'

'Seriously, huh? I don't know. Maybe we should make a little bet on it.'

'I don't bet on things like that.' The furrow above his nose deepened. 'Not any more.'

He didn't bet on what? Relationships? Because of her?

That wasn't what she wanted for Max. His childhood had been rough as it was, devoid of affection… love. He deserved to be happy, and she wanted that for him. Even now.

'We never really talked about it. What happened all those years ago.' Suddenly she wished she'd chosen a place a little less loud as she fingered the plastic placemat in front of her.

'I seem to remember a *lot* of talking. Most of it angry.'

Yes, there had been the arguments. Especially at the end, when he'd found her journal, the smoking gun that she was still hoping against hope that she would become pregnant.

Even before that, though, Max had become someone she didn't recognise. Impatient. Short. And somehow sad. That was the worst of all the emotions she'd seen in him. She'd tried so hard to have a child, thinking it would make everything better between them. That it would bind Max to her in a physical way—give him a sense of roots. Instead, it had only made things worse. The pregnancy attempts had ended up becoming a vicious cycle of failure and then increased desperation. Instead of binding them together, her attempts had torn them apart.

The waitress came and set their drinks in front of them. 'Are you ready to order?' Her voice wasn't nearly as friendly this time.

'Fish and chips for me and a glass of water, please.' Annabelle was craving good, old-fashioned fare.

'I'll have the same. And a dark ale to go with it, please.'

Annabelle didn't remember Max being a big drinker. Not that two drinks constituted an alcoholic. He just seemed...harder, somehow. Less approachable. Like his parents?

Once the waitress was gone, Annabelle picked up her wine, sipping with care.

Max, however, lifted his own glass and took a deep drink. 'I haven't had one of these in a long time. This place was a good choice.'

'Ella and I like to come here every once in a while. It's out of the way and loud enough that you don't have to think.'

He seemed to digest that for a moment. 'Not as loud as some of the places I've been.'

Interesting.

'Where *have* you been? If you don't mind my asking.' She didn't feel like talking about the arguments or failures of the past.

'I don't. I joined up with Doctors Without Borders. In between contracts in England, I've gone wherever they've needed me. Kenya, a time or two, but mostly the Sudan. I spent the last six months there.'

Annabelle listened, fascinated, as he shared what he'd done in the years since he'd left their flat. Some of the stories were horrifying. 'Isn't it hard to see that?'

'Yes.'

'And yet you keep going back. After this contract is up and Sienna is back from maternity leave, will you return there?'

The waitress arrived with their food and drinks, quickly asking if they needed anything else.

'I think we're good, thank you.'

When they were alone again, he drank the last of his whisky. 'I don't know what I'm going to do once this contract is up. I've been thinking about settling someplace on a more permanent basis.'

From what he'd told her, he'd hopped from city to city, country to country as the whim took him.

She was on her first bite of fish when he asked, 'How long have you lived in Cheltenham?'

It took her a second to chew and swallow. 'A year. I went to live with my mum for a while after…well, after you left.'

'Suzanne told me you didn't stay in the flat for long.'

Annabelle had missed their cleaning lady. 'Did you think I would?'

'I didn't really know what you would do. I went back after my first trip, almost a year later, and you were gone.'

'I just couldn't…stay.'

'Neither could I.' He paused. 'Even if you hadn't asked me to go, I would have. Things were never going to change.'

This was the most she'd ever been able to drag out of him. And she wasn't even having to drag. Back then they would fight, and then Max would clam up for days on end, his tight jaw attesting to the fact that he was holding his emotions at bay with difficulty.

He'd once told her that his parents had been the same way with him—their anger had translated into silence. He'd struggled with breaking those old patterns their entire marriage. But in the last six months of it, those habits had come back with a vengeance. If she'd tried to probe or make things right between them—with the offer of physical intimacy—he'd always seemed to have some meeting or suddenly had a shift at the hospital. She'd finally got the message: he didn't want to be with her, except when absolutely necessary for the in-vitro procedures. And then, after her last miscarriage, he was done trying for a baby.

Actually, Max had been done. Full stop. He'd left their relationship long before he'd actually walked out of the door.

She took another sip of her water to moisten her mouth as she got ready to tackle the most difficult subject of all.

'You haven't signed the papers.'

There was a pause.

'No. I've been overseas on and off.' He shrugged. 'After a while, I forgot about them.'

That stung, but she tried not to let it. 'Doesn't it make going out on dates awkward?'

'I've been busy. No time—or inclination—to jump back into those waters.'

His answer made Annabelle cringe. 'I'm sorry if I'm the reason for that.'

'I just haven't seen many happy marriages.'

'My parents are happy.'

He smiled at that. 'They are the exception to the rule. How are they?'

'They're fine. So are my sisters. Jessica had another boy while you were gone—his name is Nate.' She didn't want to delve into the fact that her parents' and siblings' relationships had all seemed to work out just swimmingly. Except for hers.

'That's wonderful. I'm happy for them.'

Popping a chip into her mouth, she tried not to think about how different their childhoods had been. Max's parents had seemed unhappy to be tied down with a child. They'd evidently loved to travel, and he had cramped their style.

Annabelle's home, on the other hand, had been filled with love and laughter, and when her parents had travelled—on long road trips, mostly—their kids had gone with them. She had wonderful memories of those adventures.

She'd hoped she and Max could have the same type of relationship. Instead, she'd become so focused on a single aspect of what constituted a family that she'd ignored the other parts.

Had she been so needy back then that she'd damaged Max somehow?

Well, hadn't their breakup damaged her?

Yes, but not in the way she'd expected. Annabelle had grown thicker skin over the past three years. Before, it seemed as if her whole life had been about Max and their quest to have a family. When that had begun breaking down and she'd sensed a lack of support on Max's side to continue, she'd become more and more withdrawn. She could see now how she'd withheld love whenever Max hadn't done exactly what she'd wanted. Just as his parents had.

She regretted that more than anything.

'So what do you want to do about it?'

He set his glass down. 'About what?'

Did she need to spell it out? 'About the paperwork. Maybe this is the reason we've been thrown back together. To tie up loose ends.'

A smile tilted up one side of his mouth. 'So I'm a loose end, now, am I?'

Nothing about Max was loose. He'd always been lean and fit, but now there was a firmness to him that spoke of muscle. Like the biceps that just peeked out from beneath the polo shirt he'd changed into before leaving the hospital.

They'd checked on Baby Hope before taking off. She was still holding her own, against all odds. But if a donor heart was not found soon...

She shrugged off the thought. 'You're not a loose end. But maybe I'm one of yours. You could be happy, Max. Find the right woman, and—'

'You're not a loose end, either.' His hand covered hers, an index finger coaxing hers to curl around it. The sensation was unbearably intimate and so like times past that she was helpless not to respond to the request. Their fingers twined. Tightened. The same heat from the exam room sloshed up her neck and into her face.

'Are you done with your meal?'

Her eyes widened. 'Yes. Why?'

'Would you mind coming with me for a minute?' He threw some notes onto the table, and, without even waiting for the bill, got to his feet.

She swallowed hard, wondering if he'd had enough of this conversation. Maybe he even had his signed divorce papers back in his office. If so, she hoped she wouldn't burst into tears when he presented her with them.

But he'd just told her she wasn't a loose end. And he'd held her hand in a way that had been so familiar it had sent a sting of fear through her heart.

So she picked up her coat and followed him through the pub, weaving through tables and people alike. When their waitress made to stop them, Max murmured something to her. She nodded and disappeared back among the tables of customers.

At the door, Max helped her into her coat and they went out into the dark night. It was chilly, but it wasn't actually as cold as she expected. When Max kept on walking, rather than stopping to let her know why they'd left the restaurant, she remained by his side. She had no idea where they were going, but right now she didn't care.

A taxi stopped at the kerb. 'You looking for a fare?'

'I think we're okay.' Max glanced at her as if to confirm his words. She gave a quick nod, and the cab driver pulled away in search of another customer. The bar was probably a perfect spot to do that, actually, since anyone who'd had a few too many drinks would need a way to get safely back to their flat. Putting her hands in her pockets, she waited for him to tell her why he'd brought her out here. Maybe something was wrong with him physically. Could that be why he'd come home from the Sudan?

A few minutes later, she couldn't take not knowing. 'Is everything okay?'

'It's still there, isn't it, despite everything?'

She frowned, moving under one of the street lamps along the edge of a park. 'What is?'

'That old spark.'

She'd felt that spark the second she'd laid eyes on him all those years ago. But he wasn't talking about way back then. He was talking about right now.

'Yes,' she whispered.

She wished to hell it weren't. But she wasn't going to pay truth back with a lie.

'Anna…' He took her hand and eased them off the path and into the dark shadows of a nearby bench.

She sat down, before she fell down. His voice… She would recognise that tone anywhere. He sat beside her, still holding her hand.

'You've changed,' he said.

'So have you. You seem…' She shook her head, unable to put words to her earlier thoughts. Or maybe it was that she wasn't sure she should.

'That bad, huh?'

'No. Not at all.'

He grinned, the flash of his teeth sending a shiver over her. 'That good, then, huh?'

Annabelle laughed and nudged him with her shoulder. 'You wish.'

'I actually do.'

When his fingers shifted from her hand to just beneath her chin, the shiver turned to a whoosh as all the breath left her body, her nerve endings suddenly attuned to Max's every move. And when his head came down, all she felt was anticipation.

Max wasn't sure what had come over him or made him want to leave the safety of the bar, but the second his lips touched hers all bets were off. The fragrance of her shampoo mixed with the normal sterile hospital scents, and it was like coming home after a long hard day.

His fingers slid up her jawline, edged behind the feminine curve of her ear and tunnelled into her hair. Annabelle's body shifted as well, turning into him, her arms winding around his neck in a way he hadn't felt in far too long. Or with any other woman.

The truth was that simple. And that complicated. No woman would ever be able to take Anna's place—so he'd never even tried to find one.

He deepened the kiss, tongue touching her lips, exulting in the fact that she opened to him immediately. No hesitation.

They'd always been good in bed, each instinctively knowing what the other wanted and each had been more than willing to oblige. Soft and sweet or daring and adventurous, Anna had always been open to trying new things. Until it had become all about...

No. No thinking about that right now.

Not when she was clutching the lapels of his jacket as if she could tug him into her very soul.

He angled his head, thrusting a little deeper into the heat of her mouth. Maybe they should just forget about the cold park and head back to the warmth of his cottage and the heat they'd find in his bed. There were taxis on practically every corner.

That was what he wanted: to have her. In bed. Skin to skin. With nothing between them but fire and raw need.

Just as he was getting ready to edge back enough to ask her to go with him, the sound of voices broke through the haze of passion.

Not Anna's voice, but someone else's. Close enough that he could tell they were man and woman.

Annabelle beat him to the punch, pulling back so suddenly that it left him reeling for a few seconds. She glanced at him and he looked back at her. They both smiled. Young medical students caught necking. It had happened before, when they'd been dating. Only that had been a police officer, who'd not been quite as amused by their antics.

'Caught again,' he murmured.

'So it would seem.'

He looked over to see who was walking past and his smile died, icy fingers walking up his spine. It was indeed a man and a woman, but they were pushing a pram. Bundles and bundles of blankets were piled on top of what had to be a young infant. And their faces.

God. They were happy. Incredibly happy.

His gaze went back to Anna's to find that all colour had drained from her skin, leaving her pasty white. The young man threw them a smile and a quick hello.

Somehow Max managed to croak something back, but the mood was spoiled. He could tell by Anna's reaction that she'd been thrown back to the tragedy that had been their shared past. At least that was what he took her stricken gaze to mean—the way her hungry eyes followed that pram as it went past and disappeared into the darkness.

His teeth gritted together several times before he had the strength to stand up and say what needed to be said. 'I think we've both had a little too much to drink. Maybe it's time to call it a night.'

Anna's one glass of wine and his two weightier beverages did not constitute drunkenness by any stretch of the imagination. Unless you considered being drunk on memories of the past as over-imbibing. It had to be all the reminiscing they'd done in the restaurant and the way her face had softened as she'd looked across the table at him. He'd always had trouble resisting her, and tonight was no exception. After one smile, he'd been putty in her hands. But he'd better somehow figure out how to put a stop to whatever was happening between them before one of them got hurt.

He'd opened his heart to her once before only to have it diced into tiny pieces and handed back to him. Never again. He would do whatever it took to keep that stony organ locked in the vault of his chest.

Far out of reach of her or anyone else.

CHAPTER FIVE

'I JUST HEARD. There's a heart. Get to the hospital.'

It took several seconds before a still-groggy Annabelle realised who was on the phone and what he was talking about. Once she did, she leaped to her feet, glancing at the clock on her nightstand to see what time it was. Three a.m.

Once a donor organ was located time was of the essence. It had to be transplanted within hours. 'I'm on my way.'

Scurrying around as fast as she could, she found clothes and shoved her limbs into them, not worrying about how she looked other than a quick brush of her teeth and putting her hair up into a high ponytail. Then she was out of the door and on her way to Teddy's. It was pitch black as she pulled her car out onto the roadway, and there were almost no other vehicles out this late. Blinking the remaining sleep from her eyes, she thought about the tasks she needed to do once she arrived.

Max evidently wasn't at the hospital yet, since he'd said he'd just heard. Which meant they'd tracked him down at home. Wherever that was.

Last night after that disastrous kiss, he'd seen her

home in a taxi, before giving her a tight wave as the driver pulled away. What had she been thinking letting him kiss her?

Letting him? More like her yanking him to her as tightly as she could. Once his lips had made contact with hers, he'd have been hard pressed to get away from her. She'd been that desperate to have him keep kissing her on into eternity.

Only that hadn't happened.

She tightened her grip on the steering wheel. No, that couple with the baby had walked by ruining everything. It hadn't been their fault, nor could they have known that Max's face had hardened instantly, reverting back to the mask she remembered from the end of their marriage. Was he remembering how badly he'd wanted what she couldn't deliver? No, he'd told her he no longer wanted children—maybe he didn't want to see reminders of what could have been.

And the way he'd looked at her after the young couple had walked away...

As if he couldn't wait to get away from her. He'd pulled her up from that bench so fast her head had spun. And no mention of when they would see each other again.

They wouldn't, obviously. Not outside the hospital. Or outside surgical suites. Last night had been a mistake. A remnant of embers long since extinguished. Except for one tiny spark...

Wasn't that what he'd called it? A spark?

Why had he even called her about the heart? He could have operated on Hope in the middle of the night, and she would have known nothing about it until the next morning. Had he been worried about how upset she would be that he hadn't told her?

Or was it simply the courtesy of a doctor to another member of a patient's medical team?

That was probably it.

Well, it didn't do any good to think about it now. This call was what Annabelle had been waiting for during the past two weeks. News that this particular baby might have a chance to live and grow.

She could put aside any discomfort working beside Max might bring. He and Sienna were both top in their field. She halfway wondered if the other doctor would be performing the transplant surgery. But Sienna had turned the case over to Max. Which meant he would be doing it.

Would he let her in the operating room? She wasn't a surgical nurse, but she had done a rotation in the surgical suite. And she wanted to be there for Hope, even though the baby would have no idea she was there. And wouldn't care.

She reached the hospital and made her way to the staff car park area. From the looks of the empty spaces, people still hadn't recovered from the virus. Hopefully Max would be able to find enough healthy bodies to be able to perform the surgery in the middle of the night. Well, by the time things were all prepped, it would probably be closer to six o'clock in the morning. Still early, but not so far out that it would be hard to talk people into coming in to assist.

Hurrying to the main entrance, she was surprised to find Max waiting for her. 'I thought you'd be in prepping for surgery.'

'We're still waiting on the medevac to get here with the heart.'

She walked with him, his long steps eating the distance. 'Do you know anything about it?'

'It typed right for Hope. The donor was an infant… the victim of a drunk driver. The family signed off just a few hours ago.'

Signed off. Such an impersonal term for what was a very personal decision. That baby had been someone's pride and joy. Their life. She'd mourned the foetuses she'd miscarried. But how much more would she ache if she'd held those children in her arms only to have them taken away by a cruel set of circumstances?

Kind of like the devastation her sister had experienced when she'd tried to adopt. But at least that child was still alive somewhere in the world.

A telltale prickle behind her eyelids warned her to move her thoughts to something else. Like the way Max had sounded saying Baby Hope's name.

Max had always been good at making sure parents knew that he thought of his tiny patients as people, painstakingly remembering even the names of extended family members. It was one of the things she'd truly loved about him. How special he made people feel.

It was what had drawn her to him when they'd first met. He'd acted as if she were the most beautiful girl in the room. Well, Max had certainly been the best-looking guy she'd ever laid eyes on, and when he'd said her name it had made her—

'Anna? You okay?'

She scrubbed her eyes with her palms. 'Still fighting the last bits of sleep, but I'll be fine.'

It was a lie. Annabelle was wide awake, but she was

not going to tell him that she'd been standing there remembering the way they'd once been together.

'Well, you'd better finish waking up. We have a lot of work to do before that heart arrives.'

'Were you able to assemble a transplant team?'

He nodded, looking sideways at her as they continued down the brightly painted corridor. Annabelle had always loved the way Teddy's was so cheerful, almost as if it were a wonderful place for kids to laugh and play rather than a hospital that treated some of the most desperately ill children in the area.

'You're part of that team.'

Annabelle stopped in her tracks. She'd hoped he would include her in some way, but to put her on the actual team… That strange prickling sensation grew stronger. 'Are you serious?'

'I wouldn't have said it if I weren't.'

'Thank you. You don't know what this means to me.'

'I think I do.' He smiled, no hint of awkwardness in his manner, unlike Annabelle, who could barely look at him without remembering what had happened last night. 'But I didn't put you on it out of some sense of pity. I need you. You know Hope better than probably anyone else here at the hospital. I want you monitoring her, letting me know of anything out of the ordinary you see as we get her ready. And I want a sense of how she is when the surgery is finished, and she's coming out of the anaesthetic.'

More beautiful words had never been spoken. Max acted as if it were a given that the baby would survive the surgery and actually wake up on the other side. As if there were no question about it. Done for her sake? Or because he really believed it? 'You've probably studied her case as much as I have.'

'I've studied it, but you've lived it, Anna.'

She *had* lived it. Some of it joyful, like when Hope opened those sweet blue eyes of hers and stared into Annabelle's. Some of them terrifying…like the day before yesterday when she had gone into respiratory failure. Annabelle had thought for sure those were the last moments of the baby's life. And now this. The sweet sound of hope…for a precious baby who was fighting so hard to live.

And now she just might get that chance.

'Thank you. For letting me be a part of it.'

Max started moving again, his steps quicker, more confident. 'I wouldn't have it any other way.'

'Ready for bypass.'

Max glanced back at the perfusionist seated at the table across from him, its myriad tubing and dials enough to make anyone nervous. But Gary Whitley—an expert in his field, Max had been told—was at the helm, his white goatee hidden beneath the surgical mask. 'Tell me when.'

Once they put Baby Hope on the bypass machine, the race with time would begin once again. The sooner the donor heart was in place and beating, the better chance the baby had for a good outcome. The risk for post-perfusion syndrome—the dreaded 'pump head'—grew the longer a patient was on bypass. Most of the time, the symptoms seemed to resolve after a period of weeks or months, but there were some new studies that suggested the attention and memory problems could be long-reaching for some individuals. Hopefully the baby's young age would preclude that from happening.

'Let's start her up.'

Gary adjusted the instrumentation and looked up just as the centrifugal pumps began whirling, sending the blood through the tubes and over into the oxygenator. 'On bypass.'

Max then nodded at Anna, who noted the time. She would keep an eye on the maximum time allowable and notify the team as they arrived at certain critical markers: one-quarter, the halfway mark and the three quarters mark, although he hoped they didn't cut it that close.

Using a series of clamps and scalpels, they finished unhooking Hope's defective heart, and, after checking and double checking the great vessels, they removed the organ from the opening in her chest wall.

'Ready for donor heart.' The new organ carefully changed hands until it reached Max. He checked it for damage, despite the fact that it had already gone through rigorous testing. He preferred to inspect everything himself...to know exactly what he was dealing with.

Was that one of the reasons he'd asked Annabelle to be involved in the surgery? Because he knew what to expect when they worked together?

Yes. But it was also because he knew this patient meant so much to her. Leaving her out after all the time, effort, and—knowing Annabelle—love she'd put into Baby Hope seemed a terrible act. Almost as if he were discarding her once she'd served her purpose.

That thought made him wince, but he quickly recovered.

Everything looked good. He measured the new heart

for fit on the patient's left atrium and trimmed a tiny bit of tissue to ensure everything went together as it should. Then he set about the painstaking process of suturing it all back together.

'One half.' Annabelle's voice was calm and measured, giving no hint of what must be going through her mind. Things like, *Are we on track?* Or, *How long until I see those beautiful eyes of hers open?*

Max knew those fears all too well. He experienced them on each and every surgery. But for him to do his job, he had to put those thoughts aside and move systematically through the process. The worst thing he could do was waste precious time worrying about each and every possible outcome.

But Max couldn't help giving her a tiny piece of reassurance. 'We're a little ahead of schedule. As soon as I finish these final sutures we can begin warming her up.'

In his peripheral vision, he saw Annabelle's eyelids close as if she was relieved by the words. Then she squared up her shoulders and continued to watch both him and the clock.

When the last stitch was in place, Max looked at every vessel and each part of the heart, making sure he'd forgotten nothing. Only when he was completely satisfied did he give Gary the okay to start the warming process and begin weaning Hope off the bypass machine. Sometimes the weaning process itself would coax the new heart into beating, the return of blood flow triggering the electrical impulses, which would then start firing. The surgical suite was silent until Annabelle's voice again counted down the time. 'Three quarters.'

This time there was the tiniest quaver to her tone. *Don't worry, sweetheart. Just give her a few minutes.*

Sweetheart?

He hadn't used that endearment when thinking about her in ages. And he shouldn't be thinking it now.

His gaze zeroed in on his patient's open chest to avoid glancing up at Annabelle, knowing something in his expression might reveal emotions he wasn't even aware of having.

Two more minutes went by. If the heart didn't start soon, they would have to shock it with the paddles. Even if it came to that, they could still have a good outcome, but something made him loath to use more aggressive measures.

Just one more minute. Come on. You can do it.

This time he couldn't resist glancing at Annabelle. Her face was tight and drawn, no colour to be seen, even in her lips. It was as if she were sending her own lifeblood over to the baby so that she could live.

His assessment of his wife's thoughts was interrupted by a quick blipping sound from a nearby machine. Everyone's attention rocketed to the heart monitor. *Blip-blip.*

Looking directly at the new heart, he saw a beautiful sight. The organ contracted so strongly it seemed to want to leap out of its spot.

Within a few more seconds, it had settled into a normal sinus rhythm. Strong. Unfaltering. Unhesitating. The most beautiful sight he'd ever seen.

'It's working.'

There were cheers of relief throughout the operating theatre, but one voice was missing. When he looked up to see why, Annabelle's hand was covering her mouth and tears were streaming down her face. His instinct was to go to her, wrap her in his arms and say everything was going to be okay. But he couldn't promise her that. Not ever again. It was why they were no longer together, because he couldn't bring himself to say those words. He'd been at the end of himself by that point and had to let her go in order to save her.

At least that was Max's reasoning at the time.

Had it been valid?

It didn't matter now. What was done was done. There was no going back. Not that he wanted to.

So he turned his attention to the patient in front of him, assessing her needs and checking the sutured vessels for any sign of leakage. Everything looked tight and steady. And that beautiful heart was still beating.

Five minutes later, the decision was made to close her up. Max could have passed that work over to someone else. In fact it was customary after a long surgery to let an intern do the final unglamorous job. But Max wanted to do it himself. Needed to follow the path all the way to the end before he would feel right about passing her over to the team of nurses who would watch over her all night long.

'Let's finish it.'

Soon the room was alive with different staff members doing their appointed tasks, the atmosphere much different now than it had been twenty minutes ago when that heart had sat in Baby Hope's chest as lifeless as her old heart was now. They would start the immuno-suppressant medication soon, to prevent her body from turning on her new organ and killing it, mistaking it for an invader. She'd be on medication for the rest of her life, which Max hoped would be a long and healthy one.

He set up the drainage tube system and then closed the sternum, using a plating technique that was made up of tiny screws and metal joiners. He carefully tightened each and every screw. Once that was done, muscle was pulled back into place and finally the skin, leaving space for the tubes that would drain off excess fluid. And the ventilator would remain in place for the next day or so, until they were sure everything was still working the way it should.

An hour later, an exhausted but jubilant Max cleared the baby to head to Recovery and then to the critical care ward to be closely observed over the next couple of days. Six hours of surgery had seemed like an eternity, at least emotionally. He was worn out.

When the baby was wheeled away, he congratulated his team, aware of the fact that Annabelle was standing in the corner. She looked as tired as he felt. A cord tightened in his gut as he continued thanking everyone individually.

The last person he went to shake hands with was the perfusionist, who had done his job perfectly, with stellar results. Only when he reached the man, his head was swivelled to the side, looking with interest at...

Annabelle.

He frowned.

Max peeled off his gloves and tossed them in the stack of operating rubbish that sat in a heap a few feet away, watching Annabelle. She was gathering instruments, seemingly unaware of the other man's gaze.

Gary's attention finally swung back to him and he smiled, stretching his hand out. 'Were you waiting for me? Sorry. It was great working with you.' He nodded in Annabelle's direction. 'I was just wondering who the nurse was. She looks vaguely familiar, but I don't think I've seen her in surgery before.'

One of his biceps relaxed, and he accepted the man's quick handshake.

She wasn't using her married name any more, but he decided to use a tactful approach and see if the perfusionist understood his meaning. 'That's Annabelle Brookes-Ainsley. She works down in the neonatal unit, but was interested in this particular case.'

'Because…' The drawn-out word said Gary hadn't connected the last names yet.

'Because she's been working with this patient. And it's my first surgery here at the hospital. It was a chance to see me in action.' He connected the two phrases, even though one had nothing to do with the other. He certainly didn't want to spell out that Annabelle was his wife. He was pretty sure she wouldn't appreciate that, but the guy had put him in a tough spot.

'To see you in…' Gary's eyes widened and a hint of red crept up his neck. 'Of course. I should have realised.'

'Not a problem. I'll let you get back to what you were doing, but I wanted to come over and say how much I appreciate the smooth handling of this surgery.'

'I—well, I appreciate it.'

With a ghost of a smile, Max swung away from the man and spoke briefly with the intern who'd been observing, answering a couple of questions he had. He kept that easy smile, but his insides were churning to get to Annabelle before she disappeared. And she would, if he knew her. She would want to go see how Baby Hope was doing.

The heart transplant marked the third patient 'crisis' that she'd assisted him with, and in each instance she'd done her job with precision and without hesitation. Max found it amazing that two people who'd been through what they had could still pull together and work for the good of someone else.

No rancour. No snide remarks, just an uncanny ability to know what the other was thinking, probably ingrained from years of living together. Whatever it was, they'd worked well together.

Except it evidently didn't carry over to their 'off times' because Max had no idea what she was thinking now. He answered one final question and then glanced at where Annabelle had been a second ago. Except, just as he'd suspected, she wasn't there. She'd already left the room. Without a single word.

CHAPTER SIX

ANNABELLE WASN'T SURE where she was going, but she had to get away from that room. It wasn't just the pile of bloody gauze and surgical tools that bothered her. Or the sight of Hope's still form being wheeled out of the surgical suite. It was Max's easy handling of both the case and the surgical staff.

And the aftermath of an adrenaline high that would probably send her crashing back to earth over the next hour or so. She didn't want Max to see her like that. He'd seen it enough over the course of their marriage.

She got ten steps down the hallway when she heard her name being called. Annabelle stopped in her tracks.

Max. Of course it was.

He had always been too good at ferreting out her emotional state, picking up on the nuances of what she was feeling. Maybe if he hadn't been quite so adept at it, she would have been able to hide her anguish over her repeated miscarriages. Only she hadn't. So she'd resorted to pulling away emotionally in an attempt to hide it from him. And in doing so had driven a wedge between them that had been impossible to remove.

Steeling herself, she turned to face him.

He came even with her, looking down into her face. Searching for something. She had no idea what.

'Good job in there.'

That made her lips twitch. 'I didn't have a very difficult task.'

'No, but I know you had a vested interest in that baby. It couldn't have been easy watching the clock ticking without any idea of what to expect.'

'I've watched transplants being done before.'

He frowned. 'You have? Because Gary, our perfusionist, doesn't seem to remember seeing you before.'

'I haven't actually watched one done at this hospital. Well… I mean, I've watched videos of them.' Lots of them actually. She'd wanted to see exactly what Hope would experience from start to finish.

'And did I measure up to what you saw in those videos?'

She sensed a slight hint of amusement in his voice. But yes, Max had measured up, damn him. Except she'd desperately wanted him to be as good as or better than anything that had passed across her computer screen. And he had been. His fingers had been nimble and yet gentle as he'd handled Hope, both before surgery and during it. There'd been a steely determination about him as those brown eyes had inspected the new heart. She'd seen it again as he'd waited for that same heart to begin beating. And then the smile he probably hadn't even realised he'd flashed when that tiny organ had started pumping oxygen-rich blood through Hope's tired body.

Watching him work had caused something warm to flood through her own insides. Just as the warmth had washed through Hope's veins as the surgery had neared completion. And that scared her.

'You already know the answer to that. Hope is alive because of you.'

That same devastating smile slid across his lips. 'It's been a while since I've done surgery in a hospital setting. Actually it's been a while since I've done anything in a modern hospital.'

Annabelle matched his smile. 'I'm sure it takes some getting used to after what you've seen.'

'It does.' He paused for a long moment and his eyes dipped to her mouth.

Annabelle's breath caught in her lungs. 'I can't imagine what it must have been like.'

Slowly his glance came back up to hers. 'You'd have to be there to really understand.' He paused for a moment. 'I actually have a Christmas fundraising gala to attend with Doctors Without Borders the day after tomorrow in London. If you're interested in learning more you could always come with me. Or are you slated to work two nights from now?'

'No, but…' Was he asking her to travel to London with him? Because it sure sounded like—

'I know we haven't made any hard and fast decisions about the future, but maybe we should. We could talk on the drive over.'

She stood there paralyzed, afraid to say no, but even more afraid to say yes.

'I would like you to come, Anna. Please.'

Oh, Lord. When he asked her like that, with his head tipped low to peer into her face, it was impossible to find the words to refuse him. So she didn't try. 'What about Hope?'

'We should be able to tell by tomorrow how things are going, and Sienna has already agreed to cover for me that night—along with her team, which she assures me is the best in the area. We'll just be gone overnight. Hope will never even know we're gone.'

Overnight? That word sent a shiver through her, even though it shouldn't. Memories of other nights in London swirled to life in her head despite her best efforts. Of them in their flat, making love as if there were no tomorrow.

Of course, in the end, there hadn't been.

She shook herself back to reality. This was no big deal. And they did have a lot to discuss. Most fundraisers were held at night. By the time the festivities wound down and they got back on the road it would be late. Probably much later than Max would want to drive. And if there was alcohol involved...

They could stay at a hotel. Annabelle had done that on several occasions when she'd gone into London for a seminar or lecture in her field. It was no big deal. She'd travelled with colleagues before. They'd simply taken care of their own sleeping arrangements.

Would he bring the divorce papers with him and sign them on the dotted line in front of her? If so, she should just let him. They both needed some closure, and maybe this would give it to them.

Even if the thought of taking that final step made her throat clog with emotion.

Why? It was time. Past time, actually.

'Okay, I'll go.' And she would just suck it up and muddle through the best she could. 'What kind of dress is it?'

'Black tie, actually.'

'Really? Isn't it too late to tell them you're bringing along a guest?'

'No.' He shrugged, the act making his shoulder slide against hers, a reminder of just how close he was standing. 'The invitation is for me and a guest. Most people bring a significant other.' That devastating smile cracked the left side of his mouth again. 'You're as close as I have to one of those.'

As in close, but no cigar? As in an almost-ex significant other?

'Ditto.' Her brows went up. 'I think.'

His hand came up, the backs of his knuckles trailing down the side of her face, leaving fire in their wake. 'We did good in that surgical suite. We gave her a chance that she wouldn't have otherwise had.'

'*You* did good. You made this happen.'

'Sienna could have done just as well.'

Annabelle was sure the other surgeon could have. But there had been something about the way Max had looked at that baby that had turned her inside out. Something more than simply a surgeon treating a patient. Hope had touched him as much as she'd touched Annabelle.

A wrench of pain went through her. Max would have made such a great father.

She'd wanted to do that for him more than anything. To give him what he hadn't been given by his own parents: the chance to watch a normal, happy childhood unfold. To love. And be loved. Only it hadn't worked out that way.

'Sienna didn't do it, though. You did.'

The fingers that had been slowly caressing her face curved around to the back of her neck.

Oh, Lord. He was going to kiss her. Right here in the

hospital corridor. Was that the act of a man who was about to finalise a divorce?

Maybe. Weren't there exes who had sex as they travelled down the path to divorce?

Not her.

And yet, every nerve ending was quivering with awareness. With acceptance. Her lips parted.

'Sorry. Is your last name Ainsley?'

'Yes.' Their necks cranked around at the same time, foreheads colliding as they did so. Ouch. Damn it!

Only then did she remember that she didn't go by Ainsley any more.

She slid away from Max as a male nurse came towards them, horrified that she'd been caught red-handed flirting with her ex-husband.

He's not your ex. Not yet. And she wasn't flirting. She'd been… Oh, hell, she had no idea what either of them had been doing.

The nurse's eyes went from one of them to the other. Of course. He wasn't sure exactly who he was looking for. '*Max* Ainsley?'

'That would be you,' Annabelle said, glancing sideways at Max.

The nurse frowned. 'There's been a complication with the transplant patient.'

'Oh, God.' Annabelle's stomach clenched. She should have been in that room monitoring Baby Hope, not hanging around in the corridor mooning after her ex.

She hadn't been mooning. And she'd been heading for the recovery area when Max had stopped her to talk. Had asked her to go with him to some gala. Neither of them had expected the moment to morph into something more.

Didn't it always, though, where Max was concerned?

They hurried down the hallway following the retreating nurse. 'What do you think it is?'

'I have no idea.' He took his smartphone out of his pocket. 'No one tried to page me that I see.'

They arrived in Recovery, and Max slid through the door with Annabelle close behind. 'What's the problem?'

Two nurses were at the baby's head watching the heart monitor on the side. Annabelle saw it at once.

'A-fib.'

Her eyes swung to Max, waiting for his assessment. And the concern on his normally passive face sent a wave of panic through her.

Damn it!

Max went into immediate action. While postoperative atrial fibrillation was a fairly common complication of cardiac surgeries, POAF wasn't the norm for heart transplants, and, when it did show up, it typically showed up a couple of days down the line. That made it a very big deal. Especially in an infant that had already been in crisis in recent days.

The possibilities skated through his head and were legion. Problem with the pulmonary vein? Probably not. The isolation of that vessel usually helped prevent POAF. Acute rejection? Not likely this soon after transplantation. Pericardial inflammation or effusion? Yes. It could be that. Fluid could be building around the heart—the body's reaction to inflammation. And it could cause a-fib, especially if it came on this quickly.

'Let's see if she's got some effusion going on and work from there.'

The baby, awash in tubes and bandages, looked tiny as she lay in the special care incubator, a tuft of soft blonde hair turning her from a patient into a person. He glanced to the side to see that Annabelle's face was taut with fear, her hands clenched in front of her body.

Was she worried about losing this one, the way she'd lost baby after baby due to miscarriage?

He'd been helpless to prevent those, but he damned well wasn't right now. He could do something to turn this around. And if he had anything to do with it, this baby was going to live.

He belted out orders and over the next three hours they ran several tests, which confirmed his diagnosis. They pumped in anti-inflammatories, and he and Annabelle settled in to wait for a reaction. Four hours after the initial alarm was raised, Baby Hope's heart had resumed a normal sinus rhythm.

Annabelle sank into a rocking chair, her elbows propped on her knees, her back curving as she sat there with her eyes closed. 'Thank God.'

Unable to resist, Max went over and used his palm to move in slow circles between her shoulder blades. 'We'll keep a close eye on her over the next twenty-four hours, but I'm pretty sure we've got this licked. As long as the fluid doesn't start building again, the rhythm should hold.'

'And if it starts building?'

'We'll cross that bridge when we come to it, Anna.'

The other nurses had moved on to other patients, now that the crisis was over, leaving Max and Annabelle alone with the baby.

Annabelle reached into the incubator and smoothed down that tuft of hair he'd noticed earlier. The gesture caught him right in the gut, making it tighten until it was hard to breathe. 'I think you're too close to this case. Maybe you need to take a step back.'

'Social services handed me her care.' She glanced up at him. 'Please don't make me stay away.'

He could do just that. Let someone know that her emotions were getting in the way of her objectivity. And he probably should. But Max couldn't bring himself to even mention that possibility. He hadn't been able to comfort her during those awful times in their marriage, but he could give her this. As long as it didn't take too big a toll on her.

She was a grown woman. She could make her own decisions. Unless it adversely affected their patient.

'I won't. But I'm going to count on you to recognise when your emotions are getting the better of you and to pull back.'

He didn't say the words 'or else', but they hung between them. Anna acknowledged them with a nod of her head. 'Fine. But I don't think I should go to the Christmas party with you.'

'Miss McDonald will take good care of her. If she starts taking another turn tomorrow, we'll both stay here. But it's only for one night. We'll be back the next day.'

She looked up, her hand still on the baby's head. 'Are you sure?'

Why he was so insistent on her going with him he had no idea. But these first few days at the hospital had been crazy. With the staff shortages, Annabelle had probably worked herself almost into the ground. A little Christmas cheer was in order. For both of them. They could count it as a celebration of Hope's successful surgery.

He told her as much, and then added, 'I'll tell you what. As long as she's holding her own, we'll go to London. If we hear the slightest peep out of Sienna, we'll come back immediately. It's not that long a drive.'

Her thumb brushed back and forth over the baby's tiny forehead. 'Okay.'

She probably had no idea how protective she looked right now. As if her very presence were enough to keep anything bad from happening to that baby. If it worked like that, Annabelle might have three or four children by now.

His children.

Max's throat tightened, a band threatening to cut off his airway. There would be no children. Not for Annabelle. And not for him.

That had nothing to do with this case. Or with either of them. Max needed to remember that, or the past would come back and undo all the progress he'd made over the last three years.

Progress. Was that what it was called? His stints in Africa seemed more like running away.

No. He'd helped a lot of children during those trips. Kids that might have had no chance had he not been there.

Like Baby Hope?

It wasn't the same at all. Hope could have had any number of doctors perform her transplant. He'd just happened to be here at the time.

And he was glad he was.

His fingers gave Annabelle's shoulder a squeeze. 'She needs her rest.'

A ridiculous statement, since Hope was in a drug-induced sleep. He had a feeling his words were more to help Annabelle rest than the baby.

'She's just so…helpless.'

'She might be. But we're not. She's got a great team of experts who are pretty damned stubborn.'

'Like you.'

That made Max smile, the band around his throat easing. 'Do I fall on the expert side or the stubborn side?'

'Both.' She tilted her head back and smiled up at him. 'Hope is extremely lucky to have you on her team.'

'Thank you.'

When she stayed like that, he gave in to temptation and bent down to give her a friendly kiss, hoping to hell no one was looking through the observation window at them right now.

He straightened, his fingers moving beneath her hair to the warm skin of her neck, damp despite the chilly temperatures in the room. From the stress of working to keep Hope's a-fib from turning into something worse. She had to be absolutely exhausted. 'You need to get some rest too, Anna. Before you collapse.'

'I will.' Her attention moved back to the baby. 'I just want to sit here a little longer, okay?'

He had a feeling nothing he said was going to move her out of that chair, so he did something he shouldn't have done. Something that would only test his equilibrium more than it already had been.

He pulled up a second rocking chair and settled in beside her.

'How are the quads?'

Ella and Annabelle walked towards the front doors of the local café just like they did every Friday morning.

Only today big flakes of snow were beginning to fall around them, sifting over the Christmas decorations that had been strung to the lamp posts. It should have felt festive, like something out of a postcard. But it didn't.

She had too much on her mind for that.

She tightened the scarf around her neck, needing her friend's advice today. The midwife hadn't steered her wrong when she'd convinced her to move to the Cotswolds a year ago. The change in scenery had done her a world of good. At least until Max had come barrelling back into her life. But no one could have predicted that he would be the one taking Sienna's place. Well, Sienna had known, but, from her reaction when she realised they knew each other, the cardiothoracic surgeon had had no idea who he was when the hospital had contracted him.

Annabelle just had to think about how to broach the subject. So she'd started with something work related until she could figure out how to bring up Max's name.

'They're fine so far. Mum and babies all doing well. It's very exciting.'

Ella had seemed distracted over the last couple of weeks. But every time Annabelle tried to gently probe to see what was bothering her, her friend clammed up. 'I hope everything goes well for them.'

'Me too.' Ella pushed open the door to the café and got into line along with probably ten other people who were all ordering speciality coffees and breakfast sandwiches. 'So what's going on with Max?'

Whoa. So much for casually introducing the subject after an appropriate amount of small talk. But she should have known that wasn't going to happen. Ella tended to jump right to the heart of the matter. Except when it came to talking about her own issues, evidently. But at least she seemed to be feeling better than she had a couple of days ago. Maybe she wasn't catching the virus after all.

'What do you mean?'

'Are we really going to play this game, Annabelle?'

Her? Her friend had been pretty evasive herself recently.

'I guess we're not.' She gripped the wrought-iron rail that kept customers headed in the right direction. 'It's no big deal. He asked me to go to a Christmas fundraiser with him. It's in London.'

'He did? When did this happen?' Ella's face was alight with curiosity. And concern.

Annabelle couldn't blame her. Max had only been at the hospital a few days, but he'd already managed to turn her neat and orderly world on its head. Just as he always did. She'd sworn she was immune to him, that she could stay objective.

But just like with Baby Hope, it seemed that Max had the uncanny knack of being able to separate the fibres of her emotions and stretch them until Annabelle was positive they would snap.

He'd warned her about getting too emotionally attached to Hope. But who was going to warn her about him?

Max was a master at keeping his feelings under wraps. She knew the way she—and the rest of her family—wore her heart on her sleeve made him uncomfortable. His background had made him much more cautious about big emotional displays when they'd started dating. But with a lot of work and time spent with her parents that personality trait had turned around to the point that Max didn't think twice about slinging his arm around her shoulders. That was when Annabelle knew she could love him.

His parents had died when he was in his early twenties, before he and Annabelle met. Even his grieving had been a private affair. And when she'd lost her babies...

He'd gone back to being clinical. Probably because she'd been so overwrought the first time or two. Then she'd begun pulling away as well and it had snowballed from there. She'd called him heartless that last time.

No more, Anna.

Wasn't that what he'd said?

But had he really been as heartless as she'd thought? Maybe his grief—like with his parents' deaths—had been worn on the inside.

'Anna?'

Her friend's voice called her back. She tried to remember the question. When had Max asked her to the charity event? 'He asked me yesterday, after Hope's surgery.'

When he'd almost kissed her in the hospital corridor.

If the male nurse hadn't interrupted them when he had...

God! She was setting herself up for disaster.

The redhead moved forward several feet in line. 'How did he ask you?'

'Um...with his voice?'

Ella jabbed her with her elbow. 'That's not what I mean and you know it. Was he asking you to a fundraiser? Or was he asking you to something else?'

Something else?

'I'm not sure what you mean.'

Ella turned her attention to the barista, ordering her usual beans and eggs breakfast with coffee.

Unlike her friend, Annabelle's stomach was churning too much to go for a hearty breakfast so she ordered a cup of tea and a couple of crumpets with butter and marmalade.

'What in the world are you having?' Her friend curled her nose, her Irish accent coming through full force, as it did when she was amused.

'I'm trying to eat lighter these days.'

Ella tossed her hair over her shoulder, taking the coffee the woman at the counter handed her. 'I'll go find us a table.'

It would do no good to try to hide anything from the midwife. She had always been far too good at seeing through her. Then again, there was that heart-on-the-sleeve syndrome that Annabelle just couldn't shake. The barista handed her a teapot and cup, promising that she would be along with their breakfast orders soon. There was nothing left but to join Ella and try to sort through all of her feelings about spending time alone with her husband tomorrow evening. After all the years they'd been apart, he shouldn't still leave her weak at the knees, but he did. And there was no denying it.

The second she sank into her chair, the midwife wrapped her hands around her chunky white mug and leaned forward. 'So tell me what's going on.'

'I'm not sure.'

Ella didn't respond, just sat there with brows raised.

Okay, so this was worse than just spilling her guts. 'Like I said, it's Max.'

This time her friend laughed. 'I thought we'd already established that. If the rumours about the newest—and sublimely hot—member of Teddy's tight-knit family are true, then he was spotted with his lips puckered, ready to swoop in on the always untouchable Annabelle. Some accounts of that story included a ringing slap to the face.'

Annabelle's eyes widened, shock moving through her system. 'People think I slapped him?'

'Not everyone. Some think you disappeared into the nearest supply cupboard with him.'

'Oh, heavens!' She poured tea into her cup and took a quick sip, letting the hot liquid splash into her empty stomach, hoping it would give her some kind of strength. 'Do they know who he is?'

She hoped Ella would understand the question. Did everyone at the hospital know that Max was her husband? Not that he actually was, except for on a piece of paper. The second she'd told him to get out, the marriage had been over.

'If they don't yet, they're going to work it out soon enough.' A waitress stopped by and dropped off their plates of food. 'The only thing stopping them is that you're using your maiden name. But of course, that makes it even more delicious as it heads down the gossip chain. Who wants to hear about an old married couple doing naughty things?'

'Great. So what do I do about it?'

'You might want to think about putting your own version of events out there so that you—and Max, for that matter—don't wind up with a real mess on your hands.'

'And what version of events is that? That I'm married to Max, but that we're on our way to dissolving the marriage? Talk about winding up with a mess on my hands.'

She already had. And she wasn't exactly sure what she could do to fix it. Especially since some people had evidently seen their display after the transplant surgery, when she was as sure as the next person that Max had been about to kiss her. If not for the nurse…

She presumed that he had been one of the ones to start the rumour. Then there was the situation of the actual kiss that had passed between them. But that had been outside the pub, and she was pretty sure no one from the hospital had been there. It was why she'd chosen the place.

Quickly telling Ella about that incident as well as all of the confusing feelings and emotions she'd been dealing with up to this point, she shrugged. 'Maybe I should have told him I wouldn't go to London with him.'

'Are you kissing… I mean kidding?' Ella grinned to show that the slip had been anything but an accident. 'You two have got to figure this thing out. There's obviously something there. That's what people are picking up on. Tell me you're not still in love with him.'

Annabelle didn't miss a beat, although her fingers tightened on the handle of her teacup. 'Of course not. But that doesn't mean I don't care what happens to him. I want him to be happy.'

'And you don't think he will be with you?' Ella took a deep breath. 'You've been locked in the past, Anna, whether you realise it or not. I think you have a decision to make. If you really believe you shouldn't be together, and you want him to be happy, then maybe it's time to do something about it. Remove yourself as an obstacle, as hard as that might be.'

When she'd asked Max to leave, she'd made no effort to go after him. And he'd made no effort to come back and work things out. Besides, she'd been so devastated by the fact that he wasn't willing to sit and wallow in misery with her that she hadn't been thinking straight.

But he evidently hadn't needed to wallow. He could have fought for their marriage—offered to go with her to counselling. But he hadn't. He'd simply seemed relieved it was all over with.

Her heart clutched in her chest. She'd been relieved too. And now?

Now she didn't know how she felt.

Their food was long since gone, although Annabelle couldn't remember actually eating her crumpets. But she must have since the spoon from the little pot of marmalade was sitting on her bread plate, remnants of orange rind still clinging to its silver bowl.

'Maybe you're right. Maybe it is time to do something.' She could contact her solicitor and ask him to prod Max to sign, since she couldn't seem to get the nerve up to ask him herself.

'Unless you decide you still love him. Then I say you fight.' Ella reached across and squeezed her hand. 'I know that doesn't help, but maybe you need to take a closer look at your heart. See what it's telling you to do.'

'I don't think I can.' That kiss went through her mind. He was certainly still attracted to her, he'd said as much, but Annabelle had always assumed that he'd stopped loving her when he'd left their home. So even if she cared about him, would it matter?

'Maybe that gala will give you the strength to do just that. If it does, then you have a decision to make. And this time you'd better act on it, one way or the other. Unless you're content to remain in stasis for the rest of your life.'

No. Of that Annabelle was sure. She had been locked

in a kind of suspended animation for three years now. It was time to move forward.

Even if that meant leaving Max behind. For ever.

CHAPTER SEVEN

MAX SAT ON the stairs, listening to his parents argue.

Again.

For the first time in his fifteen years he was scared about what might happen to him. Would they leave him here by himself?

'I am going on that cruise, whether you come with me or not.'

His dad's angry voice carried easily, just as it always did. Even if Max had been upstairs in his room, he would have heard those words.

'And what about Maxwell?'

'What about him? If you're worried, ask your aunt Vanessa to come and stay with him. I'm sure she'll be happy to lounge around the pool and do nothing.'

'Doug, that's not fair.'

'What's not fair about it? I consider it an equitable trade. I worked hard for this bonus, and I'm not going to give it up.'

There was a pause, and he held his breath as he waited for his mother's answer. 'Okay, I'll ask her. But we can't keep doing this. Vanessa has accused me more than once of not wanting him.'

'Just ask her.'

No reassurance that his parents actually did want him. They never took him on any of their so-called trips.

His hands tightened into fists as they rested on his knees. Then he slowly got up from his spot and crept back up the stairs. To pretend he didn't care.

Except when he got to his room and opened the door there was someone already in there. A woman... crouched on the floor beside his bed, crying. She looked up. Blue eyes met his.

Annabelle!

Suddenly he was grown up and his childhood bedroom morphed into the bathroom of their London flat. Anna held a small plastic stick in one hand, her eyes red and swollen. When he went to kneel down beside her to comfort her, she floated away. Through the door. Down the stairs, where everything was now eerily quiet. No matter how hard he tried to reach her, she kept sliding further and further away, until she was a tiny blip on the horizon. Then poof! *She was gone. Leaving him all alone. Just as his parents had.*

Max's eyes popped open and encountered darkness. He blinked a couple of times, a hand going to his chest, which was slick with sweat.

God. A dream.

He sat up and shoved the covers down, swinging his legs over the side of the bed.

Well, hell!

He didn't need a dream to tell him what he already knew.

But maybe his subconscious had needed to send him a clear and pointed message about going to that Christmas party with Anna: that he needed to tread very, very carefully.

* * *

Baby Hope was still holding her own. And he'd finally shaken off the remnants of that dream he'd had that morning.

He'd also received some positive news about the accident victims they'd treated a couple of days ago. Several of the patients had already been released to go home, and the rest of them were expected to recover. Sarah, who'd been one of the most badly injured, might have to have surgery to stabilise the sternal fracture. But everyone was hopeful that she'd heal up without any lasting damage.

That was some very good news.

He hadn't seen Annabelle yet this morning. Which was another good thing.

Right, Max. Just because you've passed the entrance to the hospital multiple times since your arrival this morning, means nothing.

A thought hit him. Maybe she'd come down with the same virus that had plagued other hospital staff.

It didn't seem likely. A few of those had trickled back to work today, and no one else had called in sick. At least, that was what one of the nurses had told him. So it seemed that the outbreak might be dying down. A good thing too. The closer they got to Christmas, the more patients they'd probably be seeing. Everywhere he looked, there were doctors and nurses whose faces appeared haggard and tired.

Frayed nerves were evident everywhere, including the operating room this morning, where he'd had to repair a hole in a young patient's heart. The anaesthetist had snapped at a nurse who'd only been trying to do her job. He'd apologised immediately afterward, but the woman had thrown him an irritated glance, muttering under her breath. It was probably a good thing that he'd understood none of the words.

All of a sudden, Annabelle came hurrying down the hall, a red coat still belted tightly around her waist. When she caught sight of him and then glanced guiltily at the clock to his right, one side of his mouth cranked up in spite of himself. She was late.

The Annabelle he knew was never late. Ever.

He moved a few steps towards her. 'Get held up, did you?'

'I'm only six minutes late.'

For Anna, that was an eternity. He held up his hands to ward off any other angry words. 'Hey, I was only asking a friendly question.'

'Sorry, Max. It's just been quite a day already.'

'Yes, it has.' His had started off with that damned nightmare, followed by a surgery at five o'clock this morning. Fortunately, the procedure had been pretty straightforward, and he'd been out of the surgical suite an hour later.

Her glance strayed to his face. 'What time did you get here?'

'A few hours ago.'

'I thought shift changes were at eight.' Her fingers went to her belt, quickly undoing the knot.

He nodded. 'They are. I had an emergency to see to, so I came in early.'

Her breath caught with an audible sound, her hands stopping all movement. 'Hope?'

'No, another surgery. It was urgent, but it came out fine.'

'I'm so glad.' She finished shifting out of her jacket

and stepped into her office, where she hung the garment on the back of the door. Her lanyard was already hanging on a cord around her neck. 'Have you been to see Hope yet?'

'Once. She's still stable. I was just getting ready to check on her again. Care to join me?'

'Yes. I was halfway afraid something would go terribly wrong during the night.'

A cold hand gripped his heart. It had indeed. He shook off the thought.

'I would have called you, if something involving Hope had come up.'

She nodded. 'Thank you.'

'So your day has already been tough?'

'Kind of. I've been on the second floor.'

'Oncology?' Some kind of eerie premonition whispered through his veins.

'Yes.' Her voice quavered slightly. 'We found out this morning that one of my nephews has been diagnosed with a brain tumour. I went to ask Dr Terrill a few questions about the type and prognosis. Just so I could hear first-hand what he might be facing.'

He hadn't yet met any of the doctors or nurses on the second floor, as each area was kind of insulated from each other. 'I'm sorry, Anna. Who is it?'

'It's Nate. Jessica's son…the one I mentioned.'

A band tightened around his chest. 'How old is he?'

'Just two.'

Jessica, the youngest of Annabelle's sisters, had already had a couple of children by the time he'd left. In fact, the huge size of Anna's family was one of the things that had created such pressure on her to have children of her own. She would never admit it, but with each new niece or nephew the shadows in his wife's eyes had grown. She'd wanted so desperately what her sisters had…what her parents had had. If the family hadn't been so close, it might not have mattered quite so much. But they were—and it did.

He wanted to ask what Dr Terrill had said, but, at two years of age, the tumour had to be something that didn't take years to emerge.

'Jessica noticed he wasn't keeping up with his peers on the growth charts like he should. And recently he'd been complaining that his head hurt. So they ran a series of tests.'

Headaches could be benign or they could signal something deadly. 'Do they have the results?'

Annabelle could say it was none of his business. And it wasn't. Not any more. He'd lost the right to know anything about her family when he'd walked out of their home and flown to Africa.

'A craniopharyngioma tumour. They're in discussing treatment options with their doctor today.'

He went through the catalogue in his head, searching for the name.

Found it.

Craniopharyngiomas were normally benign. But even though they didn't typically spread outside the original area, they could still be difficult to reach and treat.

'Why don't you get someone to cover you for a few hours, so you can be on hand if they need you? Or maybe you should go to London early.'

That might solve his dilemma about the Christmas party.

'I need to work. And Mum and Dad are there with

Jessica and her husband. At this point there are too many people. Too many opinions.'

Kind of like with Annabelle's in-vitro procedures. There had always been someone in her family stepping up with an opinion on this or that. It hadn't bothered him at first, but as things had continued to go downhill Max had come to wish they would just mind their own business. A ridiculous mind-set, considering Max himself had hoped to have a family as large and connected as Annabelle's had been—and evidently still was.

'If you'd rather not go to the party—'

'I want to go. It'll give me a chance to run by and check in on Nate while I'm in London.'

'Of course.'

Well, if fate didn't want to help him, he was stuck. Besides, he didn't blame her for wanting to go, if it meant making a side trip to see them. It was doubtful her family would want him there, though. Not with everything that had happened. But he could think about that later.

He decided to change the subject. 'Are you ready to go see Hope?'

'Yes, just let me check in and make sure there are no other urgent cases I need to attend to.'

Five minutes later, they were in Hope's room, gowned and gloved to minimise exposure to pathogens that could put the tiny girl in danger. She was still sedated, still intubated. But her colour was good, no more cyanosis. Something inside Max relaxed. Her atrial fibrillation hadn't returned after the scare yesterday, and her new heart was beating with gusto.

The empty chair next to the baby's incubator made a few muscles tense all over again. This child would never have a concerned loved one sitting beside her to give her extra love and care. At least not her mum.

As if Annabelle knew what he was thinking, she lowered herself into that seat, her gaze on the baby inside. She murmured something that he couldn't hear and then slid her hand through one of the openings of the special care cot. She stroked the baby's hair, cooing to her in a quiet voice. More muscles went on high alert.

Had she done this for each of her nieces and nephews? The fact that she would never hold a child she'd given birth to made him sad. And angry. Sometimes the world was just cruel, when you thought about it. Here was a woman who could give unlimited amounts of love to a child, and she couldn't have one.

But life wasn't fair. There were wars and starving children and terrible destructive forces of nature that laid waste to whole communities.

Annabelle glanced up at him. 'The difference between how she looked thirty-six hours ago and right now are like day and night.'

He remembered. He also remembered how they'd almost lost her an hour after her surgery.

But this tiny tyke was a fighter, just as Anna had said she was. She wanted to live. Her body had fought hard, almost as if she'd known that if she held on long enough, relief would come.

And it had.

Maybe life was sometimes fair after all.

He laid a hand on top of the incubator. 'And so far she's handling all of this like a champ.'

'Where will she go after this?'

The question wasn't aimed at him. But he felt a need to answer it anyway. 'I'm sure there are a lot of people who would take Hope in a second. She'll get a lot of love.'

'I hope so.'

'There's no chance that her mum will come back and want her later?'

'It's been over two weeks. She knew that Hope was born with a heart defect. There's always a chance, but if she'd wanted to find her, surely she would have come back to the hospital by now?'

He nodded. 'What do social services say?'

'That if her mum doesn't return, she'll be placed in a foster home and then put up for adoption.'

That brought up another point. He took his hand off the cot. 'You've never thought again about adopting?'

That had been another sticky subject towards the end of their marriage. She'd refused to even entertain the idea.

'My sister's experience made me afraid of going that route. But after spending so much time with Hope, I'm more open to it than I was in the past. Not every case ends in heartache, like Mallory's did. I don't know if I'd be able to adopt Hope, but surely they would let me consider another child with special needs. I love my nieces and nephews, but...' She stopped as if remembering that she had a very ill nephew.

She withdrew her hand, staring into the special care cot.

'But it's not the same. I get it.' He wanted to make sure she knew that there was nothing wrong with wanting someone of your own to love. He'd once felt that way about Anna. That she made his life complete in a way nothing else could, not even his work in Africa, as worthy as that might be. But in the end, his dream had been right about one thing: she hadn't wanted him to stay.

'You've probably seen plenty of needy children in Africa.'

'Yes. There are some incredible needs on that continent. I've sometimes wished…' He'd sometimes wished he could give a couple of kids a stable home without poverty or fear, but with the way his parents had been… Well, it wasn't something he saw himself tackling on his own.

Then there was the unfinished business with Annabelle. It didn't lend itself to making a new start. Especially when the previous chapter was still buzzing in the background. It was another thing his dream had got right. Annabelle was out of reach. She had been for a long time. He needed to sign those papers. Only then could he move forward.

He'd been thinking more and more along those lines over the last several days. She was here. His excuse of old was that he wasn't quite sure where to find her. But that no longer held water.

He couldn't have hired a solicitor to track her down back then? Or have gone through her parents?

Probably. But he'd believed if she wanted that divorce badly enough, she would find him.

'You've sometimes wished what?'

'That I could make life better for a child or two.'

She swivelled in her chair, her face turning up to study his. 'You once told me you no longer wanted children.'

Yes, he had. After her last miscarriage, he'd told her that to protect her health and to save what was evidently unsalvageable: their marriage. So he'd told a lie. Except when he'd said the words, they hadn't been a lie. He'd just wanted it all to stop.

And it had.

'I was tired of all the hoops we had to leap through. Of all of the disappointment.'

'I'm so sorry, Max.' Her face went from looking up at him as if trying to understand to bending down to stare at the floor.

What the hell?

Realising she might have misunderstood his words, he knelt down beside her in a hurry, taking her chin and forcing her to look at him. 'I wasn't disappointed *in* you, Anna. I was disappointed *for* you. For both of us. I wanted to be able to snap my fingers and make everything right, and when I couldn't… It just wore me down, made me feel helpless in a way I'd never felt before.'

'Like Jessica must feel right now with Nate.' Her eyes swam with moisture, although none of it spilled over the lower rim of her eyelids.

'She has a great support network in you and the rest of the family.' Something Max hadn't felt as if he'd given to Annabelle. He'd withdrawn more and more of his emotional support, afraid to get attached to a foetus that would never see the light of day. And towards the end, that was what he'd started thinking of them as. Foetuses and not babies. And he'd damned himself each time he'd used that term.

'She does. Her husband has been her rock as well.'

Unlike him? His jaw tightened, teeth clenching together in an effort to keep from apologising for something that he couldn't change.

Her eyes focused on him. And then her hand went to his cheek. 'Don't. I wasn't accusing you of not being there, Max. I was the one who pulled away. You did what you could.'

'It wasn't enough.'

Her lashes fluttered as her lids closed and her hand fell back to her side. 'Nothing would have been enough. I was a mess back then. I'm stronger now.'

She was. He saw it in the way she cared for Baby Hope and the rest of her patients. She'd called Jessica's husband a rock. She could have been describing herself.

'You were always strong. They were just difficult days.'

Baby Hope stirred in her cot, one of her arms jerking to the side until her fingers were pressed against the clear acrylic of the incubator. Annabelle touched her index finger to the barrier separating her from the baby. 'This is the strong one. I'm envisioning a bright future for her.'

'She has a great chance.'

Annabelle sucked down a deep breath and let it out in a rush. 'Thank you for all you did to help her.'

'She did most of the work. She stuck around until we could find a donor heart.'

'Yes, she did.'

Max stood up and held out his hand, the ominous warning of his dream fading slightly. 'Let's let her get some rest.'

'Good idea. I need to get to work and then check in with my sister.' She took his hand, their gloves preventing them from feeling each other's skin, but it was still intimate, her grip returning his. He found himself continuing to hold her hand for several seconds longer than necessary. 'You'll let me know if there's any change in her condition, won't you?'

'You know I will.' He paused, not sure how she would feel about what he was about to say. 'You'll let me know about Nate, won't you? I know I've never met him, but I care about your family.'

He had loved her parents and siblings, had liked seeing what it was like to be part of a large and caring family. It had had its downsides as well, the births of her nieces and nephews seeming to increase Annabelle's anguish over her own lack of having babies, but that hadn't been anyone's fault. As upset as he'd been at times over what he'd seen as meddling, he was grateful her family had been there to give her the support he'd never had as a child and couldn't seem to manage as an adult.

'I will. And thank you.'

With that, Annabelle peeled off her gloves, threw them in the rubbish bin, and went out of the door.

'You go to the party, honey.'

Annabelle clenched her phone just a little tighter. 'Are you sure, Mum? I can spend the night there with you instead.'

'Don't do that. Nate is fine. He's resting comfortably right now.'

'And Jessie and Walter?' Her sister had to be frantic with worry. With a husband who travelled five days a week, it couldn't be easy to deal with a child's health crisis while his father worked to make a decent living.

'Walter is staying home this week. They're setting up timetables with their team of doctors. It looks like Nate's prognosis is better than it could have been. The tumour is not malignant, and they're hopeful they can get all of it with surgery.'

Even though it wasn't malignant, meaning it wouldn't spread wildly through Nate's body, it could still regrow, if they didn't get absolutely every piece of it when they operated. But resecting a tumour and differentiating between tumour cells and healthy tissue was one of the hardest jobs a surgeon had. At least with Baby Hope's surgery, once the transplant was done, there was no growth of foreign tissue to contend with. There were other problems that could arise, yes, like her a-fib, but cells of the old heart wouldn't hang around and cause trouble later. Once it was out of the body, it was gone for good.

She hadn't told her mum yet that Max was working at her hospital or that he was the one she was going to the party with. Somehow she needed to break the news to her. But she wasn't sure if she should do it now, with the worry of Nate hanging over her head. The last thing her mother needed was to lose sleep over another of her children. Her family had been shocked—and horrified—when they'd heard that she and Max had separated. So she had no idea how her mum would react. She'd probably be thrilled...and hopeful. Something else Annabelle didn't want her family being. She and Max were not getting back together.

'Who are you going with? Ella?'

Oh, great. Here it came.

'No. Not Ella.' She'd better just get it over with. 'I'm actually going with Max.'

There was a pause. A long one. Annabelle could practically hear the air between their two phones vibrating.

'Mum? Are you there?'

'I'm here.' Another hesitation. 'I didn't know he was back in England.'

'He came back a week ago.' She bit her lip. This was turning out to be harder than she'd expected.

'Okay, then. I didn't know you'd been in contact with him.'

Oh, yes. Much harder.

'By coincidence, he's come to work at the same hospital as I am, here in Cheltenham.' Before her mother could jump to conclusions, she hurried to finish. 'He wound up here quite by accident. He's taking another surgeon's place while she goes on maternity leave.'

'You're positive he didn't know you were there?'

And there was that note of hopefulness she'd been hoping to avoid.

'Yes, I'm absolutely positive.'

'I wonder…' Her mother let whatever she was going to say trail off into nothing. Then she came back. 'Why don't you and Max come to London a little earlier? We're just getting ready to put up the tree and decorate it. You didn't help us put on the ornaments last year, and you know everyone would love to have you there. And Max, of course. Nate… Well, he would love it.'

Oh, Lord, how was she going to get out of this? She'd had no idea her mother would suggest she come over and help decorate the tree. Especially not with her ex in tow.

'I'm not sure Max will want to—'

'It certainly can't hurt to ask. And if he doesn't want to join us, he can just pick you up at the house later and off you'll go to the party.' Another pause, quicker this time. 'What kind of party did you say it was?'

'A Doctors Without Borders fundraiser.'

'Isn't that who Max left—I mean worked with?'

Her mum was right. Annabelle might have been the one to ask him to leave, but Doctors Without Borders had been Max's escape route. They had used to talk about going and working together. But in the end, Max had gone alone.

'Yes.'

'Is he going back with them once he's finished his contract at the hospital?'

Something in Annabelle's stomach twisted until it hurt. No, that had been her, clenching her abs until they shook. She'd asked him that same question at the pub. 'I don't know what his plans are after that, Mum.'

'So this might be our last chance to see him for a while?' Her mum called something to her father, but she couldn't hear what it was. Great. She could only hope that she wasn't telling him that Max was back and that it would be good to have the family together again.

Her mum knew that Max had left, but she'd never told her that she'd served him with divorce papers soon afterwards. It had been a painful time in her life and she'd kept most of it to herself. And then as time had gone on and Max hadn't sent his portion of the paperwork back, it was as if Annabelle had put it to the back of her mind like a bad dream that had happened once and was then forgotten.

This probably wasn't a good time to bring up the fact that a reconciliation was highly unlikely. Max had given no indication that he wanted to get back together with her. In fact, even when he'd towed her from the restaurant and kissed her in the park, he'd referred to what was going on between them as 'the spark'. Physical attraction. People could be attracted to each other without it going any deeper than that.

'I'll ask him. But don't be disappointed if he'd rather not come, Mum.'

'I won't. But you'll come, even if he chooses not to, won't you?'

There was no way she was going to be able to get out of it. And actually she didn't want to. This was a family tradition that she'd participated in every year except for the last one, when she'd just been getting situated at Teddy's and had been too busy with all the changes to be able to take a train home to London. With Nate's diagnosis, though, she had to go. 'I'll be there, Mum, but I probably won't be able to stay for dinner.'

'Of course not. Tell Max I'm looking forward to seeing him.'

Okay. Hadn't she just explained that he might not want to come?

She would invite him. And then let him decide what he wanted to do. And if he agreed to go? Well, she'd have to decide how to tell him that her family wasn't privy to one small detail of their relationship: that not only had she asked him to leave, but she'd also asked him for a divorce. And the only thing lacking to make that happen…was Max's signature on a piece of paper.

'You what?'

Sitting in front of Annabelle's mum and dad's house, Max wasn't sure what on earth had possessed him to say yes to this crazy side trip. Because he was suddenly having second thoughts.

Especially now.

'You didn't tell them we're divorcing?' The words

tasted bitter as he said them, but how could she have neglected to tell her parents that their marriage was over, and that it had been her choice?

Surely they'd realised, when he'd never come home…

'There just never seemed to be a good time to mention it. Someone was always being born. And then my aunt Meredith passed away a year and a half ago. My dad retired six months after that. It's just been—'

'Life as usual in the Brookes' household.' He remembered well how frenetic and chaotic things got, with lots of laughter and some tears. It had taken him a while to get used to the noise—and there was a lot of it—but the love they had for each other had won him over. Especially when they had drawn him into the fold as if he'd always been a part of their close-knit group. It was what he'd always wanted, but never had. He'd been in heaven. While it lasted.

'Please don't be angry. I'll tell them eventually. Probably not tonight, since it's Christmas time, and with Nate's illness…'

'It's okay. Maybe it's easier this way. They did know we weren't living together any more.'

'They knew we'd separated, yes, of course. I left our flat and came home before moving to the Cotswolds.'

'Yes, the flat…' He almost laughed. Well, he guessed they were even, then, because there was something he hadn't told her either. That he hadn't sold the flat once she'd moved out of it, even though his monthly cleaning lady had called him to let him know Annabelle was moving home and that she'd said he could do what he wished to with the flat. Those words had hit him right in the gut. Somehow he'd never been able to picture her moving out of the place they'd turned into a home.

He'd assumed he would sign the place over to her once the paperwork was finalised. But then she'd moved out. And the paperwork had never been signed.

Why was that?

'What about it?' Annabelle turned to him, her discomfiture turning to curiosity.

'We still have it, actually.'

Her head cocked. 'Still have it?'

'I never got around to selling it.'

Her indrawn breath was sharp inside the space of his small sports car. 'But why?'

That was a question he wasn't going to examine too closely right now. 'I was overseas on and off and it got pushed to a back burner. As time went on, well, it just never happened.'

'Who's living there?'

'No one. I never sublet it. Suzanne cleans it once a month, just like always. When repairs are needed, her husband comes over and does them.' He shrugged. 'I halfway thought maybe I'd return to London at some point.'

Except every time he'd got close to thinking about his home city, he somehow hadn't been able to bring himself to come back and visit. Instead, he'd landed in several different cities in between his stints with Doctors Without Borders.

Annabelle smiled and it lit up the inside of the car. 'I'm glad. I loved that place.'

'So did I.' Well, they were going to look awfully out of place at a tree-decorating party with their fancy clothes on. But she'd seemed so uncomfortable when she'd relayed her mother's request that he hadn't wanted to make her feel even worse—or have to go back to her mum and tell her that he'd refused to take part. That would have been churlish of him. At least now he knew why the invitation had been extended. If they'd been divorced, Max was pretty sure he'd have been persona non grata in this particular family, even if he hadn't been the one to initiate it.

Climbing out of the car, he went around to Annabelle's side and opened it for her. Out she stepped, a vision in red. Until she tried to move to the side so he could close the door and tripped over the hem of her gown, careening sideways. He grabbed her around the waist, his fingers sliding across the bare skin of her back as he did so.

Her momentum kept her moving and her arms went around his neck in an effort to regain her footing. 'Oh! Max, I'm so sorry...'

Just then the front door to the house opened, and people poured out of the opening, catching them tangled together.

Not good.

Because it didn't look as if he'd just been saving her from a fall. It looked as if they were having a private moment.

Not hardly.

Annabelle saw them at the same time as he did and quickly pulled back. So fast that she almost flung herself off balance all over again. He kept hold of her for a second or two longer to make sure she had her footing. Then they were surrounded by her family, and Annabelle was hugging various adults and squatting down to squeeze little ones of all sizes. He couldn't prevent a smile. This was the Annabelle he remembered, uncaring of whether or not her dress got dusty. The people she loved always came first.

Just as he once had.

He'd forgotten that in all of the unhappy moments that had passed between them. These had been good times. Happy times. And…he missed them.

George Brookes came around and extended his hand. 'Good to see you, Maxwell.' His booming voice and formal use of his name was just like old times as well. There wasn't a hint of recrimination on the man's face. Or in his attitude. Just a father welcoming his son-in-law for a typical visit.

Max squeezed his hand, reaching over to give him a man's quick embrace, then gave himself over to greeting the family he'd once been a part of.

Bittersweet. He shouldn't have come. And yet he was very glad he had.

Jessica came up to hug him. He held her shoulders and looked into her face. 'How are you and Walter holding up?'

Her chin wobbled precariously, but she didn't start crying. 'We're doing better now that you and Annie are home.'

Home.

Yes, he'd once considered this the home his childhood abode never was. And the Brookeses had been the family he no longer had. Despite his own parents' faults, he suddenly missed them. Regretted never once visiting their graves.

Once he'd lost the right to be a part of Annabelle's family, the children of Africa had become his family. And they had loved more freely and with more joy than anything he'd ever seen. They'd taught him a lot about unconditional love.

Something he'd never really given to anyone. Even Anna. He'd always held something back, afraid of being hurt. And in the end, he'd demanded she give up something she dearly wanted.

He'd been wrong in that. Even though he'd told himself time and time again that it had been to save Annabelle the pain of future miscarriages, maybe he'd been more interested in saving himself.

He didn't have time to think about it for long, though, because he was soon whisked back into the bosom of a family he'd dearly missed, sitting on the arm of the sofa while Annabelle and her sisters held up ornament after ornament, reminiscing about where each had come from. Some were home-made. Some were fancy and expensive. But each held some kind of special meaning to this family.

Anna was gorgeous in her flowing red gown. Off the shoulder, but with some loose straps that draped over her upper arms, it fitted her perfectly, the snug top giving way to a full loose skirt that swished with every twitch of her hips. And they twitched a lot. Every once in a while she threw him a smile that was more carefree than any he'd seen from her in a long, long time. He knew that smile. She'd once worn it almost constantly. When he'd come home from work. When they'd gazed at each other across the dinner table. When they'd made love deep into the night…

His throat tightened, and he dipped a finger beneath his bow tie in an effort to give himself a little more room to breathe, even though he knew that wasn't the problem. In his hands, Max held the long white gloves

Anna planned on wearing to the party, but had taken off so she wouldn't drop and break any ornaments. In the back of all their minds was Nate and his diagnosis, but when Max looked at the little blond boy, he was smiling and laughing on the floor as he played with his siblings and cousins. Suddenly Max wished he could commit this scene to memory so that he would never forget this moment.

When Nate got up from his place on the floor and came to stand in front of him, looking at him with curious eyes, the tightness in his throat increased.

'Where's my ball?'

He blinked. Max wasn't sure why the boy was asking him, but he was not about to refuse him. 'I don't know.'

'You help find?'

'Sure.' Getting to his feet, he tucked Anna's gloves into his pocket and held out a hand to the little boy. As he did, his doctor's mind took in the subtle signs of illness. Nate's small stature, the frailness of his fingers beneath Max's. Jessica sent him a look with raised brows.

'He's looking for his ball?' Max had to raise his voice to be heard.

'It's in the basket by the far wall in the dining room.' Jessica glanced at her son, the raw emotion in her eyes unmistakable. 'Thanks, Max.'

'Not a problem.'

Together he and the boy made their way into the dining room. It looked the same as it always had, polished cherry table laid with glistening china and silver for the meal they would be having later. Gloria had never been worried about breakage, even with such a large and active family. His own mum had rarely set out the good china.

'There's the basket, Nate. Let's see if Mum was right.'

A white wicker chest was pushed against a wall, a large contingent of photographs flowing up and around it until they filled the space with black and white images.

Above the pictures ornate black letters gave a message to all who dined there.

In Stormy Seas,
Family Is A Sheltered Cove.

And it was. This family represented safety. Too many faces to count, but there must have been thirty frames, each telling a story. The birth of a child. The winning of trophies. The weddings of each of the girls. Jessica and Walter, Paula and Mark, Mallory and Stewart...

No. His heart caught on a stuttered beat, and he couldn't stop himself from moving closer. Annabelle and Max.

That day was pinned in his memory, superseding even his most recent ones. Anna, fresh from his kiss, was staring up at him with eyes filled with love. And he was... He had his arm wrapped around her waist as if he was afraid she might wander away from him if he didn't keep her close.

And she had. They'd both wandered.

Annabelle said she hadn't told her parents about the divorce. He wasn't sure if Gloria just hadn't had a picture to replace this one with, or if she'd left it up in hopes that one day he and her daughter might mend their fences and get back together.

Little did she know that those fences had been irrevocably broken. His gaze moved over the rest of the pictures. There were no others of them. Maybe because they hadn't had all that much to celebrate during their marriage.

Part of that was his fault. They'd been fixated on having a baby for so long, they'd never made time to look at the other things they'd shared.

A small hand tugged on his. 'My ball? In basket.'

That was right. He'd forgotten about Nate and his ball. Forcing the lump in his throat to shift to the side, he gave the child a smile. 'Let's see if it's where Mum said it was.'

He opened the basket to find children's toys of every shape and size. Gloria must keep them for all of the grandkids to play with while they visited. And all of Annabelle's sisters now had children. Except for her.

He glanced through the doorway to see her still helping to decorate the tree, laughing at something someone had said. She was truly beautiful. Inside and out.

She seemed to have made her peace with not having kids. At least from what he could tell. So maybe it was time for him to accept that as well and start finding the joy in life. Turning back to his task, he found Nate trying to lean over the basket to get a green spongy ball the size of a football. 'Is that it, buddy?'

Grabbing the object from the chest, he handed it to Nate, who let go of his hand and gripped the item to his chest. 'Ball!'

'I guess we got the right one. Watch your fingers.' He carefully lowered the lid and latched it to keep small hands from getting pinched. They made their way back to the room and Nate went straight to Jessica, showing her his prize.

'Wonderful. You've found it!' She glanced up at Max with a mouthed, 'Thank you.'

He gave her a nod in return. Annabelle handed an ornament to her dad, who still stood ramrod straight and tall, probably from his days in the military. He gave her a quick hug and took the item, stretching up to put it on the very top of the tree. The man then turned towards the rest of the people assembled. 'Shall we light it before Annie and Max have to leave?'

A roared 'Yes!' went up from all the kids, making the adults smile. He glanced at his watch. Seven-thirty. The gala started in half an hour, so they did need to leave soon, since the party was on the other side of the city.

Annabelle came over to stand beside him.

With the flick of a switch all the lights in the living room went off, leaving them in darkness. An affected *'oooooh'* went up from the people gathered there.

Max stood there, the urge to put his arm around Anna's waist almost irresistible. The way he'd done in years past. He fought it for a moment or two, then gave up. His contract wasn't for ever. Once Sienna came back from maternity leave, he would be on his way again. So why not do this while he still could?

He slid his hand across the small of her back, the warm bare skin just above the edge of the fabric brushing against his thumb. Curving his fingers around the side of her waist, he was surprised when she reciprocated, her arm gliding around his back, leaning into him slightly as she smiled at something else her father was saying.

Then, just as suddenly as the overhead lights had been turned off, another set of lights flicked on. Swathed in layers of tiny glowing bulbs, the Christmas tree lit up the whole room like magic.

Not 'like' magic. It *was* magic. The tree. The night. The family. It was as if he'd never left three years ago. He didn't know whether to be glad or horrified. Had he not moved forward even a little?

No, he'd done nothing to forge a life without Anna. But he needed to either do just that, or…

Or try to do something to make things right between them.

Only, Max wasn't sure that was a good idea. They'd wounded each other without even trying. Wouldn't they just take up where they'd left off and do it all over again, if given half a chance? Wouldn't she ask him to leave once again?

He didn't know. All he knew was that he wanted to live here in this moment. Surrounded by Annabelle's family and the life and love they shared between them.

Except they needed to leave, if they were going to make it to the gala in time.

As if reading his thoughts, Annabelle looked up at him, her eyes shining with a strange glow that was probably due to the lights on the tree. 'We should go.'

'Are you sure you don't want to stay here and eat with your family?'

She lifted a handful of the fabric of her dress. 'We got all dressed up, so let's just enjoy the night. Okay? No expectations. No preconceived ideas.'

That shocked him. Annabelle was by nature a rigid planner. The attempts to get pregnant had been accomplished with clinical precision—the spontaneity wiped out more and more with each new wave of treatment.

If she hadn't just said those last words, he would

have assumed she was following through with what they'd planned to do. But something about the way she said it…

Well, if that was what she wanted, who was Max to disagree? And maybe it was the twinkle lights messing with some rational part of his brain, or the fact that her dress clung in all the right places, but he suddenly wanted to have Annabelle all to himself.

CHAPTER EIGHT

THE GALA HAD some twinkle lights of its own. Everywhere she looked there were signs of Christmas. From the garland-draped refreshment tables to the large ornate tree in the corner, filled with presents. Those boxes, mostly filled with toys and hygiene supplies, would make their way to needy kids all over the globe. Max had brought a small gift too, placing it gently under the tree.

'What is it?'

'A couple of toy cars.' He smiled at her. 'Not very practical.'

She smiled back at him, touched by his thoughtfulness. 'Some little boy is going to love it. Especially since it's *not* practical.'

When Max had suggested staying at her parents' house, she'd heard what she thought was a note of yearning in his voice. She'd been so tempted to just fall back into old patterns, but her parents might have started asking some harder questions if they'd stayed for the meal. Questions she didn't have the answers to. Or maybe she simply hadn't wanted to face those answers.

So here she was, with her ex-husband, at a party. And she had no idea what she was going to do about him.

No expectations. Wasn't that what she'd said?

Yes. So she was simply going to enjoy this night. Max was right. She'd worked herself into the ground over the last couple of weeks. Didn't she deserve to just let her hair down and have a little fun? He'd suggested using this time to celebrate Hope's successful surgery, so she would. And maybe she'd even send a wish up to the universe that the baby have a long and happy life.

That was what she'd do. She'd worry about what happened tomorrow when it came.

But for now, they had the whole evening in front of them, and she intended to enjoy it.

'Do you want something to drink?' Max's voice brought her back from wherever she'd gone.

'I'd love a glass of red wine, if they have it.'

'Wait right here. I'll go and see.'

He went off in the direction of the bar where there was quite a large crowd waiting to get something. He'd be up there for a while. She took the opportunity to study her surroundings.

Were all of these people doctors who volunteered with the organisation? Surely not. Some of them must just be donors who were here to pledge their support. Or people like her who simply wanted to know more about what happened in the places those volunteers served.

A leader board hovered over the raised platform to the left. Annabelle assumed they would unveil an amount at the end of the evening. There were also wooden boxes at all of the doors where you could drop in either a pledge card or a one-time donation. She'd gone to do just that when they'd arrived at the building, but Max had stopped her. 'I didn't bring you here for that.'

'I know you didn't.'

She'd wanted to give. Annabelle had often thought of going on one of the medical missions with the organisation, but, once she and Max had separated, the idea had been put on a back burner. Maybe she should rethink that. She glanced at the bar again. He was still waiting so maybe she could find some more information in the meantime.

She took the opportunity to move over to one of the doors where the boxes were, along with some colourful brochures about the organisation. Taking her purse out of her clutch bag, she pulled out several notes and dropped them into the slot of the box in front of her, then she went to peruse the pamphlets.

'What can I help you with?' A voice to her right made her look up.

A man in a tuxedo stood there, hand outstretched. 'I'm Dale Gerrard.' He flashed a set of very white teeth. 'I should warn you that I'm a recruiting agent for Doctors Without Borders. And I'm very good at my job. Are you in the medical profession?'

'I'm a nurse.' She accepted his handshake, although it felt weird doing so with her long white gloves in place.

The man epitomised the meaning of 'tall, dark and handsome.' With raven-black hair and tanned skin, he probably had more than his share of female admirers. He smiled again, giving her hand a slight squeeze before releasing it. 'Have you been on a mission with us before?'

'No. But I've thought about it in the past.'

'Really?' His level of interest went up a couple of notches. 'What stopped you?'

And that was something she wasn't about to tell him.

It was too personal. And too painful. She glanced back at the line. Max was still over there. But just as she caught sight of him he suddenly turned, his eyes sweeping the crowd. Probably wondering where she'd gone.

And then he saw her. Just as the man next to her touched her arm to get her attention. Even from this distance she saw Max's brows pull together.

She looked away in a hurry, trying to focus on what the person beside her was saying. He was trying to hand her a clipboard and a pen.

Taking it with fingers that suddenly shook, she tried to corral her emotions. So what if Max had seen her? Surely he didn't think she'd stood around pining for him year after year.

What had started off as an enjoyable evening morphed into something different as a wave of irritation slithered through her innards. They weren't together any more, so Max had no say in her life. None.

Lifting her chin, she focused again on the man next to her. 'Yes, I would love to fill one out.'

'Great. Why don't you come behind the table with me and you can have a seat while you do?'

So Annabelle did just that, following Dale around the edge of the table where there was a line of seats, although no other representatives were there at the moment.

She sat down, suddenly glad to let her shaking legs have a break. Then she ducked her head and did her best to concentrate on the questions on the form, filling them in and hoping that Max didn't storm over here and embarrass her.

He wouldn't.

Her ex had never been a particularly jealous type.

And there was no reason for him to start now. Especially since they were no longer a couple.

She was scribbling something in the box of the sixth question when a glass of red wine appeared in front of her. Swallowing hard, she glanced up. How had he got back that fast?

Sure enough, Max was standing in front of the table, taking a sip of whatever amber liquid was in his glass. 'Are you thinking of going on a medical mission?'

'I… Well, I…'

Dale, probably realising something was amiss, smoothly filled in the blanks. 'Annabelle was filling out a form to get more information on what we do.' He glided to his feet and offered his hand. 'I don't know if you remember me. I'm Dale—'

'I remember you. You were in Sudan with me two years back.'

'That's right. I haven't been back in a while. I'm doing recruiting work now.'

Max was gracious enough to smile at the man. 'And you're doing a great job of it, from what I can see.'

Looking from one to the other of them, Dale thanked him, and then said, 'I take it you two know each other.'

'You could say that.' His smile grew. 'Annabelle and I are married.'

'You're…' All the colour leached out of the man's face, leaving it a sickly grey colour. 'I didn't realise…' He glanced down at the form she was filling out. She had indeed put Annabelle Ainsley. She'd thought about using her maiden name, like at the hospital, but Ainsley had just seemed to flow out of the pen of its own accord. She had no idea why, but right now she could clobber Max for making this poor man feel like an idiot. Except a tiny part of her wondered why he'd spoken up and claimed she was his wife. He could have just played it off with a laugh and said that, yes, they knew each other from long ago. It would have been the truth, and it might have saved everyone some embarrassment. And yet he hadn't. He'd spoken the truth, without actually speaking it. Because they had not been husband and wife for almost three years.

Dale recovered, though. 'Well, maybe you can go on the next mission together, then. And since you already know the ropes, I'll let you help Annabelle finish filling out the form. I'm sure you can answer any questions as well as I can.'

With that, the man headed over to another person who was glancing at the literature, engaging him in conversation.

'Why did you do that?' She peered up at him.

'He's a flirt. I was trying to save you from being hit on.'

'Maybe I wanted to be hit on.' That was unfair. She didn't want to be. But she also didn't want Max taking it upon himself to be her rescuer when he hadn't been in her life for almost three years.

His gaze hardened. 'Did you?'

And it now came down to telling the truth. Or lying just to get back at him. 'No. But I could have handled it on my own.'

'I'm sorry, then.'

Annabelle let her emotions cool down. No harm done. And maybe he really had been trying to keep her from landing in an awkward situation. 'It's okay. And thank you for the wine.' She picked up the glass and took a sip.

'Did you really want to fill out a form?'

'I did. I've thought about volunteering in the past, but it never worked out.'

Max came around the table and dropped into the chair that Dale had vacated. 'I remembered us talking about it years ago. I thought you only said that because it was something I wanted to do.'

'It's been in the back of my mind for a while. I just never got around to doing anything about it.'

The sleeve of his tuxedo brushed against her upper arm as he leaned over to see what she'd filled out so far, his warm masculine scent clinging to her senses in a way that no one else's ever had. If Max had been worried about Dale, he needn't have. She had no interest in the other man. While she could recognise that the recruiter was good-looking and charming, she'd felt no spark of attraction.

In fact, those sparks—as Max had called them— had been few and far between. And they'd never been strong enough to make her want to be with someone else. Not while there was still a piece of paper that had gone unsigned for far too long.

Maybe it was time to confront the issue. 'Do you want to sign the divorce papers? Is that why I'm here?'

His gaze darkened, lips thinning slightly. 'I brought you here so you could see what I've been doing with myself for the past three years. If I remember right, you were the one who expressed an interest.'

The soft anger in his voice made her fingers clench on the pen. Okay, so maybe it had been rude to come out and ask, but the subject was like the elephant in the room that no one wanted to talk about.

And evidently, Max still didn't want to talk about it.

Something in her heart became lighter, though, at the words. So he wasn't any more anxious than she was to finally close the chapter on their failed relationship.

But why?

Did she really want to sit here and dissect all the possible reasons? Or was she simply going to take another sip of wine and go back to filling out the papers? She lifted the glass to her lips.

A few seconds went by, and then a warm hand touched her arm. 'Hey. I'm sorry. I didn't want to come here alone, and you were the person I chose to bring. Can't that be enough?'

Yes. It could.

She drew in a deep breath and let it out in a whisper of sound. 'I'm sorry. And I wanted to come too. So yes, let's just leave it at that for now, shall we?'

His fingers moved slowly down her arm, along her glove, until his hand covered hers on the table. 'Then as soon as you're finished with that form, will you dance with me?'

Letting her fingers circle his for a brief second, she lifted them with a nod. 'Yes. I'd love to.'

Max's hand slid around her waist and swung her around the room for a second time, the music pulling him into a world where nothing else existed but her touch and the synchronised movements of their bodies as they danced together. It had been ages since he'd held her like this.

It felt good and right, and he wasn't exactly sure why. What he did know was that he didn't want this night to end any time soon.

Maybe it didn't have to.

Annabelle had said she didn't want any expectations or any preconceived ideas.

Had she meant that she didn't want the past to stand in the way of them being together tonight? He had no idea. But if she was willing to just take tonight as it came, then maybe he should be okay with doing the same.

And with her cheek pressed against his left shoulder, he wasn't in a hurry to do anything to change the situation.

He'd been an idiot about Dale being there with her at the table. But the man—a general physician—had somehow charmed his way into more than one bed when they'd served on the medical mission in Sudan that year. The women hadn't complained, but back then Max had been too raw from his own heartache to take kindly to someone jumping from one person to the next.

He'd fielded some veiled invitations of his own from female volunteers, but he hadn't taken any of them up on their offers. In reality, he hadn't wanted anyone. The sting of rejection when Anna had asked him to leave had penetrated deep, leaving no room for anything else but work. In reality, he'd been happy to be alone. It was a condition he was well acquainted with.

And something he didn't want to think about right now.

'Are you okay?' He murmured the words into her hair, breathing deeply and wondering what the hell he was playing at.

'Mmm.'

It wasn't really an answer, but the sound made something come alive in his gut. How long had they been here, anyway?

Not that he wanted to look at his watch. In fact, he didn't want to leave at all. But they couldn't stay here all night, and once they left…

It was over.

'Anna?'

'Yes?'

He paused, trying to figure out what he wanted. 'Are you still okay with spending the night in London?'

Her feet stopped moving for a second. 'Yes. I can stay with my folks if you don't want me at the flat, although I didn't ask Mum if she had room.'

'We can share the flat. I just wasn't sure if you'd decided you wanted to get back to Cheltenham—'

'No. As long as we can check on Hope at some point, I have no plans until my shift starts midday tomorrow.' She eased back to look into his face. 'Unless *you've* changed your mind.'

Not hardly.

But he should have told her he had. Because holding her brought back memories of dancing with her other times, when life was simpler and all that mattered was their love for each other. Seeing that picture on the wall at Anna's parents' house had made all those feelings come back in a rush. He'd been having trouble tamping them down again, but he'd better work out how.

Because, as of now, he and Anna were going to be sharing their flat one last night.

And the memories and feelings that haunted that place were a thousand times more powerful than anything he might have felt as he'd looked at that wall of pictures. His heart thudded heavy in his chest as the music changed, the singer they'd hired shifting to a lower octave, his voice throaty with desire. The mood in the place changed along with it, dancers beginning to hold each other a little closer.

Right on cue, the arms around his neck tightened just a hair, bringing his face closer to hers. And suddenly all he wanted to do was kiss her.

'Anna...'

Her eyes slowly came up and focused on his. He saw the exact same longing in them that he felt in his gut. Tired to hell of fighting what he'd been wanting to do for days, Max lowered his head and pressed his lips to hers.

Nothing was fast enough.

Annabelle's body couldn't keep up with the ricochet of emotions as Max spun her back into his arms the second they were inside the lift at their old flat, heading towards the fourth floor. Thank heavens no one else was in the compartment, because it felt as if she were on fire, and the only one who could quench the blaze was having none of it. He was keeping the flames fanned to inferno-like proportions.

Her gloved fingers gripped the expensive fabric of his tuxedo jacket as she tried desperately to return kiss for kiss...to respond to his murmured words. In the end, all she could do was hang on and pray they reached the flat before the dam totally broke and the camera caught them doing something that could get them arrested.

Ping! Ping!

Finally. The soft sound signalled they had arrived at their destination. The only thing left was to... The doors opened.

'Max.' His name came out as half chuckle, half moan as she tried to tug him to the side. 'We need to get off.'

His fingers tunnelled into her hair, his lips nibbling on the line of her jaw and making her shiver with need. 'And if I don't want to move out of the lift?'

'Then…*ooh!*…then we're going to be stuck riding it for the rest of the night.'

'Bloody hell.' His pained smile put paid to his words, but he stuck a hand between the doors just as they were getting ready to close. 'The image of you "riding it for the rest of the night…"'

They slid into the foyer, a ring of doors lining the fourth floor. She tried to call to mind the number of their flat, but, with her head this fuzzy with need, she was having trouble. 'I don't—'

'Four-oh-three.'

Gripping her hand as if afraid she might try to flee before they made it inside, he came up with a set of keys from one of the pockets of his trousers.

No way. She wasn't about to run.

Somehow Max got the key fitted into the lock and turned it. They practically fell inside the door.

Home!

No, not home. But close enough.

Dumping the keys onto the marble table in the foyer, he navigated through a hallway, switching lights on as he went, towing her behind him. She glanced around as they went through the flat.

It was immaculate. He'd said that Suzanne came once a month to clean. Annabelle didn't even want to think about how much money that added up to over the course of the last couple of years.

The place looked just as she'd left it. Her mum had told her to take the furniture with her to her new flat, but Annabelle hadn't wanted anything to do with the sad remains of their marriage. So she'd just left it all for Max to dispose of. It looked as if he hadn't wanted to be left in charge of that task any more than she had.

Down the hallway, past a bathroom and two guest bedrooms, until they arrived at their old room. Three years later, the brown silk spread still adorned the bed, looking brand-new. It could have been a mausoleum preserving a slice of her life that had been both happy and filled with anguish.

'I can't believe it's all still here.'

That seemed to stop Max for a moment. He looked around as if seeing it all for the first time. 'I haven't been here in ages. I always meant to change things, but...'

He hadn't been able to any more than she had.

'Let's not think about that right now.' She wrapped her arms around his waist, unwilling to ruin what had been building between them ever since they'd come face to face in the corridors of Teddy's. It seemed as if every tick of the clock had been leading to this.

Whatever 'this' was.

He cupped her face in his hands. 'Let's not,' he agreed before moving in to kiss her once more.

Again and again, his lips touched hers until the fire was back and this time there was nothing to hold them back.

Annabelle pushed his tuxedo jacket from his shoulders, moving to catch it when it started to drop to the floor.

'Leave it.' His knuckles dragged up the length of her neck, smoothing along the line of her jaw until he reached her ear. He toyed with one of her chandelier earrings, making it swing on her lobe in a way that made her shudder. He'd always known exactly how to make her melt like a pot of jelly that had been exposed to a heat source.

And he was the ultimate heat source, his body generating temperatures that threatened to scorch her until nothing was left but smouldering embers.

And she was fine with that.

He reached around and found the zipper on her dress—began edging it downward.

'Wait!'

She wasn't sure quite why she said that word, other than the fact that she wasn't wearing a bra under the gown, and if he got her dress off—well, she would be standing there in only her underwear while Max was almost fully clothed.

He evidently misunderstood because he went very still. Too still.

'Max?'

'Do you want me to stop?' He leaned back to look at her face.

'Yes. I mean no.' She shook her head, trying to form her words in a way that wouldn't sound completely off the wall. 'I'm not wearing…um…anything under this. I was hoping to even up the odds a little bit first.'

'You're not wearing *anything*?' He took a step back and dragged a hand through his hair. 'I am very glad I didn't know that while we were out on the dance floor. Or driving over here. Or in the lift.'

'I'm not totally naked. There was just no way to wear a bra with the back of the dress the way it is.'

He moved in again, his fingers trailing up the length of her spine and then walking back down it. 'Very glad I didn't know that, either. But now that I do…' His fingers again reached for the zipper and tugged it down, while Annabelle scrambled to hold up the front of her dress.

'What happened to evening up the odds?'

'I kind of like the odds the way they are.'

'You mean when they're in your favour?'

Max grinned at her but took a step back and began undoing the knot of his bow tie. 'You want even? You've got it.'

Not fair!

'But I wanted to do that.'

'It's much safer this way.' He pulled the tie through the starched white collar of his shirt and let it drop on top of his jacket.

'Safer for whom?'

'For me. And for you.' His fingers went to the first button of the shirt.

This time she groaned. Then a thought came to her. He'd done this on purpose. If she was holding up the front of her dress, she wouldn't be able to touch him, which meant...

That the thought of her doing so was making him as crazy as he was making her.

Well, two can play at that game, Max Ainsley!

'Oh, Max...' She let his name play over her tongue.

His hands stopped where they were, his brows coming together.

With what she hoped was a saucy smile, she let go of her dress, glad when it whispered down her body and pooled at her feet, instead of just staying put and forcing her to awkwardly push it to the ground.

His reaction was more than worth it. A blast of profanity-laced air hissed from his mouth as he stood there and stared. And when she started to move a step forward, he lurched backwards.

Annabelle was glad she'd decided to wear her laciest underwear ever, the red matching her dress to a tee. They rode high up on her hips and, while not quite a thong, they'd been advertised as Brazilian cut, which meant there was only a narrow band of fabric that covered her behind.

She peeled one of her gloves off in a long smooth move, and then the other, letting each of them land on top of her dress. 'Now the odds are even, don't you think?' She moved forward again, and this time Max stayed put. Maybe he was just incapable of thought right now, which had been her exact intent. She pressed her palms against his chest, gratified to feel the pounding of his heart beneath her touch. 'Let me help you with those buttons, since you seem to be having trouble.'

He still didn't say anything as she somehow managed to flip open one white button after another, until she reached the one at the top of his cummerbund. Pressing herself against his chest and gratified to hear yet another gust of air above her head, she reached around him to find the fastening at the back that held the wide satin band in place. It too hit the floor.

Evidently, Max had had all he could take, because his hands wrapped around her upper arms and eased her away from him. 'You're a witch, you know that?'

'Mmm-hmm. Be careful, or I might cast an evil spell on you.'

'A spell? Yes. I think you already have.' He swooped her up into his arms and dumped her in the middle of the bed, the brown silk rippling out from her landing spot. 'Although whether it's evil or not is yet to be seen.'

Max backed up several paces and made short work of the rest of his buttons, undoing the fastening on the front of his black trousers. And this time it was Annabelle who got to enjoy the show, as his strong chest appeared along with those taut abs. Off came his shoes and black socks.

The man made her mouth water. Even his feet were sexy.

Then he hesitated, and her attention shot back to his face.

'What are you doing?'

His smile this time was a bit forced, the lopsided gesture she loved so much tipped a little lower than normal. 'I'm trying to hold it together.'

Annabelle's relieved sigh was full of pure joy. He wasn't having second thoughts. He wanted this just as much as she did. 'Then why don't you come over here and let me hold it for a while?'

'Did I call you a witch yet?' His laughter came out sounding choked, but at least his voice had lost that weird edge he'd had moments earlier.

'Yes.' She leaned up on one elbow and crooked a finger at him. 'Time to stop stalling and let me help you finish.'

'That's exactly what I'm afraid of, Anna: that you'll help me finish before I'm ready.'

'Hmm…we can take care of that on the next round.'

'Next?' He came forward until he was close enough for her to go into action. She sat up and scooted her butt to the edge of the bed until he stood between her thighs.

'Yes, next.' She said the word with conviction, reaching again for his waistband. This time the zipper went down, and he made no effort to stop her. Pushing his trousers down his legs, she let him kick them out of the way. 'And now, Maxwell Ainsley, we're finally even.'

They both still had their underwear on.

'You first, then.' Max leaned over her, planting his hands on the bed on either side of her thighs, but he made no effort to strip her bare. Instead, his lips found hers, his touch soft and sweet and somehow just as erotic as the more demanding kisses had been. She tipped her head up, absorbing each tiny taste, each brush of friction as they came together over and over. Soon, though, the V between her parted legs began to send up a protest, a needy throbbing making itself known. She pushed herself even closer to the edge of the bed, her thighs spreading further. It didn't help.

Well, his 'you first' might mean she was supposed to strip him first, right? So that was exactly what she would do. Hooking her thumbs in the elastic band on his hips, she gave a quick tug before he could say or do anything, pushing them down to his knees.

'Cheater,' he murmured, not moving from his spot, every syllable causing his lips to brush against hers.

'We never set any ground rules, if I remember right. And if you'll just stand up, I'll finish the job.'

'I don't trust you.'

'No?' She gave him a smile full of meaning. 'Well, there's more than one way to skin a cat...or undress a man.'

With that she lay back on the bed, kicked off her high-heeled pumps and slid her bare feet up the backs of his calves. When she reached the spot where his boxers were still clinging to his legs, she pushed them as far down as she could. Max still hadn't moved a muscle...except for the one currently ticking away on the side of his jaw.

What she didn't expect was for his hands to whisk up her sides and cover her breasts, the warm heat and promise of his touch making the nipples harden instantly. He didn't stay there, however; his fingers were soon travelling down the line of her belly until he reached her own underwear and dragged them down her thighs, moving backwards as he inched them over her legs, across her ankles and finally pulled them free of her body. He stepped out of his boxers while he was at it. Or at least she assumed he did, since she couldn't actually see him do it.

This time when he parted her legs, there was no mistaking his intent.

'You want to play with fire, Anna? Well, you've got it.'

With that, he put his hands beneath her bottom and tugged. Hard. Hard enough that she slid forward to meet his ready flesh. 'Is this what you want?'

The part of her that had been throbbing in anticipation clenched, thinking he was going to give it to her right away. Instead, he slid up past it, eliciting a whispered complaint from her. It ended in a moan when he found that nerve-rich area just a little higher.

He repeated the act. Words failed her, a jumble of sensations eclipsing her ability to think, much less talk.

Her eyes fluttered closed, the release she'd sought just seconds ago now rushing at her much too quickly.

His voice came from above her. 'I think it is.'

His fingertips found her nipples once again and squeezed, the dual assault wracking her body with a pleasure so sharp it made her arch up seeking him. 'Max.'

He gave her what she wanted then, thrusting forward and finding her immediately. The movement was so sudden it made her gasp, her fingers clutching his shoulders as he set up a quick rhythm that didn't give her any room to catch her breath. Instead it tossed her high into the air and held her there for several seconds, and then she was over the edge, her body spasming around his. Max groaned, his mouth finding hers as he plunged again and again before finally slowing, the sound of his heavy breathing wonderfully loud in her ears.

She wrapped her arms around his neck, holding him tight as the emotions she'd been holding back finally bubbled over, tears slipping silently down her cheeks. Annabelle came to a stunning realisation.

She loved her husband.

She didn't just *love* him. She was *in* love with him. She'd never stopped being in love with him. She'd submerged the truth—buried it far out of sight—and tried to lose herself in caring for sick children instead. Only it hadn't worked. Not entirely.

Because here it was. In plain sight.

Annabelle loved him. Deeply. Entirely. And she had no idea what she was going to do about it.

CHAPTER NINE

IT HADN'T FELT like goodbye sex.

The deep sleep that had finally pulled Max under in the early hours of the morning released him just as quickly.

He blinked a couple of times, trying to bring to mind exactly what had happened last night, but it all blurred together to form a scene of decadence and exhausting satisfaction.

Annabelle.

He turned his head to look at her side of the bed only to find it empty—the nightstand bare of anything except a clock. No note. He frowned before remembering that they'd come to London together, so it wasn't likely that she'd slipped out and caught a train back to Cheltenham. So she was still here. Somewhere.

She was here.

He relaxed and rolled onto his back, settling into the pillows with his hands behind his head. It was just seven in the morning. They might even have time for another session before they had to be on their way.

And do what afterwards?

He wasn't sure. But maybe they could start again. In the crush of timetables and thermometers and ovulation charts, Max had forgotten just how good sex—real sex, not something with a goal in mind—had been between them. Last night had brought it all rushing back. Their first year had been out of this world. They'd been so in tune with each other's needs that it had seemed nothing would be able to come between them.

Until it had.

Maybe they could get back to the 'before' part of the equation.

Was he actually thinking of getting back together with her? Could they erase what had torn them apart and start over? If so, they could just put off signing any papers for a while and wander down this lane for a few miles and see what happened.

Unless Annabelle didn't want to do that.

Didn't someone say that couples who were getting divorced would sometimes fall into each other's arms one last time as a way of saying goodbye or having closure? What they'd done hadn't seemed like that. At least not to him.

Vaguely he was aware of the sound of running water. Ah, that answered the question as to where she was. She was taking a shower.

Naked.

She probably had soap streaming down her body. *Naked.*

When the word popped up a second time, he smiled. Hadn't he just thought about how it was still early?

Well, they could kill two birds with one stone. He could soap her back, while doing a few other things.

Throwing the blankets off, he realised the flat was chilly. The heat must be turned down, since Suzanne hadn't expected anyone to be living here.

He'd have to call her this morning and let her know he'd spent the night so she didn't come into the flat, realise someone had been in there and assume there'd been an intruder. And he'd promised he would call the hospital first thing to see how Baby Hope was doing. This was a good time to do that.

Bringing up the number on his smartphone, he rang the main desk of the hospital.

'This is Mr Ainsley. Is Miss McDonald in yet?'

'Let me check.'

The voice clicked off and became elevator music as he was put on hold. The shower was still running. Even if she came out before he was done with his call, he would just coax her back under the spray.

The music stopped and Sienna's voice came over the line. 'Hi, Max. Everything okay?'

It was more than okay, but that wasn't something he was going to tell anyone. Not yet.

'Fine. I'm just checking on our patient.'

He could practically hear a smile form on the other doctor's lips. 'We have several patients. Which one are you referring to?'

This time the smile was on his end. 'A certain young transplant patient.'

'She's fine. No more episodes of a-fib.' There was a pause. 'I do seem to remember telling you I would call you if there was any change.'

'You did. But I wanted to be able to tell…' This time it was Max who stopped short. He wasn't really ready for anyone to know that he and Annabelle had spent the night together. 'I just wanted to see if I needed to rush back this morning or not.'

'No need to rush at all. She's doing brilliantly.'

'Good. Thank you for taking over her case during my absence.'

'Not a problem at all. Are you coming back today?'

'Yes.' Which brought back to mind what he'd set out to do when he got out of bed. 'I'll be in around four o'clock this afternoon. Call me if you need me.'

'I will. Have a safe trip.'

'Thank you.'

Max rang off, scrubbing a hand through his hair. And now back to his previous thoughts of Annabelle and that shower.

Before he headed for the bathroom, though, he made a quick detour down the hallway and turned the heating up to a tolerable level—the amazing thing was they hadn't noticed the cold last night when they'd been making love. Then he padded back to the bathroom, stopping just outside the door.

The shower was definitely running.

He hadn't put on any clothes before falling asleep so that saved him a step. His mouth watered. He could certainly use a shower. Now more than ever.

Trying the doorknob and finding it unlocked, he eased into the room. Steam enveloped the space. She'd been in here a while. But then again, he remembered Annabelle had loved long, luxurious baths and showers. Her skin would be soft and moist...

Gulping, he removed his watch and placed it on the counter and then turned towards the shower enclosure. He could just barely make out Annabelle's form through the frosted glass. His body hardened all over again. How did she do that to him?

It was almost as if they'd been given a clean slate. Something he'd needed—they'd both needed.

With that thought in his head, he wrapped a hand around the handle of the door just as the water switched off.

Damn!

Yanking the door open, he found a pink-faced Annabelle, her hair streaming down her back, eyes wide with surprise.

'Max! I thought you were still asleep.'

'I was. But then I heard the shower and thought I might take one too.'

Her slow smile lit up the enclosure. 'I think I might have left you a little hot water. If you can be quick.'

'Did you forget? We had an on-demand unit put in. I can be as slow as I want to be.'

'Can you?' Her smile widened. 'I may have missed a spot or two, then. Do you mind if I join you?'

'I was counting on it.'

With that, Max closed the door and turned on the shower. Then, with the sting of hot water pelting his back, he put everything else out of his mind as he moved to turn on Anna.

Annabelle stretched up to kiss Max's shoulder one last time, her body warm and limp as she stood on the warm tiles of the shower enclosure. 'Were you able to call the hospital yet?'

'How did I know you were going to ask that?' He gathered her hair in his hand and squeezed the excess water out. 'I've missed doing this.'

'Showering?'

'Showering...with you.'

'I've missed it too. Along with...' Her hands swept

down his chest, heading to regions below, only to have him catch her before she reached her destination.

'Witch. Is that all you've missed?'

Was there a hint of insecurity in that voice? Impossible. Max was never insecure. He always knew exactly what he wanted. Or didn't want.

A chill went over her.

No. He'd said he'd missed her. Or had he? Hadn't his exact words been that he'd missed showering with her? Having sex with her?

Not exactly. He'd stopped her from stroking him. Had asked if that was all she'd missed. Maybe he was seeking reassurance.

'No, it's not all I've missed. I've missed…us.' She tried to let the sincerity in her voice ring through.

Threading his fingers through hers, he nodded. 'So have I. And yes, I called the hospital. Hope is doing fine.'

'Thank God. Maybe this will be a happy Christmas after all.' She wasn't above seeking a little reassurance herself.

'I'm hoping it will.' Letting her go, he stepped out of the shower, leaving her alone. Just when the worry centres began firing in her head, he came back, a thick white towel in his hands. Another one was wrapped around his waist.

'I guess this means fun time is over?'

'Didn't you say you had a shift this afternoon?'

'Oh! That's right.' How could she have forgotten that? Maybe because when Max was around, she tended to forget everything.

When she went to grab the towel from him, he held

it just out of reach. 'Not so fast. There's something else I've missed.'

With that, he opened the fluffy terry and proceeded to pat her dry, starting with her face and gently moving down her body, until he was kneeling before her, sweeping the towel down her thighs and calves. A familiar tingling began stirring in her midsection. 'You'd better be careful, or I'm never going to let you out of this room.'

'I can think of worse things than being kept as your prisoner.'

The towel moved between her legs, teasing more intimate territory.

A low moan came from her throat before she could stop it. 'That's so not fair. You didn't let me touch you.'

His eyes came up to meet hers. 'You have more control than I do.'

'Wanna bet?' She tangled her fingers in his hair, letting the warm moist strands filter between them. 'I've never been able to resist you. I really do need to get to work, though.'

He stood. 'See? More control. Bend over.'

'Wh…what?' The word sputtered out on a half-laugh.

'Naughty girl. Not for that.' He grinned, the act taking years off his face. 'Now bend over.'

She did as he asked, and Max flipped her hair over until the strands hung straight down. Then he wrapped the towel around her head and twisted it, enveloping her wet locks in it. A glimmer of disappointment went through her. Max had it all wrong. She had no control when it came to him. She wanted him. All the time.

And now that things seemed to be easing between them, maybe she'd be able to have him whenever she wanted him. At least that was what she hoped. Surely he felt the same way as she did.

She tightened the towel and then stood upright again, letting the end of it slide down the back of her head. Luckily there was still a hairdryer in the flat. She'd found it when searching through the drawers.

Max opened the shower door for her and let her step out. A wave of steam followed her as he wrapped her in a second towel. 'Good thing we don't have an alarm that is triggered by heat.'

'Yes, that's a very good thing.' He encircled her waist and pulled her back against him. 'I can think of several times during the night when we might have set it off, if so.'

'I can think of several times that you went off too.'

He dropped a kiss on her hair, and she felt something stir against her backside. He gave a strangled laugh. 'Maybe we'd better not talk about that right now.'

Maybe they shouldn't. Because the tingling that had started when he'd towel-dried her was getting stronger. 'Okay, let me get dressed and dry my hair, and I'll be ready.'

He tipped up her head and gave her a soft kiss. 'Okay, but it's under duress.' Letting her go, he dragged his hands through his own wet hair, which settled right into place.

'That is so not fair. You don't have to do anything to look great.'

'Neither do you.' He tapped her nose with his finger. 'You are perfect just as you are.'

'I don't know about that, but I do feel perfectly satisfied.' She went over and opened a drawer, finding the hairdryer she'd discovered earlier. She picked it up, laughing as a thought hit her. 'After all those contortions we did years ago, wouldn't it be funny if last night or this morning did what all the hormone treatments couldn't? So...do you want a boy or a girl?'

It was only when she picked up her hairbrush that she realised Max wasn't laughing. He had gone very still.

He slipped his watch around his wrist, before looking up. His eyes were completely blank, although a muscle ticked in his jaw. 'A boy or a girl?'

A sliver of alarm went through her at the slow words. Where was the man who had just made love to her as if he couldn't get enough?

She forced a smile to her face. One she didn't feel. 'It's just that it would be ironic, if I got pregnant when we weren't even trying.'

Actually, it wouldn't be funny. Or ironic. Or anything else. Why had she even said that?

Max turned and went into the bedroom. With a panicked sense of déjà vu, Annabelle followed him, finding the bed was perfectly made. So perfectly that if she hadn't remembered writhing like a maniac beneath those sheets, she might have thought it was all a dream.

Only that exquisite bit of soreness in all the right places said it had been very real.

Except there was that weird vibe she'd picked up after joking about getting pregnant. He hadn't looked or sounded like someone who would be thrilled about that happening. Maybe she should put his mind at ease. She moved closer.

'Hey, are you afraid I might get pregnant because of what we did?'

His pupils darkened, expanding until they seemed

to take up his entire iris. 'I think the more appropriate question would be: are you afraid you *won't* get pregnant?'

She blinked. 'No, of course not. I was joking.'

'Were you? Because right now, I don't feel like laughing.'

Neither did she. She had no idea why the pregnancy thing had crossed her mind. Maybe because it had been so long since they'd had sex that was totally spontaneous.

Nothing like bringing up a whole slew of bad memories, though.

He turned away and picked up his overnight bag, setting it on the bed.

Annabelle caught at his arm, forcing him to face her again. 'Look, I'm sorry. Obviously it's still a touchy subject.'

'Touchy would be an understatement.' The thin line of his mouth was a warning she remembered from days past. 'Is this why you were so eager to get back to the flat last night—were you trying to hit a certain magic window? If so, you've got the wrong man.'

'I wasn't doing anything of the sort! You're being ridiculous.'

It was as if everything they'd done last night had been swept away, dropping them back into the same angry arguments from their past.

'I'm being ridiculous?' His tone was dangerously soft. 'Funny you should say that, because I seem to remember a whole lot of ridiculousness that went on during our marriage. That journal you kept being one of them.'

The words slapped at Annabelle, leaving her speechless for several seconds. He considered their attempts to have a baby 'ridiculousness'?

The pain in her gut and the throbbing in her chest were duelling with each other, seeking the nearest available exit: her eyes. But she couldn't let the gathering tears stop her from trying one last time.

'Max, I wasn't serious about what I said in the bathroom.'

It was as if he hadn't heard her at all. 'We should have used some kind of protection. I meant what I said three years ago. I don't want children.'

His words stopped her all over again.

'Ever?'

'Ever. I thought I made that perfectly clear.'

He had. But that had been three years ago. A lot had changed since then. Maybe more than she'd thought. He'd never once mentioned still loving her. Not last night. Not this morning. The closest he'd come was the word 'spark'.

Oh, God, how could she have been so stupid? And just to prove that she was, the words kept pouring out.

'I don't understand what you're saying.'

'No? I'm saying this was a mistake, Annabelle.' He glanced one last time at the open bag on the bed. 'When we get back to Cheltenham, I'm going to find those divorce papers and sign them.' There was a long pause, and she suddenly knew the hammer was going to fall and crush her beneath its blow. 'And if you haven't already, I'm going to ask that you sign them too.'

'Please don't say that, Max. Let's talk about it.'

'There is nothing to talk about. You wanted a divorce? Well, guess what, honey, so do I.'

CHAPTER TEN

THE TRIP BACK to Cheltenham had been made in total silence. She could have tried to plead her case, but she doubted that Max would have heard anything she had to say.

Just as in their marriage, he had shut down emotionally. His face and the tight way he'd gripped the wheel had seemed to confirm that, so Annabelle had stared out of the window at the passing countryside, doing her best not to burst into tears.

He wasn't any more willing to fight for her—for *them*—than he had been three years ago. And she was done trying.

She loved him, but she was not going to kneel at his feet and beg him not to leave.

After working her afternoon shift—during which she hadn't seen Max a single time, not even to check on Hope—she'd spent a long sleepless night, first in her bed, and when that hadn't worked she'd lain on the sofa.

This morning, she was exhausted, but resigned. If he wanted to sign the papers, she was going to let him. She unpacked her bag, staring at herself in the mirror for a long time.

Was he right? Had some subconscious part hoped she

might become pregnant because of what they'd done? Maybe. And if she was honest with herself, there was probably some long-lost side of her that would always harbour a tiny sliver of hope. How could she just extinguish it?

She couldn't. And evidently Max would not be able to love the side of her that wanted children.

Okay. She would just deal with it, as she had the last time.

She went to the shelf and picked up the manila envelope, blowing three years' worth of dust off it. Sitting at her desk, she withdrew the papers inside, her hand shaking as she laid them out flat, realising she'd never really looked at what her solicitor had sent over. Max wasn't the only one who had put off walking this through to the end.

Petition for dissolution of the marriage between
Maxwell Wilson Ainsley
and
Annabelle Brookes Ainsley

She was listed as the petitioner and he was the respondent. In other words, she was asking for the divorce and it was up to Max to respond.

Which he had, yesterday.

The night before last she'd felt such hope. And now here she was, back where she'd started three years ago.

Only worse. Because back then, when he'd issued his ultimatum about discontinuing the IVF attempts, she hadn't completely believed him. Until she'd caught him looking at that ovulation journal. She'd seen his face and had known it was over.

But that was all in the past. At least she'd thought so until yesterday. She'd had no idea he harboured such terrible resentment of their time together.

After they'd made love, Annabelle could have sworn that those old hurts had been healed. Obviously she'd been wrong.

Annabelle stared at the document.

She was the petitioner.

The word swirled through her mind again and again. Just because someone asked for something didn't mean the other person had to give it to them, did it? No, but Max seemed more than willing to let her have what she wanted. Only she wasn't sure she wanted it any more.

Why? Because he'd hurt her pride? No. That hurt went far deeper than that.

What if she, the petitioner, *withdrew* her request? Was that even possible? She could try to stop the process and, if Max insisted, let it turn into a long drawn-out battle in the courts. She could try to hurt him the way he'd hurt her. But that wasn't what Annabelle wanted. She didn't want to hurt him. Or to fight with him.

She didn't want to fight at all.

But that didn't mean that wasn't what should happen.

Hadn't her parents always taught her to fight for what she believed in? And wasn't that what she'd expected of Max all those years ago?

Yes.

Even now, despite his angry words, she believed they had a chance if they let go of the past. But did Max believe the same thing? After yesterday, she wasn't sure.

Why had he got so angry after she'd joked about her getting pregnant?

Because he thought she still wanted children and he didn't?

That was what he'd implied when he'd mentioned hitting the 'magic' window: *If so, you've got the wrong man.*

She didn't know for sure, because Max had *refused to talk to her*!

So, she had a choice. Let him sign and be done with it. Or go and have it out with him. Whether he wanted to or not.

Where? She had no idea if he'd even gone in to work yesterday afternoon.

She could always go to his house. If she knew where that was. She realised she didn't have a clue where he lived.

But she knew someone who did.

Max circled his living room for what seemed like the hundredth time, trying to find some kind of peace with his decision. If he could leave the country, as he had three years ago, he would. But he had a contract to fulfil, and he was dead tired of running.

He loved Annabelle. More than life itself.

But the thought of standing by a second time while she destroyed her health and more over a dream that was never going to come true was a knife to the heart. That time she'd retained fluid and had been so sick, he'd been afraid he was going to lose her. It had all turned into one huge ball of misery. The empty promises from fertility doctors. The tears. The torment. There had been no holy grail. No miracle.

And when she'd finally realised he was serious that last time? She'd told him to leave. Had sent him packing, cutting him off from the only real and good thing he'd ever known. And he'd been willing to walk away to make it all stop.

His statement about there being no miracle wasn't entirely true. There had been. But it hadn't been in what he or any of the doctors could give to Anna. It was what Anna had given to him: a love like none he'd ever known.

And what had he done? He'd thrown it away a second time. Because he'd been afraid.

Could he undo the things he'd said? Maybe, but how did he convince her to be happy with what she had? With him?

A cold hand clutched his chest. Was that what it had been? Had he been jealous of her attempts to have a child?

No. He could answer that honestly. That wasn't his reason for walking out on her yesterday. And yes, even though he hadn't physically left the vicinity, he had walked away from the burgeoning hope of a new beginning.

And for what?

For a few careless words uttered in a bathroom? Had he really stopped to listen to what she was saying, or had he simply assumed she was headed down the same old path?

The problem was, he hadn't actually heard her out, he'd simply blurted out that he didn't want children and that he wanted to finalise the divorce.

Was she waiting for him to sign the papers? Was she even now informing her solicitor to finish what she'd started?

His throat tightened until it was difficult to breathe.

She should. She should leave him far behind and forget all about him.

But he didn't want her to.

So what should he do?

Probably what he should have done three years ago. Stand in front of her and listen to her heart, rather than issue ultimatums. Hear what it was she wanted out of life. If it came out that they wanted completely different things, then he could walk away with no regrets. It was just that Max wasn't so sure they did. They had worked together—had loved together—in a way that had made him hope that this time might be the charm.

Weren't those almost the exact same words that Annabelle had said in that bathroom?

Yes.

So why was he standing here wondering if he'd done the right thing? He needed to find her and pray that he wasn't too late.

Opening his wardrobe, he grabbed a leather jacket and headed towards the front door. He could always camp in front of Baby Hope's hospital room and wait for Annabelle to show up. Because if he knew one thing about the woman it was that she loved that baby. She had fought for the infant's survival time after time. Maybe it was time that someone—him—decided to fight for Annabelle.

Just as he reached for the doorknob his bell rang, startling the hell out of him.

He frowned. *Come on. I really need a break here.*

Wrenching the door open to tell whoever it was that he didn't have time for chit-chat, he was shocked to find the person he'd just been thinking about standing on his front mat.

No. That couldn't be right.

He forced his gaze to pull the image into sharp focus. Still the same.

'Anna?' Her eyes looked red, and she carried a packet under her arm. 'Are you okay?'

'No. No, I'm not, actually.' She took a deep breath and then held up an envelope. 'But I brought my copy of the divorce papers. If you have yours, you can sign them, and I'll take them both to my solicitor.'

His throat clogged with emotion. He was too late. He'd brought the axe down on something that could have made him happy for the rest of his life. He should tell her he wasn't going to sign them, that it wasn't what he wanted at all, but somehow the words wouldn't form.

Because she was going to leave him all over again.

It's not like you didn't tell her to.

'Are you going to ask me in?'

Realising she was standing in the cold, he took a step back, motioning her inside his cottage.

'Let me take your coat and hat.'

Annabelle shed both items, handing the gear to him, but retaining her hold of the envelope. 'Thank you.'

He led her into the living room and made her a cup of tea, while she perched on the couch, the packet resting across the knees of her jeans. He wanted to take it from her and toss it into the gas fireplace he'd switched on, but hadn't he decided to listen to her heart? To hear her out without jumping to any conclusions?

But she said he could sign his copy of the papers right there in front of her.

If he wanted to.

He waited until she'd had her second sip of tea before wading into the waters. 'You didn't have to bring your copy. I have one of my own.'

He couldn't imagine saying anything more stupid than that.

'I know. But I wanted to come by and get a few things off my chest. In person.'

Taking a gulp of his coffee and feeling the scald as it went down his throat, he paused to let her talk.

Reaching deep into her handbag, she pulled out a notebook. Max recognised the green floral cover and immediately stiffened. Why did she even still have that?

'When I was packing my things to come to Cheltenham, I found this, and realised the enormity of the mistake I'd made all those years ago. Keeping this a secret was wrong on so many levels.' Her chest rose as she took a deep breath. 'What I said in the bathroom had nothing to do with this. I meant the words as a joke, but they backfired horribly and ended up shooting me in the heart. I wasn't scheming to get pregnant after the fundraising party, I swear.'

'I'm just beginning to realise that.' One side of his mouth tilted slightly. 'I think you used the word "ridiculous" to describe my reaction. You were right.'

Her eyes searched his. 'I never should have said that. And just so you understand, I know I'm not going to get pregnant from having sex with you. Not two days ago. Not three months from now. Not ten years from now. I'm sorry if you thought that was what I was after. I'm not. Not any more.'

A pinpoint of hope appeared on the horizon. 'So you're not interested in having a baby?'

'If it happened, I would be ecstatic. But I'm not going to chase after it ever again. Especially knowing you don't want kids.'

'I never said that.' Even as the words came out, he realised he had. He'd said that very thing. Maybe he wasn't the only one who'd misunderstood. 'Okay, I did. But I meant I didn't want to go through the procedures any more. It hurt too much to see how they ripped you apart emotionally. Physically. Especially after that last attempt.'

He swallowed hard, forcing the words out. 'I thought you were going to die, Anna. And in the end, that's why I agreed to leave.'

'What?' The shock on her face was unmistakable.

He nodded. 'I've never done anything harder than walk through that door. The only thing that kept my feet moving was the thought that I might be saving your life. With me gone, you'd have no reason to go through any more treatments.'

'I—I never knew.'

If he'd been hoping she'd leap into his arms after that revelation, he was mistaken. Instead, she looked down at the journal in her hands, smoothing her fingers over the embossed cover. 'You hurt me, Max, when you came into that bathroom all those years ago and issued an edict that it was over. That I wasn't to try to get pregnant any more. I felt I had no control over anything, not even my own decisions.'

He knew he'd hurt her. 'You're right. We should have discussed it together.' He stood and walked towards a bank of windows that overlooked a park, stuffing his hands into his front pockets. 'It's just that seeing you in such torment… Well, it ripped my heart out.'

'And it killed me that I couldn't give you what you wanted.'

'What *I* wanted?' He turned back towards her.

'A family. You used to talk about how you wanted a big family, just like mine. So you could give our children what your parents hadn't given to you. And I wanted so desperately for you to have that. Then, when it came down to it—' her voice cracked '—I couldn't give it to you.'

He sat down next to her on the couch, horrified by her words. Had she really thought that? 'Anna, *you* were my family. Yes, I was disappointed that you couldn't get pregnant. But only because it seemed to be something you wanted so desperately.'

'I wanted it because of you.'

Could it be? Had he misread the signs all those years ago? Had he been so focused on the fights that had swirled around her efforts at conceiving that he'd missed the real reason she'd been so anguished after each failed attempt?

'I had no idea.' He took one of her hands.

'I asked you to leave because I was hurt and trying to protect myself the only way I knew how. I took the coward's way out.'

'You're not a coward.' He took the journal from her, his thumb rubbing the edges of the little book. 'I am. Because I love you too much to watch you go through this again.'

'You love me?'

He stared at her. 'You didn't know?'

'I thought I did. At one time. But now?' She swallowed. 'I'm not sure.'

He set the journal on the coffee table and caught her face in his hands. 'I'm so sorry, Anna. Hell, I…' He bowed his head, trying to control the stinging in his eyes. Then he looked back up at her. 'I screwed everything up back then. And I screwed it up again at the flat yesterday morning.'

'So you don't want a divorce?'

He had to tread carefully. He wanted there to be no more misunderstandings. 'I don't. But I have to be sure of what you want out of life.'

'You aren't the only one who screwed up, Max. I wanted so badly to give you the things you didn't get as a child: roots and a huge amount of love.'

'You gave me those when you married me. That, along with your amazing, crazy family.'

'They all love you, you know. It's one of the reasons I couldn't bring myself to tell them about the divorce.' His eyes weren't the only ones stinging, evidently, judging from the moisture that appeared in hers. 'So where do we go from here?'

He thought for a minute.

'Maybe we should look at counselling. Find out how to handle everything we've been through. And after that?' He picked up her left hand and kissed the empty ring finger. 'I'd love to put something back on this.'

'I still have my rings.' She smiled. 'I don't think I've ever quite given up on us. It's why I never asked my solicitor to find you and demand those signed papers back. I think I was hoping that one day you would find your way home. And you did.'

He smiled back, linking his fingers with hers. 'It

would seem we have fate—and Sienna McDonald—to thank for that. Although I would like to think I would have come to my senses if your solicitor ever *had* hunted me down.'

She leaned her head on his shoulder. 'I guess I should have sicced him on you sooner, then.'

'Maybe you should have.' He dropped a kiss on her temple. 'I have to tell you that picture of us in your parents' dining room brought back memories of how happy we were. Of how things could have been had not things got so…'

'Insane.' She finished the sentence for him.

'I don't mean that in a bad way.'

'I know. But it was.' She lifted her head and motioned to the packet. 'That brings me back to my original question. Do you want me to hold onto these just in case it doesn't work out?'

'No.' Max got up from his seat and went over to a cabinet under his television. Opening the door, he retrieved an envelope that looked identical to hers. He sat back down, but didn't take the papers out. Instead, he folded the packet in half, trapping the journal in between. 'May I?'

He held out a hand for her envelope. When she gave it to him, he opened the flap and dropped the other items inside. Then he got up from the sofa. 'What I really want to do is toss these into the fireplace and watch them burn to ashes, but, since it's a gas fireplace, I'm afraid I'd set the cottage on fire.'

'That wouldn't be good.'

'No, it wouldn't. Especially since I'm hoping to move out of it very soon. I might not get my security deposit back.'

'Y-you're moving?' The fear on her face was enough to make him pull her from the sofa and enfold her in his arms.

'I'm sorry. I didn't mean I was moving away. I'm just hoping to change locations.'

'I don't understand.'

'Well, it might seem a little odd to your family and everyone at the hospital if you put your rings on and we continue living in separate homes, don't you think?'

Wrapping her arms around his neck, she pressed herself against him. 'Yes. It would. If you're thinking of coming to live at my place, I have to warn you that it's not as fancy as our flat in London, and—'

'It will be perfect, Anna. Just like you.'

With that he led her into the kitchen and stopped in front of the rubbish bin. Pushing the foot pedal, he waited until the top lifted all the way up. 'It's not as impressive as sending them up in a puff of smoke, but it'll be just as permanent. Once this lid falls, I don't want to mention these papers ever again.'

'Deal. But let's both do it.' She held one side of the envelope, while Max kept hold of the other end. Then they dropped it, along with all the hurts from the past, right where they belonged. Where they could never again poison their relationship.

Max released the pedal and let the lid drop back into place. 'Maybe in a couple of years we could move back to London. Or talk about adoption.'

'Adoption? You'd be okay with that?'

'As long as you are. I know with your sister—'

'I'm definitely open to that option.' She squeezed his hand. 'You might even be able to talk me into going on a medical mission, just like we used to dream about.'

'Are you serious?'

'Yes. I want to see what you've seen. Walk where you've walked. And I know that, this time, we'll be right in step with each other.'

He turned her until she faced him. 'I would be honoured to work alongside you, Mrs Ainsley.'

'And I, you.'

'How long before you have to be at Teddy's?'

She glanced at her watch. 'I have about two hours. I wasn't sure how long this was going to take or what state I would be in by the end of it.'

'Hmm… I think I might be able to answer both of those questions.' He gripped her hand and started leading her through the living room. 'This will take just about two hours…or however long you have left. And as for the state you'll be in by the end of it—I'm hoping you'll be in a state of undress and that you'll be very, very satisfied.'

'That sounds wonderful.' She caught up with him and put her arm around his waist. 'As for the satisfied part, I can't think of how I could be any more satisfied than I am at this very moment.'

They went through the bedroom door and he pushed it shut behind them. 'In that case, I plan to keep you that way for the rest of your life.'

EPILOGUE

ON EITHER SIDE of her, a small hand clutched hers as she walked slowly towards the waiting plane. After a ton of paperwork and countless trips to their solicitor's office, Annabelle and Max finally had their answer. Two boys with special needs were on their way to a brand-new life on a brand-new continent. Ready to join their sister, who was being cared for by Annabelle's mum.

Six months after Hope's surgery, the baby had come home to live with Annabelle and Max. The same solicitor who had handled this adoption had done a bit of digging and found a similar case where a preemie baby had been adopted by her nurse. It was enough to convince the courts that Hope belonged with them. Now two years old, she was growing and thriving and had brought such joy into their lives.

She glanced to the side where Max was making the final arrangements for the flight back to England. He stood tall and proud, no sign of the angry, frustrated man who'd walked out of her door all those years ago. And Annabelle had finally made her peace with never having a biological child. If it happened, it happened.

They'd compromised on that front. Max had agreed to not using birth control—with a sexy smile as they'd lain in bed after making love one night—and she'd agreed not to seek extraordinary means to have a child.

The life they now had was enough. More than enough.

Max meant the world to her. As did Hope, who had given them the best Christmas gift of all: a chance to rekindle their romance and to fix what was broken between them.

And now these two small gifts had come into their lives, both with heart defects that had needed surgery. Max and Annabelle had met Omar and Ahmed on a brief Doctors Without Borders trip they'd made four months earlier. A colleague of Max's had performed the surgeries and Annabelle had fallen in love. With those two boys, and with Max all over again. His selfless need to help ease the suffering of others had been more than evident. Then and now.

They'd both vowed to communicate. And they'd learned how with the help of a counsellor right after they'd moved into Annabelle's home. At the end of the process, Max had promised to stick with her no matter what. As had she.

'Baba anakuja!' said Omar, and he gripped her hand even tighter.

Annabelle glanced up, her eyes watering to see that 'Papa' was indeed coming towards them. It was the first time one of the boys had referred to Max that way, and she envisioned many more years of it as they all grew to know one another even more.

He came and stood in front of her, his gaze searching her face. 'You're sure this is okay?'

'Do you even need to ask? Hope will be so happy to finally meet them. So will the rest of the family.'

Glancing down at the two kids flanking her, he then leaned in and kissed her, his lips warm with promise. A small giggle burst from Ahmed at the PDA.

'It means we'll have even less privacy.' He tucked a strand of hair behind her ear, the gesture making her smile.

'No, it just means we'll have to be more inventive.'

'More? I don't see how that's possible.' Luckily the kids didn't have a strong grasp of English yet, but they would learn. Just as they would learn about their own heritage, possibly even returning to Africa one day to give back to their culture.

'You'll just have to wait and see. I have some ideas.'

Max leaned in and kissed her again. 'I think we'd better leave this topic of conversation for another time, or I'm going to be pretty uncomfortable on the trip home.'

Home.

Max had explained how seeing their wedding photo on her parents' wall had made something inside him shift, had made him realise he still loved her.

That picture now hung over their bed as a reminder of what they stood to lose. It was something that Annabelle kept in mind each and every day.

There were no more jokes about getting pregnant. She knew just how painful a subject it was, and she was more than willing to leave it behind. For Max's sake.

Besides, they were complete just as they were. Adding Omar and Ahmed to their household was just icing on an already beautiful cake.

And Nate… Her nephew's surgery had been a complete success, and there was no reason to think the brain tumour would ever return. Jessica was ecstatic, as was everyone else. It seemed they'd all got their happy endings.

It's enough.

Those two words were now the motto of her life. No matter what her problems or difficulties, she would weigh everything against that phrase. Because it was true. Life with Max, no matter what it brought, was enough.

She wanted to reach up and touch him, but the fingers squeezing hers prevented it. But there were other ways to touch. 'I love you.'

'I love you too, Anna.' He kissed her again before moving to the side and gripping Ahmed's hand, forming an unbreakable, unified line.

Then they walked towards the open door of the plane, knowing it would soon carry them to a brand-new phase of their lives.

Where they would wake up to face each and every day.

Together.

* * * * *

Look out for the next great story in the
CHRISTMAS MIRACLES IN MATERNITY *quartet*

THE MIDWIFE'S PREGNANCY MIRACLE
by Kate Hardy

And there are two more fabulous stories to come!

If you enjoyed this story,
check out these other great reads
from Tina Beckett

A DADDY FOR HER DAUGHTER
WINNING BACK HIS DOCTOR BRIDE

THE MIDWIFE'S
PREGNANCY
MIRACLE

BY
KATE HARDY

MILLS
BOON

Published in Great Britain 2016
By Mills & Boon, an imprint of HarperCollins*Publishers*
1 London Bridge Street, London, SE1 9GF

© 2016 Harlequin Books S.A.

*Special thanks and acknowledgement are given to Kate Hardy
for her contribution to the* Christmas Miracles in Maternity *series.*

ISBN: 978-0-263-91521-1

Dear Reader,

This book is all about a Christmas miracle.

Ella struggled against the odds to become a midwife, and then discovered that it was almost impossible for her to have a baby. Oliver was badly hurt by a previous partner who took away something precious. Neither of them is prepared to have a serious relationship, and they bury themselves in work, suppressing how they really feel about each other.

But one unexpected night leads to an even more unexpected consequence.

And they discover that miracles really do happen.

I hope you enjoy their journey!

With love,

Kate Hardy

For Scarlet, Susanne and Tina—
really enjoyed working with you all on our quartet!

Kate Hardy has always loved books, and could read before she went to school. She discovered Mills & Boon books when she was twelve and decided this was what she wanted to do. When she isn't writing Kate enjoys reading, cinema, ballroom dancing and the gym. You can contact her via her website: katehardy.com.

Books by Kate Hardy

Mills & Boon Medical Romance

Her Real Family Christmas
200 Harley Street: The Soldier Prince
It Started with No Strings…
A Baby to Heal Their Hearts
A Promise…to a Proposal?
Her Playboy's Proposal
Capturing the Single Dad's Heart

Mills & Boon Cherish

Falling for Mr December
Billionaire, Boss…Bridegroom?
Holiday with the Best Man

Visit the Author Profile page at
millsandboon.co.uk for more titles.

PROLOGUE

Hallowe'en

ALMOST AS IF someone had called his name, Oliver Darrington found himself turning round and looking at the doorway.

Ella O'Brien, one of the junior midwives from his department, was standing there. Despite the fact that she was wearing a mask that covered half her face—because tonight was the annual Hallowe'en Masquerade Ball, the glitziest fundraiser in the Royal Cheltenham Hospital's social calendar—he recognised her instantly.

Desire shimmered at the bottom of his spine and he dragged in a breath. He really needed to get a grip. Ella was his colleague. His friend. He'd been attracted to her since the very first moment she'd walked into Teddy's, the centre for birth and babies at the Royal Cheltenham Hospital. Her striking red hair, worn tied back in a scrunchie, had snagged his attention. Then he'd noticed her clear green eyes and the soft curve of her mouth. He'd wanted her immediately, though he'd held himself back. Since the fallout from dating Justine, Oliver didn't do serious relationships; plus he hadn't wanted to risk making things awkward on the ward between them, so he'd managed to keep things strictly professional between himself and Ella.

Though several times when they'd worked together, his hand had brushed against hers and it had felt as if he'd been galvanised. And sometimes he'd caught her eye and wondered, did she ever feel that same secret pull?

Though he'd dismissed it: Ella O'Brien was one of the most grounded and independent women he'd ever met. He knew she was dedicated to her career and she wasn't the type to let herself be distracted by a fling—which was all he could offer. Besides, over the last eighteen months, he'd discovered that he liked Ella: she was easy to work with, being both sharply intelligent and yet able to empathise with the mums on the unit. He didn't want to risk spoiling that.

But tonight…

Tonight was the first time he'd ever seen her all dressed up, and it threw him. At work, Ella wore uniform or scrubs, and on team nights out she'd always dressed casually in jeans and a T-shirt. Oliver couldn't quite square the no-nonsense midwife he was used to with the woman in the navy satin prom dress. Her dress had a sweetheart neckline and was drawn in sharply at the waist to highlight her curves before flaring out again to the knee, and she was wearing high heels which made her legs look incredibly long. She looked utterly gorgeous. Right at that moment, Oliver really wanted to pull her into his arms and kiss her until they were both dizzy.

'Stop being so shallow, Darrington,' he chided himself.

And then he realised that Ella had hesitated in the

doorway; she was clearly scanning the room, trying to work out where the rest of the team was. For just a moment, she looked vulnerable—which was odd for someone who was always so confident and cheerful at work. And that look of uncertainty made him go straight to her rescue.

'Good evening, Ella. You look lovely,' he said as he joined her in the doorway.

Her fair Irish skin turned a delicate shade of pink. 'Thank you, Oliver. But you're not supposed to recognise me with a mask on, are you?'

'Your hair's a tiny bit of a giveaway.' That glorious dark red. And tonight it was in a sophisticated updo, with a few loose, soft curls framing her face, making him want to release the pins and let it fall like silk onto her shoulders... Oh, for pity's sake. Now was definitely not the time to start fantasising about her. He forced himself to concentrate. 'So how did you recognise me?' he asked.

'Your voice is pretty distinctive.'

As was hers, with that soft Irish accent. 'Fair cop,' he said easily. 'The rest of the team from Teddy's is over there.' He gestured in the direction of their table. 'Come and have a glass of champagne.'

Even though Oliver was a good six inches taller than she was, Ella noticed that he kept his stride short to match hers as they skirted round the edge of the dance floor. She was really grateful; the last thing she wanted to do was to make a fool of herself by walking too fast and tripping over in her unfamiliar high heels. Especially here, at such a glamorous do. Right now, she felt seriously out of her depth. She'd never really been much of a one for parties and balls; at university, she'd missed out on most of the big events, because she'd been concentrating so hard on her studies. It had been such a struggle to get to university in the first place, she hadn't wanted to jeopardise her career by partying when she should've been studying. And it was one of the reasons why she was still a virgin at the age of twenty-six: she'd concentrated on her studies rather than on serious relationships. Part of her felt ridiculously self-conscious about it; in this day and age, it was so old-fashioned to still be a virgin. Yet, at the same time, she felt that sex ought to mean something. She didn't want to have a one-night stand with someone just for the sake of it.

Last year, she'd been on duty so she hadn't been able to make it to the famous Royal Cheltenham Masquerade Ball; this year, she was off duty so she didn't have a good excuse to avoid it. But either Oliver hadn't noticed that she was a bit flustered, or he was too sensitive to make an issue of it. He simply chatted to her as they crossed the dance floor to join the rest of the team.

Ella, you look lovely.

Typical Oliver: charming and kind. It was one of the skills that made him popular to work with on the ward, because he always managed to make their mums-to-be feel more at ease and stop worrying. Just as he was clearly trying to put her at her ease now.

Ella had worked with the consultant for the last eighteen months; although she'd been instantly attracted to him, she'd been very careful not to act on that attraction. Although there had been moments when they'd accidentally touched at work and it had made her feel as if her heart was doing a backward flip, and sometimes she'd caught his eye in an unguarded moment and wondered if he felt that same pull, she hadn't acted on it because Oliver Darrington was way, way out of her league. According to the hospital grapevine, the string of women he dated all looked like models or had aristocratic connections; no way would he be interested in a junior midwife who came from a very ordinary family in County Kerry. So she'd kept things strictly professional between them at work, not even confessing to her best friend Annabelle how much she liked Oliver.

And she'd be strictly professional tonight, too.

Which was a real effort, given how gorgeous Oliver looked right now. He usually wore a suit to work, but she'd never seen him wearing evening dress before. He reminded her of Henry Cavill in his *The Man from U.N.C.L.E.* role: tall and handsome, debonair even, with his dark hair perfectly groomed. Except Oliver's eyes were grey rather than blue, and his mouth was even more beautiful than the actor's...

Get a grip, Ella O'Brien, she told herself, and she managed to smile and say the kind of things everyone expected to hear when she and Oliver joined the rest of the team.

The warmth of their welcome dispelled the remainder of her nerves, and she found herself chatting easily.

'Dance with me?' Oliver asked.

This was the stuff dreams were made of: waltzing around a posh ballroom with Oliver Darrington.

Except Ella couldn't dance. She'd always been horribly clumsy. The only thing that she was worse at than dancing was spelling, thanks to her dyslexia. And she'd spent so many years as a child believing that she was stupid and slow and hopeless at everything that she didn't trust herself not to make a mess of dancing with Oliver.

'I should warn you that I have two left feet,' she said. 'And I've never danced to this sort of music.' She gestured to the jazz trio on the stage. 'I've only ever watched *Strictly Come Dancing* on the telly. So on your head—or toes—be it, if you *really* want me to dance with you. But now's your chance to escape with all your toes unbruised.'

'You won't bruise my toes.' He smiled. 'Just follow my lead and it'll be fine.'

Was it really going to be that easy? Ella didn't share his confidence. At all.

But then Oliver led her onto the dance floor and they actually started dancing together.

It felt like floating on air. The way he guided her meant that she was moving in the right direction and her feet were always in the right place. And she'd never, ever experienced anything so magical. It was even better than she'd dreamed. Right at that second she felt like a fairy-tale princess in her swishy-skirted dress, dancing with the handsome prince. And she loved every moment of it. Being in his arms felt so right—as if this was where she'd always belonged. It made her feel warm and safe and cherished; yet, at the same time, there was the slow, sensual burn of attraction, dangerous and exciting.

Oliver danced with her for three songs in a row; and she was greedy enough to want to dance with him all night. Except this was the hospital's charity ball and Oliver was a consultant. He should be mixing, like the rest of the senior staff.

'Shouldn't you be—well—dancing with someone

else?' Ella asked, feeling guilty both for being selfish and for wanting Oliver all to herself.

His eyes glittered behind his mask. 'No. It's up to me to decide who I dance with—and I want to dance with you.'

Her heart skipped a beat. Was Oliver telling her that he'd noticed her, the way she'd noticed him over the last few months? That for him, too, this had been building up for a long time? Or was she misreading him and hoping for too much?

'Though would you rather be dancing with someone else?' he asked.

'No, no—not at all.' Though she rather thought that Oliver might have spoiled her for dancing with any-one else, ever again. Not that she was going to admit that to him.

'Good.' He kept her in his arms, and Ella's pulse went up a notch as they moved round the dance floor.

Oliver knew he shouldn't be doing this. He'd meant to dance with Ella once, to be polite and friendly, then keep his distance.

The problem was, he really liked the feel of her in his arms. Which again was ridiculous, because Oliver didn't do proper relationships. Not since Justine. He was well aware that the hospital grapevine had labelled him a heartbreaker, a playboy who had an endless string of one-night stands. There was a grain of truth in the ru-mours, because he never got involved with anyone for the long term; but he really wasn't a heartbreaker and he was picky about who he slept with. He always made sure that every woman he dated knew the score right from the start: that it was just for fun, just for now and not for always. He definitely didn't leave a trail of broken hearts behind him, because that would be unkind and unfair.

But there was something about Ella that drew him. A simplicity of heart, maybe?

Which was precisely why he ought to make an excuse and get her to dance with someone else. Put some space between them until his common sense came back. He didn't want to mess up their working relationship. Even though right now he really, really wanted to dance her into a quiet corridor and kiss her until they were both dizzy.

Then he became aware that she was speaking and shook himself. 'Sorry, Ella. I was wool-gathering. What did you say?'

She gave him the sweetest, sweetest smile—one that made his heart feel as if it had just turned over. 'Nothing important.'

'I guess I ought to stop monopolising you and let you dance with someone else,' he said.

Which was Oliver being nice and taking the blame for her social mistakes, Ella thought. 'Yes,' she agreed. She kept the bright smile pinned on her face as they went back to join the rest of the team. Then Charlie Warren, one of the other doctors from Teddy's, asked her to dance. Although Charlie was usually quite reserved, his offer was genuine enough, so she accepted.

'So are you enjoying the ball, Ella, or here under sufferance like me?' Charlie asked.

'I'm enjoying myself.' In fact, much more than she'd expected to. Though she had a nasty feeling that Oliver was the main reason for that. 'I'm sorry you're not.'

'I never do, really,' Charlie began, then grimaced when she trod on his toes.

'Sorry,' she said instantly. 'I'm afraid I have two left feet.'

'I thought all Irish people were supposed to be natural dancers? I guess you have *Riverdance* to blame for that.' It was an attempt at humour, as he was obviously trying to make polite conversation, but for as long as Ella had known Charlie, he'd always been distant with everyone at work. Quite the lone wolf.

'Sadly, that gene bypassed me,' she said. 'I'm more Flatfeet than Flatley.'

'I think my toes have already worked that one out for themselves but, even though we're no Fred Astaire and Ginger Rogers, you look lovely tonight, Ella.'

'Thank you,' she said smiling. 'I think you look more like James Bond than Fred Astaire anyway.'

'You're very sweet, Ella.' He gave her a shy half-smile. 'And you've made an otherwise dull evening much nicer.'

Ella found herself going through a similar routine with the colleagues she danced with from the Emergency Department.

'You know, we're going to have to set up a special broken toe department in the unit, just for the men you've danced with tonight,' Mike Wetherby teased.

'So I'd be better off sticking to delivering babies than dancing, hmm?' she teased back, knowing that he meant no harm by the comment.

'You can dance with me any time you like, Ella O'Brien,' Mike said. 'As long as I have fair warning so I can put on my steel-toe-capped boots first.'

She just laughed. 'In steel-toe-capped boots, you'd be clomping around the dance floor as badly as me.'

'Then we'd be the perfect match.'

'Yeah, yeah.'

And then Oliver rested his hand on Ella's shoulder. 'The next dance is mine, I believe.'

The warmth of his fingers against her bare skin sent a shaft of pure desire through her. She reminded herself crossly that this was a charity ball and Oliver had danced with at least half a dozen other women. He'd treated them in just the same way that he'd treated her, with courtesy and gallantry, so she was kidding herself and setting herself up for disappointment if she thought that his behaviour towards her tonight was anything more than that of a colleague. And she wasn't going to embarrass herself by throwing herself at him and being turned down.

Was it wishful thinking or did the lights actually dim slightly as they moved onto the dance floor?

Oliver drew her closer, and she shivered.

'Cold?' he asked.

'No, I'm fine,' she said, not wanting him to guess that her reaction had been something so very different.

He pulled back slightly and looked her in the eye. For a second, Ella could've sworn that the same deep, intense yearning she felt was reflected in his eyes. But that had to be imagination or wishful thinking. Of course he didn't feel like that about her. Why would he?

She stared at his mouth, wondering for a crazy second what it would be like if Oliver kissed her. It must be that second glass of champagne affecting her, she thought, vowing to stick to water for the rest of the evening.

But dancing with Oliver was headier than any

amount of champagne. And she noticed that, although she'd been clumsy with her other partners, with Oliver she didn't seem to put a foot wrong. Dancing with him made her feel as if someone had put a spell on her—but a nice spell, one that made her feel good.

And when he drew her closer still, she rested her head on his shoulder and closed her eyes. Just for these few moments, she could believe that she and Oliver were together. Just the two of them, dancing cheek to cheek, with nobody else in the room. Just them and the night and the music...

At the end of the evening, Oliver said casually, 'I think you're on my way home, Ella. Can I give you a lift?'

The sensible thing to do would be to smile politely and say thanks, but she'd be fine—though she hadn't remembered to book a taxi, and there was bound to be an enormous queue so she'd have to wait for ages in the cold. It was a twenty-minute drive from here to her flat. She could manage that without making a fool of herself and throwing herself at Oliver, couldn't she?

'Thank you. That's very kind of you,' she said. 'It'll save me having to wait ages for a taxi.'

'Pleasure,' he said. 'Shall we go?'

She walked with him to his car. It was icy outside, and the thin wrap she'd brought did nothing to protect her from the cold.

'Here,' he said, shrugging out of his jacket and sliding it across her shoulders.

'But you'll be cold,' she protested.

'Not as cold as you,' he said.

Typical Oliver: gallant and charming. But she appreciated the warmth of his jacket, and tried not to think about the fact that it had been warmed by Oliver's body heat.

Just as she'd half expected, his car was sleek and low-slung. When he opened the door for her, Ella nearly tripped getting in and was cross with herself for being so stupid and clumsy.

'Ella, relax. There aren't any strings. This is just a lift home,' he said.

More was the pity, she thought, and was even crosser with herself for being such an idiot.

'Sorry. Too much champagne,' she fibbed.

When she fumbled with the seat belt, he sorted it out for her. Her skin tingled where his fingers brushed against her.

Stop it, she told herself. He doesn't think of you in *that* way. And you're too busy at work to get involved with anyone—especially a colleague who apparently never dates anyone more than twice. Keep it professional.

'What's your postcode?' he asked.

She told him and he put it into the sat nav. Then he switched on the stereo and soft classical music flooded the car. 'Do you mind this?' he asked. 'I can change it, if you like.'

'No, it's lovely. I like piano music,' she said. 'We have a piano at home.'

'You play?'

'No, Mam does. I meant home in Ireland, not here,' she said. 'Mam's a music teacher. She plays the piano at school in assembly and in the Christmas Nativity plays for the little ones.'

'Did you ever think about being a teacher?' he asked.

'No.' Everyone had thought that little Ella O'Brien

was very sweet but not very bright, and would never get through her exams. Until the new biology teacher had started at her school when Ella was fifteen, worked out that Ella was dyslexic rather than stupid, and batted her corner for her. 'I always wanted to be a midwife, like my Aunty Bridget.' Everyone had thought that Ella was being a dreamer when she'd said what she wanted to do, but she'd put in the effort and worked so hard that she'd managed to get through her exams with good enough grades to get a place in London to train as a midwife. 'It's so special, sharing those first few minutes of a new life coming into the world.' She paused. 'What about you? Did you always want to be a doctor?'

'Yes.' Though there was something slightly shut-tered in Oliver's voice, and Ella wondered if he'd had the same kind of struggle she'd had about her choice of career. Although her parents supported her now, they'd worried throughout the whole of her degree and her training as a midwife, even though her tutors knew about her dyslexia and were really supportive. Her parents had told her all the time that she ought to give it up and come home to Ireland—particularly when she'd had her operation for a ruptured ovarian cyst and fallen be-hind in her studies. Thankfully Ella had been stubborn about it, and her parents had eventually come to terms with the fact that she was staying in England. She tried to make it home for a visit every couple of months, as well as video-calling them at least once a week through her laptop. And nowadays she knew her parents were more proud of her than worried about her.

Oliver didn't elaborate on his comment, and she felt too awkward to ask anything more. Particularly as she was so physically aware of him sitting next to her.

Well, she was just going to have to be sensible about this. But, when he pulled up on the road outside her flat, her mouth clearly wasn't with the programme, because she found herself saying, 'Thank you for the lift. Would you like to come in for a coffee?'

This was where Oliver knew that he was supposed to say no. Where he was supposed to wish Ella goodnight, wait until she was safely indoors and then drive away. But he discovered that his mouth wasn't working in partnership with his common sense, because he found himself saying yes and following her into her flat.

Her tiny flat was on the ground floor in one of the pretty Regency squares in Cheltenham.

'Come and sit down.' She ushered him into the living room. 'Black, one sugar, isn't it?'

'Yes. Thanks.'

'I'll be two seconds,' she said, and disappeared off to what he presumed was her kitchen.

He glanced around the room. There was enough space for a small sofa, a bookcase full of midwifery texts, and a very compact desk where there were more textbooks and a laptop. It looked as if Ella spent a lot of time outside work studying.

There was a framed photograph on the mantelpiece of her at graduation with two people who looked enough like her to be her parents, plus several others of a large group of people in a garden. Clearly she was at some family party or other, and everyone seemed to radiate love and happiness. Oliver felt a momentary pang. His own family wasn't like that, though perhaps part of that was his own fault for distancing himself from them. He could hardly be close to his brother while avoiding his parents, though; and when he saw his parents he was always on the receiving end of their disappointment.

Sometimes he thought that most parents would've been proud of their son for sticking through fourteen years of training and qualifying as an obstetrician. But the Darringtons had had rather different expectations for their son...

He really ought to make his excuses and leave. Ella was the last person he should get involved with. Apart from the fact that she was obviously much closer to her family than he was to his, she was his colleague and he didn't want things to get messy at work. Nothing could happen between them.

But when he went into her small kitchen to tell her that he needed to go, she turned round and smiled at him and all his common sense fled. Her beautiful green eyes held him spellbound. And right at that moment he felt the strongest connection to her. Her mouth looked warm and sweet and soft, and he really wanted to kiss her. When his gaze flicked up to her eyes again, he realised that she was doing exactly the same: looking at his mouth. So was she, too, wondering...?

Instead of saying goodnight, he stepped forward and brushed his mouth very lightly against hers—just as he'd wanted to do all evening. Not just all evening, if he was honest with himself: he'd wanted to kiss her for weeks and weeks and weeks.

Every nerve-end in his lips tingled, so he couldn't stop himself doing it again.

And this time she kissed him back.

'Ella,' he said when he broke the kiss. 'I've wanted to do that for months.'

'Me, too,' she whispered.

So she'd noticed him in the same way?

His common sense made a last-ditch bid to extract him. 'We shouldn't do this.'

'I know—we work together and we ought to be sensible,' she agreed.

'Exactly,' he said, relieved that he hadn't quite ruined their working relationship by giving in to that mad urge to kiss her. They could still salvage a professional friendship after tonight.

But then she rested her hand against his cheek. Her touch was light and gentle, and he found himself twisting his head to kiss her palm.

Her beautiful green eyes darkened.

Then the kissing started all over again, this time in earnest, and Oliver forgot all his good intentions. He loosened her hair, the way he'd wanted to do all evening, and let it tumble down to her shoulders.

Her eyes widened. 'Oliver!'

'I know.' He kissed her again. 'But I can't help this—I really want you, Ella. I have done since the first time I met you.'

'Me, too,' she said.

His whole body tingled with desire. She wanted him as much as he wanted her?

'So what are we going to do about this?' she asked.

'Right now, I can't think straight,' he admitted. 'I just want to make love with you.'

For a moment, he thought she was going to back away. But then she inclined her head very slightly and took his hand to lead him to her bedroom.

'Are you sure about this?' he asked softly as she switched the bedside light on.

'I'm sure,' she said, her voice low and husky.

He kissed her, and it made his head spin. Hardly able to believe this was happening, he slid the zip down at the back of her dress. Seconds later, he stroked the material away from her shoulders and it fell to the floor.

She undid his bow tie, then unbuttoned his shirt with shaking fingers, smoothed the material off his shoulders and let it fall to the floor next to her dress.

He unsnapped her bra. 'You're beautiful. All curves.'

She gave him a shy smile. 'You're beautiful, too. All muscles.'

And suddenly the faint awkwardness was gone—there was just Ella, kissing her, and feeling the warmth of her skin against his.

Oliver wasn't sure which of them finished undressing whom, but the next thing he knew he was kneeling between her thighs and her hair was spread over the pillows, just as he'd imagined it.

And then he stopped. 'Protection. I don't have a condom.'

'You don't need one,' she said, flushing slightly.

So she was on the Pill? Part of him remembered Justine's treachery and the repercussions. But he knew that Ella wasn't like Justine. The woman he'd got to know over the last eighteen months was open and honest. She wasn't going to cheat on him with someone else, get pregnant, and then try to make him believe that the baby was his. He knew that without having to ask.

'Oliver?' She looked worried, now. 'I don't sleep around. I'm not...' The colour in her cheeks deepened. 'You know.'

'I know.' He stroked her face. 'And the rumours about me aren't true. I don't have sex with every single woman I date.' He shouldn't be having sex with Ella, either; but right now her skin was warm against his, this had been a long time coming, and he wanted to do this more than he'd wanted to do anything in years.

'I know,' she said, and kissed him.

That kiss made him relax with her, and he slowed the pace down, wanting to explore her. He kissed and stroked his way down her body, starting with a dip beneath her collarbones and paying attention to exactly what made her sigh with pleasure, from the curve of her inner elbow to the soft undersides of her breasts, then starting with the hollows of her anklebones and feathering his way upwards until she was making tiny, involuntary noises and clutching at his shoulders.

'Now?' he asked softly.

'Now.' Her voice was raspy and husky with desire. Which was exactly what he'd wanted.

As he eased into her, he felt her tense.

'OK?' he asked.

She nodded. 'I just never thought it would be like…'

Her words slammed into his brain and he realised the implication of what she'd just said.

Ella was a virgin. And he'd just taken her virginity.

Oh, hell. But it was too late now. He couldn't reverse what he'd done. All he could do was try to make this as good for her as he could.

'Oliver?' And now she looked panicky. As if she thought she'd done something wrong.

It wasn't her. He was the one in the wrong. He should've thought. Should've checked. Should've walked away, instead of giving in to that desperate need to be close to her.

'You're beautiful,' he said, staying perfectly still so her body would have the time and space to get used to him, and kissed her. Because then he wouldn't have to talk and make a mess of things.

Slowly, she relaxed again, and kissed him back. And he paid close attention, finding out what made her whimper with desire, taking it slowly until he finally felt her body rippling round his and it tipped him into his own climax.

He held her close. 'Ella. I feel so guilty about this.'

'Don't. You didn't do anything wrong.' She stroked his face.

'But you were a—'

'Virgin. I know.' She bit her lip. 'Which is so stupid in this day and age. It makes me feel… Well, who on earth is still a virgin at the age of twenty-six?' She grimaced.

He knew the answer to that. 'A woman who's waiting for the right person.'

'There's no guarantee that Mr Right will ever come along.'

Or Ms Right. She had a point.

And right now she was clearly embarrassed by the situation, because her fair skin was flushed.

'I'm not judging you,' he said awkwardly. 'Ella, you're lovely.'

The 'but' was a mile high in flashing neon letters, and she obviously saw that straight away. 'But you don't do relationships,' she said. 'I know.'

'I'm sorry. I should go.' He dragged in a breath. 'But at the same time I don't want to leave you. I don't want to leave it messy like this.'

'I'm not expecting anything from you, Oliver.'

But he'd seen the flicker of disappointment in her eyes before she'd managed to hide it. She'd just given

him her virginity. To simply walk away from her immediately after that would make him feel like a real lowlife.

Plus he didn't actually want to go. Having Ella in
his arms felt so *right*.

'Can I stay for a bit and just—well, hold you?' he
asked.

'Why?'

One answer slammed into his head, but he wasn't
ready to consider that. He took a deep breath. 'Because
I feel horrible. I can't just get up and leave you. I just
took your virginity, Ella.'

'That isn't an issue.'

He rather thought it was. 'I feel bad about it.'

'Don't. It was my choice.' She paused. 'But you don't
want a relationship with me.'

Trust Ella to hit the nail on the head instead of avoiding the issue. His no-nonsense colleague was back. 'It's
not *you*. It's anyone.' He raked a hand through his hair.
'I've got an interview for the Assistant Head of Obstetrics job next week. If I get the post, then all my attention's going to be on my new job. It's the wrong time
for me to get involved with anyone.'

'And I'm not your type anyway.'

Actually, she was exactly his type, warm and sweet
and lovely; though his family wouldn't agree with him.
His brother would be fine, but his parents would see
her as the girl from a very different background—an
unsuitable background. Not that anyone at work knew
about his family. He'd been careful to keep his background very quiet. The fact that his father had a title
had absolutely nothing to do with Oliver's ability to do
his job, and he wanted people to judge him for himself,
not for whose son he was.

He took her hand. 'Ella. I like you a lot. I respect you. And I've been attracted to you ever since the first time I met you. What happened tonight... I think it's been a long time coming.'

'It has.'

So she felt that weird, almost elemental pull, too?

'But we're not going to repeat it.'

He couldn't tell a thing from her expression or from the tone of her voice. Everything was neutral. 'It's not you, Ella. It's me.' The last thing he wanted was for her to take the blame. He knew the whole thing was his fault. He should've kept himself under his usual control.

'As far as everyone else is concerned, you gave me a lift home from the ball—as your colleague—and you stayed for a cup of coffee,' she said. 'And that's it.'

'Thank you.' She really was letting him off the hook—and it was a lot more than he deserved.

'If you, um, need the bathroom, it's next door. The towels are clean. Help yourself to anything you need.'

'Thanks.' He pulled on his underpants and padded to the bathroom.

When he returned from his shower, with the towel still wrapped round his waist, she'd changed into a pair of pyjamas. Totally unsexy striped flannel pyjamas that buttoned right up to the neck.

And how bad was it that he wanted to unbutton them and slide the material off her skin again? To kiss every centimetre of skin he uncovered and lose himself in her warmth?

Then again, those pyjamas were also a statement. She was dressed—and he was wearing only her bath towel. 'Do you want me to go?' he asked.

'I think it would be best,' she said.

He knew she was right, and that leaving would be the sensible thing to do, but he still felt bad. As if he should've stayed a bit longer, and at least held her until she fell asleep. Going now felt as if he was deserting her.

'I'm sorry,' he said.

'I'm not.' She lifted her chin. 'We did nothing to be ashamed of.'

He had. He'd taken her virginity without a second thought. But if he pressed the issue, he had a feeling she'd take it the wrong way and think he was ashamed about sleeping with her—that she was the problem, not him. Which wasn't true.

'Uh-huh,' he said awkwardly. Normally he was good with words, but tonight that ability had completely deserted him. 'Ella—we've worked together well for eighteen months. I don't want that to change.'

'It won't. Nobody at the hospital needs to know anything about what just happened.'

She didn't meet his eye, he noticed. So that comment about not being ashamed had obviously been sheer bravado.

'I'm not a good bet when it comes to relationships, Ella,' he said softly. Though he didn't want to tell her why. How stupid was he not to have realised that Justine had been seeing someone else, and that he was her golden ticket to the good life for her and the baby that wasn't his? He knew that Ella wasn't a gold-digger, the way Justine had been; but he still couldn't face taking a risk with a relationship again. Making another mistake. Having his heart trampled on again. So it was better to stay exactly as he was, where everyone knew the score and that all his relationships were just for fun.

* * *

Not a good bet when it comes to relationships.

Neither am I, Ella thought ruefully.

What did she have to offer anyone? Thanks to the endometriosis that had dogged her for years and caused the ovarian cyst to grow and rupture, Ella couldn't have children. It was one of the reasons why she'd avoided relationships; what was the point of starting anything when you knew you were taking someone's future choices away? Who would want a wife who couldn't give him a family? She'd seen first-hand from her own best friend's experience how the pressure of infertility could cause even the strongest marriage to crack.

So she knew she was better off as she was. She'd come to terms with the situation over the last few years; now she had the chance to concentrate on her job and prove that she was better than her grades at university suggested—that she was worthy of her job. And her job would be enough for her.

'I don't want a relationship with you, Oliver,' she said. It wasn't strictly true, but she wasn't stupid enough to long for something she knew she couldn't have. 'Except a working one.'

The relief in his expression was so dazzling, it almost blinded her.

Well, she could be just as bright and chirpy. She wasn't going to let him see how much his relief had hurt her. 'Shall I make you a cup of tea while you're getting dressed?'

'No, it's fine, thank you. I'd probably better go.'

'I'll, um, let you get changed,' she said, and headed for the kitchen to give him some space.

The two mugs of instant coffee—never made—sat

accusingly in front of the kettle. She tipped the coffee granules in the bin, rinsed out the mugs and made herself a strong cup of tea. Mam's solution to everything, she thought wryly. Though she had a feeling that it would take an awful lot more than a cup of tea to sort this out.

She'd just have to pretend that tonight had never happened. And hopefully things wouldn't be awkward between Oliver and her at work.

CHAPTER ONE

Saturday 3rd December

'EXCUSE ME, PLEASE. I'll be back in a second.' Ella held her breath and made a dash for the door. This was hardly professional behaviour, but it would be better than throwing up in front of the poor mum-to-be and her partner.

She made it to the staff toilet with seconds to spare. And then, weirdly, as she leaned over the bowl, she stopped feeling sick.

Huh?

If she was coming down with the sickness bug that was sweeping its way through the hospital and leaving all the departments short-staffed, she should've been throwing up right now. Big time. But the queasiness that had left her feeling hot and sweaty in the consulting room seemed to have vanished.

She frowned. The last thing she'd been aware of was how strong the dad-to-be's aftershave had been.

Sensitive to smells and feeling sick...

Had any other woman listed those symptoms, Ella would've suspected early pregnancy. But she knew that she couldn't possibly be pregnant. Her doctor had given her the bad news more than five years ago, after her ovarian cyst had ruptured. Between the cyst and the endometriosis that had dogged Ella and caused her to fall behind in her studies, her Fallopian tubes were in a bad way and she'd been told she'd never have children of her own.

How ironic that she'd specialised in midwifery. Cuddles with a baby she'd just delivered, or with a friend's or cousin's child, were all she would ever have. But after a lot of heartache and tears she'd come to terms with the situation. She loved her job. Trying to find a Mr Right who wouldn't mind that she couldn't ever give him a baby of his own—well, that was just being greedy and expecting too much.

She splashed water on her face, took a deep breath and returned to the consulting room to finish the antenatal appointment with her parents-to-be.

But when exactly the same thing happened at her next antenatal appointment, Ella began to wonder quite what was going on.

She and Oliver hadn't used protection, the night of the Hallowe'en masked ball. But she'd thought it wouldn't matter.

Of course she wasn't pregnant. She couldn't be.

As for the fact that her bra felt a bit too tight and her breasts felt slightly sore… That was purely psychological. Her imagination was simply running riot and coming up with other pregnancy symptoms. There was no way this could be a miracle baby. No way at all.

But, now she thought about it, her period was late. A quick mental count told her that it was two and a half weeks late. She hadn't had time to notice because they'd been so short-staffed and busy in the department lately. Actually, that was probably the reason why her period was late in the first place; she'd been rushed off her feet and working crazy hours, so it wasn't surprising that her menstrual cycle was protesting.

'Ella O'Brien, you're being a numpty,' she told herself crossly. 'Of course you're not pregnant.' All the same, during her break she took one of the pregnancy test kits from the cupboard. Just to prove to herself once and for all that she was being ridiculous, and then she could get on with the rest of her life.

She peed on the stick, then waited.

A blue line appeared in the first window, to show that the test was working properly.

And then, to her shock, a blue line appeared in the second window.

But—but—this couldn't be happening. It *couldn't*. How could she possibly be pregnant?

She sat there staring at the test, in turmoil, emotions whirling through her.

The test result was clear: she was expecting a baby. The one thing she'd been told would never happen, by specialists she'd trusted absolutely. From what they'd said, the odds were so stacked against her falling pregnant, she'd have more chances of winning a huge prize on the lottery.

Though in some ways this felt better than winning the lottery. A baby. The gift she'd never dreamed she'd ever be able to have, except from the sidelines. Although she'd smiled and been genuinely pleased whenever one of her cousins or one of her friends had announced she was pregnant, a tiny part of Ella had mourned the fact she'd never know the joy of being a mum. And now she was actually going to be a mum. Have a baby of her own. For a moment, sheer joy flooded through her. Despite almost impossible odds, she was going to have a baby. A Christmas miracle.

But then panic took over. What about her career? She'd already lost a lot of ground during her studies, thanks to the combination of her dyslexia and the pain of the endometriosis. Some days, the pain had been so debilitating that she hadn't been able to sit through lectures, and she'd had to borrow notes from friends instead of recording the lectures, and struggled as the words danced across the page. Even when her doctor had finally found some medication to help deal with the pain, things hadn't got much better, because then she'd had the ruptured cyst...

She'd worried that if her tutors knew the truth about her illness, they'd make her drop the course. They knew about her dyslexia and they'd already given her so much help, letting her record lectures so she could listen to them and absorb the knowledge that way. She couldn't possibly ask for yet more help. It'd be greedy and self-ish. Ella almost gave in to her parents' suggestion to forget all about being a midwife and go home to Ireland. But then she'd had a work placement and she'd loved working on the ward so much. It had made her more determined to follow her dream of being a midwife, so she'd struggled on and scraped through her exams.

And she was always aware that she should've done better as a student, that her grades had let her down. It drove her to work harder on the ward, to prove to every-one round her that she was better than her exam results said she was. All the way through her medical career, she'd asked to use computer software to dictate notes rather than rely on her terrible handwriting, she'd used coloured lenses in her glasses so she could manage with bright paper or a screen, and she'd asked colleagues to proofread her notes—because she'd never, ever put a patient at risk by not double-checking that everything in the notes was absolutely correct. And, even though people weren't supposed to discriminate against you at work if you had a medical condition, Ella had always felt the need to work extra hard, just to prove that her dyslexia wouldn't make any difference to her ability to do her job.

But going on maternity leave in six months' time would have a huge impact on her career. She'd lose experience and study time. And what would happen when her maternity leave had ended? Juggling work and still managing to spend a decent amount of time with the baby, as a single parent, was going to be tricky. Arranging childcare to fit round her shifts would be tricky, too.

Though she wasn't the baby's only parent.

And that was something else that worried her.

There was only one man who could be the father, because she'd only ever slept with Oliver.

Once.

How, how, *how* had she managed to get pregnant? Then again, how many times had a young mum-to-be cried on her shoulder that it had been the first time she'd had sex and she'd been so sure you couldn't get pregnant if it was your first time?

But, that night, Ella had told Oliver it was safe not to use a condom. Her doctors had been so sure that she couldn't have children—that her Fallopian tubes were so badly damaged that she probably wouldn't be able to have children even with the help of IVF—that she really *had* believed it was safe not to use a condom.

And now here she was: single, and pregnant with Oliver's baby after a one-night stand. How on earth was she going to tell him about the baby?

She had absolutely no idea what Oliver would say or how he'd react to the news. Since the night of the ball, things between them had cooled considerably. She wasn't sure which of the two of them was the more embarrassed about what had happened. He'd really reacted badly once he'd realised that she'd been a virgin. Working together had been awkward, and both of them had made excuses to avoid work social events where the other might be there.

Things had cooled even more when it turned out that Oliver had got the job as Assistant Head of Obstetrics. Although he wasn't directly Ella's boss, he was very much her senior. The last thing she wanted was for him—or anyone else at Teddy's—to think that she'd slept with him in an attempt to boost her career. She'd never do anything like that.

At least Oliver wasn't dating anyone else, as far as she knew, so that was one less complication to worry about. But how did you tell someone that you were expecting his baby, when you weren't even in a relationship with him and you had no idea how he'd react?

She couldn't even begin to frame the right words.

She knew she wasn't going to get a happy-ever-after, where Oliver went down on one knee with a hand clutched to his chest, declared his undying love for her and asked her to marry him. Though she wasn't naive enough to expect that. And if he did ask her, she certainly wasn't going to marry a man who didn't love her, just for the baby's sake. That wouldn't be fair to any of them.

But Ella did want Oliver to be involved with the baby. She'd had a really happy childhood. She'd been an only child, but her parents had both come from big families and she'd had plenty of cousins around, so it had been almost as good as having siblings. She wanted that for her baby, too: that feeling of being loved and wanted, of being part of a family. And, even though she wasn't expecting Oliver to resurrect anything more than a distant kind of friendship with her, she hoped that he would at least be there for their child as the baby grew up. It would be a terrible shame for either of them to miss out on any of that.

But what if Oliver didn't want anything to do with the baby at all? What if he expected her to have a termination?

Then she'd have to rethink her situation at the Royal Cheltenham. Seriously. She already knew that she absolutely didn't want a termination. Though working with Oliver in any way, shape or form would be impossible if he expected her to take that option. She'd have to leave the hospital and find a job somewhere else.

Even though she loved her job here at Teddy's, Ella knew she would need some support with the baby. Even if Oliver didn't expect her to have a termination, if he didn't want to be involved with the baby, then she'd have no choice but to go home to Ireland. Although her parents would be shocked and a bit disappointed in her at first, she knew they loved her and wanted the best for her. And she knew how much they'd wanted to be grandparents, even though they'd assured her that of course they weren't bothered by her infertility. They'd be on her side and help her with the baby, and maybe she could work part-time as a midwife in Limerick. Have the best of both worlds.

She cupped her hands protectively around her abdomen. 'Right at this moment, I have no idea how this is going to work out, baby,' she said softly. 'But one thing I do know: I definitely want you. I never dreamed I'd be lucky enough to have you, and I'm so glad I am. You're the best thing that's ever happened to me—and I'm going to try my hardest to be the best mum to you I can.'

She splashed water on her face, wrapped the test kit in a plastic bag and stored it in her pocket, then returned to the ward.

'Are you all right, Ella?' Annabelle, her best friend and the head neonatal nurse on the ward, asked.

'I'm fine,' Ella fibbed. 'You haven't seen Oliver anywhere, have you?'

'I think he's in a meeting. Is it urgent, or can one of the other doctors fill in for him?'

It wasn't urgent exactly—her pregnancy wouldn't show for a few weeks yet—but absolutely nobody else could fill in for him on this. Not that she could tell Annabelle without telling her the rest of it. And, given the reasons why Annabelle's marriage to Max had collapsed, Ella wanted to choose her words carefully so she didn't rip open her best friend's old scars. Particularly as Max was now working at Teddy's, easing in to a role as Sienna's maternity cover. Annabelle had opened her heart to Ella about the situation, the previous day, and Ella just couldn't say anything that might hurt her best friend.

'It'll wait,' Ella said, trying to keep her voice light.

And it was probably for the best that Oliver wasn't

available right now. It would give her some space and time to think about how she was going to tell him the news.

The afternoon was also filled with antenatal appointments; one mum in particular was really worried.

'So this baby's in the same position that her brother was in?' Sara Reynolds asked.

'Back to back—yes,' Ella confirmed.

'So that means another long labour followed by an emergency section?' Sara grimaced. 'I know I agreed to a trial of labour, but I'm so scared my scar might come open halfway through and I'll have to be rushed into the operating theatre. And the idea of being in labour for two days again and then being stuck in bed for a week, feeling as bad as I did last time, when Jack's so lively...' She shook her head. 'I can't do it. I can't, Ella.'

'It's not going to be like that,' Ella reassured her. 'We'll keep a really close eye on you, and we're not going to let you struggle. Though you're right about a back-to-back labour taking longer, and this little one's been very happily settled in that position for the last three appointments.'

'You don't think she'll move round?'

'At this stage, no. I'll go and have a word with your consultant,' Ella said, 'but I'm pretty sure he'll agree with me in the circumstances that we should be able to offer you an elective section.'

'But if I have a section, doesn't that mean I'll be stuck in bed for a week and I won't be able to drive for a month?' Sara looked worried. 'And I need the car to get Jack to nursery. It's four miles away and there isn't a bus.'

'Last time,' Ella said gently, 'you'd had a two-day

labour before the section. It's not surprising that it took it out of you. This time round, you won't have to go through that first, so it'll be easier and you'll be a lot more mobile. Nowadays we say you can drive when you feel ready, though if you can give it three weeks to let yourself heal that would be good. Maybe one of your family or friends nearby can help with the nursery run?'

Sara bit her lip. 'My cousin said she'd come and help.'

'Well, that's great.' Ella smiled at her and squeezed her hand. 'Give me five minutes and I'll have a chat with your consultant.'

Who *would* have to be Oliver, she saw with dismay as she looked at Sara's notes on the computer screen.

Provided she didn't let herself think about the situation she hadn't had a chance to discuss with him, she should be able to deal with this. Her patient had to come first.

Thankfully, Oliver was out of his meeting. Ella could see him sitting at his computer, typing away and looking slightly grim. Working on notes following his meeting, maybe? Hopefully he wouldn't mind the interruption. She rapped on his open door. 'You look busy, but please can I interrupt you for three minutes on behalf of one of my mums, given that you're her consultant and you need to be the one to sign off on the decisions?'

'Sure.'

He didn't smile at her, but that was OK. This was work. She ran through the brief. 'The mum is Sara Reynolds, thirty-six weeks, second baby. Last time round, the baby was back-to-back and she had a two-day labour followed by an emergency section. This baby's been in the same position for the last three appointments, and I don't think she's going to move now.

Sara originally agreed to a trial of labour, but she's really worried that she'll end up with another long labour, and she'll have to have another emergency section that'll leave her unable to function for weeks. Given the baby's position and that Sara's got a really lively toddler to cope with as well, I really think she'd be better off having a planned section.'

'Let me look at her notes so I can bring myself up to speed with exactly what happened last time,' Oliver said.

'OK.' And please don't let him be long, Ella thought. She was starting to pick up the smell from his coffee cup and it was making her stomach roil.

But clearly his computer system was on a go-slow when it came to retrieving the patient's notes, and it got to the point where she couldn't bear the smell of coffee any more.

'Excuse me a moment,' she said, and fled to the toilet. Thankfully it was queasiness again rather than actually being sick, and she splashed water onto her face until she felt able to cope again.

When she got back to Oliver's office, he'd clearly had time to review Sara's notes.

'Are you all right?' he asked.

'Yes. I just felt a bit…' No, now really wasn't the time for her to tell him that it was morning sickness. She stopped. 'I'm fine.'

'If you're going down with that sickness bug, I want you off the ward right now before you pass it on to anyone else,' he said. 'Go home, Ella.'

'It's not that.' She didn't want to tell him the real reason right now. It wasn't the time or the place, and she still didn't have the right words to explain the situation to him. 'So do you have an answer for Sara?'

'Yes. I agree with you, so I've marked on her notes that I'm happy for her to have an elective section. I'll get it booked in with Theatre. Do you want me to come and have a word with her?'

'No, it's fine.' Especially as that coffee was making her feel queasy again and she didn't want to have to dash off to the toilets again and risk him working out what was really going on. 'Thanks. I'd better get back to my patient. Catch you later.'

Ella was acting really oddly, Oliver thought. Rushing out of his office like that. Yet she'd been adamant that she wasn't going down with the sickness bug that was sweeping through the hospital.

So what was the problem?

Things had been awkward between them ever since the night of the masked ball. The night when he'd taken her virginity. He still felt guilty about it; and as a result he'd probably been even more cool with her than she was being with him.

He really ought to have a chat with her and try to get things back on an even keel between them. Especially as he was the Assistant Head of Obstetrics now. There was absolutely no way they could get involved with each other; although he wasn't directly her boss, he was her senior. Though it would be nice to salvage some kind of working relationship, so they were at least on semi-friendly terms in the department. He *liked* Ella. He missed the easiness between them.

As for anything more… Well, he'd told her the truth. He wasn't a good bet when it came to relationships.

Even though Ella was the one woman he thought might actually tempt him to try, it just couldn't happen. It would all go wrong and wreck their working relationship for good.

He knew she'd be writing up her notes after her appointments, so he quickly typed out a message on the hospital's internal email system.

We need to have a chat. Come and see me when you're done today.

Before he hit 'send', he added 'please', so she'd know he wasn't being cold and snooty with her. And hopefully they could sort things out.

We need to have a chat. Come and see me when you're done today, please.

Oh, help. That sounded very formal and very ominous, Ella thought as she read the email at the end of her shift. Why did Oliver want to see her?

She hadn't put a foot wrong in her job ever since she'd moved from London to Teddy's eighteen months ago. But, now Oliver was Assistant Head of Obstetrics, he was bound to have read everyone's file, to help him get a handle on the team and see where anyone might need more training. If he'd read her file, then he'd know that she'd only just scraped through her exams at university. Was this why he wanted to see her? Did this mean he was going to expect her to prove herself all over again?

Great. Just the thing to start off a Saturday evening. Not.

Dreading what he was going to say, she went to Oliver's office. 'You wanted to see me?'

He looked up from his desk. 'Yes. Close the door, please.'

Now that was *really* worrying. Was he about to tell her that he was reorganising the team and there wasn't a space for her? She couldn't think why else he would reverse his usual open-door policy.

Adrenalin slid down her spine, and she did as he'd asked.

'We need to talk,' he said, gesturing to the chair opposite his.

'Right.' She sat down.

'Coffee?'

Even the thought of it made her gag. She tried really hard to stop the reflex, using the trick her dentist had taught her last time she'd had to have an X-ray by making a fist of her left hand, squeezing her thumb with her fingers. Except it didn't help and she still found herself gagging.

'Are you all right, Ella?' Oliver asked.

'Mmm,' she fibbed. 'Maybe some water would help.'

He narrowed his eyes at her. 'What aren't you telling me?'

Oh, help. She wasn't ready for this conversation. At all. And it made it worse that every time she looked at him, she remembered what it felt like to be in his arms. What it felt like to kiss him. What it felt like when his bare skin was sliding against hers...

And this wasn't the time and the place for remembering that, either. 'Why did you want to see me?' she asked instead of answering his question. 'Am I losing my job?'

'Losing your job?' Oliver looked surprised. 'Of course not. Why would you think that?'

'Your note was pretty ominous.'

He frowned. 'It was meant to be polite.'

'And you just asked me to close the door...'

'I'm not sacking you, Ella, and this isn't a disciplinary meeting, if that's what you're thinking.' He raked a hand through his hair. 'Things are a bit strained between us and I wanted to clear the air, that's all. Look, let me grab you some water or some coffee, and we can—' He stopped abruptly. 'Ella, you've gone green. Are you quite sure you're not going down with the sickness bug?'

'I'm sure.'

'Then what's wrong?'

She couldn't see her way out of this. She was going to have to tell him at some point, so it might as well be now. And she'd had all afternoon to think about how to tell him and still hadn't come up with the right words. Maybe short and to the point would be the best option. 'I'm pregnant,' she said miserably.

Pregnant?

Oliver's head spun and he actually had to shake his head physically to clear it.

Pregnant.

He'd been here before. With Justine. Except the baby hadn't been his, because Justine had lied to him all along. He knew Ella was nothing like Justine; but the past still haunted him.

The last time those words had been said to him, he'd been just as shocked. The baby hadn't been planned and he'd still been studying for his specialist exams. He hadn't been ready for the extra responsibility of parenthood, but of course he'd done the right thing and stood by Justine. It was his duty.

And then, when Justine had finally told him the truth, he'd been let off the hook. Except by then he'd started to think of himself as a dad. Having that taken away from him had hurt even more than Justine's betrayal. He'd been shocked by how isolated and lost he'd felt—and he'd sworn that never again would he let himself get emotionally involved or in a position where someone could hurt him like that.

Now here he was again, hearing a woman tell him that she was expecting his baby. Even though Ella came from a completely different background, and he'd worked with her for long enough to trust her on a lot of levels—the situation brought back all the hurt and mistrust.

'How pregnant?' he asked carefully.

'My last period was the middle of October. I'm nearly three weeks late.'

'Seven weeks, then,' he said, calculating rapidly. They'd had unprotected sex on the night of the Hallowe'en ball. That would've been two weeks after the start of her last period, from what she'd just said. Which meant they'd had sex right in the middle of her cycle: the most fertile time.

And she'd been a virgin—something that made him feel guilty and protective of her at the same time. And which put all kind of inappropriate memories in his head: the way her voice had gone all husky with arousal, the way her pupils had gone wide and dark with desire, the way it had felt when he'd finally eased into her...

Oh, for pity's sake. He couldn't think of that now. She'd just told him she was pregnant.

Of course it was his baby. There was no question that it was anyone else's baby. Everyone knew that Ella was completely devoted to her job—come to think of it, she hadn't dated anyone since he'd known her.

Except for that one snatched evening with him. And he'd been the only man who'd ever shared her bed like that—with the ultimate closeness. Which made it special, because Ella wasn't the sort to sleep around.

She looked anxious. 'So you believe me?'

'That you're pregnant? Or that it's mine? Obviously the dates tally. And, given the situation, it's pretty obvious that the baby's mine.' He looked at her. 'I assume you've done a test, to be this sure about it?'

She nodded. 'Today.'

'And you didn't suspect anything before today?'

She frowned. 'No.'

'Even though your period was late?'

'I put that down to stress,' she said. 'You know it's been crazy round here, with so many people off sick, plus Sienna's going off on maternity leave really soon and it'll take Max a while to settle in properly. We're all rushed off our feet.'

'So what made you decide to do a test today?' Then he remembered how she'd run out of his office, admitting afterwards that she'd felt a bit sick. He'd assumed she was going down with the bug. But it hadn't been that at all. 'You started getting morning sickness,' he said, answering his own question.

She nodded. 'I can't bear the smell of strong after-shave and coffee. That's what made me...' She swallowed hard, obviously feeling queasy at just the thought of the scents.

He grabbed one of the bottles of water he kept in his desk drawer and pushed it across the desk at her. 'Here.'

'Thank you.' She unscrewed the cap and took a sip of water. 'Oliver, I didn't mean this to happen. I wasn't trying to trap you, or try to sleep my way up the ladder or anything like that. It wasn't planned.'

'Too right it wasn't planned,' he said grimly. He wasn't angry with her, but he was furious with himself. Why hadn't he taken proper responsibility when it came to precautions? More to the point, why had he made love with her in the first place, when he'd managed to keep his hands to himself and his libido under control for the last eighteen months? Why had he given into temptation that night, let the single glass of champagne he'd drunk go completely to his head and wipe out his inhibitions enough to let him kiss her and take her to bed?

Though he really wasn't prepared to answer those questions right now.

Instead, to cover up his guilt and confusion, he snapped at her. 'So what was it? The Pill didn't work?'

She flinched. 'I'm not on the Pill.'

What? He could hardly believe what he was hearing. 'You led me to believe you were.' So, in a way, she'd been as devious as Justine. Clearly his judgement was incredibly poor when it came to relationships.

'I didn't say I was on the Pill.'

'You hinted at it.' He remembered it very clearly. 'You said I didn't need a condom. Why would you say that unless you were taking the Pill?'

'Well, that lets you very nicely off the hook, doesn't

it? Because it's all my fault. That's fine. I accept the entire blame for the situation.' She screwed the cap back on the water bottle. 'Don't worry, Mr Darrington, I'm not expecting anything from you. I just thought you had the right to know about the baby.' She stood up. 'I'm officially off duty right now, so I'm going home.'

'Wait. Ella.' He blew out a breath. 'You've just told me you're expecting my baby. At least give me time to process the news. And what do you mean, you're not expecting anything from me? As the baby's father, of course I'll support you financially.' Just as he'd supported Justine when he'd thought that she was pregnant with his baby. A Darrington always did the right thing.

'I don't want your money.'

'Tough. Because I have no intention of letting you go through this unsupported and on your own.' He stared at her. One thing he was very sure about: this time he wasn't going to have fatherhood snatched away from him. This time he was exercising his rights, and he was going to have *choices*. 'It's my baby, too, Ella. So that means I get a say. In *everything.*'

'I never had you pegged as an overbearing bully,' she said, 'but you're behaving like one right now. I'm telling you about the baby purely out of courtesy, and I know you're not interested in being with me so I don't expect anything from you. And now, if you'll excuse me, I've already told you I'm off duty and I want to go home. Goodnight.'

This time, she walked out.

By the time Oliver had gathered his thoughts enough to think of going after her, Ella was nowhere to be seen.

Great.

If he ran after her now, everybody would notice. The

last thing either of them needed right now was to have the hospital speculating about their relationship—or, worse still, actually guessing that Ella was pregnant with his baby.

He needed time to think about this. To get used to the idea. To work out exactly what he was going to do.

So much for thinking that he and Ella could smooth over what had happened that night and try to repair their working relationship. Her bombshell had just changed everything. And right at that moment he didn't have a clue what to do next, or even what to think. She hadn't even told him why she hadn't been on the Pill, and he needed to get to the bottom of that. His head was spinning.

He'd finish all the admin here and then go for a run to clear his head. And then, maybe, he'd be able to work out the best way forward. For all three of them.

The run cleared his head a bit. But then the reality slammed home. He was going to be a father.

Oliver took a deep breath. He'd been here before, but this time he had no doubts at all. The baby was his, and so was the responsibility. OK, so she'd told him he didn't need to use protection, and that had turned out not to be true—but it took two to make a baby. Plus Ella's family lived hundreds of miles away in Ireland; although her best friend lived in Cheltenham, it basically meant that Ella was on her own. She and the baby needed him to step up to the plate and be responsible.

He could start by making sure that she was taking folic acid and eating properly. Which was hard in the early stages, when you had morning sickness and couldn't face the smell or taste of certain foods. He now knew the smell of coffee was a trigger for her, so he needed to find something that was bland, yet nutritious and tempting at the same time. Decaffeinated tea might be easier for her than coffee; he knew she usually drank tea at work. And maybe some fresh strawberries, pasteurised yoghurt and granola.

He dropped in to the supermarket on his way home, trying to ignore the piped Christmassy music and the stacks of Christmas chocolates and goodies displayed throughout the shop. Right now it didn't feel much like Christmas. It felt as if the world had been shaken upside down and he wasn't quite sure what day it was. Though he rather thought he might need some kind of Christmas miracle right now.

He concentrated on picking out things he thought might tempt Ella to eat, and added a box of vitamins specially formulated for pregnant women. Then he came to the large stand of flowers by the tills. Did Ella even like flowers? He didn't have a clue. He knew some women hated cut flowers, preferring to let them bloom in a garden or on an indoor plant. And there was the scent issue. Something as strong as lilies might set off her morning sickness.

But it would be a gesture. A start. A way of showing her that he wanted to be on the same side. Maybe something not over-the-top and showy, like the large bouquets sprinkled with artificial snow and glitter. Something a little smaller and bright and cheerful with no scent, like the bunch of sunny yellow gerbera. Although he didn't have a vase at home, he could stick them in a large glass of water overnight so they'd still look nice in the morning. Hopefully Ella would like them.

Then maybe tomorrow they could talk sensibly about

their options. Hopefully Ella would tell him what she really wanted. She'd said that she was only telling him about the baby out of courtesy, but did she really mean that? Did she want him to be part of the baby's life— part of *her* life? Or did she really mean to do what their colleague Sienna seemed to be doing, and go it alone?

And what did he want?

Since Justine's betrayal, Oliver had major trust issues when it came to relationships. He didn't date seriously. He hadn't even wanted a proper relationship, thinking that the risks of getting hurt again were too high. But the fact that Ella was expecting his baby changed that. He knew he definitely wanted to be a part of his child's life.

And Ella? He'd fought against his attraction towards her for months, keeping it strictly professional between them at work. Then, the night of the charity ball, he'd danced with her; it had felt so right to hold her in his arms. To kiss her, when he'd driven her home. To make love with her, losing himself inside her.

If he was honest with himself, he wanted to do it again. And more. He wanted to wake up with her curled in his arms. Being with Ella had made him feel that the world was full of sunshine. That snatched evening was the first time he'd felt really connected with anyone for years. He could actually see them as a family: Ella nursing the baby at the kitchen table, chatting to him about his day when he got home from work. Going to the park, with himself pushing the pram and Ella by his side—maybe with a little dog, too. Reading a bed- time story to the baby together and doing all the voices between them.

They could give their baby the kind of childhood he hadn't had. One filled with warmth and love.

But then reality slammed in. Did she feel the same way about him? Did she want to make a family with him, or did she just want financial support, the way Justine had? OK, so she didn't know who his parents were, and she'd said earlier that she didn't want his money—but was it true?

Had it meant anything to her, giving him her virginity? Or had it all just been a nuisance to her, an embarrassment, something she wanted to get rid of and he'd happened to be in a convenient place to do her a favour? And why had she been so adamant that they didn't need contraception—especially as it now turned out that she hadn't been on the Pill?

He didn't have a clue. In normal circumstances, that would be a difficult conversation to have. With pregnancy hormones clouding the issue, it was going to be even harder.

Tomorrow.

He'd sleep on it and hope that the right words would lodge themselves in his head by tomorrow.

CHAPTER TWO

ON SUNDAY MORNING, Oliver drove over to the pretty little square where Ella's flat was and rang her doorbell.

She opened the door wearing pyjamas, sleepy-eyed and with her hair all mussed. 'I'm sorry. I didn't mean to wake you,' he said.

'It's almost half-past nine, so it's my bad,' she said wryly. 'What do you want?'

He held up the recyclable shopping bag. 'I brought breakfast. I thought maybe we could talk.'

'Breakfast?'

'And these.' He handed her the gerbera. 'I hope you like them.'

Unexpectedly, her beautiful green eyes filled with tears. 'Oliver, they're gorgeous. I love yellow flowers. Thank you. Though you really didn't have to do that.'

'I wanted to,' he admitted. And right now, seeing her all warm and sleepy, he really wanted to take her in his arms and hold her close and tell her that he'd protect her from the world.

Except he wasn't sure how she'd react, and he knew he needed to take this slowly and carefully until he had a better idea of what was going on in her head. He wasn't going to end up in the same place he'd been after Justine, where he'd been in love with her but she hadn't loved him back.

'Come in. I'll put the kettle on.' She ushered him through to her living room. 'I'll go and have a quick shower and get dressed, and then I'll put those lovely flowers in water.'

'You don't have to change on my behalf.'

She gave him a speaking glance. 'I can't be sitting here at my kitchen table in pyjamas, with you all dressed up like a magazine model.'

'Apart from the fact that I'm not all dressed up, I don't mind if you stay in your pyjamas.'

'Well, *I* do.'

He really didn't want to sit around doing nothing. It wasn't his style. He'd always preferred keeping busy. 'Shall I make breakfast, then, while you're showering?'

He could see that she was torn between insisting that it was her flat so it was her job to make breakfast, and letting him do something. 'All right,' she said finally. 'I normally eat in the kitchen, if that's all right with you.'

'OK. I'll see you when you're ready.'

By the time Ella had showered and changed into jeans and a cute Christmassy sweater with a reindeer in a bow tie on the front, Oliver had laid two places at the tiny bistro table in her kitchen and had arranged everything on the table: freshly squeezed orange juice, granola, yoghurt and a bowl of hulled and washed strawberries. It looked amazing. And she couldn't remember the last time anyone apart from her parents had made this kind of fuss over her. Right now she felt cherished—special—and it was a good feeling.

'No coffee,' he said.

'Thanks. I really can't bear the smell of it.'

'And that's why I held off on the croissants. Just in case they affected you, too.' He gestured to the teapot. 'The tea's decaf—I thought it might be easier for you to manage.'

'That's so sweet.' He'd made all this effort just for her, and her heart melted. 'This all looks so nice. Thank you.'

'I had to guess because I didn't really know what kind of thing you like for breakfast.'

She blushed. 'You didn't stay for breakfast when… Well, you know.'

'Uh-huh.'

Right at that moment, he looked just as embarrassed and awkward as she felt. She'd been stupid to bring up the issue.

'I just wanted to do something nice for you,' he said.

'And I appreciate it,' she said meaning it.

He poured her a mug of tea. 'No sugar, right?'

She loved the fact that he'd actually noticed how she took her tea. 'Right.'

'So how are you feeling?' he asked.

'Mostly fine. Just as long as I avoid strong smells.' She smiled. 'And that should get better in about six weeks, or so I always tell my mums.'

'It's usually better by the second trimester,' he agreed.

'I thought Sienna was teasing me when she told me that tin cans actually smell when you're pregnant,' Ella said, 'but she's right. They do.' She shuddered, and took a sip of the orange juice. 'This is lovely. Thank you so much. I feel totally spoiled.'

* * *

'It's the least I could do.' Again, Oliver could imagine having breakfast with Ella on Sunday mornings. A lazy breakfast, with toast and tea and the Sunday papers, and then taking the baby out together for a late-morning walk in the park… It shocked him to discover how much he actually wanted that.

A real relationship.

With Ella and their baby.

Thankfully she hadn't noticed him mooning about, because she asked, 'So is everything OK with you?'

'Yes.'

'And you're settling in well to your new job?'

'Just about,' he said, smiling back at her. Maybe this was going to work out. They could at least make polite conversation. And they'd been friends before the masked ball. They respected each other as colleagues. He really believed they could salvage something from this now.

He kept the conversation going until they'd finished breakfast and he started clearing the table; then he noticed that there was still something left in the bag he'd brought with him. 'Oh, I meant to give you this earlier.' He took the box of vitamins from the bag and handed them to her.

She frowned. 'What's this?'

'Folic acid—obviously now you know about the baby, you need to start taking it.'

'Uh-huh.' Her face shuttered. 'Did it occur to you that I might already have bought a pregnancy vitamin supplement with folic acid?'

'I—' He stared at her. No. He hadn't given it a second thought.

'Oliver, I'm a midwife. It'd be a bit stupid of me to ignore my years of training about the best way for pregnant women to look after themselves and their babies, wouldn't it?'

She sounded really put out, though he couldn't for the life of him understand why. All he'd done was buy her some vitamins. 'I was just trying to help. To look after you.'

'To take over, more like,' she said.

'But—'

'Do you think I'm suffering from "pregnancy brain" and I'm completely flaky?' she asked. She shook her head, narrowing her eyes at him. 'And, for your information, "pregnancy brain" is a total myth. I came across a piece on the news the other day that said actually women's brains are sharper when they're pregnant.'

What? Where was all this coming from? He didn't understand. 'Ella, I didn't accuse you of anything of the sort.'

'No, but you bought me folic acid without even thinking that I might already have some. There's a huge difference between asking me if you can pick something up for me, and just presenting me with it as if I'm too stupid to have thought of it for myself.'

'You're overreacting.'

'Am I?' She folded her arms. 'If this is how it's going to be for the next seven and a half months, with you looking over my shoulder all the time and making decisions for me without even bothering to discuss things with me first…' Again, she shook her head. 'That's really overbearing and that's not what I want, Oliver. Actually, right now I think I'd like you to leave and give me some space.'

He stared at her in disbelief. 'All I want to do is to protect you and the baby, and provide for you. How's that being overbearing?'

Could he really not see it? Ella wondered. 'It's overbearing because you're not discussing anything with me. You've made the decision already and you're expecting me to just shut up and go along with it.' She'd been there before: when everyone thought that little Ella wasn't bright enough to train as a midwife. She hated the way Oliver seemed to be falling into those same attitudes and thinking he knew what was best for her. She'd had years of feeling undermined and useless, and she wasn't going to let it happen again. 'And if you *dare* say that's just pregnancy hormones making me grumpy, I'll... I'll...' She was too angry to think of what she'd do next. So much for thinking he wanted to cherish her. What an idiot she was, letting herself fall a little more in love with a control freak who wanted to boss her around.

'Ella, this is—'

'I need some space. Thank you for the flowers and breakfast, because that was very nice of you, but I'd really like you to leave now. Please.'

'What about the washing up?'

'I think I might just about be capable of sorting that out for myself.' She stood up and gestured to the doorway. 'Would you give me some space, please?'

Maybe making a tactical retreat would be the best thing to do right now, Oliver thought. 'All right.'

He wasn't sure whether her reaction had made him more hurt or angry. He'd tried to do the right thing, but

Ella was being totally unreasonable. He'd never called her intelligence into question. Why on earth would she think he had?

Despite her protests, he was pretty sure that pregnancy hormones were affecting her mood.

He'd try to talk to her again later and hope that she'd be in a better frame of mind. More receptive.

Going to the gym and pounding the treadmill didn't help. Neither did going to his office and spending a couple of hours catching up on paperwork.

Was he really being overbearing and making decisions without asking her? Oliver wondered.

A simple box of vitamins really shouldn't cause this much trouble.

Justine had been more than happy for him to make a fuss of her and buy things for her while she was pregnant. Then again, she'd had her reasons. But Ella was seriously independent. Brave enough to travel to London at the age of eighteen to study midwifery, so far from her family home in Ireland that she wouldn't be able to just pop home for the weekend like most of the other students could. And she'd be brave enough to bring up this baby on her own.

Except she didn't have to.

He wanted to be there. For her and for the baby.

He didn't want to tell her about Justine—not just yet—but he could try to build a bridge. Try to see things from Ella's point of view.

It didn't take him long to drive back to her flat.

This time, when she answered the doorbell, she didn't smile.

'Hear me out?' he asked. 'Please?'

She said nothing, but at least she didn't slam the

door in his face. 'I was going to get you flowers as an apology, but I already bought you flowers this morning and I don't want you to think I'm going over the top—especially as you already think I'm being overbearing. I had no idea what to get you. I don't know what you like, so I just…' Oliver hated feeling so clueless and awkward. Normally he was in charge and he knew everything would go smoothly. This was way out of his comfort zone.

'It doesn't matter. I don't need you to buy me things.'

Another difference between Ella and the women he usually dated: they expected presents. Expensive presents.

'The most important thing is that I'm sorry for being bossy. I don't mean to be and I'll try not to be. But,' he said, 'old habits die hard, and I can't promise that I won't mess up in the future.'

Her face softened, then, as if she understood the jumble of thoughts filling his head, and she stepped back from the doorway. 'Come in and I'll make some tea—and, for the record, I'm perfectly capable of filling a kettle with water and boiling it.'

'I know,' he said. He'd got the message that Ella liked her independence. 'But is there anything I can do to help?'

'Just sit down and let me do it myself.'

He waited on the sofa in the living room, feeling more and more antsy as the seconds passed.

Finally, she came in with two mugs of tea.

'Thank you,' he said, accepting one of the mugs.

She inclined her head in acknowledgement and sat down at her desk rather than next to him on the sofa. Making a point, he supposed.

'It must be difficult for you, being in this situation,' she said.

That was an understatement. She didn't know anything about the memories it was bringing back, and right at the moment it wasn't something he wanted to share. 'It's not exactly a picnic for you, either,' he said, trying to see it from her point of view. 'All I need to do is to get my head round this properly.' *All*. He was struggling enough with that. 'But it's worse for you because you get all the morning sickness and what have you as well.'

'Thanks for reminding me,' she said dryly.

'Ella, I want to be there for you and the baby.'

'I understand that. But it doesn't give you the right to push me around.'

He hadn't been trying to push her around, but he didn't want to argue. Now was probably not the right time to ask difficult questions about the contraception issue, either. He wanted to get their relationship on a less rocky footing, first. Instead, he asked carefully, 'So have you thought about what kind of care you want, and whether you want to book in at Teddy's or if you'd rather go somewhere else?'

'I know all the staff at Teddy's and I know I'll get the best care there, so it makes sense to book in to our department,' she said. 'Though it does mean everyone's going to know. And at a really early stage.'

'Is that a problem?'

She looked thoughtful. 'I guess not—I mean, everyone's been great about Sienna. After the initial gossip, wondering who the baby's father is.'

'Would you prefer people not to know I'm the baby's father?'

'I don't want people thinking I slept with you to get an advantage at work.'

He smiled. 'Ella, nobody would ever think that of you. You work hard enough for two people as it is.' He paused. 'What about a scan?'

'I already know I'm about seven weeks.'

'Which is about the right time for a dating scan—not that I disbelieve you on the dates, just…'

She nodded. 'Though it'll mean people will know now, not later on.'

'Yes, and they'll cut you a bit of slack—this is the stage where you're likely to feel really tired and need a break.'

'I'll still be part of the team, and being pregnant doesn't alter that.'

Why was she being so difficult about this? 'I'm not saying that you're not part of the team—just that maybe you could cut back a bit on your shifts for a while.'

Her face darkened. 'No.'

'Ella—'

'I said before, please don't push me around. You're not my keeper, Oliver.'

'I know. I'm just trying to do what's best for you.'

'Because I'm not bright enough to know what's best for me?'

'No, of course not.' He didn't get why she was being so prickly. 'Ella, is there something you're not telling me?'

'How do you mean?'

'You and me—we've always got on well. Until—well.' He didn't want to embarrass her by putting it into words.

But she clearly wanted to face it head-on. 'Until we slept together.'

'I feel guilty about that. You're not the sort who does one-night stands—and I took your virginity.'

'Which isn't an issue.'

'It is for me.'

She looked confused. 'Why?'

'Because it makes me feel dishonourable.'

She scoffed. 'Oh, get over yourself, Oliver. What are you, the Lord of the Manor?'

Not far off it. But he needed to get back on reasonable terms with her before he dropped that particular bombshell. 'I'm sorry. I did warn you I'd mess up on the control freakery stuff.'

'I guess. And maybe I need to cut you some slack, too—but how would you feel if I suggested you cut back on your shifts, just because you'll have a baby in seven months' time?'

He nodded. 'I get it.'

She rubbed her stomach reflectively. 'So is there a new girlfriend who might not be very happy to hear the news?'

'No, there isn't.' And the question stung. 'Do you really think I'm that shallow?'

'No, but you never seem to date anyone for long.'

'Strictly speaking, I didn't actually date you,' he pointed out. 'We both got carried away, that night.'

'I guess.' She paused. 'So why do you avoid proper relationships?'

Something else he didn't want to discuss. 'Let's just say I've been a bit burned in the past.'

'And you're still brooding over it enough not to give someone else a chance? She must've hurt you a lot.'

'Yes. She did,' he admitted.

'I'm sorry that you got hurt. But I'm nothing like the usual women you date.'

'Usual?'

She grimaced. 'I haven't been gossiping about you. But the hospital grapevine says you pick women who look like models, women from a much posher background than mine.'

He stared at her. 'You think I'm a snob?'

'No. You treat all our mums the same, whether they're ordinary women or royalty or celebs,' she said. 'I guess what I'm saying is I'm me, so don't go thinking I'll be like her.'

'You're not like her.' He trusted Ella, for a start. Professionally. But letting her into his heart would take a lot longer. Justine had left him with a lot of baggage.

Though he really didn't want to talk to Ella about Justine right now. Especially given their circumstances. How did you tell someone who was expecting your baby that you'd been here before—but the baby hadn't been yours? She'd start reading all kinds of things into that and what he might be thinking now, and he was having a hard time explaining it to himself; he certainly couldn't explain his feelings to her. Wanting to change the subject, he asked, 'What about you?'

Her eyes widened. 'You seriously think I'd date someone else when I'm pregnant with your baby?'

He winced. 'That sounds bad. I mean… You only just found out about the baby. You might've met someone between Hallowe'en and now.'

'No. There isn't anyone.'

'OK.'

And actually the hospital grapevine said she didn't

date. Ella was dedicated to her work. Oliver assumed that someone had hurt her badly in the past and she didn't trust love any more, the same way that he didn't trust love. But he could hardly grill her about it. That would be intrusive; besides, right now their relationship was so fragile he didn't want to risk saying the wrong thing and making it worse. 'Have you told your parents?' he asked.

'Not yet. I think I'd prefer to do that face to face—video-calling isn't good enough for news like this,' she said. 'I'm going home for two days at Christmas. I'll tell them then.'

'How do you think they'll take it?'

With sheer disbelief, Ella thought. Her parents knew the situation with her endometriosis and the ruptured cyst. They'd resigned themselves to never having grandchildren, though she'd seen the wistfulness in her mum's eyes every time one of her sisters became a grandmother again. Not that she wanted to discuss any of that with Oliver. Not right now. Because if he knew about her medical issues from the past, he'd try even harder to wrap her in cotton wool and it would drive her crazy.

'They'll be supportive,' she said. She knew that without having to ask. They might be shocked, but they'd definitely be supportive. 'How about yours?'

'It's complicated,' he said.

Another stonewall. Oliver had been hurt by someone in the past and his family situation was complicated. Did that mean maybe his ex had dumped him for his brother, or something? Did he even have a brother or a sister? But, even if she asked him straight out, she knew he'd evade the subject. 'You don't give anything away, do you?'

'I...' He blew out a breath. 'I'm making a mess of this.'

'Yes, you are,' she said. 'It's always better to be honest.' Which was pretty hypocritical of her, considering what she was keeping from him.

He raked a hand through his hair. 'Ella, right now all that matters to me is you and the baby.'

Why couldn't she let herself believe him?

When she didn't say anything, he sighed. 'I'd really like to be there at the scan. But it's your call.'

That was quite a capitulation—and one that clearly hadn't come easily to him. He was used to being in charge at work, so of course he was going to be bossy outside work as well. And maybe she had overreacted a bit. Maybe he really *had* meant to be helpful and trying to look after her, rather than making her feel stupid. But she didn't want to whine about her dyslexia. Plenty of people had more to deal with than she did.

Maybe she should capitulate a bit, too. 'I'll let you know when I've seen my doctor and got a date through,' she said.

'Thank you.' He finished his tea. 'I guess I should let you have the rest of your afternoon in peace. But call me if you need anything, OK? And I'm not trying to be bossy. I'm trying to be supportive.'

'Uh-huh.'

When she'd shown him out, she tidied up and washed up the mugs. She had absolutely no idea how this was going to work out. Oliver was clearly intending to do the right thing and stand by her—but she didn't want him to be with her out of duty. She wanted him there because he *wanted* to be there.

He hadn't said a word about his feelings. He hadn't asked her about hers, either. Which was just as well, because she was all mixed up. The attraction she'd felt towards him hadn't gone away, but she was pretty sure it was one-sided. She didn't want him to pity her for mooning about over him, so she'd been sharper towards him than normal. But then again, if it was that easy to push him away, he clearly didn't want to be with her in the first place.

'It'll work out,' she said quietly, cradling her abdomen protectively with one hand. 'If the worst comes to the worst, I'll go back home to my family in Ireland. But one thing I promise you, baby: even though you weren't planned, you'll always, *always* be loved. And if you're a girl I'm going to call you Joy, because that's what you are to me.'

CHAPTER THREE

ELLA WAS ON a late shift on the Monday morning, and called her GP's surgery as soon as they were open. To her surprise and delight, the GP was able to see her that morning before her shift.

'How are you feeling?' the GP asked when Ella told her she was pregnant.

'Fairly shocked,' Ella admitted. 'I didn't think this would ever happen, after what the doctors told me in London. But, now I've had a couple of days to get used to the idea, I'm thrilled.'

'Good.' The GP smiled. 'Congratulations. Are you having any symptoms?'

'A bit of morning sickness—it's not much fun if one of the dads-to-be on the ward is wearing a ton of aftershave, or if anyone at work's drinking coffee,' Ella admitted.

'I don't need to tell you that you should feel a lot better by the time you're twelve weeks.'

Ella smiled back. 'No. It's weird, because I'm usually the one giving that advice.'

'And you've already done a test?' the GP asked.

'Yes.'

'Then there's not much point in doing a second one,'

the GP said. 'Given your medical history, though, I'd like to send you for an early scan. As you work at Teddy's, would you rather go there or would you prefer to book in for your antenatal care somewhere else?'

'Teddy's is fine,' Ella confirmed.

'Good. I'll put a call through to the ultrasound department this morning. Reception will contact you with the date and time.'

'That's great—thank you very much.'

By the time Ella got to Teddy's, the GP's surgery had already sent her a text with the date and time of her scan. Ella wasn't sure whether she was more relieved or shocked to discover that the scan was tomorrow morning, an hour before her shift was due to start.

Someone was bound to see her in the waiting room for the ultrasound, so the whole department would know about the baby very quickly. Which meant that Ella needed to find Annabelle and tell her the news herself. The last thing she wanted was for her best friend to hear about the baby from hospital gossip, especially as she knew what Annabelle had been through over the last few years.

Annabelle was in her office, clearly writing up some reports. Ella knocked on the door, opened it slightly and leaned through the gap. 'I can see you're really busy,' she said, 'but can I have a quick word?'

'Sure,' Annabelle said. 'Is everything all right?'

'Yes—there's just something I wanted to tell you.' Then Ella looked more closely at her friend. 'There's something different about you.'

'How do you mean, different?' Annabelle asked.

'You look happier than I've seen you in a long, long time.'

Annabelle smiled. 'That's because Max and I are back together. For good.'

'Really?' Thrilled for her friend, Ella leaned over the desk and hugged her. 'That's fabulous news.'

'All those years I thought I'd failed him because I couldn't give him children.' Annabelle blew out a breath. 'But he says I'm enough for him, Ella. He doesn't need a family to feel we're complete.'

'I'm so pleased.' Ella paused. 'So this means you're not going to try IVF again?'

'No. We might consider adopting in the future, but we need time to think about it. And time just to enjoy each other,' Annabelle said. 'So what's your news?'

Even though Annabelle seemed to be OK with the idea of not trying for a family, Ella knew that this was still a sensitive subject. 'There isn't an easy way to say this.'

'Oh, no. Please don't tell me you're leaving Teddy's.'

'No.' At least, she hoped she wasn't going to have to leave. 'Annabelle, I wanted you to know before anyone else on the ward does—because everyone's going to know after tomorrow. And I really don't want this to upset you.'

'Now you're really worrying me. Is it another cyst?' Annabelle bit her lip. 'Or—and I *really* hope it isn't—something more sinister?'

Ella took a deep breath. 'No. Nothing like that.'

'Then will you please put me out of my misery?'

'I'm pregnant.'

'Pregnant?' Annabelle's blue eyes widened. 'That's the last thing I expected *you* to tell me. But—how?'

Ella squirmed. 'Basic biology?'

'Apart from the fact that you're not dating anyone—

or, if you are, you haven't told me about him—there's your endometriosis and that ruptured cyst and all the damage to your Fallopian tubes,' Annabelle pointed out. 'I thought the doctors in London said there was no chance of you conceiving?'

'They did. But I guess there was a billion to one chance after all.' A Christmas miracle. One Ella had never dared to dream about.

'I don't know what to say. Are you…well, happy about it?' Annabelle asked cautiously.

Ella nodded. Yet, at the same time, part of her was sad. This wasn't how she'd dreamed of things being when she was a child; she'd imagined having a partner who loved her. That definitely wasn't the situation with Oliver.

'Congratulations. I'm so pleased for you.' Annabelle hugged her. 'How far are you?'

'Seven weeks.'

'Your mum will be over the moon at the idea of being a granny.'

Ella smiled. 'I know. I'm going to tell her at Christmas when I go back to Ireland. Or maybe I'll take a snap of the scan photograph on my phone and send it to her tomorrow.'

'You've got a dating scan tomorrow? That's fantastic. Do you want me to come with you?' Annabelle asked.

'That's lovely of you to offer, but it's fine.'

'Of course. I guess the dad will want to be there.'

Dear Annabelle. She was clearly dying to know who it was, but she wasn't going to push her friend to share all the details until Ella was ready.

'The dad,' Ella said, 'is being just a little bit bossy at the moment and trying to wrap me up in cotton wool.'

Annabelle raised an eyebrow. 'He doesn't know you very well, then?'

'It's complicated.' Ella took a deep breath. 'I'm not actually dating him. And I'm not sure I'm ready for everyone to know who it is.'

'Sienna, mark two?' Annabelle asked wryly. 'Well, that's your right if you want to keep it to yourself. And you know I have your back.'

Ella smiled. 'I know.' Which was precisely why she was going to tell her best friend the truth. 'Obviously this is totally confidential—it's Oliver.'

'Oliver?' Annabelle asked in a scandalised whisper. 'As in our Assistant Head of Obstetrics?'

Ella winced. Was it so unlikely? 'Yes.'

'But… When?'

'The night of the charity ball. We danced together. A lot. He drove me home. And we…' She shrugged. 'Well…'

'I had no idea you even liked him.'

'I've liked him since the moment I met him,' Ella admitted. 'But I never said anything because I always thought he was way out of my league.'

Annabelle scoffed. 'You're lovely, and anyone who says otherwise has me to answer to.'

'But you know what the hospital gossip's like. They say he only dates people a couple of times—and they're usually tall, willowy women who look like models or movie stars. As in the opposite of me.'

'You're beautiful,' Annabelle said loyally.

'Thank you, but we both know I'm not Oliver's type. I'm too short and too round. And he… Well.' Ella had absolutely no idea how Oliver felt about her. He was being overprotective, but was that because of the baby?

'So what are you going to do?' Annabelle asked.

'I'm still working that out,' Ella admitted.

'Is he going to support you?'

'He's pretty much driven me crazy—presenting me with a box of folic acid, telling me to cut back on my shifts...'

'Ah. The protective male instinct coming out. And you sent him away with a flea in his ear?'

Ella nodded. 'You know how hard I worked to get through my exams. I'm not going to give all that up now.'

'So what do you want him to do?'

'Be part of the baby's life,' Ella said promptly. 'And not boss me about. Except I want him to be there because he wants to be there, not just because he thinks he ought to be there.'

'What does he say?' Annabelle asked.

'It's—' But Ella didn't get the chance to finish the conversation, because one of their colleagues came in, needing Annabelle to come and see a patient.

'We'll talk later,' Annabelle promised, on her way out of the door. Except Ella had a busy shift, starting with a normal delivery and then one that turned complicated, so she didn't have time to catch up with Annabelle.

Everything was fine in her second delivery; there were no signs of complications and no signs of distress as she monitored the baby.

But, as the mum started to push, Ella realised that she was having difficulty delivering the baby's face and head. The classic sign of the baby having a 'turtle neck' told her exactly what the problem was: shoulder dystocia, meaning that the baby's shoulder was stuck behind the mum's pubic bone. And in the meantime it meant that the umbilical cord was squashed, so the baby had less oxygenated blood reaching her.

'Sophie, I need you to stop pushing,' Ella said calmly. She turned to the trainee midwife who was working with her. 'Jennie, please can you go and find Charlie? Tell him we have a baby with shoulder dystocia, then get hold of whichever anaesthetist and neonatal specialist is on call and ask them to come here.'

'What's happening?' Sophie asked, looking anxious.

'Usually, after the baby's head is born, the head and body turns sideways so the baby's shoulders pass comfortably through your pelvis. But sometimes that doesn't happen because the baby's shoulder gets stuck behind your pubic bone,' Ella explained. 'That's what's happened here. So we need a bit of extra help to get the baby out safely, and that's why I've asked our obstetrician to come in. There will be a few people coming into the room and it'll seem crowded and a bit scary, but please try not to worry. We're just being super-cautious and making sure that someone's there immediately if we need them, though with any luck we won't need any of them.'

'Does this happen very often?' Sophie asked, clearly in distress.

'Maybe one in a hundred and fifty to one in two hundred births,' Ella said. 'Try not to worry, Sophie. I've seen this happen a few times before, and we can still deliver the baby normally—but right now I'm going to have to ask you to stop pushing and change your position a bit so we can get the baby's shoulder unstuck and deliver her safely.'

'Anything you say,' Sophie said. 'I just want my baby here safely.' A tear trickled down her face.

'I know.' Ella squeezed her hand. 'I promise you, it's all going to be fine. Now, I want you to lie on your back, then wriggle down so your bum's right at the very edge of the bed. Can you do that for me?'

'I think so.' Sophie panted a bit, clearly trying to hold back on pushing, and then moved down the bed according to Ella's directions.

Charlie came in with Jennie, followed by the anaesthetist and neonatal specialist. Ella introduced everyone to Sophie. 'Charlie, I want to try the McRoberts manoeuvre first,' she said quietly. It was the most effective method of getting a baby's shoulder unstuck, and would hopefully avoid Sophie having to have an emergency section.

'That's a sound decision,' Charlie said as he quickly assessed the situation. 'I've got another delivery, so if you're confident with this I'll leave you and the team. I'll be in the birthing suite next door—my patient's waters have just broken.

'I'm good, Charlie,' Ella said, then turned her attention back to Sophie as Charlie departed, leaving her to manage the birth.

'Sophie, I'd like you to bend your knees and pull your legs back towards your tummy,' Ella said. 'Jennie's here to help you. What that does is to change the angle of your spine and your pelvis and that gives the baby a little bit more room, and then hopefully we'll be able to get her shoulder out a lot more easily. You'll feel me pushing on your tummy—it shouldn't hurt, just feel like pressure, so tell me straight away if it starts to hurt, OK?'

'All right,' Sophie said.

While Jennie helped move Sophie's legs into position, Ella pressed on Sophie's abdomen just above her pubic bone. It wasn't quite enough to release the baby's stuck shoulder, and she sighed inwardly. 'Sophie, I'm afraid her shoulder's still stuck. I'm going to need to give you an episiotomy to help me get the baby out.'

'I don't care,' Sophie said, 'as long as my baby's all right.'

Which was what Ella was worried about. There was a risk of Sophie tearing and having a postpartum haemorrhage—but more worrying still was that the brachial plexus, a bundle of nerves in the baby's shoulder and arm, could be stretched too much during the birth and be damaged.

'OK. You'll feel a sharp scratch as I give you some local anaesthetic,' Ella said as she worked. 'And you won't feel the episiotomy at all.' Swiftly, she made the incision and then finally managed to deliver the baby's head.

'Here we go—I think someone's all ready to meet her mum.' She clamped the cord, cut it, and handed the baby to Sophie while mentally assessing the baby's Apgar score.

'Oh, she's so beautiful—my baby,' Sophie said.

The baby yelled, and everyone in the room smiled. 'That's what we like to hear,' Ella said softly. 'Welcome to the world, baby.'

While Ella stitched up the episiotomy, the neonatal specialist checked the baby over. 'I'm pleased to say you have a very healthy little girl,' she said. 'She's absolutely fine.'

Ella helped Sophie get the baby latched on, and the baby took a couple of sucks before falling fast asleep.

'We'll get you settled back on the ward, Sophie,' Ella said. 'But if you're worried about anything at all, at any time, you just call one of us.'

'I will. And thank you,' Sophie said, tears running down her face. 'I'm so glad she's here.'

Oliver called in to one of the side rooms to see Hestia Blythe; he'd delivered her baby the previous evening by Caesarean section, after a long labour that had failed to progress and then the baby had started showing signs of distress.

'How are you both doing?' he asked with a smile.

'Fine, thanks.' Hestia smiled back at him. 'I'm a little bit sore, and I'm afraid I made a bit of a fuss earlier.' She grimaced. 'I feel so stupid, especially because I know how busy the midwives are and I should've just shut up and let them get on with helping people who really need it.'

'You're a new mum who needed a bit of help— you're allowed to make a fuss until you get used to doing things,' Oliver said. 'Nobody minds.'

She gave him a rueful look. 'I needed help to get my knickers on this morning after my shower and it was so, so pathetic. I actually cried my eyes out about it. I mean—how feeble is that?'

'You're not the first and you definitely won't be the last. Remember, you had twenty-four hours of labour and then an emergency section,' Oliver said. 'I'd be very surprised if you didn't need help with things for a day or two. And the tears are perfectly normal with all the hormones rushing round your body.'

'That's what that lovely midwife said—Ella—she was so kind,' Hestia told him. 'She said it was the baby blues kicking in early and everything will seem much better in a couple of days.'

'She's right. When you've had a bit of sleep and a chance to get over the operation, you'll feel a lot more settled,' Oliver agreed. And, yes, Ella was lovely with the patients. He'd noticed that even the most panicky new mums seemed to calm down around her.

'May I have a look at your scar, to see how you're healing?' he asked.

Hestia nodded. 'You kind of lose all your ideas of dignity when you have a baby, don't you?'

He smiled. 'We do try not to make you feel awkward about things, so please tell me if anything I say or do makes you uncomfortable. We want to make your stay here at Teddy's as good as it can be.'

'I didn't mean that,' she said, 'more that you don't feel shy or embarrassed about things any more—you get used to people looking at all the bits of you that aren't normally on view!'

'There is that,' Oliver agreed. He examined her scar. 'I'm pleased to say it looks as if you're healing very nicely. How's the baby?'

'He's feeding really well,' Hestia said. 'I found it a bit tricky to manage at first, but Ella sat down with me and showed me how to get the baby to latch on. She was really patient with me.'

'That's great. May I?' He indicated the crib next to the bed.

'Of course.'

Obviously she saw the goofy smile on his face when

he looked at the baby because she said, 'You can pick him up and have a cuddle, if you like.'

'Yes, please.' Oliver grinned. 'This is one of my favourite parts of the job, cuddling a little one I helped to bring into the world. Hello, little man. How are you doing?' He lifted the baby tenderly and stroked the baby's cheek.

The baby yawned and opened his gorgeous dark blue eyes.

It was always a moment Oliver loved, when a newborn returned his gaze. But today it felt particularly special—because in a few months he knew he'd be doing this with his own baby. 'He's gorgeous, Hestia.'

'You're a natural at holding them,' Hestia said. 'Is that from your job, or do you have babies of your own?'

'My job,' he said. Though now he was going to have a baby of his own. And, the more he thought about the idea, the more it brought a smile to his face.

A baby.

His and Ella's.

Right now they weren't quite seeing eye to eye, but he'd make more of an effort. Because this really could work. He liked Ella and he knew she liked him. They were attracted to each other, or Hallowe'en wouldn't have happened. And love…? Oliver had stopped believing in that a long time ago. But he thought they could make a good life together, for the baby's sake.

He just needed to convince Ella.

'I was wondering,' Hestia said. 'My husband and I were talking, this morning, and you were so good with us last night. If it wasn't for you, we might not have our little boy now. And we'd like to name the baby after you. If that's all right?' she added.

'I'd be honoured,' Oliver said. 'Though I wasn't the only one in Theatre with you, so it'd be a bit greedy of me to take all the glory.'

'You were the one who saved our baby,' Hestia insisted. She peered over at his name tag. 'Oliver. That's such a lovely name.'

Oliver stared down at the baby. If Ella had a boy, would she want to call him Oliver? Or maybe Oliver as a middle name?

The baby started to grizzle and turn his head to the side. 'It looks as if someone's hungry.' He handed little Oliver over to his mum. 'Are you OK latching on now, or would you like me to get one of the midwives?'

'I'll manage—you've all been so great,' Hestia said.

'Good. If you need anything, let us know OK?'

'I will,' she promised. 'But right now all I can think about is my little Oliver here. And how he's the best Christmas present I could've asked for.'

Oliver smiled at her and left the room.

The best Christmas present I could've asked for.

In a way, that was what Ella had given him.

Needing to see her, he went in search of her.

'She's writing up her notes from her last delivery in the office,' Jennie, one of their trainee midwives, told him. 'The baby had shoulder dystocia.'

Which meant extra forms, Oliver knew. 'Did everything go OK?'

'Yes.'

'Good.' He headed for the midwives' office. Ella was sitting at the desk; as usual, she'd dictated something first into her phone, and it looked as if she was listening to her notes and then typing them up a few words at a time. Oliver knew from reading Ella's file that she was dyslexic; he assumed that this was the way she'd learned to manage it, and it was also the reason why she wore coloured glasses when she was reading notes or sitting at a computer.

He rapped on the glass panel of the door to get her attention, then opened it and leaned round it. 'Hi. I hear you just had a baby with shoulder dystocia.'

She nodded. 'There were absolutely no signs of it beforehand. The baby weighed three and a half kilograms and the mum didn't have gestational diabetes.'

'Prediction models aren't much help, as they're based on the baby's actual weight rather than the predicted weight, so don't blame yourself for it. In half of shoulder dystocia cases, we don't have a clue in advance, plus not all of them are big babies or from diabetic mothers,' Oliver said. 'How did it go?'

'Fine. As soon as I realised what was happening, I asked Jennie to get Charlie, the anaesthetist and the neonatal specialist. The McRoberts manoeuvre didn't quite work so I had to give her an episiotomy and guide the baby out, but the baby was fine and there's no sign of a brachial plexus injury. I'm going to keep an eye on Sophie—the mum—for postpartum haemorrhage.'

'Good job.' She looked so tired right now, Oliver thought. Having to concentrate on typing must be hard for her. 'Do you want a hand filling in the shoulder dystocia form?'

She narrowed her eyes at him. 'I'm not that hopeless, Oliver.'

And then the penny dropped. She obviously worried that people thought she was less than capable because of her dyslexia. Maybe in the past people had treated her as if she was stupid; that would explain why she'd overreacted to him buying the folic acid, because it had made her feel that he thought she was stupid.

'You're not hopeless at all, but you look tired,' he said, 'and filling in forms is a hassle even if you don't have to struggle with dyslexia as well.' He remembered what Ella's tutor said in her reference: ignore the exam results because Ella was an excellent midwife and could always tell you every last detail of a case. It just took her a lot longer than most to write it up. The exams must've been a real struggle for her, even if she'd been given extra time or the help of a scribe during the papers. And yet she'd never once given up. 'You could always dictate it to me and I'll type it up for you,' he suggested.

She narrowed her eyes even further. 'Would you make the same offer to anyone else on your team?'

She was worried about him showing favouritism towards her because of the baby? 'Actually, yes, I would,' he said. 'That's the point. We're a team, at Teddy's. And I'm responsible for my team's well-being. Which includes you.' He pulled up a chair next to her, brought the keyboard in front of him and angled the screen so they could both see it. 'Right. Tell me what to type.'

Again she looked wary, and he thought she was going to argue with him; but then she nodded and dictated everything to him. Just as he'd expected, she was meticulous and accurate.

'Thank you,' she said when he'd finished typing.

'Any time. You know your stuff and you pay attention to our mums, so you made that really easy for me.' But she looked so tired, almost forlorn, and it worried him. He wanted to make things better. Now. He gave in to the impulse and rested his palm against her cheek. 'Tell me what you need.'

'Need?'

Her pupils were suddenly huge and his mouth went dry. Was she going to say that she needed him? Because, right now, he needed her, too. Wanted to hold her. Wanted to kiss her.

When she said nothing, he rubbed his thumb lightly against her skin. 'Cup of tea? Sandwich? Because I'm guessing the staff kitchen is a no-go area for you right now.'

'I'd love a cup of tea,' she admitted. 'And a sandwich. Anything really, really bland.'

'Give me five minutes,' he said. 'And, for the record, I'm not trying to be bossy. You've had a busy shift with a tough delivery, and I bet you haven't had the chance of a break today. I want to be there for you and our baby, Ella.'

He'd said the magic word, Ella thought as she watched Oliver leave the office. 'Our', not 'my'. So maybe she wasn't going to have to fight him for her independence.

He came back with the perfect cup of tea, a cheese sandwich and an apple that he'd cored and sliced for her. Ella felt her eyes fill with tears. 'Oh, Oliver.'

'Don't cry.'

But she couldn't stop the tears spilling over. He wrapped his arms round her, holding her close and making her feel cherished and protected, and that only made her want to cry more.

Hormones, that was all it was. And if someone came into the office and saw them, people might start to talk. Although Ella dearly wanted to stay in his arms, she wriggled free. 'Oliver. People are going to start gossiping if they see us like this.'

'No—they'll think you're tired after a long shift, and I'm doing exactly what I would for any colleague. Being supportive.'

'I guess.' She paused. 'I've got an appointment through for the scan.'

He went very still. 'Are you asking me to come with you?'

'If you want to.'

There was a brief flash of hunger in his eyes. Did that mean he wanted to be there, or did he think it was his duty? She didn't have a clue how he felt about her, and she wasn't ready to ask—just in case the answer was that he saw it as his duty.

'But if anyone asks why, it's because you're supporting your colleague,' she said. 'I'm not ready for the world to know about—well.' She shrugged. There wasn't an 'us'. What should she call it? A fling? A mistake? The most stupid thing she'd ever done in her life?

And yet the end result had been something she'd always thought was beyond her reach. The most precious gift of all. Something that made her heart sing every time she thought about the baby.

'Noted,' he said, his voice expressionless. 'What time?'

'Eleven.'

'I'll be there,' he said. 'Do you want me to meet you in the waiting area outside the ultrasound room, or here?'

'I think the waiting area would be best.' If they went together from here, their colleagues were bound to start speculating, and she really didn't want that. Not until she knew what was really happening between her and Oliver.

'All right.'

'I guess I'd better finish writing up my notes,' she said. 'And then I want to check on Sophie—the mum—to see how she and the baby are doing. And I promised to give a hand with putting up the Christmas decorations in the reception area.'

'I'll let you get on, then.' For a moment, he looked as if he was going to say something else. Then he shook his head as if he'd changed his mind. 'I'll catch you later.'

CHAPTER FOUR

THE NEXT MORNING, Ella woke with butterflies in her stomach. The pregnancy test she'd taken had been positive; but as a midwife she knew that there were all manner of things that could go wrong over the next few weeks. One in four pregnancies ended in a miscarriage. And would the scarring in her Fallopian tubes have caused a problem with the baby?

She managed to force down a slice of toast and was sitting in the waiting room outside the ultrasound suite at five minutes to eleven, having drunk the requested one litre of water. There were Christmas cards pinned on the cork board in the reception area, and some of the tables had been moved to make way for a tree. All the couples sitting in the waiting room now were clearly looking forward to the following Christmas: the first Christmas with their new baby. Right now, Ella didn't know if she and the baby would still be here in Cheltenham with Oliver, or whether they'd be back in Ireland with her family, and it made her feel slightly melancholy.

Would Oliver be on time for the appointment? Or would he need to be in with a patient and have to miss the scan?

She reminded herself that it didn't matter if he couldn't be there; she could manage this perfectly well on her own. She tried to flick through one of the magazines left on the table to distract people who were waiting, but the paper was too shiny for her to be able to read the words easily.

And that was another worry: would her baby inherit her dyslexia? Ella knew that a daughter would have a one in four chance of inheriting the condition, and a son would have a three in four chance. She hated the idea that she could've passed on something that would cause her child difficulties in the future; though at least she was aware of what to look out for, so if necessary she'd be able to get help for her child much earlier than she'd received help, and her child wouldn't go through most of his or her education feeling as clumsy and stupid as Ella had.

She'd just put the magazine back on the table when she heard Oliver say, 'Good morning.'

She looked up and her heart skipped a beat. He really was beautiful: the walking definition of tall, dark and handsome. And she'd never reacted to someone as strongly as she reacted to Oliver.

'Good morning,' she said, trying to sound cool and collected and hoping that he didn't pick up how flustered he made her feel.

'Are you all right? Is there anything I can get you?'

'Thanks, but I'm fine. And, before you ask, yes, I've drunk all the water they asked me to.'

'Let's hope they're running on time so you're not uncomfortable for too long. May I?' He gestured to the chair next to her.

'Of course.' And how ridiculous it was that she

longed for him to take her hand, the way that the partners of the other pregnant women in the waiting room seemed to have done. She had to remember that their relationship was limited to an unplanned and inconvenient shared status as a parent: they weren't a proper couple. They probably never would be. The best she could hope for was that Oliver would be there for the baby as he or she grew up. It would be stupid to dream that the man who'd held her yesterday afternoon when she'd cried, the man she was falling for just a little more each day, felt the same way about her. Yesterday he'd been kind, that was all.

A few minutes later, they were called into the ultrasound suite. As they walked into the dimly lit room, the sonographer said, 'Oh, Mr Darrington! I didn't expect to see you.' She looked speculatively at Ella. 'I didn't realise—'

'I'm supporting Ella,' Oliver cut in, 'as I'd support any member of my team whose family lives a long way away.'

'Oh, of course.' The sonographer blushed. 'I'm sorry for—well, making assumptions.'

Ella had wanted to keep everything just between the two of them, but at the same time she felt a prickle of hurt that Oliver hadn't acknowledged the fact that this was his baby, and had fudged it in a way so that he hadn't lied directly but had definitely misdirected the sonographer. She knew it was contrary and ridiculous of her to feel that way, and it was probably due to all the pregnancy hormones rushing round her system. How many times had she had to comfort a pregnant woman in their department who was upset for a totally irrational reason?

Following instructions, she lay on the couch and bared her stomach. The sonographer tucked tissue paper round Ella's clothes to stop them being covered in gel, then put radio-conductive gel on her stomach.

'It's warm,' Ella said in surprise. 'The gel is always cold if we do a scan on the ward.'

The sonographer smiled. 'It always is warm down here because of all the machinery heating up the room. I think it makes things a bit more comfortable for the mums.'

'I agree. We'll have to think of a way of doing that on the ward,' Ella said to Oliver.

The sonographer ran the head of the transceiver over Ella's stomach. 'Good. I can confirm there's just one baby here.'

Ella hadn't even considered that she might be having twins. She had no idea if twins ran in Oliver's family, but she could hardly ask him right then—not without adding to the hospital rumour mill.

'The baby's growing nicely,' the sonographer said, and took some measurements on the screen. 'It's about thirteen millimetres long, so I'd say you're about seven and a half weeks.'

'That ties in with my dates,' Ella said.

'You can see the baby's head and body very clearly.' The sonographer turned the screen round to show them a bean-shaped blob; there was a flicker which Ella knew was the baby's heartbeat. And she was shocked by the rush of sheer emotion that burst through her at the very first sight of her baby.

'The baby's heart rate is one hundred and fifty beats per minute—which you'll know as a midwife is absolutely fine. It's too early to measure the fluid behind the neck for a Nuchal test, as we'd usually do that at about eleven weeks, but we can do a combined screening test for Down's then,' the sonographer said.

Ella only realised then that she'd been holding her breath, waiting to know that everything was all right and her fertility problems hadn't also caused a problem for the baby. 'Thank you. It's really good to know all's well.'

There was a knock on the door and another member of the ultrasound team put her head round the door. 'Sorry to interrupt—can I have a quick word?'

The sonographer went over for a brief discussion. 'I'm so sorry,' she said. 'I just need to pop next door for a moment. I'll be back very soon.'

'Not a problem,' Ella said, feeling a tug of sympathy for whoever was in the other ultrasound room. For the senior sonographer to be called in, it meant the team needed a second opinion on a potential complication.

As the door closed, Oliver took her hand. 'Our baby,' he said in wonder, looking at the screen. 'I've seen so many of these scans since I started working as an ob-gyn, and even performed a few of them myself, but this... This is special.' His voice sounded thick with emotion.

'I know.' It had affected Ella in the same way, and she was amazed by how strongly she felt. She'd only known about this baby for three days and it had turned her world upside down; but at the same time it was the most precious gift anyone could've given her and she was already bonding with the tiny being growing in her womb. She couldn't help tightening her fingers round his.

'Our baby, Ella,' he said again, his voice hoarse, and cupped her face with his free hand.

His touch sent a tingle through her. 'Oliver,' she whispered.

He dipped his head to kiss her; it was soft and sweet and full of longing.

When he broke the kiss, he pulled back just far enough so they could look into each other's eyes. Ella noticed that his pupils were huge. Was it because of the low light in the ultrasound room, or was it because he felt as emotional as she did right at that moment? Did he feel this same pull towards her that she felt towards him? Did they have a chance to make it as a couple—as a family?

'Ella,' he said softly, and kissed her again.

Her heart felt as if it had just done a somersault.

But then they heard the click of the door starting to open, and pulled apart again. Ella felt her cheeks burning, and really hoped that the sonographer hadn't seen anything—or, worse still, that she looked as if she'd just been thoroughly kissed.

Oliver looked both shocked and horrified. Ella could tell instantly that he was regretting the kiss and shrivelled a little inside. How stupid of her to hope that the kiss meant he felt something for her. Clearly he'd just got carried away by the rush of the moment.

'Sorry about that,' the sonographer said brightly. 'I guess as you work in Teddy's, Ella, you already know the answers to the kind of questions my mums normally ask, but is there anything you'd like to ask?'

Ella smiled. 'I'm not going to ask to know whether the baby's a girl or a boy, because apart from the fact I know it's way too early for you to be able to tell, it doesn't matter either way to me.' Though, she wondered, did it make a difference to Oliver? 'But would it be possible to have a photograph, please?'

'Sure. Let's see if we can get you a slightly less blurry picture,' the sonographer said with a smile. Once she'd got a picture she was happy with, she asked, 'How many copies do you need?'

'Two,' Ella said. 'How much are they?'

Before Oliver could embarrass them both by trying to pay, she took out her purse and handed over the money.

The photographs were printed while she wiped her abdomen free of gel and restored order to her clothes.

'Thank you for your support, Oliver,' she said. 'I know you're really busy, so you don't have to hang around and wait for me.'

It was practically a dismissal. So Ella was obviously regretting their kiss, Oliver thought. And she was probably right. They could do with some space. He'd got carried away in the heat of the moment, overwhelmed by seeing the baby on the screen. Right now he needed to take a step back from Ella, metaphorically as well as literally.

'Thanks. I'll see you later on the ward,' he said.

But before he had a chance to leave the sonographer was called next door again.

'Ella,' he said, his voice low and urgent. 'What happened just now—it shouldn't have done. I apologise.'

'Uh-huh.' Her voice was very cool.

And he deserved that coolness. It was all his fault. 'I guess I lost my head a bit. It was the excitement of seeing the baby on the screen and hearing the positive news.'

'We both got carried away,' Ella agreed. 'It won't happen again.' She gestured to the prints. 'I assume you'd like one of these?'

'I would.' It shocked him how very much he wanted the picture. *Their baby.* 'Thank you,' he said when she handed one to him.

'It's the least I could do.'

'I owe you—' he began.

'It's fine. A print of a scan isn't going to bankrupt me.'

That wasn't what he'd meant at all. 'Ella...' He sighed, seeing the determined set of her jaw. 'OK. I'll see you later. And thank you for the photograph.' He wasn't ready to share the news with anyone yet, but having the picture made everything so much more real. He tucked it into his wallet and left the room.

And he'd really have to get his head together.

He'd had no right to kiss her. The reason her fingers had tightened round his was purely because she was emotional about the baby. Seeing the little life they'd created, the strength of the baby's beating heart. That was all.

She wasn't in love with him.

And he wasn't in love with her, he told himself firmly. The attraction he felt towards her was because of the baby, rooted in responsibility rather than passion. He needed to be fair to her and leave her free to find someone else. Someone who hadn't put their heart in permafrost and would be able to give her the love she deserved.

But he'd meet every single one of his responsibilities

towards the baby, and he needed to find a good working relationship with Ella, so their child never felt unwanted or a burden. They definitely needed to talk. Later—he really needed to gather his thoughts first.

Annabelle beckoned Ella into her office as she walked past. 'So how did it go?'

Ella beamed and took the scan picture from her purse. 'Look at this! I know, I know, it's too soon to see anything more than a bean-shaped blob.'

'It's gorgeous,' Annabelle said, looking slightly wistful.

Ella bit her lip. 'Oh, Annabelle, I'm sorry. I didn't mean to open up old wounds.' But she'd so wanted to share the picture with someone who'd understand how excited she was.

'You haven't upset me in the slightest.' Annabelle hugged her. 'I'm thrilled for you. Really, truly and honestly.'

'Thank you.' Ella tucked the picture back into her purse.

'So what's the situation between you and Oliver?' Annabelle asked.

'Complicated,' Ella admitted. Even though Annabelle was her best friend, Ella wasn't going to tell her about that kiss today. Oliver had apologised for it and said he'd got carried away in the heat of the moment and it was a mistake, so it'd be pointless for her to wish that it had meant anything more.

'Are you a couple, or not?'

'Not,' Ella said.

'Do you want to be?' Annabelle asked.

That was the crunch question. And the worst part

was that Ella couldn't really answer it. 'I don't know. I like him, Annabelle—I like him a lot—but I don't want to lose my independence. I worked so hard to qualify as a midwife, and I hate the way Oliver just expects me to cut back on my shifts and do whatever he says. He obviously hasn't even thought about what it's going to do to my career.'

'I think,' Annabelle said, 'you need to talk to him.'

'You're right. I know,' Ella agreed.

'But, before that,' Annabelle said gently, 'you need to work out what you really want.'

And that was going to be the really hard part. Because right at that moment Ella wanted everything—and she knew that was way too much to ask.

That evening, when she got home, Ella video-called her parents.

'Is everything all right, darling?' Roisin O'Brien asked. 'You always call us on a Thursday, and today's only Tuesday.'

'I know. Mam, I have some news.'

Roisin beamed and asked hopefully, 'You're coming back to Ireland and going to work in the hospital in Limerick?'

Ella smiled. 'Mam, you know I love it here at Teddy's. No, it's not to do with work. Is Da there? Because I need to talk to you both together.'

'Is everything all right?' Roisin asked again.

'Yes.' And no, but she wasn't going to say that.

'Joe! Joe, our Ella's on the computer to talk to us,' Roisin called.

Joe appeared on Ella's screen, next to his wife. 'And how's my beautiful girl, then?'

Ella felt the tears well up. 'Oh, Da.'

Joe looked horrified. 'Ella? Whatever's the matter? I'll hop on the plane and be right over. You just say th—'

'No, Da, it's fine,' she cut in. She swallowed hard. 'Mam, Da—there isn't an easy way to say this, so I'll do what you always say and tell it to you straight. You're going to be grandparents.'

There was a stunned silence for a moment, and then Roisin said, 'But, Ella, the doctors in London said...' Her voice trailed off, and Ella knew what her mother didn't want to voice. The doctors in London had said Ella would never be able to have a child of her own.

'They got it wrong.' Ella picked up the scan photo and held it so her parents could see it. 'I had the scan today—I'm seven and a half weeks. You can't see a lot, just a bean shape, but the sonographer said everything looked fine and the baby's heart was beating just right.'

'We're going to be grandparents.' Joe and Roisin hugged each other.

'You're not angry with me?' Ella asked. 'Because—well, this wasn't supposed to happen?'

'So the baby wasn't planned. It doesn't mean he or she won't be loved to bits,' Roisin said. 'Lots of babies aren't planned. It's grand news, Ella. What about the baby's da? When do we get to meet him?'

Ella hadn't even considered that. 'I'm not sure,' she said carefully. 'It's complicated.'

'Do I need to come and talk to the lad and remind him of his responsibilities?' Joe asked, folding his arms.

'No, Da, and that's not why I called. I just wanted you both to know about the baby. It's early days and a lot of things could still go wrong—but I love you so much and I couldn't keep the news to myself any longer.

Please don't say anything to anyone else in the family, not yet—not till I'm twelve weeks, OK?'

'All right. And we love you, too, Ella,' Roisin said. 'If you want us to move over to England to help you with the baby, you just say the word. Or if you want to come home, you've always got a home with us and so has the baby.'

'Oh, Mam.' Ella swallowed back the tears.

'So what does the young man in question have to say for himself?' Joe asked.

'He was at the scan with me today. He's very responsible,' Ella said, guessing what her father was worrying about. She smiled. 'He's trying to wrap me up in cotton wool as much as you do.'

'With about as much success, I'll bet,' Roisin said. 'You get your independent streak from your Granny O'Connor.'

'And your Granny O'Brien,' Joe added, not to be outdone.

Ella laughed. 'Oh, I miss you both so much.'

'You'll be home in a couple of weeks for Christmas,' Roisin said, 'and we can give you a proper hug then. Are you keeping well in yourself?'

'Just a bit of morning sickness.'

'You need crackers by your bedside,' Roisin began, then laughed. 'Hark at me trying to give a midwife advice on pregnancy.'

'You're my Mam,' Ella said. 'Of course you'll tell me, and when I get home you know I want to know *everything* about when you were pregnant with me.'

'She'll talk the hind leg off a donkey,' Joe said.

'As if you won't, too, Joe O'Brien,' Roisin teased back.

'You sort things out with your young man,' Joe said,

'and you bring him home with you for Christmas so we can give him a proper welcome to the family.'

'I'll try,' Ella said. And she knew her parents meant it. They'd definitely welcome Oliver. Her 'young man'. She couldn't help smiling. If only. 'I love you, Da. And you, Mam.'

'We love you, too,' Roisin said. 'Can we have a copy of that photo—our first picture of our grandbaby?'

'I'll scan it in and send it tonight,' Ella promised. 'As soon as we've finished our video call.'

'Good night, darling,' Roisin said. 'And you call us any time, you hear?'

'I hear. Love you,' Ella said, and ended the call.

It had made her homesick, and she was tearful again by the time she scanned in the photograph and emailed it over to her parents. Part of her wanted to call Oliver and ask him to come with her to Ireland for Christmas; but he probably already had plans. Plans that wouldn't include her. She'd just have to take this whole thing day by day, and hope that things would get easier between them.

Oliver brooded about the situation with Ella and the baby for the rest of Tuesday. It didn't help when he had a text from his mother, asking him if he could please confirm whether he was going to come to the drinks party at Darrington Hall on Thursday night.

He hadn't been to his parents' annual pre-Christmas drinks party for years. But maybe it was time he tried to thaw out his relationship with his family. Particularly as he was about to become a father.

How would his family react to the news? He had no idea. Would they expect him to settle down? Would they try to use the baby as an excuse to make him leave the hospital and spend his time working with his brother, instead of doing the job he'd trained for years and years to do? Would it be the thing that brought them back together again? Or would their awkward relationship be like a marriage under strain and crack even further under the extra pressure of a baby?

It was all such a mess.

It would help if he knew what Ella wanted. Did she regret what had happened between them? Or would she be prepared to try and make a life together?

He didn't have a clue.

And he didn't even know how to begin to ask.

CHAPTER FIVE

By WEDNESDAY MORNING, the frustration was too much for Oliver. Usually he was self-contained, but right now he really needed to talk this over, preferably with someone he could trust to keep this to themselves.

The best person he could think of was Sebastian. Prince Sebastian Falco of Montanari had been one of his best friends since they'd met during Seb's first week at university, when Oliver had been nearing the end of his medical degree; they'd hit it off immediately, despite the four-year difference in their ages. Given his position as the heir to the kingdom of Montanari, Sebastian knew about the importance of privacy. And it didn't matter that Sebastian and Oliver hadn't actually seen each other for a few months; they always picked up their friendship exactly where they'd left off.

Oliver looked at the scan photograph again, then picked up his mobile phone and called Sebastian's private number.

To his relief the prince answered immediately. 'Hello, Olly. How are you?'

All over the place. Not that Oliver was going to admit it. 'Fine, fine,' he fibbed. 'Seb, have I caught you in the middle of something, or do you have a few minutes?'

'I've probably got about ten minutes,' Sebastian said ruefully, 'and then I really do have to be in a meeting. It's good to hear from you, Olly. How are things?'

'Complicated,' Oliver said wryly.

'Would this be as in female complications?' Sebastian asked. 'Or is it the new job?'

'Both—and thank you for the case of champagne, by the way.'

'It's the least I could do,' Sebastian said. 'So what are these complications? I take it that's why you're ringing me—to get an impartial point of view?'

'And a bit of perspective.' Oliver blew out a breath. He really didn't know where to start. Or maybe he should just do the whole mixed-up lot at once. 'It's crazy at work, what with the winter vomiting virus wiping out half the staff, and Sienna's going on maternity leave any day now. And I'm going to be a father.'

There was silence on the other end of the line.

'Seb? Are you still there?'

Was his friend really that shocked by the news of Oliver's impending fatherhood? Oh, hell. That didn't bode well for his family's reaction. Sebastian was much more laid back than Oliver's parents.

'Sorry, Olly. Someone needed me for a second. You were saying, half of your department's having babies?' Sebastian asked.

'Not half of us—that's the virus wiping everyone out—though it does feel as if everyone's going on leave. Just Sienna. Obviously you know her from when she did the training at the hospital for you.'

'Yes. She did a good job—thank you for recommending her.'

There was something in Sebastian's voice that Oliver couldn't quite work out. Or maybe it wasn't the best line. He didn't always get great mobile phone reception in his office.

'So Sienna got married when she came back to England?' Sebastian asked.

'No, she's still single. But she knows we're all there for her and she's got a very willing rota of babysitters when the baby arrives. It's due somewhere around the beginning of February.'

'I see.' There was a pause. 'So you're going to be a dad. Should I be offering congratulations or commiserations?'

'Both,' Oliver said wryly. 'Though at least this one's definitely mine.'

'Not a repeat of Justine, then.'

Trust Sebastian to come straight to the point. It was one of the things that Oliver appreciated about his friend: his ability to focus on the important thing and cut through all the irrelevancies. 'No. And Ella's nothing like Justine. She's open and honest. And very independent.'

'So she won't let you boss her about.'

Oliver knew his friend was teasing him—or was he? Was he really as overbearing and bossy as Ella said he was?

'When's the baby due?' Sebastian asked.

'In seven and a half months.'

'It's very early days, then.'

'Yes. Ella only told me a few days ago. She had the dating scan yesterday. Seeing the baby's heart beating on the screen...' It had been a real game-changer. Because now everything was real. *His baby.* And he wanted to be a much better father than his own father had been.

Yet wasn't he making the same mistakes? Insisting that everything should go his way? It was a knee-jerk reaction to the way Justine had behaved—and Ella deserved better.

'So what's the complication with the baby's mum?' Sebastian asked.

Trust the prince to ask the awkward question. 'It's tricky. I'm not her direct boss, but I'm the Assistant Head of the Department.'

'Well, it wouldn't be the first workplace romance in history.'

When Oliver didn't reply, Sebastian continued, 'I assume it *is* a romance?'

'Yes and no.' Oliver sighed. 'I admit, I've been attracted to her since the moment I met her. She's gorgeous—all soft curves and red hair and green eyes.'

'The way you describe her makes her sound like a Picasso painting,' Sebastian commented dryly.

Oliver laughed. 'Hardly. It's not just how she looks—I'm not that shallow. She's *nice*. I can be myself with her. But you know I don't do relationships. So I've kept it platonic.'

'Obviously something changed, or you wouldn't be preparing for fatherhood in seven and a half months' time,' Sebastian pointed out.

'I danced with her at the annual Hallowe'en charity ball. Then I gave her a lift home.' Which sounded pathetic. 'I meant to see her safely indoors and leave, but she invited me in for coffee. And then I just gave in to the urge to kiss her, and…' Oliver sighed. 'I guess one thing led to another.'

'How does she feel about you?'

Good question. One Oliver had been asking himself rather a lot, and he hadn't quite worked out the answer. 'I don't honestly know. Obviously there's something there between us, or we wouldn't be in the position we're in now. But the baby has complicated things a bit. I don't know whether she wants me for *me*,' he said, 'or if she wants me for the baby's sake.'

'Have you tried asking her?'

'No—because, if I'm honest, it's the same for me. I don't know if I want to be with her because I want her, or because I feel responsible for the baby.' Though he wasn't going to tell Sebastian about the kiss during the scan. That complicated things even more. Had they both been caught up in the moment, the excitement of see-ing the little life on screen? Or were they both trying to deny the inevitable? Were they meant to be together?

And then there was the issue of why she'd been so sure that he hadn't needed to use contraception. He still hadn't got to the bottom of that. He didn't think Ella was a gold-digger, but there was definitely something she was keeping from him, and he hadn't found the right way to ask her about it without causing a fight. 'Right now, everything's mixed up.'

'I guess only time will tell,' Sebastian said. 'Just make sure you keep the lines of communication open.'

Oliver knew that was sound advice. 'I will.'

'Have you told your family yet?'

'No. It's too early.'

'Fair enough.' Sebastian paused. 'Does Ella know about your family?'

The crunch question. Sebastian knew Oliver kept his background quiet at work, and why. 'No,' Oliver admitted.

'You're going to have to tell her at some point. And them. Especially if she's going to be a part of your future.'

'I know.' He'd been thinking about that. He needed to introduce Ella to his family; and, given that they seemed to be reaching out to him right now, maybe their attitude towards his career might have mellowed and they'd accept him for who he was rather than who they wanted him to be. 'My mother wants me to go to the annual Darrington pre-Christmas cocktail party.'

'Then go,' Sebastian said.

'You know I haven't been for years.' He hated all that meet-and-greet stuff.

'Things are different now. You need to introduce Ella to them. And,' Sebastian counselled, 'a party where there are a lot of people around would be a useful way of doing that.'

'You mean, it's in public so my parents will have to behave impeccably, and there will be enough other people there to dilute them?'

'I didn't say that.' But Oliver could almost hear the smile in his friend's voice, because they both knew what his family was like. Appearances mattered to the Darringtons. Sebastian, being a prince, was perfect friend material in their eyes. Ella came from a very different background, and it probably wouldn't go down well.

Oliver didn't need his parents to approve of Ella. Their relationship—if they could make it a real relationship—was just between the two of them. But he was starting to realise that family was important. Was there a place for his family in his future? Could they learn from the mistakes of the past and build some bridges?

'Olly, I really have to go,' Sebastian said. 'Sorry. I'll call you back when I'm out of my meeting.'

'I'll probably be in a meeting then myself, or in Theatre,' Oliver said. 'But you don't need to call me back, Seb. I think you've already helped me work out the best way forward. Thank you.'

'Any time. Good luck,' Sebastian said. 'And keep me posted on how things go.'

'I will. And thanks again.'

Once he'd put the phone down, Oliver texted his mother.

Confirm will be there on Tomorrow. May I bring a guest? There's someone I'd like you to meet.

The reply came back.

Of course. Look forward to meeting her.

Grilling her, more like, he thought. He definitely wouldn't leave Ella on her own at Darrington Hall. Even if she did protest that he was wrapping her in cotton wool.

'Mummy, look, it's Santa!' The little boy tugged at his mum's hand and pointed to the room on the other side of the floor, and Ella couldn't help smiling at the excitement on his face.

'Santa'—often one of the consultants in a borrowed

suit—paid a brief visit to Teddy's every Wednesday afternoon in December, to see the siblings of all the new babies on the ward. The Friends of the Hospital group had raised money for gifts appropriate for different ages—a soft toy, colouring pencils and a pad, or a reading book—and it helped to make the older siblings feel that they were still special despite the new arrival in the family.

So who was it today? Oliver? Max?

Definitely not Oliver, because a couple of minutes later he came striding along the corridor. He paused in the doorway when he saw Ella, and smiled. 'OK?'

Ella nodded, and glanced back at the mum she'd been checking over. She was busy with the baby and talking to her toddler, so Ella stepped out for a second. 'You?'

'Yeah.'

'I wondered if you were, um, helping our friend in the red suit.'

He smiled. 'That would be next week.' For a moment, he took her hand and squeezed it. 'Next year, our baby will see Santa.'

His voice was low enough so that nobody else would've heard. And that touch, combined with the expression in his eyes and what he'd just said, sent a thrill right through her. Especially when he added, 'And I can't wait. I know five months is still a bit young, but...'

Did that mean he wanted to take the baby to see Santa on his own? Or did he mean the three of them as a family? Not that she could ask. Yesterday, he'd kissed her; but then he'd said it was a mistake. Right now they seemed to be taking one step forward and two steps back.

Or maybe this was her chance to sound him out a

little more. 'The year after will be better,' she said. 'Because by then the baby will be talking and know what's going on.'

'We're so getting a train set for the second Christmas,' he said. 'Whether we have a girl or a boy. Wooden trains are the best fun.'

And she could just see him kneeling on the floor with their baby, helping their little one put the train tracks together. Her heart constricted. But would she be there with him?

'You're going to be an amazing mum,' he said. 'Singing nursery rhymes and telling stories with all the voices.'

He'd been thinking about the future, then? Just the baby, or about them too? She let herself get carried away with the fantasy that it was all of them. 'And you're going to be the dad who does all the scary stuff—the highest slide in the park, pushing the swings as fast as they'll go.'

'That sounds good to me,' he said. 'But not that scary. I'll always keep my own safe.'

Right at that second she wasn't sure whether he was talking about the baby or her. And she so wanted it to be both of them.

'Ella—can I borrow you for a second?' Jennie, their trainee midwife, asked.

Oh, help. Ella really hoped that Jennie hadn't overheard any of that conversation.

'Sure,' she said, keeping her fingers crossed that she didn't sound flustered. 'I'll just let my mum know I'll be with you for a little while before I finish writing up her notes. I think they're next for Santa, so they won't miss me. Catch you later, Oliver.'

'Later,' he agreed with a smile.

It was just a work pleasantry, that was all, she reminded herself. She might not even see him again before the end of her shift. But at least they hadn't been fighting. That had to be a start.

Once Ella had helped Jennie and finished writing up her notes, she was called to the birthing suite for another delivery. This was the best job in the world, she thought, watching the little family in front of her: the dad with tears of pride and joy in his eyes, the mum looking tired but radiant, and the baby cuddled up between them. To be able to share these first few precious minutes of a new life was so amazing.

The delivery had been free from complications, the baby had had a perfect Apgar score, and now the three of them were settled back on the ward.

Would Oliver cry when their baby arrived, the way this baby's dad had cried with sheer joy? Or would he be perfectly cool, calm and collected? Given what he'd said to her when Santa came onto the ward, she had a feeling it would be the former. And he had talked about next Christmas, so it sounded as if he wanted to be part of the baby's life.

There was still a lot they weren't saying to each other, but at least they weren't arguing. So maybe they'd manage to work things out between them.

She left the little family to bond and went to write up her notes in the quiet of the office.

She was halfway through when there was a rap on the door. She looked up to see Oliver standing in the doorway.

'Can I have a word?' he asked.

Her heart skipped a beat as she thought about the way he'd kissed her in the ultrasound room yesterday; but then she remembered how quick he'd been to dismiss it as a simple reaction to seeing the baby and hearing the good news. Despite what he'd said to her earlier today about their baby and next Christmas, they hadn't actually resolved their relationship. And she had to be objective about this. Oliver Darrington might be the father of her baby, but he wasn't in love with her. She'd be a fool to dream it would ever happen. She damped down the flare of desire. 'Sure,' she said, as coolly as she could. 'Though I'm in the middle of writing up the birth notes.'

'Did it go well?'

'Very. There were no complications, and I left the new mum and dad bonding with their little girl.' She smiled. 'The dad cried when she was born. It was so lovely to see how happy they were.' And oh, she had to stop talking. The last thing she wanted was for Oliver to guess how she was feeling. 'You wanted something?'

'Yes. What are you doing tomorrow?'

'Cleaning my flat,' she said, 'as it's my day off. And I really ought to do a bit of Christmas shopping. I'm a bit behind, this year.'

'Are you busy in the evening?' he asked.

'Why?'

'Because my parents are having a cocktail party.' He looked awkward. 'I wondered if you'd like to come with me.'

He wanted her to meet his parents?

Ella stared at him in surprise. 'Are you sure? I mean... They didn't invite me.'

'They have now. I asked if I could bring you.'

So he'd already talked to his family about her? Had he told them about the baby, despite the fact he'd suggested she shouldn't tell anyone until she was past the first trimester?

She pushed down the rising panic. Cocktail party, he'd said. She didn't know anyone who actually held cocktail parties. She knew that Oliver had quite a posh accent. But how posh exactly were they? Would she fit in?

As if he'd guessed what she was thinking, he said, 'It's not a big deal. Just a drinks party they hold every year before Christmas.'

It was an annual event? That sounded even scarier. 'It sounds a little bit fancy,' she said.

Oliver's face shuttered. 'All right. So you don't want to meet my family.'

She shook her head. 'No, that's not what I meant, Oliver. I was just thinking that it sounds like quite a big party and your parents will be busy. Wouldn't it be better if I met them at something a bit quieter and more low-key rather than a big event?' And something she could escape from more easily. 'Like, I don't know, meeting at a café in town for a cup of tea?'

'It's probably better,' he said, 'if there are a lot of people there.'

That sounded ominous. Did that mean he thought they were going to hate her, especially when they found out about the baby? Or did they already know about the baby and they weren't pleased?

Clearly her worries showed in her face because he said, 'What I mean is that my family can be a little bit pushy—I guess that's where I get my overbearing streak. I think the first time you meet them will be better if they're a bit diluted. They're the problem, not you.'

That didn't calm Ella's worries in the slightest. Particularly as she knew that her own family would welcome Oliver warmly when she introduced him to them. They'd draw him straight into the middle of things and treat him as if they'd known him for years and years. Her father had already said they wanted to welcome him to the family.

Clearly Oliver's family was very different, and she'd have to tread very carefully.

'Have you told them about the baby?' she asked.

'Not yet.'

'Because they won't approve of me?' The question burst out before she could stop it.

'Because,' he said, 'it's still early days. I'd prefer to wait until you're safely through the first trimester before we tell my family about the baby.'

That was sensible; though it made her feel guilty that everyone in the department already knew. It felt wrong to be sharing this with their colleagues and not Oliver's family, especially as she'd already shared the news with her own family. But how could she explain that? 'OK.' She paused. 'So what do I wear? If it's a big cocktail party...'

'I'll buy you a dress,' Oliver said.

She frowned. 'No—and that's not why I asked. Is the dress I wore to the masked ball suitable?'

'Yes, but I can b—' he began.

'No,' she cut in. 'You really don't need to buy me a dress, Oliver. It's a total waste to buy something you're only ever going to wear to one thing.'

He sighed. 'I'm being bossy again?'

She nodded.

'Got it,' he said. 'Will you allow me to drive you to the party?'

'Yes, but only because you know the way.'

'All right.' His grey eyes were unreadable. 'I'll pick you up tomorrow, then.'

'What time do I need to be ready?'

'The party starts at half-past seven, and it takes about an hour to get there. So I'll pick you up at half-past six.'

'I'll be ready. Should I have dinner first?'

'There will be nibbles there—but yes, I'd say grab a sandwich or something before I pick you up,' Oliver said.

Ella noticed that he didn't suggest eating together first, and pushed down the feeling of hurt. After all, she'd already accused him of being bossy. He'd probably thought she'd bite his head off if he suggested it. 'All right. I'll see you tomorrow then.'

She watched him walk out of the door. Had he just asked her on a date of sorts? Was he thinking about trying to make a go of things between them, and introducing her to his family was the first step? Or was this some kind of test she needed to pass?

'You're overthinking it, you numpty,' she told herself crossly. She knew Oliver didn't play games. He was simply introducing her to his family. Not as the mother of his child, but as... She didn't quite know what as, but it was most likely he'd say she was his colleague or maybe his friend. And then, when he'd worked out how his family reacted to her, he'd find the right way to break the news about the baby. It was nothing to worry about.

'We're going to be just fine,' she said, resting her

hand where her bump wasn't even visible yet. 'If they don't like us—well, that's their problem, and we'll deal with it if and when we have to.'

CHAPTER SIX

DESPITE HER BRAVE intentions of the night before, Ella spent Thursday feeling really nervous. What would Oliver's parents be like? Would they accept her? He'd said that his relationship with them was complicated. Would the baby make things worse? Or was he hoping that the baby would be a bonding point?

But then again, how many people thought that having a baby would paper over the cracks in their relationship, only to find instead that the pressure of having a newborn made the cracks burst wide open? And that would be true of any family relationship, not just that of the baby's parents.

She tried not to think about it too much while she cleaned her flat, and it made her feel slightly better when Annabelle sent her a text during her break on the ward.

Good luck for tonight. Am sure O's parents will love you.

Then she went into Cheltenham to do her Christmas shopping, and all her fears came back. Everywhere she looked, she seemed to see new mums proudly pushing a pram with their partners by their side.

Tears pricked her eyelids. She *missed* her parents. And she knew they'd both be doting grandparents, always ready with a cuddle and a story. Would Oliver's parents feel the same way about the baby? Or would it make their strained relationship with Oliver more difficult?

Plus it was still very early days in her pregnancy—especially given the complications of her own medical history, which she hadn't yet felt comfortable enough to share with Oliver. The sonographer hadn't said anything, but what if there was a cyst on her other ovary? What if it grew during the pregnancy and she ended up needing an operation to remove it? She knew that kind of operation wasn't usually done until halfway through the pregnancy, to protect the baby—but what if the cyst ruptured, like the other one had?

'Stop it. You're borrowing trouble, and you know that's stupid,' she told herself crossly.

It had to be hormones making her all tearful and miserable like this, because Ella had never been a whiner. Even on days when the pain of her endometriosis had made it hard for her to crawl out of bed, she'd tried her best to pretend that everything was just fine.

And she needed to be on top form tonight, all smiley and cheerful, so Oliver's family would like her.

Oliver.

Should she get him a Christmas present? They weren't in a relationship exactly, but he was her baby's father. Though Ella didn't have a clue what to buy him. He never shared anything personal at work. Although she knew from the night of the Hallowe'en ball that he liked piano music, she didn't know what he already owned. And she didn't want to buy him something bland and impersonal like a bottle of wine.

She shook herself. She'd worry about that later. For now, she needed to think about meeting his family and hoping she could make them like her.

The shopping and the cleaning took it out of her, and she ended up falling asleep over her books. She had only just enough time to get ready, grab a sandwich and do her hair and make-up before Oliver arrived at precisely half-past six.

'You look lovely,' he said.

'Thank you.' So did he, in a dinner jacket and bow tie—just as he'd worn to the ball. Evening dress suited him.

And she remembered exactly what it had felt like to slide that shirt off his shoulders and trace his pectoral muscles with her fingertips—and how it had felt when he'd unzipped the dress she was wearing right now...

Oh, help. She really had to keep her imagination and her memory under strict control. Tonight she needed to be on her best behaviour—and that didn't mean doing what she really wanted to do most at that moment and kissing Oliver until they were both dizzy with need and ended up back in her bed. Especially as she wasn't sure at all how he felt about her.

Hormones, she reminded herself. This is all just hormones rushing round and I need to be sensible. 'Um—would you like a drink?' she asked.

'Tea would be good, thanks.' He looked slightly wary. 'I need to talk to you about something.'

This didn't sound good. 'Come in and sit down.' She busied herself making tea; he didn't say anything, which made her feel even more awkward. But she wasn't a coward; she'd face this head on. 'What did you want to talk about?'

'My family,' he said, surprising her. 'I know I don't have to ask you to keep this confidential.'

Because he trusted her? That was a good thing. If he was going to tell her why his relationship with his parents was tricky, it might stop her accidentally making things worse tonight. 'Of course I'll keep whatever you tell me to myself,' she said, wanting to reassure him.

'I don't mention my family at work,' he said, 'because I want people to see me for who I am, not whose son I am.'

She frowned. 'Your dad's famous?'

He coughed. 'My father's the Earl of Darrington.'

It took her a while to process it. 'You mean your family's like a real-life version of the one in *Downton Abbey*?'

'Yes.'

She stared at him, not quite able to believe this. She'd known Oliver was posh, but *this* posh? Oh, help. She didn't quite know how to deal with this.

'So should I have been calling you Lord Darrington all these months?' she asked carefully.

'No. I'm not the oldest son, so I'm just the Hon Oliver Darrington,' he said. 'Addressed as plain Mr Darrington, just as you're addressed as Miss O'Brien.'

'Ms,' she corrected. And as for his 'just the Hon'—she didn't know anyone else who was an Hon. And then a really nasty thought struck her. 'Oliver, you don't think I'm a gold-digger, do you? Because I had absolutely no idea you were—well, from that kind of background.'

Shock spread across his face. 'Of course you're not a gold-digger, Ella. Apart from the fact that nobody at work knows about my background, you're completely open and honest.'

That wasn't quite true. She hadn't been totally honest with him about her past, because she hadn't wanted him to pity her. Guilt trickled through her—but the worry was uppermost. 'So this party tonight's going to be really, really posh?'

He grimaced. 'A bit. And I understand if you'd rather not go. I probably should have told you when I asked you to come with me.'

'I wish you had, because at least then I could've maybe found something more suitable to wear while I was out shopping today.' She gestured to her dress. 'Everyone's going to take one look at me and know this was a sale bargain and probably cost less than their underwear. I'm not going to fit in. And your parents are going to think I'm just after your money. Which,' she added, just in case he was under any kind of misapprehension on that score, 'I'm not.'

Oliver came to stand before her and pulled her to her feet. 'Ella O'Brien, you look beautiful. Nobody whose opinion matters will think anything about what you're wearing other than the fact that you look lovely. You're more than good enough to hold your own at any party, whether it's the pub quiz between Teddy's and the Emergency Department, or the ballroom at Darrington Hall full of...' He spread his hands. 'Well.'

'Lords and ladies?' she asked wryly.

'Not all of them will have a title,' he said. 'But yes. You're more than good enough, Ella.'

There was a slash of colour across his cheeks, telling her that he felt really strongly about this. He really did believe that she could fit in.

And then, the expression in his eyes changed. Turned from fierceness to heat. Achingly slowly, he dipped his head to brush his mouth against hers. There was a sweetness to his kiss, just like when he'd kissed her in the ultrasound room, and Ella found herself melting against him and returning his kiss.

'You're wearing the same dress you wore that night,' Oliver whispered against her mouth. 'That night we made love. The night we made our baby.'

His hand slid down to rest protectively over her abdomen, and Ella's pulse speeded up a notch. On impulse, she rested her hand over his, and he moved slightly so that her fingers were entwined with his, united and protective.

'And you're wearing that suit,' she whispered back. 'I can remember taking your shirt off.'

His eyes darkened. 'Ella. I can't stop thinking about that night. How it felt to be with you.' He stole another kiss. 'The scent of your hair. The feel of your bare skin against mine.' His teeth grazed her earlobe as he whispered, 'I haven't stopped wanting you. And now you're carrying our baby, it makes me want to…'

'Yes.' Oh, yes. She wanted it, too. That shared closeness she'd only ever known with him. Except this time it would be different. Because they'd created a new life, and when he explored her he'd notice the tiny, subtle changes. And she knew he'd tell her about every single one in that amazingly sexy posh voice.

Right now her skin felt too tight. Especially when

he kissed her again, pulling her close against him, and her hardened nipples rubbed against him.

'Oliver,' she breathed.

But, when Ella felt Oliver's fingers brush the skin on her back as he began to slide the zip of her dress slowly downward, common sense kicked back in. Yes, she wanted to make love with him. Desperately. But she was supposed to be going to meet his family. She needed to make a good impression. Turning up late, looking as if she'd just had sex, with her mouth all swollen and her hair all mussed—that most definitely wouldn't be the right impression.

'Oliver. We *can't*. We're going to be late.'

He stroked her face. 'Or we can skip the party.'

'But your parents are expecting us. It's rude not to turn up.'

'I know. But I can say I was held up at work.'

'Which isn't true.'

'It's a white lie.'

It sounded as if he didn't want to go to the party, and not just because he wanted to carry her to her bed. She narrowed her eyes at him. 'What else aren't you telling me, Oliver?'

He sighed. 'Nothing, really.'

'You said things were strained between you and your parents. Is not turning up going to make things worse? Or will it be worse when they meet me and realise I'm not from your world?'

He rested his palm against her cheek. 'Trust you to hit the nail on the head. OK. Let's just say that they had other plans for me, so they're not brilliantly happy that I went into medicine.'

She couldn't understand why. 'But you're Assistant Head of Department at a ridiculously young age. Doesn't that tell them how good you are at what you do?'

'I didn't actually tell them about the promotion,' he admitted.

'Why? For pity's sake, Oliver, aren't they massively proud of you? Because they ought to be! You're really good at your job. What you do is *important*.'

Ella was batting Oliver's corner for him, and it made him feel odd. He'd never, ever dated anyone who'd backed him like that before. With Justine, he was always the one doing the protecting; but Ella was different. She was his equal.

Strictly speaking, he and Ella weren't actually dating. But there was more to their relationship than just the shared unexpected parenthood. And the fact that she was backing him like this… Maybe she was the one that he could trust with his heart. The one who'd see him for who he really was. 'You really think that?' he asked.

She put her hands on her hips and rolled her eyes at him. 'Oliver Darrington, you're the one who makes the difference in a tricky birth between someone having a baby, and someone losing their baby. You've saved babies and you've saved their mums, too. And if that's not more important than—than—' She waved a hand in disgust. 'Than having a title, then I don't know what is.'

Even with her lipstick smudged and her hair slightly mussed from their shared kiss, Ella looked magnificent. A pocket Amazonian.

'You,' he said softly, 'are amazing. Never let anyone else ever tell you otherwise.'

'So are you,' Ella said fiercely. 'So we're going to this party, and your family can see that for themselves.'

'Right.' He stole another kiss. 'Though you might want to put some more lipstick on and fiddle with your hair.'

'Give me two minutes,' Ella said.

And she was ready in the time it took him to wash up their undrunk mugs of tea.

Ella didn't manage to get much more out of Oliver about his family on the journey, other than that his older brother Ned was married to Prue and they had three girls. Her bravado dimmed a bit when Oliver explained that Ned was the heir to the earldom and he was the 'spare' until Ned and Prue had a son—particularly when she worked out that if Ned and Prue didn't have a son and something happened to Ned, Oliver would be the future Earl of Darrington; and then if her baby was a boy he would be the heir, which would make her the mother of an earl. Her nerves threatened to outweigh the bravery completely when Oliver drove down the long, narrow driveway lined with trees and she saw just how big Darrington Hall was. Her worries grew as he parked his car among what she recognised as Rolls-Royces and Bentleys. No way could she fit into this kind of world. If his parents didn't approve of his job, they'd approve even less of her.

He helped her from the car, and led her up the steps to the porticoed entrance. They were greeted at the door by a butler wearing white gloves, who took their coats. 'Good to see you again, Master Oliver,' he said, dipping his head in acknowledgement.

'Thank you, Benson,' Oliver said with a smile.

'Everyone's in the ballroom, Master Oliver,' the butler said.

'Thanks, Benson. This way, Ella,' Oliver said.

The reception hall was massive, with a huge sweeping staircase, polished wooden floors, a carpet that looked as if it was an antique worth hundreds of thousands of pounds, and a whole gallery of portraits in heavy gold frames.

'Are they...?' Ella asked, gesturing to them.

'The Earls of Darrington, yes. My father's the one over there.'

The newest portrait. The current Earl had a stern face, Ella thought. And he was wearing very formal dress; she imagined it was what he'd wear in the House of Lords.

He really, really wasn't going to approve of her.

There were serving staff dressed in black and white, carrying silver trays filled with glasses of champagne or exquisite canapés. The trays looked as if they were real silver, Ella thought, rather than the polished chrome used in a restaurant.

She felt even more out of place when they walked into the ballroom itself. Again, the room was massive, with wooden-panelled walls, a huge marble fireplace, more oil paintings in heavy frames and the most enormous crystal chandelier. There was a baby grand piano in the corner of the room, and the man sitting on the piano stool was playing soft jazz, not quite loudly enough to disturb the hum of conversation. And the only time she'd seen a Christmas tree that big was in one of the posh London stores. It looked professionally decorated, too—not like the Christmas trees in her family, strewn with decorations made over the years at school by each child. All the reds and golds of the different decorations matched, and the spacing between baubles was so precise that someone must've used a tape measure.

But then Oliver tucked her hand firmly in the crook of his arm and was walking her over towards a couple at the other side of the room.

'Olls! I thought Mama had been at the sherry when she said you were turning up tonight,' the man said, clapping him on the back.

Even without the words, Ella would've guessed that this was Oliver's brother, because they looked so alike.

'Very funny, Ned. I'd like you to meet Ms Ella O'Brien. Ella, this is my elder brother Ned, and how he managed to persuade lovely Prue here to marry a scoundrel like him is beyond me,' Oliver said, laughing.

'I—um—how do you do, Lord Darrington?' Ella said awkwardly, holding out a hand, really hoping that she'd got the etiquette right. Or should she be curtsying to him? She only just resisted the urge to kick Oliver very hard on the ankle for not giving her anywhere near enough information about how to deal with this.

Viscount Darrington shook her hand. 'Delighted to meet you, Ms O'Brien, or may I call you Ella?'

She could see where Oliver got his charm from, now. 'Ella's fine,' she said, cross with herself for squeaking the words.

'And you must call me Ned,' he said with a warm smile.

'And I'm Prue. We don't stand on ceremony, whatever nonsense Olls might have told you,' Viscountess Darrington said. Then she shook her head in exasperation. 'Did he not even let you get a drink, first? That's terrible. Olls, your manners are shocking. Come with me, Ella—let's leave these heathens to sort themselves out. What would you like? Some champagne?'

'Thank you,' Ella said, 'but I'm on an early shift tomorrow, so I'd rather not be drinking alcohol tonight.'

'Let's sort you out with something soft, then,' Prue said with a smile. 'And I'm sure we have you to thank for Olls actually coming to the party. He normally wriggles out of it.'

'I…um…' Ella didn't know what to say.

'And it's really bad of him to drop you right in the middle of this without any warning,' Prue said. 'This place is a bit overwhelming, the first time you see it—and with all these people about it's even more intimidating.' She shook her head again and tutted. 'I'm so sorry, Ella. If he'd actually told us he was bringing you, I'd have suggested meeting you in Cheltenham for lunch first—somewhere quiet, where we could have had a proper chat and got to know each other a bit before tonight.'

Ella really hadn't expected Oliver's family to be so welcoming, not after he'd said things were strained between them. But Prue Darrington was a real sweetheart, and Ella began to feel just the tiniest bit better about being here.

'I think the invitation was all a bit last-minute,' she said.

Prue rolled her eyes. 'The Darrington men are all the same—they're total rubbish at communicating. But I'm so glad you've come. It's lovely to meet you. And I do like your necklace. It's so pretty.'

Ella wasn't sure whether Prue really meant the compliment or was just being kind, but she was grateful that at least someone here wasn't looking down on her. 'Thank you.'

'I take it you work with Olls?' Prue asked.

Ella nodded. 'I'm a midwife.'

'What a wonderful job to have—to see those first precious moments of life,' Prue said.

'I love it,' Ella confided shyly. 'Oliver says you have three girls?'

'We do. Rose, Poppy and Lily—aged five, three and thirteen months respectively.'

'They're very pretty names,' Ella said.

Prue grinned. 'That's the great thing about having a girl Darrington. You actually get to choose her name yourself.'

Ella blinked. 'You mean, if you'd had a boy, you wouldn't have been able to choose his name, even though you're his mum?'

'The firstborn boy is *always* Edward.' Prue winked. 'Though if we ever have a son, I plan to rebel and always refer to him by his middle name.'

As they walked by a towering floral display, Ella discovered that the heavy perfume of lilies brought on a rush of morning sickness.

'Are you all right?' Prue asked.

'Fine,' Ella fibbed.

'No, you're not. You've gone green. Come on, let's get you a glass of water and somewhere quiet to sit down.'

Prue was as good as her word, and Ella felt better when she'd had a sip of water.

Prue lowered her voice. 'So how far along are you?'

'I don't know what you mean,' Ella said, inwardly horrified that Prue had guessed her secret already.

'Ella, you're a midwife and I have three girls. When someone female goes green at the scent of lilies, either they have hay fever—in which case they'll start sneezing the place down within two seconds—or...' Prue squeezed Ella's hand. 'If it makes you feel any better, I'll tell you a secret. If the party had been last week instead of tonight, I would've turned green as well at the scent of those lilies.'

'You're...?'

Prue nodded, and lifted a finger to her lips. 'Ned and I promised each other not to tell anyone until I'm twelve weeks.'

And that gave Ella the confidence to admit the truth. 'Me, too. Almost eight weeks. But please don't tell anyone,' she said. 'Not even Ned.'

'OK. I promise. But you have to make the same promise,' Prue said. 'You can't even tell Olls for the next three weeks.'

'I promise,' Ella said.

'But this is such fabulous news,' Prue said. 'Our babies will be practically the same age. Which means they'll have a great time romping around this place together.'

'I used to play with my cousins all the time, when I was young,' Ella said. And she loved the idea of her baby having a built-in family like this, just the way that she had.

'My cousins all lived too far away for us to see them that often. And I was the only one, so I was determined to have lots and lots of children,' Prue said. 'Ned's desperate for a boy. Not because of the entailment and all that nonsense about a son and heir, but because he says he's going to need some support when the girls are teens and we all have PMT at the same time and he'll be terrified of us.'

Ella couldn't help laughing. She really, really liked Oliver's sister-in-law, and she had the feeling they were going to become good friends. 'I bet the girls wrap him round their little fingers.'

'They do,' Prue confirmed. 'And you should hear him read them a bedtime story. It's so cute.'

Would Oliver be like that as a father, totally involved with their baby?

Then again, she and Oliver weren't a proper couple—despite the way he'd kissed her tonight.

Ella pushed the thought away as Ned and Oliver came over to join them.

'I wondered where you'd both disappeared to,' Ned said.

'Sorry. I just needed to sit down for a moment,' Ella said. 'It's been a crazy shift at work today. I had a mum with a water birth, and then a scary one where the cord was wrapped round the baby's neck. Luckily there was a happy ending in both cases.' It wasn't strictly true—although that particular shift had happened, it had been a fortnight ago rather than today—but she hoped that the story would keep Ned off the scent.

'We really have to circulate, darling, or Mama will be on the warpath,' Ned said to Prue with a grimace. 'Ella, please excuse us—but do make sure you find us later, because I'd love to get to know you a bit better. And make sure Prue has your mobile number so we can arrange dinner.'

'I will,' Ella promised.

'Are you really all right?' Oliver asked when his brother and sister-in-law had gone.

'Yes.' She gave him a wan smile. 'The lilies got to me.'

'Right.' Understanding filled his gaze.

'Sorry for telling the fib about work.'

'No. I understand. You needed to—otherwise you'd have had to tell them.'

And she'd already told Prue, she thought, feeling guilty. 'I like your brother and sister-in-law,' she said.

'They're good sorts,' Oliver said. He looked her straight in the eye. 'Are you feeling up to meeting my parents?'

Even the idea of it made butterflies stampede through her stomach. It was so important that she got this right and made a good impression, for Oliver's sake. But Prue and Ned had been so nice and welcoming. Surely Oliver's parents would be the same, even if things were strained between them and Oliver? 'Sure,' she said, masking her nerves.

He led her over to the other side of the room. 'Mama, Papa, I'd like to introduce you to Ella O'Brien,' he said.

His voice was much more formal and cool than it had been when he'd introduced her to his brother and sister-in-law, and Ella's heart sank. This didn't bode well.

'Ella, this is my father Edward, the Earl of Darrington, and my mother Catherine, the Countess of Darrington,' Oliver continued.

Instead of greeting her warmly, the way Ned and Prue had, the Earl and Countess of Darrington simply stood there, looking very remote. The Earl nodded at her and the Countess just looked her up and down.

Were they expecting her to curtsey? Did you curtsey to an earl and a countess? Unnerved and flustered, Ella did exactly that. 'Pleased to meet you, Lord and

Lady Darrington,' she said awkwardly, hoping she'd got it right.

'Indeed,' the Earl of Darrington said, his voice cool.

Ella noticed that he didn't invite her to use their given names, the way Prue and Ned had done; his approach was much more formal. And she felt as if she'd already made a fool of herself. Perhaps curtseying had been the wrong thing to do.

'So how do you know Oliver?' the Earl asked.

'I'm a midwife. We work together at Teddy's,' she said, acutely aware of the difference between her soft Irish accent and the Earl's cut-glass tones.

'Of course. What do your parents do?' the Countess asked.

'Mama, that's hardly—' Oliver began.

'It's fine,' Ella said. Of course they'd want to know that. 'Mam's a music teacher and Da's a farmer.'

'So you have land in Ireland?' the Countess asked.

'No. Da's a tenant farmer,' Ella said, lifting her chin that little bit higher. She wasn't in the slightest bit ashamed of her background. As far as she was concerned, it didn't matter what your parents did or how much land or money they had—it was who you were as a person and how you treated other people that counted.

And she could understand now why Oliver had a tricky relationship with his parents, and not just because they hadn't wanted him to be a doctor; she knew he thought the same way that she did about people. From his expression, she could tell that he was horrified and angry about the way his parents had reacted to her.

'Ella's a very talented midwife,' Oliver said, his voice very clipped. 'Everyone thinks very highly of her at Teddy's.'

'Indeed,' the Earl drawled. Making it very clear that whatever anyone else thought of her, the Earl and Countess of Darrington didn't think that the daughter of a tenant farmer and a teacher was anywhere near good enough for their son.

'I'm afraid we really ought to mingle. We have rather a lot of guests we haven't welcomed yet,' the Earl said. 'Excuse us, my dear.'

And he and the Countess walked away without even a backward glance.

'I'm so sorry about that,' Oliver said, grimacing.

She swallowed hard. 'It's OK.' Even though it wasn't. Oliver's parents had just snubbed her. Big time. 'I kind of expected it.'

'My parents,' he said, 'aren't the easiest of people. It really isn't you. That was just plain *rude* of them. Maybe it's because they're stressed about holding a big party.'

Ella didn't think that something as simple as a party would stress the Earl and Countess of Darrington, especially one that had clearly been held every year for a very long time. They would simply snap their fingers and expect things to be done as they ordered. What could there be to worry about? Oliver was just making excuses for them.

Then again, what else could the poor man do?

She was just glad that her own family would be much, much nicer towards Oliver than his parents had been towards her.

Oliver raked a hand through his hair. 'Come on. I'll introduce you to a few others.'

Most of the people at the party seemed to be the movers and shakers of local businesses, plus local landed gentry: the kind of people Ella didn't usually mix with and had nothing in common with. Everyone seemed polite—at least, they weren't as openly hostile towards her as the Earl and Countess had been, but they were still quite reserved with her. It was very obvious that Ella wasn't going to fit into Oliver's world, even though his brother and sister-in-law were nice.

And why did all the men have to wear what smelled like half a bottle of super-strong aftershave? It made her feel queasy again, so she went to splash her face with water.

When she came out of the bathroom, the Countess was waiting outside.

'Feeling a little under the weather?' the Countess enquired, her expression unreadable.

Perhaps Oliver's mother thought she'd been downing too much champagne. Which couldn't have been further from the truth—but the truth was something Ella knew Oliver didn't want the Countess to know yet. 'It's been a busy day,' Ella prevaricated.

'Perhaps I should offer you some coffee.'

Even the thought of it made Ella gag, and she wasn't quite quick enough to hide the reflex.

'I thought as much,' the Countess said. 'I knew there was a reason why Oliver would want to bring someone, especially as it's been a few years since he's turned up to our pre-Christmas drinks party. How far gone are you?'

Faced with a direct question, Ella couldn't lie. 'It's still early days.'

'Hmm. Obviously Oliver will insist on a paternity test, to make *quite* sure. Both he and Ned have known their fair share of women who, let's say, would like to take advantage of their positions.'

What? Oliver's mother actually thought that Ella was

lying about Oliver being the baby's father, and that she was some sort of gold-digger—because her parents were ordinary rather than titled? That was outrageous! But Ella couldn't let rip and give the Countess a piece of her mind. She could hardly make a scene in front of everyone at the party, because it would embarrass Oliver hugely.

So she was just going to have to put up with this. And she really hoped that Oliver would think that she'd been gone a little too long and come in search of her, then rescue her from his mother.

'Of course, if it *is* his,' the Countess continued, 'then as a Darrington the baby will have a position to maintain. If it's a boy, he'll go to the same prep school and public school as Edward and Oliver.'

Over my dead body, Ella thought. No way was she dumping her baby in a boarding school. She wanted her child to go to the local school, where he or she would fit in to a normal world. And her child would most definitely grow up feeling loved and wanted, rather than being palmed off on a nanny.

'And,' the Countess said, 'in that case Oliver will have custody of the child.'

What? The baby was so tiny right now that you couldn't make out more than a bean-shape on an ultrasound scan, and the Countess was already planning to take the baby away from her?

Ella opened her mouth, about to say, 'Absolutely *not*,' when the Countess cut in.

'I'm glad we had this little chat, Miss O'Brien. I think we understand each other now.'

The Countess didn't understand her at all, Ella thought, and clearly didn't want to.

'I'll leave you to think about it,' the Countess finished, and swept off.

That told Ella everything she needed to know.

Even though Prue and Ned had been so nice, there was no way she'd ever fit in here. The last thing she wanted was to deepen the divide between Oliver and his parents. So, even though she was angry on his behalf, she wouldn't tell him what his mother had said and risk things getting even worse. Right now the best thing she could do would be to cool things between them instead of letting herself dream that she and Oliver could possibly have a future. It wasn't going to happen.

But this baby was hers and no way was she going to let Oliver's mother take the baby away from her, whatever the Countess might think. If the Countess tried, then she'd have a real fight on her hands. One which Ella had no intention of losing.

Ella had been gone a little too long for Oliver's liking. Had she got lost in the house? Or had something happened? Worried, he excused himself from the people he was talking to and went in search of her.

He found her in a corridor on the way back from the bathroom.

'Are you all right?' he asked.

'Fine,' she said.

She didn't look fine to him. She looked upset. 'Has something happened?'

'No—I'm just a bit tired,' she said.

The baby. Of course. He should've realised. And she'd already excused herself a couple of times to splash water on her face. Clearly something was triggering her morning sickness again. The lilies, maybe? She'd mentioned them earlier.

'Do you want to go?' he asked.

'It's fine,' she said. 'I'm happy to wait until you're ready.'

'I'm ready,' he said. Although it had been good to see Ned again, Oliver was seriously upset by the way his parents had been so cool to Ella, dismissing her. Maybe they were worried he was going to get hurt again, the way he had with Justine—but, as they'd been the ones to introduce him to Justine in the first place and had put so much pressure on them to get together, they were hardly in a position to judge Ella. And he was still furious about the way his mother had grilled Ella about her background. As if it mattered in the slightest what her parents did.

'I really ought to find your parents and thank them for inviting me,' she said.

Oliver would rather leave right now, but he knew Ella was right. Manners were important. It was a pity that his parents seemed to have forgotten that tonight. Though he'd make that point to them later, when Ella wasn't around to be embarrassed by his bluntness.

Thankfully they managed to keep their leave-taking really brief. But Ella was quiet all the way back to Cheltenham. And, when he parked outside her flat, she didn't invite him in for coffee.

Maybe she was tired. It was common for women to be really, really tired in early pregnancy, he reminded himself.

Yet he couldn't shake the feeling that something was wrong. Before the party, he'd kissed her—and she'd definitely responded. Kissed him back. They'd been very close to him picking her up and carrying her to her bed. And the way she'd been so firmly on his side about his career, making him feel that they were in an equal partnership and she'd fight his corner just as hard as he'd fight hers… He'd felt that they'd moved closer, were nearer to understanding each other better and getting to the point where they could agree to make a go of things. And now he realised he knew what he wanted: to be part of her life as well as the baby's. To make a proper family with her.

Right now she'd become remote again. This felt like one step forward and two steps back. Was it because his parents had been so awful? Did she really hate the world he came from? He knew if he asked her what was wrong, she'd say everything was fine. If he tried to kiss her, he had a feeling that this time she wouldn't respond—that he'd be deepening the chasm between them.

How could he get her to talk to him without making things worse?

'Thank you for this evening,' she said politely. 'I'll see you on the ward.'

Maybe the best thing to do now would be to give her some space. 'Sure,' he said, and waited until she was safely indoors before he drove back to his own place.

Was he overreacting, or was Ella going cool on him?

No. He was being ridiculous and paranoid. She'd told him she was tired. And Ella was straightforward. He was just seeing things completely out of context, because seeing his parents always rubbed him up the wrong way. He'd hoped that tonight he could re-establish a better relationship with his parents, or at least the beginnings of one. But they hadn't changed. Right now, he was just out of sorts and seeing shadows where there weren't any. Tomorrow, he'd see Ella on the ward and she'd be her usual sunny self, and everything would be just fine.

It *would*.

CHAPTER SEVEN

ELLA SLEPT BADLY that night. She kept waking up, shivering, after horrible dreams of Oliver delivering the baby and then his mother snatching the child before he could give it to Ella and slamming the door behind her.

When her alarm clanged, Ella was feeling out of sorts and upset. A shower and washing her hair didn't make her feel much better, and she could barely face a single slice of dry toast for breakfast.

She drove in to work and was relieved to discover that Oliver was in a meeting, so she wouldn't have to face him. Even though part of her wanted to tell him about what his mother had said—and to get a bit of reassurance about her nightmare—she knew that wouldn't be fair to him. It'd be like asking him to choose between her and his family. Annabelle was off duty, so Ella couldn't discuss it with her, either. Annabelle had texted her that morning.

How did it go?

Ella had texted back with a total fib, saying it was all fine. She didn't want to burden her best friend, especially as she knew how hard things had been for Annabelle and Max. She was glad it had worked out for them, but at the same time she felt slightly wistful, as she couldn't see how things could ever work out between herself and Oliver. Prue and Ned had been kind, but his parents would never accept her, and Ella didn't want to be responsible for the final rift between Oliver and his parents.

'Hey, sweetie. Are you doing OK?'

Ella looked up to see their heavily pregnant neonatal cardiothoracic surgeon, standing before her. 'Morning, Sienna. Of course I'm OK. Why wouldn't I…?' Her voice tailed off as she realised what Sienna meant. 'Oh. You know.'

''Fraid so.' Sienna patted her arm. 'You've replaced me as the hottest topic of gossip at the Royal Cheltenham, right now.'

Ella bit her lip. 'Hopefully everyone will find something else to think about soon.'

'Of course they will. How did the scan go?'

'Good, thanks. Everything's positive.'

'That's great.' Sienna smiled at her. 'I'm glad that Oliver supported you, too.'

Oh, help. They'd used the cover story that her family was far away so Oliver was supporting her, but had everyone guessed the truth—that Oliver had been there as the baby's father? 'He's the Assistant Head of Obstetrics, so I guess he feels responsible for his staff,' Ella said hesitantly.

'He's a good man. He offered to go with me for my scans, too.'

So Sienna *didn't* know that Oliver was the father of Ella's baby. Which meant that nobody else did either—

because Ella knew that Annabelle would've kept her confidence. 'Thanks for not asking.'

'About who the dad is?' Sienna laughed. 'Given my situation, I could hardly be that hypocritical. Sometimes this is just how things happen—and it's much better for a baby to have one parent who really loves them, than two who fight all the time.'

That sounded personal, but Ella wasn't going to intrude by asking. 'Yes, you're right.'

'I just wanted to say, if you need a confidential ear at any time, you know where I am—I know I'm going on leave soon, but I'll still be around.'

'Thanks, Sienna.' It was kind of her to offer, even though Ella thought that the doctor was going to be way too busy with her newborn baby. 'And I'm still on your babysitter list—the bump won't change that.'

'Glad to hear it.' Sienna patted her arm again. 'It'll be good practice for you. We're both used to newborns, but we're also used to handing the babies over and I think it's going to be a bit of a shock to our systems.'

'Ah, but I get to teach new mums how to change nappies and put on a sleep suit,' Ella pointed out.

'Then you have the advantage over me. I know who to call when I get stuck, then.' Sienna smiled. 'Right, I'm due in Theatre. I just wanted to catch you first and see how you were getting on.'

Tears pricked Ella's eyelids. 'That's so kind.'

'And invest in tissues,' Sienna advised. 'You wouldn't believe the stupid things that are going to make you cry. Or how often.'

'I believe you—especially now, because you were right about tins smelling, too,' Ella admitted wryly.

'It'll be fine,' Sienna reassured her. 'See you later.'

* * *

'Ella, could we have a wo—?' Oliver began.

She lifted her hands as if shoving him away. 'Sorry—I've been called down to Ultrasound.'

He couldn't argue with that.

But the next time he saw her in a corridor, Ella couldn't stop to have a quick word because she was in a rush on the way to help Jennie, their trainee midwife.

Was he being paranoid, or was she avoiding him?

And she'd been so quiet on the way back to Cheltenham last night.

He'd shared a part of his life with her that he'd always kept private; but, instead of bringing her closer to him, it seemed to have driven her further away.

The third time Oliver tried to talk to Ella, she was backing away as soon as he started speaking. 'Sorry, Oliver. I can't talk right now. I've been called to the Emergency Department.'

'If that was to see the mum with the suspected placental abruption,' he said grimly, 'then you're working with me.'

She bit her lip. 'Oh. I thought I'd be working with Charlie.'

So yet again she'd been hoping to avoid him. 'No. He's in the middle of a complicated delivery.' Hurt made him snap at her. 'So you'll just have to put up with it being me, won't you?'

She gave him a speaking look, but said nothing.

Oliver sighed inwardly. He hated to think that their working relationship was as bad as their personal relationship right now. He knew he should apologise for being abrupt with her, but her coolness had really got to him.

'Ella,' he said when they got into the lift. 'Are you going to be OK with this?'

'An abruption? I've come across them before,' she said coolly.

Oh, great. She'd misunderstood and was about to go prickly on him. 'I don't mean clinically. I know you know your stuff,' he said. 'I meant emotionally. You're pregnant and this might not have a good outcome. If you'd rather someone else took this case, I'll organise that for you.'

'No, it's fine.' She took his hand and squeezed it briefly. 'But thank you for thinking about that.'

Her touch flustered him so much that he didn't say a word until they were in the Emergency Department with Mike Wetherby.

'Courtney Saunders, age thirty-six, and she's currently thirty-four weeks,' Mike explained. 'This is her second baby; her last pregnancy and birth were straightforward, and this pregnancy's been straightforward so far but today she slipped on the ice while she was getting off the bus and had quite a bad fall. She tried to protect the baby by throwing herself sideways; she banged her hip and her head. I've sorted that side of it out for her, and obviously there's still a bit of tachycardia but I think that's probably stress.'

Though it could also be a precursor to other complications, Oliver knew. 'How's the baby doing?'

'That's why I called you,' Mike said. 'She says she hasn't felt the baby move much since the fall, her back hurts, and she thinks she's having Braxton Hicks.'

'But you don't think it's Braxton Hicks?' Oliver asked.

'I have a bad feeling about this,' Mike said. 'She

doesn't have any signs of bleeding but, given the fall and the length of her pregnancy, I think it might be a concealed abruption. That's why I called you guys rather than doing a manual exam myself.'

'Good call,' Oliver said. If it was an abruption, a manual exam would make things much worse. 'Have you managed to contact her partner or a friend to be with her?'

'We tried her partner, but he's in a meeting, so we've left a message for him either to call us or to come straight in,' Mike said. 'I'll introduce you to Courtney.'

Once Mike had introduced Oliver and Ella and headed off to treat his next patient, Oliver said, 'Mrs Saunders—may I call you Courtney?' At her nod, he continued, 'I'd like to examine you, if I may.'

Courtney gave her consent, and Oliver examined her gently. 'Tell me if there's any pain or tenderness,' he said.

'I'm fine. I can put up with being a bit sore and the Braxton Hicks. But I'm scared about the baby,' she said.

Ella took her hand to reassure her. 'That's why we're here. Oliver's the Assistant Head of Obstetrics, so he's really good at his job.'

'Assistant Head of Obstetrics?' Courtney looked panicky. 'Does that mean it's really serious?'

'It simply means,' Oliver said gently, 'that all my other obstetricians are in Theatre or in clinics right now and I happened to be the doctor who was free. It's nothing sinister, I promise. But what I'm going to do first is reassure you by checking the baby, OK? Once I've listened to the heartbeat, Ella's going to put some wires on you so we can monitor how the baby's doing and keep an eye on—do you know if it's a boy or a girl?'

Courtney shook her head. 'We didn't want to know. But Alex—he's my oldest—he tells everyone he's going to have a little sister.'

'Baby Saunders, then,' Oliver said with a smile. 'And we'll also measure how your contractions are doing.' He took the Pinard stethoscope and listened to the baby's heartbeat, then smiled at Courtney. 'That's a nice strong heartbeat, so that's good news.' It was a little slow for his liking, but he wasn't going to worry Courtney about that just now. Not until he'd checked the ultrasound. 'Before Ella puts the wires on, I'd also like to give you an ultrasound scan—it's just like the ones you've had before, when you came in at twenty weeks.'

And the scan showed him the one thing he'd hoped it wouldn't. He glanced across at Ella who mouthed, 'Abruption?' At his tiny nod, she mouthed, 'Line in and cross-match?'

He was glad she was so quick to pick things up— and he was even more glad that she was professional enough not to let the difficulties between them affect their patient.

He turned the screen so that Courtney could see it. 'When you fell, Courtney, it caused part of the placenta to start to come away from the wall of your womb— this dark area here shows bleeding behind the womb, which is why you're not seeing any spotting,' he said. 'It's what we call a placental abruption.'

Courtney turned pale. 'Can you stitch it back or something?'

'Unfortunately we can't reattach the placenta,' he said. 'If a mum has a small tear in the placenta and the baby's doing OK, we can send her home to wait it out, or we can admit her to Teddy's and see how things go—

but this is quite a big tear. It means that right now your baby isn't getting enough oxygen and nutrients from the placenta, and the baby's heartbeat is getting slower.'

'Is my baby going to die?' Courtney asked, her eyes wide with panic.

'We're going to do our best to keep your baby safe,' Ella said.

'And the safest thing for me to do is to deliver the baby now through an emergency Caesarean section,' Oliver finished.

'But it's too early for me to have the baby!' Courtney said. 'I'm only thirty-four weeks—there's another six weeks to go yet.'

'The baby's going to be small,' Oliver said, 'but I promise you at thirty-four weeks Baby Saunders will manage just fine. I'm going to give you steroids to help mature the baby's lungs.'

'Like bodybuilders use?' Courtney asked.

'No, they're corticosteroids, like the ones the body produces naturally or people with asthma take to help with their airways,' Ella explained. 'Babies born before thirty-seven weeks sometimes have trouble breathing because their lungs aren't developed fully. The steroids help the lungs develop so the baby doesn't have breathing problems.'

Oliver didn't chip in; he was enjoying watching Ella in action. She was so good with patients, explaining things simply in terms they could understand.

She'd be a good mum, too, he thought wistfully. But would she give him the chance to be a good dad?

He shook himself. Now wasn't the time. Their patient had to come first. But he'd try to find a good time for him and Ella to talk. They really, really needed to talk about the baby—and about them.

'What happens is we give you an injection,' Ella continued, 'and the steroids go through your bloodstream and through the placenta into the baby's body and lungs. And as well as being able to breathe better, the baby can suck better and take in more milk.'

'So the baby won't have side-effects?' Courtney asked.

'No, and neither will you,' Ella reassured her.

'But Ryan isn't here yet. He can't miss our baby being born,' Courtney said, a tear running down her cheek.

'I'll try him again,' Ella said, and squeezed her hand. 'I'm just going to put a butterfly in the back of your hand so we can give you any drugs we need, and then I'll call him myself—Mike said he was in a meeting so they left a message, but I'll make sure I actually speak to him.' She smiled at Courtney. 'I know this is really scary, but you're in the best place.'

Once Ella had put the line in, cross-matched Courtney's blood and set up continuous foetal monitoring for the baby's heartbeat and Courtney's contractions, she went off to call Courtney's partner.

'I can't believe this is happening. I wish I'd stopped work last week instead of trying to keep going a bit longer,' Courtney said.

'Hey, it could've happened anyway,' Oliver said. 'You might have slipped on your front doorstep, or when you were taking Alex out to the park.' He sat next to her and held her hand. 'There is something else I need to talk to you about, Courtney. With an abruption like this, it's possible that you might lose a lot of blood—

we can't tell from the scan how much blood you've already lost. That's why Ella cross-matched you, so we can make sure we can sort that out and give you more blood if you need it. But if I can't stop the bleeding once I've delivered the baby, I might have to give you a hysterectomy.'

Courtney looked dismayed. 'You mean—like someone who's near the menopause?'

'Sort of,' Oliver said. 'I know you're very young and you might want to have more children, so I'm hoping it'll all be straightforward. But I do need to prepare you for the worst-case scenario too—because if that happens then a hysterectomy might be the only way I can save your life.'

'So this abruption thing could kill me as well as the baby?'

'That's the very worst-case scenario,' Oliver stressed. 'In most cases it's fine. But I do need you to sign a consent form just in case the very worst happens.'

'I...' Courtney shook her head, looking dazed. 'It's a lot to take in. This morning I was planning to work for another month, and now I've fallen when I got off the bus I might die and so might the baby.'

'Very, very worst-case,' Oliver said. 'But that's why I want to deliver the baby now, to give him or her the best possible chance.'

'There isn't really a choice, is there?' she asked miserably. 'All right. I'll sign your form.'

By the time she'd signed the form and Oliver had administered the steroids, Ella came back into the room, smiling. 'I've spoken to Ryan. He's on his way now and he says to tell you he loves you and everything's going to be all right.'

A tear trickled down Courtney's face. 'Even though I nearly killed our baby?'

'You did nothing of the sort. It was an accident,' Ella reassured her. 'And your man will be here really soon. He says to tell you he's going to make the world speed record for getting across town.'

Courtney's lower lip wobbled, but she tried her best to smile.

'So what happens now is the anaesthetist is on her way. She's going to give you an anaesthetic, and then Oliver will make an incision here—' she sketched the shape on Courtney's tummy '—so he can deliver the baby.'

'Can Ryan be there?' Courtney asked.

'If he does that world speed record,' Ella said with a smile, 'then he can be there and he can cut the cord. I'll be there, too, to look after Baby Saunders. Once I've checked the baby over, you can both get to see him or her and have a cuddle.'

'What if—if it's the worst-case scenario?' Courtney asked, a catch in her voice.

'Then I'll take Ryan off to one side with the baby so Oliver can sort everything out. But he's the best surgeon I know. You're in good hands.'

If only she had as much confidence in him personally as she had in him professionally, Oliver thought. Though part of it was his own fault. He'd held back from her. If he told her about Justine, then maybe she'd understand why he was having a hard time getting his head round the fact that he was going to be a dad—and why he needed to feel that he was in control of everything. But then again, letting her close enough to meet his family had backfired.

This whole thing was a mess.

But doing the job he did, seeing how important family was to the women he helped to give birth and their partners... It was beginning to make him realise that he wanted this, too. He didn't want to be just a dad. He wanted to be a partner, too. He wanted to be loved for who he was.

But what did Ella want? Could they make a go of things together? Could they become a family, the kind of family that he hadn't grown up in but suspected that she had?

By the time the anaesthetist had administered the spinal block, Ryan had arrived for a tearful reunion with his wife. Oliver glanced at Ella and saw the wistfulness on her face. So was this affecting her, too?

Their talk would have to wait until after this operation. But Oliver was determined to sit down and talk to Ella properly and find out what she wanted—and, with any luck, it would be the same thing that he wanted. And then they could move forward properly. Together.

Thankfully, delivering the baby and the placenta stopped the bleeding, so he didn't have to give Courtney a hysterectomy. And their little girl, although tiny and in need of a day or two in the neonatal unit, looked as if she was going to do very well indeed.

Once he'd finished the operation and Courtney had gone through to the recovery room, he was on his own with Ella.

'Can we take ten minutes?' he asked. 'I'll buy you a cup of tea, if you like.'

'Thanks, but I need to be elsewhere,' she said. 'I promised to help Jennie with her studies.'

Again? His heart sank. This sounded like another

evasion tactic. Maybe he was wrong about this after all, and she didn't want the same thing that he did. 'Ella, I think we need to talk.'

'No need,' she said with a brisk smile. 'Everything's fine.'

He didn't think so; and, from the expression in her eyes, neither did she.

'How about dinner tonight?'

'Sorry,' she said. 'I really do have to go.'

Which left Oliver to walk back to his office alone.

He sat at his desk, trying to concentrate on his pile of admin, and wondering how everything between him and Ella had gone so wrong. Was it his imagination, or was she finding excuses to be anywhere but near him?

And how was he ever going to persuade her to give him a chance?

He was beginning to think that he needed a Christmas miracle. Except they were in very short supply, and in any case he ought to be able to sort this out on his own.

CHAPTER EIGHT

'You look terrible, Ella,' Annabelle informed her best friend. 'Rough night?'

'I'm fine,' Ella fibbed.

'I've known you for a lot of years now,' Annabelle said softly, 'and you're not fine. What's wrong?'

Ella grimaced. It was all so complicated. Where did she even start?

'That was a pretty stupid question,' Annabelle said. 'Obviously it's Oliver.'

'Not so much Oliver as his family,' Ella admitted.

Annabelle winced. 'I thought you said Thursday night went OK?'

'Bits of it did,' Ella said. 'His brother's nice, and so is his sister-in-law.'

'So the problem's his parents?'

Ella nodded miserably. But she couldn't tell Annabelle the whole story. It wasn't hers to tell, and it wouldn't be fair to break Oliver's confidence; Ella was the only person in the department who knew about his background. But she could tell Annabelle some of it, and maybe Annabelle would have some ideas about how to deal with it. 'His mum wants me to have a paternity test.'

'What?' Annabelle looked shocked. 'That's ridiculous.'

But it didn't bother Ella anywhere near as much as the other thing that the Countess had suggested. 'And she wants Oliver to have custody of the baby.'

Annabelle frowned. 'What does Oliver say about it?'

'He doesn't know,' Ella admitted. 'He wasn't there when she said it.'

'Then talk to him about it. Tell him what she said.'

'That's the problem. I can't,' Ella said. 'He doesn't get on that well with his parents.'

'Then obviously he'll take your side. And no way is he going to take the baby from you.'

Oh, but he could. Especially if she had a boy and Prue had a girl—because then Ella's baby could be the future Earl of Darrington. But explaining that wouldn't be fair to Oliver. 'It's complicated,' Ella hedged. 'And I don't want to make things worse between Oliver and his parents. It wouldn't be fair to make him choose sides.'

'Talk to him,' Annabelle advised. 'And if Oliver Darrington's even half the man I think he is, he'll tell his mother to back off and to start treating you with a bit of courtesy.'

'I'm not even officially his girlfriend,' Ella pointed out.

'He took you to meet his family. Which he wouldn't have done if he wasn't serious about trying to make a go of things with you,' Annabelle countered.

But Oliver hadn't said anything about his feelings. And Ella didn't want to try to make a go of it just for the sake of the baby. Sienna's words rang all too true: *It's much better for a baby to have one parent who really loves them, than two who fight all the time.*

But, before she and Annabelle could discuss it any

more, Jennie rushed over to them. 'Ella, you're needed in Room One,' she said. 'It's Georgina.'

'Georgina? As in Georgie, our mum-to-be with quads?' Ella asked. Georgina was one of Ella's special patients; after IVF treatment, the two embryos implanted had each split into identical twins, so Georgina was expecting quadruplets. 'But she's not due in for another appointment until next week.'

'She thinks she's in labour,' Jennie said.

It was way too early for Georgina to be in labour. 'I'm coming now,' Ella said. She squeezed Annabelle's hand. 'Thanks for letting me talk. I'll catch up with you later.'

'Sure. Call me if you need anything.'

'I will,' Ella promised.

She went into Room One, where Georgina was sitting on the bed, looking worried. The younger woman's face brightened when she saw Ella.

'How are you doing, Georgie?' Ella asked.

'A bit scared. I think I'm in labour,' Georgina said.

'Is Leo not with you?' Georgina's partner had been to every single appointment with her.

'He's in New York. I called him and he's getting the first plane back.' Georgina bit her lip. 'Mum's got the vomiting bug that's going round, and she doesn't want to give it to me, or she'd be here to hold my hand—but she's texted me a dozen times since I told her I was coming in.'

But texting wasn't the same as having someone with you, especially if you were scared, Ella knew. 'OK. Let's have a look at what your lovely babies are up to,' Ella said with a smile. 'Jennie, can you see if Charlie's around, please? He'll want to see his patient immediately. And can you get the portable scanner, please?'

'Sure,' the trainee midwife said.

'So are you having contractions, Georgie?' Ella asked. 'And have you timed them?'

'I'm not sure—I think I'm getting twinges or something, but it doesn't hurt as much as I expected and they're all over the place. But, Ella, my tummy feels *weird*,' Georgina said. 'It's all tight and shiny. My back aches. And I feel as if I've put on half a stone overnight.'

Alarm bells rang in the back of Ella's head. She didn't want to worry Georgina, but this didn't sound like the beginnings of labour. It sounded like a complication—and, given that Georgina was carrying four babies, this could be a very tricky complication. 'Would you mind baring your tummy for me so I can have a look?' she asked, keeping her voice light and cheery.

'Of course,' Georgina said, and pulled up her top while she leaned back against the pillows.

Georgina's abdomen definitely looked tight and shiny, as she'd said. But Ella wasn't sure this was labour. She had a nasty feeling that one of the quads might be in trouble.

'As soon as Charlie gets here,' Ella said, 'we'll have a look on the ultrasound and see if they're all waving at you this time.'

Georgina smiled, but Ella could tell that the young mum-to-be was panicking.

'I'll take your blood pressure while we're waiting for Charlie,' she said.

At least Georgina's blood pressure was normal, but Ella would be a lot happier once she'd monitored all the babies.

Just then, Oliver walked in with Jennie, pushing the portable scanner. Ella's heart skipped a beat when she saw him.

'Sorry, Charlie's in Theatre. Will I do?' he asked.

Provided they could keep their private life out of it, yes. 'Georgie, this is Oliver Darrington, our Assistant Head of Obstetrics,' Ella said. 'Oliver, this is Georgie. She's twenty-eight weeks and she's expecting quads.'

'Congratulations,' Oliver said, smiling at her.

'Thank you,' Georgina said.

'Georgie thinks she might be in labour,' Ella said. 'Her blood pressure's fine, but we need to do a scan to see what the babies are up to.'

'OK. I'm sorry, Georgie, our gel's a bit cold,' Oliver apologised. 'May I?'

'Sure.'

Once the scan of the babies was on the screen, Ella spotted the problem immediately. The two girl quads were fine, but the two boys were definitely struggling; one of them had a lot of amniotic fluid in the sac, while the other had very little and was practically stuck against the wall of Georgie's womb. The bigger boy twin had a full bladder; Ella couldn't see the smaller twin's bladder, but if her suspicions were right it wasn't full.

'Oliver, can we have a quick word?' she asked, not wanting to worry Georgina by discussing her fears in front of her.

'Sure. Would you excuse us a moment, Georgie?' Oliver asked with a smile.

Georgie nodded.

'Jennie, perhaps you can get Georgie a drink and

make her comfortable for the next couple of minutes?' Ella asked.

'Thanks,' Georgina said. 'I have been feeling a bit thirsty, the last day or two.'

It was another maternal sign for twin-to-twin transfusion, Ella knew, and her misgivings increased. She waited until they were outside the room and the door was closed before she turned to Oliver. 'I've been Georgie's named midwife since day one and Charlie's her named doctor—the quads have all been doing just fine, and Georgie was only in for a scan last week,' Ella said. 'When she told me her symptoms this morning and I examined her, I wondered if it might be twin-to-twin transfusion.'

'Good call. The scan pretty much proved that,' Oliver said.

'But how could it happen so fast? Everything was fine last week. I've kept a really close eye on her because obviously with carrying quads she's a high-risk mum.'

'She's in her last trimester,' Oliver said, 'so it's an acute form of the condition rather than a chronic one—and acute TTT can happen practically overnight.'

'So what are the options?' Ella asked. 'I've seen less than half a dozen cases of TTT in my career. Do we deliver the babies early, or do you put a hole in the membrane between the twins, or could you do laser surgery on the placenta to separate their bloodstreams?'

'It's a difficult call,' Oliver said. 'If you put a hole in the membrane so the twins share one sac, there's a risk of entangling the umbilical cords, and that's something I'd rather do at an earlier stage than Georgina's at. This has all happened really quickly, so there's a possibility that the recipient quad has a heart problem, because the excess blood and fluid will have put strain on his heart.' He frowned. 'I'd like to call Juliet Turner in.'

'Juliet Turner?' Ella asked.

'She's a neonatal specialist surgeon and she's got a fabulous reputation for her work in utero. She might be able to operate on the quads if need be.'

'What aren't you telling me?'

'She's in Australia,' Oliver admitted.

'So it'll be at least a day before she can get here— *if* she agrees to come,' Ella pointed out. 'And you're just expecting the poor woman to drop everything and travel halfway round the world to come and treat Georgie's babies?'

'Juliet's a professional.'

'Surely there's someone closer than Australia?' Ella asked.

'Juliet's the best,' Oliver said simply, 'which is the whole point of Teddy's. We can keep Georgina and the babies comfortable until she gets here.'

Ella was about to say that Juliet Turner might already have commitments which prevented her from rushing all the way from Australia to Cheltenham, but Oliver had the kind of stubborn expression that told her he'd talk the surgeon into changing any commitments for the sake of Georgina and the quads.

'OK,' she said. 'And I guess that gives Leo—the quads' dad—a chance to get here from New York. Let's tell her together.'

She went back in with Oliver and sat on the bed, taking Georgina's hand.

'Everything's not all right, is it?' Georgina asked. 'What's happening to my babies?'

'It's something called twin-to-twin transfusion,' Ella explained. 'You know you've got two sets of identical twins.'

'Two boys and two girls—Graham, Rupert, Lily and Rose,' Georgina said.

'Lovely names,' Oliver said. 'Two of my nieces are called Lily and Rose.'

'What's wrong with them?' Georgina asked.

'Lily and Rose are both fine,' Ella reassured her. 'But Graham and Rupert have a problem.

Normally identical twins share a placenta, and the blood flows evenly between the babies, so they both get the same amount of blood flow and nutrition. But sometimes there's a problem with the blood vessels so one twin gets too much and one doesn't get enough. The twin that gets too much blood wees more, and that produces more amniotic fluid round him, and the twin that doesn't get enough wees less and has less amniotic fluid. That's why it's called twin-to-twin transfusion.'

'Are they—will they be all right?' Georgina asked. 'And was it something I did?'

'It's definitely not anything you did,' Oliver said. 'It just happens, sometimes.'

'You did the best thing by coming straight in to us when you weren't feeling right,' Ella added.

'And we'll do our very best to keep them healthy,' Oliver said. 'There are several things we can do, but I'd like to bring in a specialist who's very, very experienced at doing surgery in the womb.'

'You're going to operate on one of the boys while they're still inside me?' Georgina asked, looking shocked.

'That depends on what Juliet thinks is the best thing

to do,' Oliver said, 'but it's a possibility. You can discuss your options with Dr Warren, too. I know he's been your named doctor since day one, so it's important that you talk to him.'

'So when's this going to happen?' Georgina asked. 'Today? Because I want Leo here.'

'Ella told me he's coming from New York. Don't worry, it won't be today,' Oliver said, 'so there's plenty of time for him to get here.'

'We're going to keep you in for a few days,' Ella said. 'I want to monitor the babies, so we'll be hooking you up with some wires, and we'll keep you comfortable until Juliet gets here.'

'Can't Charlie do the operation?' Georgina asked.

'Juliet has much more experience,' Oliver said. 'And I'm sure Charlie will be in to see you as soon as he's out of Theatre and he will explain everything. I'm due in clinic, but if you need me then Ella will give me a call.'

'Thank you,' Georgina said.

Charlie came in as soon as he was out of Theatre. 'I'm so sorry I wasn't here, Georgie.' Standing by the bed, he quickly read her case notes. He had been informed there was a situation on the way from Theatre. 'Ella, who diagnosed the TTT?'

Ella filled him in on everything except Juliet's potential involvement; it wasn't her place to tell Charlie.

'I understand it's a little overwhelming, Georgie,' Charlie said. 'But there are treatment options. Don't think the worst. We might not have to deliver the babies early.'

'Oliver said the babies might have an operation in my womb,' Georgina said.

'It's a possibility, but we'll discuss every option with

you and Leo and we'll go ahead the way you want us to go,' Charlie reassured her.

Ella stayed with Georgina until the end of her shift; but then she discovered that Lexie, the midwife who was meant to take over from her for the night shift, had gone down with the vomiting bug.

'Don't worry. I'll stay with you, Georgie,' Ella promised.

'But—you've been working all day.'

'That's fine,' Ella said with a smile. 'You're one of my mums, and I'm not leaving you while you're worried.'

Clearly Oliver wasn't happy about the situation when he heard about it, because he came to the door of Georgina's room. 'A word, Ella?'

'How did you get on with Juliet?' she asked, hoping to head him off.

'She'll be here on Monday. But that wasn't what I wanted to talk to you about.' He sighed. 'Ella, you can't work a double shift.'

Ordering her about *again*. 'Watch me,' Ella said grimly. 'You know the situation. Lexie's gone down with the virus.'

'Health and Safety would have the biggest hissy fit in the world.'

Ella shrugged. 'Their problem. I'm not leaving Georgie.'

'I can get an agency nurse in to cover Lexie's shift. Ella, you need to look after yourself.' His face tightened. 'And our baby.'

'Georgie's worried as it is,' Ella pointed out. 'I'm not leaving her to be looked after by someone she's never met before. She knows me and she's comfortable with me.'

'And you're putting your health at risk.'

'OK, then. I'm off duty—and I'm visiting someone in Teddy's.'

'Now you're being ridiculous.' Oliver scowled at her.

'I'm not. I care about my mums, and I'm not deserting someone who right now is on her own and worried sick about her babies. Georgie's mum has the vomiting bug, so she can't come in, and her husband's on a plane back from New York. That means that Georgie's on her own, knowing there's something wrong with one of her babies and worrying that the worst is going to happen. I'm not just walking out of that door and leaving her to it.'

Oliver sighed. Why did Ella feel that she had to prove herself over and over again? 'You're a good midwife, Ella. Everyone in Teddy's knows that.'

She lifted her chin. 'Thank you.'

'But you also have to remember that you're pregnant. You can't work a twenty-four-hour shift. I wouldn't let a non-pregnant member of staff do that, let alone one who's pregnant.'

Ella shrugged. 'Then I'm a visitor who's staying.'

A stubborn visitor. 'Just promise me you'll put your feet up, you won't rush around, and you'll eat properly.'

'I'm not stupid, Oliver.'

'I know that.'

'I'm not going to do anything reckless or anything that could hurt the baby. But I can't just walk away and leave Georgie worrying. Can't you see that?'

Yes, he could. Because Ella was sweet and kind and

was always the first to offer help. 'All right,' he said. 'You can stay with her as a visitor, provided you put your feet up and rest properly. But you are absolutely *not* working. I'll get agency cover.'

'As long as the agency midwife knows that I'm Georgie's named midwife and to run everything past me,' Ella insisted.

If he didn't agree, he knew Ella would find a way of breaking the rules and work a double shift. 'All right,' he said.

But two could play that game. And he made quite sure that Ella had a proper evening meal, because he brought it in to her himself on a tray. 'No arguments,' he said.

And he could see in her expression that she knew he'd call her on the situation in front of Georgie if she refused the meal—and he'd stay until she'd eaten it, if he had to. 'Thank you,' she said. 'That's really kind of you and it looks scrumptious.'

When Oliver had left the room and closed the door behind him, Georgie asked, 'What's with the special treatment? Are you two an item?'

Not really, Ella thought. She wished they were, but it wasn't going to happen because his parents would never accept her. So she couldn't answer Georgie's question honestly. 'Oliver looks after all his team,' she said. Which was true: sometimes she wondered what drove him to be so protective. 'And I'm pregnant.'

'Congratulations,' Georgie asked. 'When's it due? That is, I take it you're having just one and not quads?'

Ella smiled. 'No, just the one baby. It's early days. The baby's so tiny at the moment it looks like a little bean on the scan.' She took her phone from her pocket and flicked through to the photograph she'd taken of the scan picture. 'Look, that's my little one.'

'Your first?'

Ella nodded. 'And that's scary enough. I can't imagine what it's like to be expecting quads.'

'Really scary,' Georgie said. 'I never thought we'd be able to have children at all. It was a miracle that two embryos took—and even more of a miracle that both of them then became twins.'

Her baby was a miracle, too, Ella thought. Not that she wanted to discuss that. 'Two girls and two boys—and they'll all grow up close. That's nice.'

'All the way through, I've been so scared that we'd lose one of them,' Georgie said. 'All the stories you see on the Internet.'

'Which do nothing but make new mums worry,' Ella said. 'Ignore them.'

'I had—but now with this twin-to-twin thing...'

Ella took her hand. 'Try not to worry. Oliver says Juliet's the best and she'll be able to keep your boys safe.'

'I hope so,' Georgie said.

Oliver came in twice more that evening—the first to check that everything was fine, and the second to bring both Georgie and Ella a mug of hot chocolate.

And then the penny dropped for Ella.

Oliver was officially off duty right now and had been for a while, but he was still here at the hospital. Was he checking up on her? She pushed the thought away. Of course it wasn't that he didn't trust her. She'd made him aware of his bossy tendencies, so it was more likely that he was worried about her but he was trying not to make the sort of fuss that would annoy her.

'Shouldn't you be at home by now?' she asked. She saw the flash of guilt in his eyes, and knew that her guess had been right.

'I'm catching up on some paperwork, so I thought I'd take a break and keep you both company for a bit.'

'Oliver, it's ten o'clock and you're on an early shift tomorrow.'

His expression said very clearly, *Yes, and you've been in all day*.

'Go home,' she said gently, 'and get some sleep.'

'Are you sure you're going to be all right here?'

'I'm sure. And I'm on a late tomorrow, so I'm going to laze around all morning.' She knew he'd pick up what she wasn't saying in front of Georgie: *don't fuss*. Though, at the same time, it warmed her that he was concerned and trying not to be overbearing about it.

If only his family was different...

But that wasn't fair. It wasn't his fault.

'I'll see you later, then,' he said. 'Call me if you need anything.'

'I will,' she promised.

But he came in again on his way out of the department, this time carrying a blanket, which he proceeded to tuck round her. Georgie had fallen asleep, so he simply mouthed, 'Call me,' rested the backs of his fingers briefly against her cheek, and left the room as quietly as he could.

Ella had to blink back the tears. This was the man she'd fallen for—kind, considerate and caring. But his parents would never accept her in his life. She couldn't ask him to choose between them. Somehow, she'd have to find a way of backing off without either of them getting hurt.

Except she had a nasty feeling it was already too late for that.

She dozed in the chair next to Georgie's bed, waking only when the agency midwife came in to check on them, until Leo arrived at the crack of dawn the next morning. Ella talked him through what was happening with the babies, drawing diagrams and labelling them to help him understand.

'Sorry, my writing's terrible,' she said, wincing. At times like this, she really resented her dyslexia.

'It's because you're a medic,' Leo said with a smile. 'All medics have terrible handwriting.'

'I guess,' she said.

She stayed with Georgie and Leo until the midwife from the early shift took over.

'Thank you for staying with me,' Georgie said. 'That was above and beyond the call of duty.'

'Any time,' Ella said, meaning it. 'I'm going home for a nap now, but if you need me just ask one of the midwives to call me, OK?'

'You're the best, Ella,' Leo said, giving her a hug. 'Thank you.'

'No problem. Sit and cuddle your wife,' she said with a smile.

CHAPTER NINE

ELLA'S CAR HAD frozen over during the night. With a sigh, she scraped the ice off the windscreen and climbed into the car. Fortunately she was on a late today so she could go home, have a cup of tea and a bath, then set her alarm and have a sleep before her shift.

As she drove back towards her flat, she noticed a car coming up to the junction of a side road on her left. To her shock, it didn't manage to stop at the junction but slid on the ice and crashed straight into her. The impact pushed her right across the road into a line of parked cars.

She checked to see it was safe to get out of the car, then did so. She could see straight away that her car was undriveable and she'd need to call the insurance company to tow her car away.

The other driver came over to her. 'I'm so sorry, love. The road wasn't gritted and I just couldn't stop,' he said.

'The roads are pretty bad. I guess we'd better swap insurance details,' she said tiredly and reached into the car for her handbag. She took out a pen and notebook, but when she took out her reading glasses she saw that the coloured lenses had cracked during the impact. She didn't have a spare pair with her, so now she was going to make a mess of this and probably get half the numbers in the wrong place.

'Are you all right, love?' the other driver asked, clearly seeing that she was close to tears.

'I'm dyslexic,' she said, gesturing to her ruined glasses, 'and without these I'm going to get everything wrong.'

'Let me do it,' he said. 'It's the least I can do, seeing as it was my fault. You sit down in the warm, love, and I'll sort it out.'

He wrote down all the information for her, called the police to inform them about the accident and her insurance company so they could arrange to pick up her car, and waited with her until the tow truck arrived. Thankfully it turned up only half an hour later, but by then Ella was shivering and desperately tired.

'Are you sure you're all right? You've not banged your head or anything?' the tow truck driver asked.

'No, just my reading glasses are wrecked,' she said wearily. 'I was lucky. It could've been an awful lot worse.'

'We've had so many cars sliding off the road this morning—the gritters clearly didn't think it was going to freeze this badly last night,' the tow truck driver said. He took her car to the repair garage and then drove her back to her flat. 'I'm only supposed to take you to one or the other,' he said, 'but I remember you. You delivered my youngest last year. My wife had a rough time and you were brilliant with her.'

Ella was really grateful. 'Thank you so much. Do you want a cup of tea or something?'

'That's kind of you, but I'd better not. I've got half a dozen other crashes to go to,' he said wryly. 'Take care.'

Ella let herself into her flat, started running a bath and put the kettle on. Then, when she undressed, she realised there was blood in her knickers.

She was spotting.

Ice slid down her spine. She'd felt a sharp jerk across her shoulder and abdomen from the seatbelt when the other car had crashed into her, but her car's airbag hadn't gone off and she hadn't banged herself against the steering wheel. She hadn't thought the crash was bad enough to warrant going to hospital; she'd felt OK at the time, there had probably been dozens of other accidents on the icy roads and there were drivers more in need of urgent medical attention than her.

But now she was spotting, at eight weeks of pregnancy, and that wasn't a good thing.

Oh, God. Please don't let her lose the baby. It hadn't been planned, but it was oh, so wanted.

'Hang on in there, little one,' she whispered, with one hand wrapped protectively round her bump.

With shaking hands, she rang Annabelle, but her best friend wasn't answering her home phone or her mobile. Ella was sure that Annabelle was off duty today; but maybe she was out with Max somewhere and her phone was accidentally in silent mode.

Ella didn't want to ring an ambulance, because she knew how busy the hospital was right now, and someone else could need to go to the emergency department more urgently. Maybe she should get a taxi in to the Royal Cheltenham?

But right now she was so scared. She really didn't want to do this on her own.

Oliver.

Given how things were between them and that he'd

been so fed up that she'd stayed with Georgina all night after her shift, worrying that she was overdoing things and putting the baby at risk, Oliver was the last person she wanted to call. But her brain was on a go-slow and she couldn't think of anyone else. Plus he was the baby's father—he had the right to know that there was a problem.

It took her three attempts before she managed to call his mobile.

'Darrington,' Oliver said absently, as if he hadn't even looked at the screen.

'It's Ella,' she said.

'Ella? Is everything all right?'

Her teeth had started to chatter and she could hardly get the words out.

'Ella, what's happened?' he asked urgently.

'A c-car crashed into me on the way h-home, and now I'm s-spotting.'

'Are you at home?'

'Y-yes.'

'I'm on my way to you right now,' he said. 'Try not to worry. I'll call you when I'm in the car so you're not going to be on your own while you're waiting, and I'll be with you very, very soon, OK?'

Ella had had a car accident and she was spotting. That wasn't good.

Please, please don't let her lose the baby, Oliver begged inwardly.

The shock of her news had made him realise just how much he wanted the baby.

He headed out to Reception and was really grateful

that Annabelle was there; she'd changed duty at the last minute to help cover sick leave.

'Is everything all right?' she asked.

'No. Ella's been in an accident. She just called me and said she's spotting. I'm going to get her now, so please can you make sure the portable scanner's in one of the rooms and keep it free? I'm bringing her straight in to Teddy's.'

'Got you. Give her my love and tell her not to worry,' Annabelle said. 'Drive safely.'

'I will.'

As soon as he was in the car, Oliver switched his phone over to the hands-free system and called Ella as he drove to her flat. He could hear the tears in her voice when she answered; it ripped him apart that she was crying and right now he couldn't comfort her properly or do anything to fix this. But until he'd done the scan and knew what was going on, he couldn't give her the reassurance he really wanted to give her.

'Ella, I'm on my way now,' he said. 'Teddy's is on standby and Annabelle's there—she sends her love.'

'But Annabelle's off duty.'

'No, she swapped duty yesterday to help me out with sick leave cover,' he said.

He heard a sob. 'I'm meant to be on a late today.'

'Don't worry about that right now,' he soothed. 'We can sort it out later.'

'I never meant for this to happen when I stayed with Georgie,' she said. 'I would never, ever put the baby at risk.'

'I know and you did the right thing—the kind thing,' he said. 'You'd have been worrying yourself silly about

Georgie and the quads if you'd just gone home.' Because that was who Ella was: dedicated to her job.

'The crash wasn't my fault, Oliver. It really wasn't. The other driver just couldn't stop at the junction and ploughed into me.'

Why did she seem to think he was angry with her? 'Ella, I'm not going to shout at you.'

'You were near shouting at me yesterday.'

She had a point. He'd gone into overprotective mode when she'd suggested working a double shift. 'I'm sorry. I'm a grumpy sod and you have the right to tell me to shut up when I start ranting,' he said.

To his relief, he heard what sounded almost like a wry chuckle. But then there was another muffled sob. 'Hold on, honey. I'm going to be there very soon,' he said. 'And, Ella, I'm glad you called me.'

'Really?' She didn't sound as if she believed him.

'Really,' he said firmly.

He kept her talking all the way from his house to her flat. When he got there, he didn't bother about a parking permit—he'd willingly pay a dozen parking fines if he had to—but just ran over to her door and rang the bell. When she opened her door, he pulled her straight into his arms and held her close. 'Everything's going to be all right, I promise.'

'I don't want to lose the baby.' Her shoulders heaved.

'You're not going to lose the baby, not if I have anything to do with it,' he said. 'Let's go.' He locked the front door behind her, held her close all the way to his car, helped her in and then drove to the Royal Cheltenham, holding her hand between gear changes. She was trembling and he desperately wanted to hold her; but he knew that if he stopped to comfort her it would be

that much longer before he could give her a scan and
see what was going on. 'We're not going to the Emergency Department. I'll do the scan myself at Teddy's
so you don't have to wait.'

'I'm so scared, Oliver. I want this baby so much.'

'Me, too,' he said. More than that, he wanted Ella
as well. Whatever had caused her to back off from him
since the party, they could fix it—because she was more
important to him than anything or anyone else. 'It's
going to be OK, Ella. I promise you.'

She was crying silently, and he hated the fact that
he couldn't do anything more to help; but, at the same
time, he needed to get her to hospital safely.

It seemed to take for ever to get to Teddy's, even
though he knew it couldn't have been more than twenty
minutes. But at last they were there and he parked as
close to the entrance as possible, then grabbed a wheelchair from the entrance.

'I can walk,' Ella protested.

'I know, but this is faster. Let me do this, Ella. Please.
I won't smother you in cotton wool, but I want to get
you in there for that scan.' His voice cracked and he
wondered if she'd heard it and realised that he was as
emotional about the situation as she was. And, actually,
maybe she needed to know it. 'Not just for you. For me.
I need to be sure you're both all right.'

He was almost breaking into a run by the time they
got to Teddy's.

'Later,' he said to the nurse on the reception desk,
who looked at Ella in shock as he wheeled her through.
'I'll explain later.'

Annabelle had texted him to say that Room Three
was reserved for him, if she wasn't there when he

brought Ella in. Oliver wheeled Ella into the room, scooped her out of the wheelchair and laid her on the bed. The fact that she made no protest this time really scared him.

'Can you bare your tummy—?' he began, but she was already doing it.

Please, please, let the baby be all right, he begged inwardly, and smeared the gel over her stomach.

His hands were actually shaking as he stroked the head of the transceiver across her abdomen.

But then he could see the little bean shape, and the heart was beating strongly.

Thank you, he said silently, and moved the screen so Ella could see it, too. 'Look,' he said. 'It's going to be OK. There's a really strong heartbeat, not too fast and not too slow. Everything's going to be fine, Ella.'

Her shoulders heaved, and then she was crying in earnest. He held her close, stroking her hair, and re-alised that tears were running down his cheeks, too.

He wanted this baby. So did she, desperately. Surely there was a good chance that they could make a decent life together—the three of them, because now he re-alised how much he wanted that, too.

Finally Ella was all cried out—and then she realised that Oliver was still holding her. And she'd soaked his shirt. And was it her imagination, or were his eyes wet, too? She'd been so frightened that she hadn't been able to focus much on what he'd said to her, but had he said that he was scared, too?

She wasn't sure, and her first instinct was to back away in case she was making a fool of herself again. 'We ought to—well, someone else might need this room.'

'I want to admit you now and keep you in overnight,' he said, 'for observation.'

She shook her head. 'I'll be fine.'

'You're on bed-rest. Don't argue,' he said, 'and there's no way in hell you're working your shift today, so don't even suggest it.'

'But someone else might need the bed on the ward more than I do.'

'Ella, you're pregnant and you were in a car crash.'

'A minor crash. At low speed.'

'Bad enough that they had to get a tow-truck for your car,' he said. 'And you were spotting. If any of your mums came in presenting like that, what would you say?'

'Go home and rest,' she said, 'and come back if you're worried.'

'And if it was a mum you knew damn well didn't know the meaning of the word rest?'

'Then I'd suggest staying in,' she admitted.

'I know you think I'm wrapping you up in cotton wool,' he said, 'and I know that drives you mad—but what I don't get is why you won't let anyone look after you.'

'It's a long story,' she said.

He shrugged. 'I've got all the time in the world.'

He really expected her to tell him? Panic flooded through her. 'I don't know where to start.'

'Try the beginning,' he said. 'Or the middle—or anywhere that feels comfortable—and you can take it from there.'

She knew where to start, then. 'The baby. I didn't try to trap you.'

'I know. You're not Justine.'

She frowned. 'Justine?'

'It's a long story.'

What was sauce for the goose… 'I've got time,' she said. 'And maybe if you tell me, it'll give me the courage to tell you.'

He looked at her for a long moment, then finally nodded. 'OK. I'll go first. Justine was the daughter of my parents' friends. They'd kind of earmarked her for me as a suitable future wife, even though I wasn't ready to settle down and I wanted to get all my training out of the way first so I could qualify as an obstetrician. They fast-tracked me and I was just about to take my last exams when Justine told me she was pregnant.'

Ella went cold. So this wasn't the first time Oliver had been faced with an unexpected baby; it also went some way to explaining why Oliver's mother had been so disapproving about the baby, if the Countess had been in that position before. But as far as Ella knew Oliver didn't have a child. What had happened?

'I really wasn't ready to be a dad,' Oliver said. 'I'd been so focused on my studies. But I did the right thing and stood by her.'

'Like you're standing by me?' she couldn't help asking.

He didn't answer that, and she went colder still.

'So we found a nice flat, moved in together, and sorted out a room for the baby.'

Oliver definitely wouldn't have abandoned the baby. This must have ended in tragedy—or maybe Justine had refused him access to the baby and that was why the Countess had been adamant that Oliver should have custody.

His grey eyes were filled with pain and she squeezed

his hand. Clearly the memories hurt him, and she didn't want that. 'You don't have to tell me anything more.'

'Yes, I do,' he said. 'I don't want there to be any more secrets between us. I should've told you about this a long time ago.' He dragged in a breath. 'We'd planned to get married after the baby was born. But then one day she accidentally picked up my phone instead of hers and went out. I assumed that the phone on the table was mine and was about to put it in my pocket when a text came through.' He grimaced. 'Obviously I didn't set out to spy on her and read her texts, because I trusted her, but the message came up on her lock screen and I read it before I realised it was a private message for her.' He looked away. 'It was from another man, and the wording made it clear they were having an affair. I tackled her about it when she got home and she admitted the baby was his, not mine.'

'So that's why—' She stopped abruptly. Now wasn't the time to tell him that his mother wanted her to have a paternity test.

'Why what?'

'Nothing. I'm so sorry, Oliver. That was a vile thing to do to you. But why would she lie to you like that?'

He shrugged. 'You've been to Darrington Hall and met my family. I guess it was the kind of lifestyle she wanted and the other guy couldn't give her that.'

Now Ella could understand his mother's comments about gold-diggers. But did Oliver think she was a gold-digger too—despite the fact that she'd told him she wasn't? He'd been in that situation before. And now she realised why he'd been so controlling with her when she'd told him about the baby, because Justine had taken all his choices away. Ella had reacted by being stubbornly independent, and they'd been at cross purposes when it needn't have been like that at all.

'It's still horrible for you. And not all women think like that, you know.'

'I know.' His fingers tightened round hers. 'You don't.'

She was relieved that he realised that. 'Was the— was the baby all right?'

'Yes. I moved out and the other guy moved in—but from what I hear it didn't last.'

And then a really horrible thought hit her. Was Oliver still in love with Justine? Was that why he couldn't move on? She didn't want to ask him, because she was too scared that the answer might be 'yes'.

As if he'd guessed at her thoughts, he said, 'You're not Justine, and I don't have a shred of doubt that this baby's mine. I'm just sorry I haven't been able to get my head round things properly and support you the way I should've done.'

Relief made her sag back against the bed. 'Now you've told me what happened to you before, I can understand why you reacted the way you did.'

'Though I did wonder if you were lying to me,' he said, 'when you said it was safe and I assumed you were on the Pill.'

'I thought it *was* safe,' Ella said. 'I honestly never thought I'd ever get pregnant.'

'That's what I don't understand. I haven't found the right way to ask you because...' He grimaced. 'Ella, I didn't want to fight with you over it. But, once you'd told me you were pregnant, I couldn't work out why you were so sure that I didn't need contraception and yet you weren't on the Pill. I knew there was something, but asking you straight out felt intrusive and as if I was accusing you of something, and I didn't want that.'

He'd been honest with her, so now she needed to be honest with him. At least she wouldn't have to explain the medical side too much because it was Oliver's speciality and he understood it. 'I have endometriosis. It caused a lot of scarring on my Fallopian tubes over the years, and then I had an ovarian cyst that ruptured during my training. The doctors in London told me that I was infertile.'

'So that's why you said I didn't...'

'...need a condom,' she finished. 'Yes.'

'I'm sorry. Endometriosis is pretty debilitating, and to get news like that when you're so young...'

'Yes.' She'd cried herself to sleep for weeks afterwards. 'Worse was that it disrupted my studies.'

'Didn't you tell your tutors? They would've understood.'

She grimaced. 'You've read my file, so you know I'm dyslexic.'

He nodded.

'I wasn't diagnosed with dyslexia until I was fifteen. Everyone just thought I was a bit slow because I had trouble reading and I'm clumsy. I was always the last to be picked for the netball team in PE lessons, because I could never catch a ball, and you really don't want to see me trying to throw one.' She shrugged. 'Anyway, the September I turned fifteen we all knew I wasn't going to do well over the next two years, so I wasn't going to get good grades in my exams. But I was good with people and had the gift of the gab, so everyone thought

I ought to go and work in the local pub, at first in the kitchen and then in the bar when I was old enough.'

'Right.'

'Except I had a new science teacher that year, and she took me to one side after the first week and asked me all kinds of questions. She was the first teacher ever at school who seemed to think I wasn't slow.' And it had been so liberating. Suddenly it had been possible to dream. 'She said she thought I had dyslexia, because I was fine at answering questions on stuff we'd talked about in class but when she looked at my written work it wasn't anywhere near the same standard, and my writing was terrible. Nobody had ever tested me for dyslexia—they'd never even considered it. So my teacher talked to my parents and the Special Needs department at school and they got me tested.'

'And it turned out she was right?'

She nodded. 'They gave me coloured glasses and got my test papers printed on pastel colours instead of bright white, and suddenly bookwork wasn't quite so much of a struggle any more.' She smiled. 'I'd always wanted to be a midwife like my Aunty Bridget, but nobody ever thought I was clever enough to do it. But I got through my exams, I stayed on at sixth form and I actually got accepted at uni. I was already getting help for my dyslexia, because they let me record all my lectures to help me revise, so I didn't feel I could go to my tutors and say there was another problem as well. It felt like one excuse too many.'

Now Oliver began to understand why Ella was so independent. She'd had to fight hard to get where she was, and she'd no doubt been wrapped in cotton wool as the child who always underachieved—as well as being told that she was stupid by people who should never have judged her in the first place.

'And I guess,' she said, 'there was a part of me that didn't want to admit it because then I'd have to admit I wasn't a real woman—that I'd never be able to give my partner a child of his own.'

'Ella, being infertile doesn't make you any less of a woman,' Oliver said.

'That's easy for you to say, being a man,' she said softly. 'I knew my parents were desperate for grandchildren and I'd let them down, too.'

'That's seriously what they believe?'

'No, of course not! They said it didn't matter if I didn't have children,' Ella said, 'but I've seen my mum's face whenever she talks about her great-nieces and great-nephews. Just for a second there's this wistfulness. She couldn't have any more children after me, so me not being able to have children meant that she'd never have grandchildren. So she and Da were thrilled to bits when I told them about the baby.'

Oliver was shocked. Hadn't they agreed to wait to tell their family until she'd got through the first trimester? 'You've told them already?'

'I'm sorry. I just couldn't wait,' she said simply. 'I know things are tricky for you with your parents, but mine aren't like that—they're so pleased.'

She'd thought she was infertile but, because of him, she was having a baby. It was almost like the Justine situation again except there wasn't any cheating, this time. Justine had wanted the lifestyle and not him. Did Ella want the baby and not him?

He shook himself. But he wanted this baby, too. And, before the Hallowe'en Masquerade Ball, he and Ella had been friends. So maybe they could make this work, the way it hadn't with Justine.

'My parents are dying to meet you,' Ella said.

'So do I need to ask your father officially for your hand in marriage?' Oliver asked.

She blinked at him. 'What?'

'It's the practical solution,' Oliver said. 'We both want this baby. We get along well, for the most part. So we'll get married and give the baby a stable home.'

We both want this baby... Get married... A stable home.

But Oliver hadn't said a word about love. Or actually *asked* her to marry him.

And all Ella could think of was what Sienna had said about it being better for a baby to have one parent who loved it to bits than two parents who fought all the time. Given the situation with Oliver's parents, there was a good chance that she and Oliver would fight. A lot.

Marrying her meant he'd get custody of the baby: exactly what his mother wanted.

Even though Ella understood now what might have driven the Countess to take that view, she also didn't want her life taken over by the Darringtons—to have to give her baby the name they chose, send the baby to the school they chose, and give up her job to take on the role they chose.

If Oliver had said one word to her about love, it would've been different.

But he hadn't. And she couldn't marry someone who

didn't love her. It wouldn't be a real relationship. That wasn't what she wanted.

'No,' she said.

CHAPTER TEN

OLIVER STARED AT ELLA, not quite believing what he was hearing.

He'd proposed to her—and she'd refused.

'Why?' he asked.

'I'm not marrying you just for the baby's sake. And I'm perfectly happy for my baby to be an O'Brien.' Her expression was closed.

'But—this is my baby, too.' He looked at her, shocked. 'Or are you telling me…?'

She blew out a breath. 'Now I know what your ex did, I can understand why you're worrying that it's history repeating itself, but don't you know me better than that?'

He'd thought he knew her. But maybe he didn't. And maybe she did have one thing in common with Justine, then: her feelings for him weren't the same as his for her. 'I asked you to marry me.'

'For the baby's sake.' She swallowed hard. 'Like your mother—' She stopped abruptly.

'What about my mother?'

'Nothing.'

'It doesn't sound like nothing to me.'

'All right—if you must know,' Ella said, 'she wants the baby.'

'What?' He'd never heard anything more ridiculous in his life. His mother didn't even *know* about the baby.

'Provided you have a paternity test first to make quite sure it's yours,' Ella continued. 'And then you'll sue me for custody.'

This was getting more and more surreal. 'What? Why?'

'Because Darrington babies have a position to maintain.'

'That's ridiculous. Of course my mother wouldn't say anything like that,' Oliver said. 'And when did she say anything to you? I was with you nearly all the time at Darrington.'

'Not all the time. Not when I'd gone to splash my face with water.'

'You're saying my mother accosted you in the bathroom?' That definitely wasn't his mother's style.

'She'd been watching me and she'd worked out that I was going green around the lilies. And I was the first person you'd brought there in years, so there was obviously a reason why you wanted them to meet me.'

Oliver shook his head, unable to take this in.

'Believe what you like,' she said. 'But I'm not marrying you.' She turned away.

Oliver raked a hand through his hair. What the hell was going on? 'Ella—'

'I could do with some rest,' she said.

Because she'd just had a car crash and a nasty scare about the baby. And she'd been here at the hospital all night, keeping Georgie company until Leo arrived from New York.

Of course she could do with some rest. She must be exhausted, physically and mentally and emotionally.

Maybe that was why she was flinging around these wild accusations—she was sleep-deprived and still worried sick about the baby, and saying the first thing that came into her head instead of thinking about it. Maybe if he gave her some space and some time to sleep, she'd get her head round things and talk this over sensibly with him.

'I'll arrange for you to be moved to a side room,' he said stiffly, and left the treatment room.

'Is everything OK?' Annabelle asked, coming over to him as he strode through the department.

'With the baby? Yes.'

She frowned. 'Is Ella all right?'

'She needs to be moved to a side room and kept in overnight for observation,' Oliver said. 'Excuse me.'

'Oliver—'

'Not now,' he said, and headed for his office. And for once he actually closed his door. Usually he was happy to be interrupted by any member of staff who needed him, but right now he needed to lose himself in paperwork and not have to deal with another human being.

He was halfway through a pile of admin when his phone buzzed; he glanced at the screen.

Darrington Hall.

Why were his parents calling him?

For a moment, he thought about just ignoring the call. But then again it might be important. With a sigh, he answered.

'Oliver. I was just checking if you were coming home for Christmas,' his mother said.

He nearly laughed. Darrington Hall hadn't been 'home' for a long, long time. 'I'm afraid not,' he said. 'I'm on duty.'

'Can't you change it?'

'No,' he said. But something was eating at him. Had his mother really had a fight with Ella outside the bathroom? He'd thought at the time that Ella had been gone a long while. And she'd been very cool with him after that. If his mother had just warned her off him, that would explain why she'd gone cold on him. 'Mama—did you tell Ella you wanted her to have a paternity test?'

'I… Why would I do that?'

He noticed that his mother hadn't denied all knowledge of Ella being pregnant. He was pretty sure that Ella wouldn't have volunteered the information willingly, the way she had with her own family. And he knew exactly what would've driven his mother to talk about a paternity test. 'Justine,' he said succinctly.

'Well, I don't want to see you trapped again.'

It was the nearest his mother would get to admitting what she'd said. 'Ella isn't trying to trap me,' Oliver said. She'd just refused to marry him. He paused. Now he thought about it, that stuff about Darrington babies having a position to maintain sounded just like the sort of thing his mother would say. 'What position does a Darrington baby have to maintain?'

'I don't know what you mean.'

That definitely sounded like bluster. 'Mother, I'm not the heir to Darrington.'

'You will be if Edward and Prudence don't get their skates on and produce a boy.'

He let that pass. 'And, for the record, I have no intention of suing Ella for custody.'

'Custody?'

'Yes. Did you tell her we wanted custody? Because Darrington babies have a position to maintain?' he repeated.

'I—Oliver, you know it would be for the best. We could hire a nanny. There's plenty of space here—'

'No,' he cut in. 'Ella is the mother of my child, and the baby stays with her.'

'I see.' His mother's tone became frosty.

He sighed. 'Mama, I know we don't see eye-to-eye about my job. But I've been either a medical student or a qualified doctor for seventeen years now. Half a lifetime, almost. I'm not going to change my mind about what I do. And you need to start trusting me, because I'm doing what's right for me.'

'But, Oliver, Ella's—'

'Ella's lovely,' he said, 'as you'd know if you actually gave her a chance, the way Ned and Prue did. Think about it. Yes, things went wrong with Justine. On paper she was the perfect match, and you pushed us together—and it went wrong. This time, I'm making my own choice. I don't care if Ella's parents don't have the same pedigree that you do. It doesn't matter where you come from, Mama—what matters is who you are and how you treat other people.'

And he hadn't treated Ella very kindly just now.

'I'm going to be a father,' he said quietly. 'And I'd like my baby to know both sets of grandparents. Properly. I'd like to build some bridges with you and Papa. But in turn you need to respect that I'm old enough and wise enough to make my own decisions.'

'And your own mistakes?' the Countess asked coldly.

'Ella isn't a mistake,' he said. 'And neither is my career.'

'So you're giving me an ultimatum?'

'No. I'm giving you a chance to get to know the woman I love, and our baby,' he said. 'It's not going to happen overnight and we're all going to have to learn to compromise a bit, but I guess that's part of what being a real family means.'

'Oliver…'

'I'm on leave at New Year,' he said. 'Maybe we could start with lunch. Something small, informal and friendly. Just you, Papa, Ned and Prue and the girls, and us. Nobody else. Just family. You can get to know Ella a bit better—and we'll take it from there.'

'Just family, New Year,' the Countess echoed.

'A new year and a new beginning,' he said softly.

For a long time, she said nothing, and he thought she was going to throw it all back in his face.

But then she sighed. 'All right.'

'Good. I'll speak to you soon,' he said.

But, more importantly, he needed to talk to Ella. To apologise for ever having doubted her. He wasn't going to take her an armful of flowers—apart from the fact that there was a ban on flowers while the vomiting bug was still around, flowers weren't going to fix things. The only way to fix things was by total honesty.

He just hoped that she'd hear him out.

When he went back onto the ward, Annabelle was there. 'Which room is Ella in?' he asked.

'I'm not entirely sure I should tell you,' she said, narrowing her eyes at him. 'At the moment, Oliver Darrington, I'd quite like to shake you until your teeth rattle.'

He blinked, not used to his head nurse being so fierce. 'What have I done?'

She scoffed. 'Are you really that dense? You made Ella cry.'

He winced. 'I need to talk to her.'

'You need,' Annabelle said crisply, 'to grovel.'

'That, too,' he said.

'She's in here.' Annabelle indicated the side room. 'But if you make her cry any more, I'll throw you out personally, and I don't care if you're the Assistant Head of Obstetrics.'

'You won't have to do that,' Oliver said.

'Hmm,' Annabelle said, and watched him as he walked into the room.

He closed the door behind him, noting that Ella was in tears.

'Hey,' he said softly.

She looked at him and scrubbed at her eyes with the back of one hand. 'What do you want?'

'To talk. To apologise.' He paused. 'Annabelle says I need to grovel.'

Ella's face was tight. 'It doesn't matter.'

'Why are you crying?'

'It doesn't matter,' she repeated.

'Yes, it does,' he said. 'Are you crying because I walked out?'

She didn't answer.

'Because, earlier,' he said, 'you seemed to think that me walking out on you would make you happy. What do you want, Ella?'

'Something you can't give me,' she said. 'You don't do relationships. I was stupid to think that maybe I could change your mind on that score, especially now I know why you don't date anyone more than twice.'

'But that's what I want, too,' he said, coming to sit beside her. 'I want a proper relationship. I want to be a proper family. With you.'

'Your family will never accept me,' she said. 'Your brother and Prue are nice, but your mum hates me and your dad despises me, so it's never going to work. It's just going to cause endless rows between you and them, and that's going to make things difficult between you and me.'

'My parents,' he said, 'are difficult, but they're going to learn to change. And I'm sorry that my mother harangued you outside the bathroom and said I'd insist on custody after a paternity test.'

She frowned. 'But you said she wouldn't say things like that.'

'I didn't want to think she'd say it,' he said, 'but what you said rang pretty true. Oh, and she's sorry, by the way.'

Ella stared at him, looking surprised. 'You've spoken to your mother?'

'Technically, she rang me,' he said. 'So I asked her about what she'd said to you. And I told her very bluntly that you're the mother of my child and the baby stays with you.'

'So you're not going to sue me for custody?'

'I was rather hoping,' he said, 'that we could do better than that. That we could be a family.'

She shook her head. 'I'm not marrying you for the baby's sake, Oliver. That won't work, either. We'll end up resenting each other and it won't be good for the baby.'

'That isn't why I asked you, actually,' he said. 'I

asked you because I want to marry you for you. Because I love you.'

She scoffed. 'We had a one-night stand with consequences neither of us was expecting. That's not love, Oliver.'

'Agreed, but that's got nothing to do with it. I've known you for eighteen months,' he said. 'The first moment I saw you, I noticed you. That glorious hair, those beautiful eyes, and a mouth that made my knees weak.'

She looked stunned.

'And then I got to know this bright, warm midwife who's a joy to work with,' Oliver continued. 'She's great with the mums and makes them all feel a million times better when they're panicking, she's great at explaining things to our trainees and gives them confidence when they don't think they can do things, and she thinks on her feet so she can second-guess what senior staff need, too—and I admit, that's why I didn't ask you out months ago, because I know I'm rubbish at relationships and I didn't want to mess up things at work. But then it was the night of the ball—and yes, I'm shallow, because it's the first time I saw you all dressed up and I couldn't think straight. Especially when I danced with you. I wanted to go and reclaim you from every other guy you danced with,' he told her.

'Really?'

'Really,' he confirmed. 'I couldn't resist you. And then it got complicated, because I realised what I'd done, and I'd messed everything up, and I didn't know how to make things right between us again.'

'And then I told you about the baby—and that must've brought back memories of Justine,' she said quietly.

'It did, though I never doubted you for a second and

I don't want you to do a paternity test. The night of the party, when you made me feel you really believed in me and supported me—I've never had that from anyone before. It threw me. And it made me realise that maybe you were the one I could trust with my heart. Except then you started avoiding me, and when I asked you to marry me you said no.'

'Because you never said a word about your feelings,' she said. 'I thought you were asking me to marry you out of duty, just because you thought it was the right thing to do. You said we got on well and we could give the baby a stable home—but that's not enough, Oliver. You need love as well, to make a family.'

'I'm not very good at talking about my feelings,' he said. 'But I do love you, Ella. And I do want to be a family with you and the baby. Not like the way I grew up, with my parents very distant and leaving most of the care to hired staff. I want to take the baby to the park with you, and feed the ducks together, and read bedtime stories, and be there in the playground on the first day our little one starts school.'

'The local school?' she checked.

'Definitely the local school,' he said. 'I want to be a family with you and our baby.'

He meant it, Ella realised.

Oliver really did love her. He wanted to make a life with her and the baby—not because he thought it was the right thing to do, but because he *wanted* to be with them. That day on the ward when he'd talked about taking their baby to see Santa: that had been the real Oliver. The hidden Oliver.

Ella felt her heart contract sharply. 'I love you, too, Oliver,' she said. 'I fell for you months ago.'

'But you never said anything.'

'I thought I was out of your league,' she said. 'The hospital rumour mill said you only ever dated super-models.'

He laughed. 'Hardly. Anyway, you could hold your own against any supermodel.'

'I'm too short and too curvy,' she said.

'No way. You're beautiful,' he said. 'And I don't want a supermodel. I want you. I love you.'

She stroked his face. 'I love you, too.'

'Even though I'm a grumpy control freak?'

'Even though you're a grumpy control freak,' she said. 'And I guess that's why I called you today when I started bleeding, because I trust you and I knew you'd be there for me. Just as I hope you know I'll always be there for you.'

'Then I'll ask you the same question I asked earlier, except this time I'll do it properly.' He knelt down on one knee. 'Ella O'Brien, you're the love of my life and I want to make a family with you—will you marry me?'

And this time she knew he meant it. That this was going to be a real marriage, not papering over the cracks. 'Yes.'

There was a rap on the door and Annabelle came in. She frowned as she took in the tears on Ella's face. 'Oliver Darrington, I warned you not to make Ella cry,' she said, putting her hands on her hips. 'And you didn't listen. So that's it. *Out.*'

'Annabelle, I'm not crying because I'm miserable,' Ella said, hastily. 'I'm crying because I'm happy.'

Annabelle looked confused. 'So he grovelled?'

'I probably still need to do a bit more grovelling,' Oliver admitted, 'but we're getting there—and we're looking for a matron of honour. I don't suppose you know anyone who might be up for the job? Someone, say, in this room?'

Annabelle's jaw dropped and she stared at each of them in turn. 'You're getting married?'

'You're the first to know,' Ella said. 'Would you be our matron of honour?'

'And godmother to Baby Darrington?' Oliver added.

Annabelle smiled. 'Absolutely yes. To both.'

EPILOGUE

A year later

'BA-BA! DA-DA!' five-month-old Harry crowed, waving his chubby little hands as his father walked into the living room.

'Hello, Harrykins.' Oliver swept his son up into his arms and gave him a resounding kiss. 'Have you been good for Mummy today?'

'Ba-ba,' Harry said solemnly.

'I'm glad to hear it.' Oliver blew a raspberry on the baby's cheek, making him giggle, and put him back in his bouncy chair.

'And good afternoon to you, Mrs Darrington,' he said, taking Ella into his arms and kissing her. 'Guess what I managed to borrow today?'

'Reindeer? Sleigh? A snow machine?'

'Not far off,' he said. 'Wait. Close your eyes. And no peeking.'

Ella smiled and followed his directions.

'OK. You can look now,' he said. 'Ho-ho-ho.'

She burst out laughing, seeing him wearing the Santa outfit from the ward.

Harry, on the other hand, took one look at the strange

man in the red hooded suit and white beard, and burst into tears.

Swiftly, Oliver pulled the hood back and removed the beard. 'Harrykins, it's all right. It's Daddy.' He looked at Ella. 'Sorry. I had no idea it'd scare him like this.'

'He's still only five months old and he doesn't really know what's going on. Next Christmas,' she said, 'he'll be old enough to appreciate it and you'll get the reaction you were expecting today.' She scooped the baby into her arms and rocked him gently. 'Harry, it's OK. It really *is* Daddy.'

Harry simply screamed.

Thirty seconds later, the doorbell went.

'I'll go,' Oliver said.

'Oliver Darrington, why are you half dressed as Father Christmas?' the Countess of Darrington asked in crisp tones on the doorstep. 'And why is my grandson wailing like that?'

'Those two things are connected, and I'm an idiot,' Oliver said. 'Hello, Mama. I didn't realise you were coming over tonight.'

'Your father and I just collected Joe and Roisin from the airport,' Catherine said. 'Or had you forgotten they were coming?'

'He was too excited about being Harry's very first Father Christmas to remember that you're all going to be here for dinner tonight,' Ella said with a grin, walking into the doorway with a still-sobbing Harry. 'And you need to take that suit off, Oliver, and hide it before Prue, Ned and the children get here, because the girls are still young enough to believe in Santa and I don't want to spoil it for them.'

'Tsk. Go and sort yourself out, Oliver. Give the boy to me,' Catherine said, holding out her arms, and Ella duly handed over the baby. 'There, there, Harry. Nobody's going to scare you when Granny Darrington's around.'

Probably, Oliver thought, because his mother was the scariest thing around.

Two seconds later, Harry stopped crying and started gurgling at his grandmother.

And Oliver couldn't quite be annoyed that his mother seemed to have a knack for soothing the baby, because it was so nice to see his family all on such good terms.

'I'll put the kettle on,' Ella said. 'Catherine, I bought some of that horrible lapsang souchong you like, this morning.'

'Thank you, my dear,' Catherine said.

'And there's some good proper tea for me, I hope,' Roisin chipped in, walking into the hallway and overhearing the conversation.

'Of course, Mum.' Ella kissed her mother warmly.

'Your turn for a cuddle, Roisin,' Catherine said, handing over the baby. 'And I'll make the tea, Ella. That baby's had you running round all day and you ought to put your feet up.'

Oliver hid a smile. If anyone had told him a year ago that the two most important women in his life would become fast friends, he would never have believed it. But he'd gradually rebuilt his relationship with his parents, starting with the quiet family lunch he'd suggested at New Year. Things had still been a little strained between them until one day when the baby had started kicking, and Ella had gone over to Catherine, taken her hand and placed it on the bump, saying, 'Baby Darrington, say hello to Granny Darrington.' Catherine had been rewarded by some very firm kicks, and from that point on she'd warmed to Ella.

The O'Briens had instantly adopted Oliver as one of their own and, although Oliver had been wary about the first meeting between Roisin and Catherine, to his surprise they'd got on really well. Roisin was too straightforward for there to be any misunderstandings; and, once Catherine had discovered just how well Roisin played the piano, they'd bonded over a shared love of music and their future grandbaby.

Prue and Ned had also had a son, a couple of weeks before Ella had Harry, so Oliver was no longer the 'spare'. To his delight, having that pressure taken off meant that his parents had finally accepted what he did for a living. Catherine had even suggested that the next Darrington Christmas cocktail party should be a fundraiser for Teddy's. She'd been backed by Ella, Prue and Roisin; and the O'Briens had come over from Ireland this week to help with the last-minute arrangements for the party.

Life, Oliver thought, didn't get any better than this.

Knowing that his father and Joe were bringing in the luggage, and Catherine and Roisin were in the kitchen with the baby, he scooped Ella into his arms and swung her round before kissing her. 'Hey. Happy Christmas. I love you.'

She kissed him back. 'Happy Christmas, Oliver. I love you, too.' She smiled. 'I thought last year I had the best present ever, when I found out that I was expecting our Harry, but I was wrong. Because this is the best present ever—our family, all together.'

'Our family, all together,' he agreed, and kissed her again.

* * * * *

If you missed the first story in the
CHRISTMAS MIRACLES IN MATERNITY *quartet*
look out for

THE NURSE'S CHRISTMAS GIFT
by Tina Beckett

And there are two more fabulous stories to come!

If you enjoyed this story,
check out these other great reads
from Kate Hardy

CAPTURING THE SINGLE DAD'S HEART
HER PLAYBOY'S PROPOSAL

MILLS & BOON®

MEDICAL ROMANCE

THE ULTIMATE IN ROMANTIC MEDICAL DRAMA

MILLS & BOON®

EXCLUSIVE EXTRACT

Paramedic Holly Jacobs knows that her night of scorching
passion with Dr Daniel Chandler meant more than just lust.
Playboy doc Daniel has sworn off love – but he can't
resist Holly! By the time they get snowed in on Christmas
Eve Daniel finds himself asking if Holly is for life,
not just for Christmas!

Read on for a sneak preview of
PLAYBOY ON HER CHRISTMAS LIST
by Carol Marinelli

Holly wanted a kiss, Daniel knew, but he was also rather
certain she wanted a whole lot more than that. Not just sex,
but the part of himself he refused to give.

'What?' he said again, and then his face broke into a smile,
as, very unexpectedly, Holly, sweet Holly, showed another side
of her.

'Are you going to make me invite you in?'

'Yes.'

'You're not even going to try and persuade me with a kiss?'
Holly checked.

'You want me or you don't.' Daniel shrugged. 'There's no
question that I want you. But, Holly, do you get that—?'

She knew what was coming and she didn't need the
warning—he had made his position perfectly clear—so she
interrupted him. 'I don't need the speech.'

She just needed this.

Holly had thought his hand was moving to open the door
but instead it came out of the window and to her head and
pulled her face down to his.

He kissed her hard, even though she was the one standing. The stubble of his unshaven jaw was rough on her face and his tongue was straight in.

He pulled her in tight so that her upper abdomen hurt from the pressure of the open window and it was a warning, she knew, of the passion to come.

Even now she could pull back and straighten, say goodnight and walk off, but Holly was through with being cautious.

Her bag dropped to the pavement and he then released her.

Holly stared back at him, breathless, her lipstick smeared across her face, and all it made him want to do was to kiss her again.

But this was a street.

Holly bent and retrieved her bag and then walked off towards her flat. There was a roaring sound in her ears and her heart seemed to be leaping up near her throat.

Daniel closed up the car and was soon following her to the flats.

She turned the key in the main door to the flats and clipped up the concrete steps.

She could hear his heavy footsteps coming up the steps behind her as she turned and Holly almost broke into a run.

Daniel actually did!

He had thought her cute, sweet and gorgeous these past months and had done all he could not to think of her outright as sexy.

Except she was, and seriously so.

Give a 12 month subscription to a friend today!

Call Customer Services
0844 844 1358*

or visit
millsandboon.co.uk/subscriptions

MILLS & BOON®

Why shop at millsandboon.co.uk?

Each year, thousands of romance readers find their perfect read at millsandboon.co.uk. That's because we're passionate about bringing you the very best romantic fiction. Here are some of the advantages of shopping at www.millsandboon.co.uk:

* **Get new books first**—you'll be able to buy your favourite books one month before they hit the shops

* **Get exclusive discounts**—you'll also be able to buy our specially created monthly collections, with up to 50% off the RRP

* **Find your favourite authors**—latest news, interviews and new releases for all your favourite authors and series on our website, plus ideas for what to try next

* **Join in**—once you've bought your favourite books, don't forget to register with us to rate, review and join in the discussions

Visit **www.millsandboon.co.uk**
for all this and more today!